Horse and Pony Stories

Horse and Pony Stories

Edited by
Jane Carruth

CONTENTS

The editors acknowledge the contributions of the following artists:

David Godfrey 63, 160, 228, 301, 329
John Gosler 42, 96
Sandy Nightingale 12, 85, 88, 173, 247
Geoff Taylor 21, 107, 192, 320, 365, 373
Barrie Thorpe 32, 121, 153, 203, 239, 274, 309, 347, 357, 380, 394
  (*all the above represented by David Lewis*)
John Davis 72, 132, 140, 262
John Woodcock 55, 187, 216, 287

First published 1978
Second impression 1979
Reprinted 1981, 1982, 1983, 1984
Published by Octopus Books Limited
59 Grosvenor Street
London W1

ISBN 0 7064 0764 4

This arrangement © 1978 Octopus Books Limited

Produced by Boondoggle Limited
600A Commercial Road
London E1

Printed in Czechoslovakia
50358/6

THE SILVER BRIDLE

Mollie Hunter

Patrick Kentigern Keenan considered himself the smartest man in Ireland. It is true the fairy folk had the better of him when they changed him into a hare, but then he had the better of them by winning the gold necklace for Bridget, his wife. Should he now take her advice and stay quietly at home? Patrick thought he might—and then again, he might not . . .

You can't beat a woman's curiosity, and in no time at all Bridget had the story of the gold necklace out of Patrick. When she had heard the whole thing from beginning to end, she took the necklace off and one look in the mirror was enough to tell her that the beauty it had given her was gone.

'Are ye not goin' to wear it, then?' Patrick demanded. 'And me after bein' nearly killed to get it for you!'

'I'll wear it sometimes,' Bridget said. She slipped it round her neck again and smiled to see the strange and lovely face that looked back at her out of the glass. 'But only sometimes.' With a little sigh, she took the necklace off for the last time and put it carefully away. 'That way,' she said, 'it will be a greater surprise for me to be so beautiful, and a greater pleasure for you to look at me.'

Patrick grumbled on for a while but in the end, 'Ah well, maybe you're right at that,' he said, for the truth was, he was beginning to see that Bridget had a great deal of sense to her.

'And Patrick,' said Bridget, 'take a lesson from the white hare. You nearly came to grief over it, and grief's all you'll get if you go on trying

7

to prove yourself smarter than the fairies.'

'Haven't I three times met with a fairy and no harm done?' Patrick demanded. 'There's my new shoes, and the golden spoon, and now the golden necklace to prove it.'

'And the fairy got the better of you every time,' Bridget reminded him.

'I made a vow,' Patrick said stubbornly, 'and I'll keep that vow. I'll prove yet that I'm the smartest man in Ireland.'

But though he talked so big and so bold, the white hare had given Patrick a bigger fright than he cared to admit, and what with that and the greater respect he had for Bridget's good sense he was content for a while to stay at home and mind his own business. It couldn't last, of course, and in spite of all Bridget's warnings, Patrick took up with his old ways of wandering abroad again and poking his long nose into things that would have been better left alone.

And so it happened one night that he was walking late by himself when he saw a light ahead of him. It was not standing still as you might have expected, but moving slowly away, and as soon as he saw it nothing would do Patrick but he must find out where it was and what it was.

He began to walk towards it, and as he moved, the light moved so that he never seemed to get any nearer to it, but Patrick was a stubborn man and this only made him all the more determined to find out what it was. He began to run, not looking where he was going, and suddenly his feet squelched in water and he was up to his knees in a bog.

Muttering angrily to himself, he pulled one foot clear and stepped forward, but the next step was bog too, and the next, and the next again, until it dawned on him that he was in the middle of a bog and had not the least idea where to go to get out of it. Fright fairly took him by the hair then, for he realized that the light had only been a bog-light, the flame that is sometimes seen on marshes and that people say is lit by the fairies to lure men to their death in the bog.

'Ah, but they'll not get me so easy,' muttered Patrick when he had got over the first shock, 'not me that's the smartest man in Ireland.'

He felt around himself in the mud till he found a long, tough root. Then he pulled himself up on to a tussock of grass and thrust the root down into the soft, oozy ground around him, testing for the firmest spot. In this way he moved forward, always testing the next step with his foot before he ventured to leave the hold he had, and after a while he was on firm ground again, cold and wet and tired but still free of the bog and full of his own cleverness at the way he had done it.

At the same time there was no denying that he was lost, and with the bog between him and the way he had come he would have to wait for the morning light before he could find his way home, but walk he must or he would freeze in his wet clothes, and so he struck off, always keeping to the rising ground for fear of falling into a bog again. It was when he had been walking like this for an hour, stamping his feet now and then to keep warm, that he suddenly remembered what day— or rather, what night—it was. Midsummer's eve. And he had chosen that night, the night of all the year when fairies were most likely to be abroad, to wander far from home and get lost into the bargain.

Well, he said to himself, there's nothing for it but to keep a sharp lookout and be ready for trouble if it comes, and so he walked on with his ears pricked and his eyes darting hither and thither to see what they could see. The moon came up, and shone white on the grass around him, and Patrick stopped to look about.

Suddenly he heard a noise, like music, very faint and far away, and with it, another sound like thunder very far off. The sound got louder and nearer, and straining his ears to listen, Patrick realized what it was. The music was the sound of hundreds of little bells tinkling and the thunder was the sound of horses' hooves on the turf.

Common sense told Patrick to get down out of sight of whatever or whoever was coming his way, but curiosity kept him on his feet till the very last second before the horses he had heard came in sight. As they breasted the skyline, he ducked quickly into a fold in the ground and lay there, holding his breath and wishing he were back home again beside the fire with Bridget telling him all his faults, for he knew then that he was about to see what few people had ever seen, and that was a company of fairy horsemen riding abroad on Midsummer's eve.

They swept by, only a few feet away from him, and him pressed into the ground as if he was growing there like the grass, but still with curiosity fighting his fear enough to let him raise his head now and then to see what they were like. What he saw made his eyes stand out like a frog's.

Every single horse that flew past was as white as new snow; their hooves were like polished black steel and they were shod with silver, and from the bridle-rein of every horse and from the trappings of each saddle, hung dozens of little silver bells that swung and tinkled with a wild, sweet music in time with their flying hooves.

Not a sight of a face did Patrick see of the men and women that mounted the white horses, but now and then he saw the sweep of a green robe, the toe of a shining shoe, and a stream of gold as a fairy-woman's hair flew out behind her. He dared not raise his eyes further to see more, and when they had passed he kept still for a while not knowing if more of the fairy troop might be coming that way. No more horses came, but it seemed to Patrick he could hear voices. He rose cautiously to his knees and looked over the rim of the hollow. The fairy troop had stopped not a hundred yards from him, the riders had dismounted and their horses were grazing quietly a little way off from where they had gathered together. As Patrick watched, the fairy-people formed themselves into a circle and began to dance and sing, with one of their number standing in the middle of the circle and playing on a silver pipe.

'Did you ever,' said Patrick to himself, 'see the beat of that!' He lay with his chin on his hands watching the dancers twirling and jumping. There was not a soul would believe him if he swore with his hand on his heart that he had seen such a thing happen, he thought. The dance grew faster. The dancers were spinning like tops, the circle breaking and forming again with each new movement of the dance.

It was when he noticed that the dancers were moving further and further away from the horses that a wild idea came into Patrick's head. If he could capture one of these great white horses for his own there was not a man, woman or child in Ireland but would believe the tale of what he had seen.

Patrick Kentigern Keenan was a man of action. No sooner had the thought come into his head than he began to move forward on his hands and knees. Luck was with him, for as he crawled towards the herd one of the horses began to wander off on its own. Patrick changed his direction so that he would be between this horse and the herd when it tried to return, and inched along behind it hardly able to breathe with excitement.

'Just let me capture you, my beauty,' he muttered, 'and there's no one will deny that I'm the smartest man in Ireland.'

Now he was close up to it. He turned cautiously to look at the fairy company. They were still dancing in a ring, laughing and singing, with their horses cropping quietly. He was alone with the white horse.

He lay in the grass and looked long and lovingly at it; at the coat that gleamed like white satin, at the great muscles moving smoothly under the shining skin, at the mane as soft and white as dandelion floss flowing over the proud, arched neck. Light and delicate as a dancer on its long slim legs, it stepped over the grass and the little silver bells on its bridle-rein rang with faint music.

Patrick's stomach drew into a tight knot of excitement. He rose to his knees, and the white horse turned its head in his direction. Its pointed ears flicked forward.

It was now or never. Slowly and carefully he drew his feet up under him, crouched for a second as tense as a coiled spring, then leapt forward. One bound took him to the horse's side. With one hand he clutched its mane and laid hold of the pommel of the saddle with the other. It reared on its hind legs, nostrils flaring, lips drawn back over its teeth in a snicker of alarm, and as its forefeet struck the ground again Patrick was up in the saddle, his knees pressed close into the horse's flanks, the reins gathered in his left hand.

'Hup! Away!' he roared, and brought his right hand hard down on its hind-quarters, then clutched the reins with both hands and hung on for dear life as the fairy horse bounded forward as if it had been shot from a gun.

Shouts sounded behind him, and the sound of horses' hooves. A hail of arrows came over his head, whining past him like bees, tiny arrows with deadly, poison-tipped barbs, and Patrick groaning with fear when he wasn't shouting with excitement, bent low over the white horse's neck and said to himself, 'Oh, if I'm not the biggest fool in Ireland!'

But Patrick Kentigern Keenan knew horseflesh, you had to say that for him, and he had stolen the strongest and the fleetest of the fairy horses. The shouts grew fainter, the arrows began to fall short, and soon he was alone, thundering along in the moonlight, mounted as no man had ever been mounted before or since.

11

A hail of arrows came over Patrick's head, whining past him like bees . . .

Low over ditches the white horse skimmed. High it soared over hedges and plunged downwards like a thunderbolt to the earth again. The wind got up and whipped ragged clouds forward across the sky, but fast as the ragged clouds raced, the white horse outpaced them.

Uphill or downhill was all the same to it. The air whistled past Patrick's ears as it bounded forward with gigantic strides. His hat flew off, his teeth jarred with every bounce in the saddle. He tried with all his strength to pull the beast to a halt, but with a toss of its head and a powerful pull on the reins the fairy horse nearly jerked his arms from their sockets, and it began to dawn on Patrick that the white horse would never tire of the speed it was going and that no human rider could ever pull it to a halt.

The cold sweat broke out on his forehead. Could he throw himself off its back? No. At that pace he would break his neck. But what was to happen to him? Was he doomed to gallop for ever the length and breadth of Ireland astride this wild, white creature? Was that to be his punishment for stealing a fairy horse?

On and on in the white moonlight the white horse sped. Valleys and hills dropped behind them. A wide, winding river barred their path and hope shot through Patrick. But the white horse gathered itself and leapt from bank to bank as if the wide river had been a little stream. Patrick lost all count of time. His hands were numb on the reins, his head was spinning like a top. If ever I get home safe and sound, he vowed, I'll never lay hands again on a thing that's not rightfully mine. And he groaned to think that he was maybe hundreds of miles from home.

A village rose out of the darkness in front of them. The white horse took the row of houses in a bound and thundered on. The thought of people peacefully asleep in their beds and him soaring over them clinging like a burr to the back of the fairy horse sent Patrick nearly wild with temper.

'Help! Help!' he roared, twisting his neck to look back at the houses. Not a sound came from the village, not a house showed a glimmer of light. 'I'm done for!' Patrick groaned, and just at that moment a cock crowed shrilly in the distance.

The white horse stopped dead in its tracks at the sound and, taken by surprise, Patrick shot out of the saddle and clean over its head. He had just time to think as he spun through the air that this was a sad end for a great man like himself to come to when he struck the ground and knew no more. And as he lay there on the ground, the cock crowed again and the fairy horse vanished like a puff of smoke blown down the wind.

Now it would take more than a fall from a horse to kill a man like Patrick Kentigern Keenan. He opened his eyes again at last to find that the white horse had vanished and that he was lying on the soft earth of a potato patch. It was growing to full daylight now, with cocks answering the one that had crowed, from all over the place. Patrick raised himself on his elbow and looked around, and to his great astonishment saw that it was his own potato patch he had landed in.

'Well, that's great good fortune I dug this ground yesterday,' he said, 'or a fall like that would have been the end of me right enough.'

Then he saw that he was holding something in his hand, and that something was the silver bridle of the fairy horse.

'Well, if that doesn't beat all!' he said, 'I must have held on so tight the beast had to slip its bridle before it could vanish on me.'

He lay there for a while to get over his aches and pains, feeling the shine and weight of the silver bridle in his hands and admiring his own courage in holding on to it in spite of the fairy horse. Then he got up and limped into the house for his breakfast.

Bridget had plenty to say to him when he came in all covered with earth and his clothes all torn and his hat missing, but Patrick ate his breakfast with the silver bridle on the table in front of him and he was so busy thinking of the cunning and the courage it had taken to win it that he never heard a word she said.

It was not long after this that a farmer came to him with a wild young horse and asked him to break it. 'For I'll have to shoot it if you can't, Patrick,' he said. 'It's no use in the world to me the way it is for there isn't a man that can handle it.'

'You've come to the one man that can,' said Patrick, though he didn't like the wild, rolling eye of the horse nor the way it jerked its head against the halter. 'Get its head well down, man.'

The farmer pulled tight on the halter-rope, the horse's head came down, and Patrick threw the silver bridle over it. Well, as soon as the creature felt the touch of the fairy bridle it stopped its rearing and prancing and stood as still as a stone for Patrick to mount it. He walked that horse, he cantered, he galloped, and you would have thought it had been ridden for years the way it answered to his lightest touch.

'Well, if that doesn't beat all!' gasped the farmer. He was so surprised that he paid Patrick more than he had meant to, and when he got home he spread the word that there wasn't a man in Ireland could tame horses like Patrick Kentigern Keenan.

Patrick's fame as a horse-breaker spread all over the land and horses were brought from far and near for him to tame. But it wasn't long before people began to notice that the silver bridle had more to do with it than he had. He was questioned upside down and inside out to know how he had come by it but he said never a word except, 'I'm the smartest man in Ireland, and that means that I know when to hold my tongue.'

He was sorely tempted to tell the story of the fairy horse but he had sense enough to see that no one would believe it after the business of Mulhoy and the fairy cattle. 'Let them wonder,' he said to himself. 'Sure, wonder's good for the soul and there'll come a day when I can speak out loud and clear to show the whole of Connemara the cleverness that's in me.'

Bridget was the only one that ever got the true story of the silver bridle out of him, and though she didn't know what Patrick was thinking to himself, she was pleased at the way he answered all the curious questions about it. 'You're learnin' sense, Patrick,' she said, smiling. 'I do believe you're learnin' sense at last.'

And still Patrick said never a word. Which shows that he had learned a deal more sense than even Bridget gave him credit for.

THE CHAMPIONS

Sir Walter Scott

Two riders meet in the desert, the one a Christian knight, and the other an Eastern cavalier, a Moslem. There can be only one possible outcome to such a meeting! The story of their encounter comes from The Talisman, *one of Scott's most gripping novels.*

The burning sun of Syria had not yet attained its highest point on the horizon, when a knight of the Red Cross, who had left his distant northern home and joined the host of the Crusaders in Palestine, was pacing slowly along the sandy deserts which lie in the vicinity of the Dead Sea or, as it is called, the Lake Asphaltites, where the waves of the Jordan pour themselves into an inland sea, from which there is no discharge of waters.

The warlike pilgrim had toiled among cliffs and precipices during the earlier part of the morning. More lately, issuing from those rocky and dangerous defiles, he had entered upon that great plain where the accursed cities provoked, in ancient days, the direct and dreadful vengeance of the Omnipotent.

The toil, the thirst, the dangers of the way, were forgotten as the traveller recalled the fearful catastrophe which had converted into an arid and dismal wilderness the fair and fertile valley of Siddim, once well watered, even as the Garden of the Lord, but now a parched and blighted waste, condemned to eternal sterility.

Crossing himself, as he viewed the dark mass of rolling waters, in colour as in quality unlike those of any other lake, the traveller shuddered as he remembered that beneath these sluggish waves lay the once proud cities of the plain, whose grave was dug by the thunder of the heavens, or the eruption of subterraneous fire, and whose remains were hid, even by that sea which holds no living fish in its bosom, bears no skiff on its surface and, as if its own dreadful bed were the only fit receptacle for its sullen waters, sends not, like other lakes, a tribute to the ocean.

The whole land around, as in the days of Moses, was 'brimstone and salt; it is not sown, nor beareth, nor any grass groweth thereon.' The land as well as the lake might be termed dead, as producing nothing having resemblance to vegetation, and even the very air was entirely devoid of its ordinary winged inhabitants, deterred probably by the odour of bitumen and sulphur which the burning sun exhaled from the waters of the lake in steaming clouds, frequently assuming the appearance of waterspouts. Masses of the slimy and sulphurous substance called naptha, which floated idly on the sluggish and sullen waves, supplied those rolling clouds with new vapours, and afforded awful testimony to the truth of the Mosaic history.

Upon this scene of desolation the sun shone with almost intolerable splendour, and all living nature seemed to have hidden itself from the rays, excepting the solitary figure which moved through the flitting sand at a foot's pace, and appeared the sole breathing thing on the wide surface of the plain. The dress of the rider and the accoutrements of his horse were peculiarly unfit for the traveller in such a country. A coat of linked mail, with long sleeves, plated gauntlets, and a steel breastplate, had not been esteemed sufficient weight of armour; there were also his triangular shield suspended round his neck, and his barred helmet of steel, over which he had a hood and collar of mail, which was drawn around the warrior's shoulders and throat, and filled up the vacancy between the hauberk and the headpiece.

His lower limbs were sheathed, like his body, in flexible mail, securing the legs and thighs, while the feet rested in plated shoes, which corresponded with the gauntlets. A long, broad, straight-shaped, double-edged falchion, with a handle formed like a cross, corresponded with a stout poniard on the other side. The knight also bore, secured to his saddle, with one end resting on his stirrup, the long steel-headed lance, his own proper weapon which, as he rode, projected backwards, and displayed its little pennoncelle, to dally with the faint breeze or drop in the dead calm.

To this cumbrous equipment must be added a surcoat of embroidered cloth, much frayed and worn, which was thus far useful that it excluded the burning rays of the sun from the armour, which they would otherwise have rendered intolerable to the wearer. The surcoat bore, in several places, the arms of the owner, although much defaced. These seemed to be a couchant leopard, with the motto, 'I sleep; wake me not.' An outline of the same device might be traced on his shield, though many a blow had almost effaced the painting. The flat top of his cumbrous cylindrical helmet was unadorned with any crest. In retaining their own wieldy defensive armour, the Northern Crusaders seemed to set at defiance the nature of the climate and country to which they had come to war.

The accoutrements of the horse were scarcely less massive and unwieldy than those of the rider. The animal had a heavy saddle plated with steel, uniting in front with a species of breastplate, and behind with defensive armour made to cover the loins. Then there was a steel axe, or hammer, called a mace-of-arms, and which hung to the saddlebow. The reins were secured by chainwork, and the front-stall of the bridle was a steel plate, with apertures for the eyes and nostrils, having in the midst a short, sharp pike, projecting from the forehead of the horse like the horn of the fabulous unicorn.

But habit had made the endurance of this load of panoply a second nature, both to the knight and his gallant charger. Numbers, indeed, of the Western warriors who hurried to Palestine died ere they became inured to the burning climate; but there were others to whom that climate became innocent and even friendly, and among this fortunate number was the solitary horseman who now traversed the border of the Dead Sea.

Nature, which cast his limbs in a mould of uncommon strength, fitted to wear his linked hauberk with as much ease as if the meshes had been formed of cobwebs, had endowed him with a constitution as strong as his limbs, and which bade defiance to almost all changes of climate, as well as to fatigue and privations of every kind. His disposition seemed, in some degree, to partake of the qualities of his

18

bodily frame; and as the one possessed great strength and endurance, united with the power of violent exertion, the other, under a calm and undisturbed semblance, had much of the fiery and enthusiastic love of glory which constituted the principal attribute of the renowned Norman line, and had rendered them sovereigns in every corner of Europe where they had drawn their adventurous swords.

It was not, however, to all the race that fortune proposed such tempting rewards; and those obtained by the solitary knight during two years' campaign in Palestine had been only temporal fame and, as he was taught to believe, spiritual privileges. Meantime, his slender stock of money had melted away, the rather that he did not pursue any of the ordinary modes by which the followers of the Crusade condescended to recruit their diminished resources at the expense of the people of Palestine—he exacted no gifts from the wretched natives for sparing their possessions when engaged in warfare with the Saracens, and he had not availed himself of any opportunity of enriching himself by the ransom of prisoners of consequence.

The small train which had followed him from his native country had been gradually diminished, as the means of maintaining them disappeared, and his only remaining squire was at present on a sick-bed, and unable to attend his master, who travelled, as we have seen, singly and alone. This was of little consequence to the Crusader, who was accustomed to consider his good sword as his safest escort and devout thoughts as his best companion.

Nature had, however, her demands for refreshment and repose even on the iron frame and patient disposition of the Knight of the Sleeping Leopard; and at noon, when the Dead Sea lay at some distance on his right, he joyfully hailed the sight of two or three palm trees, which arose beside the well which was assigned for his midday station. His good horse, too, which had plodded forward with the steady endurance of his master, now lifted his head, quickened his pace, as if he snuffed afar off the living waters which marked the place of repose and refreshment. But labour and danger were doomed to intervene ere the horse or horseman reached the desired spot.

As the Knight of the Couchant Leopard continued to fix his eyes attentively on the yet distant cluster of palm trees, it seemed to him as if some object was moving among them. The distant form separated

19

itself from the trees, which partly hid its motions, and advanced towards the knight with a speed which soon showed a mounted horseman, whom his turban, long spear, and green caftan floating in the wind, on his nearer approach, showed to be a Saracen cavalier. 'In the desert,' said an Eastern proverb, 'no man meets a friend.'

The Crusader was totally indifferent whether the infidel, who now approached on his gallant barb as if borne on the wings of an eagle, came as friend or foe—perhaps, as a vowed champion of the Cross, he might rather have preferred the latter. He disengaged his lance from his saddle, seized it with the right hand, placed it in rest with its point half elevated, gathered up the reins in the left, waked his horse's mettle with the spur, and prepared to encounter the stranger with the calm self-confidence belonging to the victor in many contests.

The Saracen came on at the speedy gallop of an Arab horseman, managing his steed more by his limbs and the inflection of his body than by any use of the reins, which hung loose in his left hand; so that he was enabled to wield the light, round buckler of the skin of the rhinoceros, ornamented with silver loops, which he wore on his arm, swinging it as if he meant to oppose its slender circle to the formidable thrust of the Western lance. His own long spear was not couched or levelled like that of his antagonist, but grasped by the middle with his right hand, and brandished at arm's length above his head.

As the cavalier approached his enemy at full career, he seemed to expect that the Knight of the Leopard should put his horse to the gallop to encounter him. But the Christian knight, well acquainted with the customs of Eastern warriors, did not mean to exhaust his good horse by any unnecessary exertion; and, on the contrary, made a dead halt, confident that if the enemy advanced to the actual shock, his own weight, and that of his powerful charger, would give him sufficient advantage, without the additional momentum of rapid motion.

Equally sensible and apprehensive of such a probable result, the Saracen cavalier, when he had approached towards the Christian within twice the length of his lance, wheeled his steed to the left with inimitable dexterity, and rode twice around his antagonist who, turning without quitting his ground, and presenting his front constantly to his enemy, frustrated his attempts to attack him on an unguarded point; so that the Saracen, wheeling his horse, was fain to

Like a hawk attacking a heron, the Saracen renewed the charge . . .

retreat to the distance of a hundred yards.

A second time, like a hawk attacking a heron, the heathen renewed the charge, and a second time was fain to retreat without coming to a close struggle. A third time he approached in the same manner, when the Christian knight, desirous to terminate this illusory warfare, in which he might at length have been worn out by the activity of his foeman, suddenly seized the mace which hung at his saddle-bow, and, with a strong hand and unerring aim, hurled it against the head of the Emir, for such and not less his enemy appeared. The Saracen was just aware of the formidable missile in time to interpose his light buckler betwixt the mace and his head; but the violence of the blow forced the buckler down on his turban, and though that defence also contributed to deaden its violence, the Saracen was beaten from his horse.

Ere the Christian could avail himself of this mishap, his nimble foeman sprung from the ground, and, calling on his steed, which instantly returned to his side, he leaped into his seat without touching the stirrup, and regained all the advantage of which the Knight of the Leopard hoped to deprive him. But the latter had in the meanwhile

21

recovered his mace, and the Eastern cavalier, who remembered the strength and dexterity with which his antagonist had aimed it, seemed to keep cautiously out of reach of that weapon of which he had so lately felt the force, while he showed his purpose of waging a distant warfare with missile weapons of his own. Planting his long spear in the sand at a distance from the scene of combat, he strung, with great address, a short bow which he carried at his back; and putting his horse to the gallop, once more described two or three circles of a wider extent than formerly, in the course of which he discharged six arrows at the Christian with such unerring skill that the goodness of his harness alone saved him from being wounded in as many places.

The seventh shaft apparently found a less perfect part of the armour, and the Christian dropped heavily from his horse. But what was the surprise of the Saracen when, dismounting to examine the condition of his prostrate enemy, he found himself suddenly within the grasp of the European, who had had recourse to this artifice to bring his enemy within his reach! Even in this deadly grapple the Saracen was saved by his agility and presence of mind. He unloosed the sword-belt, in which the Knight of the Leopard had fixed his hold and, thus eluding his fatal grasp, mounted his horse, which seemed to watch his motions with the intelligence of a human being, and again rode off. But in the last encounter the Saracen had lost his sword and his quiver of arrows, both of which were attached to the girdle which he was obliged to abandon. He had also lost his turban in the struggle. These disadvantages seemed to incline the Moslem to a truce. He approached the Christian with his right hand extended, but no longer in a menacing attitude.

'There is truce betwixt our nations,' he said, in the *lingua franca* commonly used for the purpose of communication with the Crusaders; 'wherefore should there be war betwixt thee and me? Let there be peace betwixt us.'

'I am well contented,' answered he of the Couchant Leopard; 'but what security dost thou offer that thou wilt observe the truce?'

'The word of a follower of the Prophet was never broken,' answered the Emir. 'It is thou, brave Nazarene, from whom I should demand security, did I not know that treason seldom dwells with courage.'

The Crusader felt that the confidence of the Moslem made him ashamed of his own doubts.

'By the cross of my sword,' he said, laying his hand on the weapon as he spoke, 'I will be true companion to thee, Saracen, while our fortune wills that we remain in company together.'

'By Mohammed, and by Allah, God of the Prophet,' replied his late foeman, 'there is not treachery in my heart towards thee. And now wend we to yonder fountain, for the hour of rest is at hand, and the stream had hardly touched my lips when I was called to battle by thy approach.'

The Knight of the Couchant Leopard yielded a ready and courteous assent; and the late foes, without an angry look or gesture of doubt, rode side by side to the little cluster of palm trees.

THAT MARK HORSE

Jack Schaefer

Not that horse, mister. Not that big slab-sided brute. Take any or all of the rest, I'm selling the whole string. But not that one. By rights I should. He's no damn good to me. The best horse either one of us'll likely ever see and he's no damn good to me. Or me to him. But I'll not sell him . . .

Try something, mister. Speak to him. The name's Mark . . . There. See how his ears came up? See how he swung to check you and what you were doing? The way any horse would. Any horse that likes living and knows his name. But did you notice how he wouldn't look at me? Used to perk those ears and wing that head whenever he heard my voice. Not any more. Knows I'm talking about him right now and won't look at me. Almost ten months it is and he still won't look at me . . .

That horse and I were five-six years younger when this all began. I was working at one of the early dude ranches and filling in at the rodeos roundabout. A little riding, a little roping. Not too good, just enough to place once in a while. I was in town one day for the mail and the postmaster poked his head out to chuckle some and say there was something for me at the station a mite too big for the box. I went down and the agent wasn't there. I scouted around and he was out by the stock corral and a bunch of other men too all leaning on the fence and looking over. I pushed up by the agent and there was that horse inside. He was alone in there and he was the damnedest horse I'd ever seen. Like the rest around I'd been raised on cow ponies and this thing looked big as the side of a barn to me and awkward as all hell. He'd just been let down the chute from a box car on the siding. There were bits of straw clinging to him and he stood still with head up testing the air.

For that first moment he looked like a kid's crazy drawing of a horse, oversize and exaggerated with legs too long and big stretched-out barrel and high-humped withers and long-reaching neck. The men were joshing and wondering was it an elephant or a giraffe and I was agreeing and then I saw that horse move. He took a few steps walking and flowed forward into a trot. That's the only way to put it. He flowed forward the way water rolls down a hill. His muscles didn't bunch and jump under his hide. They slid easy and smooth and those long legs reached for distance without seeming to try. He made a double circuit of the corral without slowing, checking everything as he went by. He wasn't trying to find a way out. He just wanted to move some and see where he was and what was doing roundabout. He saw us along the fence and we could have been posts for all the particular attention he paid us. He stopped by the far fence and stood looking over it and now I'd seen him move there wasn't anything awkward about him. He was big and he was rough-built but he wasn't awkward any more even standing there still. Nobody was saying a word. Everyone there knew horses and they'd seen what I saw. 'Damn it to eternal hell,' I said, 'That's a horse.' The agent turned and saw who it was. 'Glad you think so,' he said. 'It's your horse. This came along too.' And he stuck a note in my hand.

It had my name on it all right. It was from a New York State man who ran some sort of factory there, made shoes I think he told me once. He'd been a regular at the ranch, not for any dude doings but once a summer for a camping trip and I'd been assigned to him several years running. It wasn't long. It said the doctors had been carving him some and told him he couldn't ride again so he was closing his stable. He'd sold his other stock but thought this horse Mark ought to be out where there was more room than there was back east. Wanted me to take him and treat him right.

I shoved that note in a pocket and eased through the fence. 'Mark,' I called and across the corral those ears perked stiff and that big head swung my way. 'Mark,' I called again and that horse turned and came about halfway and stood with head high, looking me over. I picked a coil of rope off a post and shook out a loop and he watched me with ears forward and head a bit to one side. I eased close and suddenly I snaked up the loop and it was open right for his head and he just wasn't there. He was thirty feet to the left and I'd have sworn he made it in one leap. Maybe a dozen times I tried and I didn't have a chance.

The comments coming from the fence line weren't improving my temper any. Then I noticed he wasn't watching me, he was watching the rope, and I had an attack of common sense. He was wearing a halter. This wasn't any western range horse. This was one of those big eastern crossbreds with a lot of thoroughbred in them I'd heard about. Likely he'd never had a rope thrown at him before. I tossed the rope over by the fence and walked towards him and he stood blowing his nostrils a bit and looking at me. I stopped a few feet away and didn't even try to reach for the halter. He looked at me and he was really seeing me the way a horse can and I was somebody who knew his name out here where he'd been dumped out of the darkness of a box car. He stretched that long neck and sniffed at my shirt and I took hold of the halter and that was all there was to it . . .

That was the beginning of my education. Yes, mister, it was me had to be taught, not that horse. The next lesson came the first time I tried to ride him. I was thinking what a big brute he was and what a lot of power was penned in him and I'd have to control all that so I used a Spanish spade bit that would be wicked if used rough. He didn't want to take it and I had to force it on him. The same with the saddle. I used a double-rig with a high-roll cantle and he snorted at it and kept sidling away and grunted all the time I was tightening the cinches. He stood steady enough when I swung aboard but when we started off nothing felt right. The saddle was too small for him and sat too high-arched over the backbone and those sloping withers. He kept wanting to drop his head and rub his mouth on his legs over that bit.

At last he sort of sighed and eased out and went along without much fuss. He'd decided I was plain stupid on some things and he'd endure and play along for a while. At the time I thought he was accepting me as boss so I started him really stepping and the instant he understood I wanted him to move that was what he did. He moved. He went from a walk into a gallop in a single flowing rush and it was only that high cantle kept me from staying behind. I'm telling you, mister, that was something, the feel of those big muscles sliding smooth under me and distance dropping away under those hooves.

Then I realized he wasn't even working. I was travelling faster than I ever had on horseback and he was just loafing along without a sign of straining for speed. That horse just liked moving. I never knew another liked it as much. It could get to him the way liquor can a man and he'd keep reaching for more. That's what he was doing then. I could feel him notching it up the way an engine does when the engineer pushes forward on the throttle and I began to wonder how he'd be on stopping. I had an idea twelve hundred pounds of power moving like that would be a lot different from eight hundred pounds of bunchy little cow pony. I was right. I pulled in some and he slowed some but not much and I pulled harder and he tossed his head at the bit, biting, and I yanked in sharp and he stopped. Yes, mister, he stopped all right. But he didn't slap down on his haunches and slide to a stop on his rump the way a cow pony does. He took a series of jumps stiff-legged to brake and stopped short and sudden with his legs planted like trees and I went forward, bumping my belly on the horn and over his head and hanging there doubled down over his ears with my legs clamped around his neck.

That Mark horse was surprised as I was but he took care of me. He kept his head up and stood steady as a rock while I climbed down his neck to the saddle. I was feeling foolish and mad at myself and him and I yanked mean on the reins and swung him hard to head for home and that did it. He'd had enough. He shucked me off his back the way someone might toss a bean-bag. Don't ask me how. I'd ridden plenty horses and could make a fair showing even on the tough ones. But that Mark horse wanted me off so he put me off. And then he didn't bolt for the horizon. He stopped about twenty feet away and stood there watching me.

I sat on the ground and looked at him. I'd been stupid but I was beginning to learn. I remembered the feel of him under me, taking me with him not trying to get away from me. I remembered how he'd behaved all along and I studied on all that. There wasn't a trace of meanness in that horse. He didn't mind being handled and ridden. He'd been ready and willing for me to come up and take him in the station corral. But he wasn't going to have a rope slapped at him and be yanked around. He was ready and willing to let me ride him and to show me how a real horse could travel. But he wasn't going to do much of it with a punishing bit and a rig he didn't like.

He was a big batch of damned good horseflesh and he knew that and was proud of it and he had a hell of a lot of self-respect. He just plain wouldn't be pushed around and that was that and I had to understand it. I claim it proud for myself that I did. I went to him and he waited for me as I knew now he would. I swung easy as I could up into the saddle and he stood steady with his head turned a little so he could watch me. I let the lines stay loose and guided him just by neck-reining and I walked him back to the ranch. I slid down there and took off the western saddle and the bridle with that spade bit. I hunted through the barn till I found a light snaffle bit and cleaned it and put it in the bridle. I held it up for him to see and he took it with no fuss at all.

I routed out the biggest of the three English saddles we had for eastern dudes who wouldn't use anything else and that I'd always thought were damned silly things. I showed it to him and he stood quiet while I slapped it on and buckled the single leather cinch. 'Mark,' I said, 'I don't know how to sit one of these crazy postage stamps and I'm bunged up some from that beating. Let's take it easy.' Mister, that horse knew what I'd said. He gave me the finest ride I ever had . . .

See what I mean, the best damn horse either of us'll ever see? No, I guess you can't. Not complete. You'd have to live with him day after day and have the endless little things happening tally up in your mind. After a while you'd understand as I did what a combination he was of a serious dependable gent and a mischievous little kid. With a neat sense of timing on those things too. Take him out for serious riding and he'd tend strict to his business, which was covering any kind of ground for you at any kind of speed you wanted.

The roughest going made no difference to him. He was built to go at any clip just about anywhere short of straight up a cliff, and you'd get the feeling he'd try that if you really wanted him to. But let him loaf around with nothing to do and he'd be curious as a cat on the prowl, poking into every corner he could find and seeing what devilment he could do. Nothing mean, just playful. Maybe a nuisance if you were doing a job where he could get at you and push his big carcass in the way whiffling at everything or come up quiet behind and blow sudden down your shirt collar. Let him get hold of a bucket and you'd be buying a new one. There'd not be much left of the old one after he'd had his fun. He'd stick his nose in and flip the thing and do that over and over like he was trying for a distance record then start whamming it around with his hooves, tickled silly at the racket. And when there'd be no one else around to see how crazy you were acting he'd get you to playing games too. He liked to have you sneak off and hide and whistle low for him and he'd pad around stretching that long neck into the damnedest places looking for you and blow triumphant when he found you. Yes, mister, that horse liked living and being around him'd help you do the same.

And work? That horse was a working fool. No. There was nothing foolish about it. The ranch was still in the beef business too in those days and he'd never had any experience with cattle before. He was way behind our knowing little cow ponies when it came to handling them and he knew it. So he tried to balance that by using those brains of his overtime and working harder than any of the others. He'd watch them and try to figure what they were doing and how they did it and then do it himself. He'd try so hard sometimes I'd ache inside, feeling that eagerness quivering under me. Of course he never could catch up to them on some things. Too big. Too eager. Needed too much room moving around. He couldn't slide into a tight bunch of cattle and cut out the right one, easing it out without disturbing the rest much. And he wasn't much good for roping, even though he did let me use a western saddle for that soon as he saw the sense to it. Lunged too hard when I'd looped an animal and was ready to throw it. Maybe he'd have learned the right touch in time but he didn't get the chance. The foreman saw us damn near break a steer's neck and told us to quit. But on straight herding he couldn't be beat. He could head a runaway steer before it even stretched it's legs. He could scour the bush for strays like a hound dog on a scent. He could step out and cover territory all day at a pace that'd kill off most horses and come in seeming damn near as fresh as when he started. I used to think I was tough and could take long hours but that horse could ride me right out of the saddle and act like he thought I was soft for calling a halt.

But I still haven't hit the real thing. That horse was just plain honest all through. No, that's not the exact word. Plenty of horses are that. He was something a bit more. Square. That's it. He was just plain square in everything he did and the way he looked at living. He looked to have things fair and even. He was my horse and he knew it. I claim it proud that for a time anyway he really was my horse and let me know it. But that meant too I was his man and I had my responsibilities. I wasn't a boss giving orders. I was his partner. He wasn't something I owned doing what I made him do. He was my partner doing his job because he wanted to and because he knew that was the way it ought to be with a man and a horse. A horse like him. Long as I treated him right he'd treat me right. If I'd get mean or stupid with him I'd be having trouble. I'd be taking another lesson. Like the time along about the second or third week when I was feeling safer on that English saddle and forgot he wasn't a hard-broke cow pony. I wanted a sudden burst of speed for one reason or another and I hit him with my spurs. I was so used to doing that with the other horses that I couldn't figure at first what had happened. I sat on the ground rubbing the side I'd lit on and stared at him watching me about twenty feet away. Then I had it. I unfastened those spurs and threw them away. I've never used the things again ever, any time on any horse . . .

Well, mister, there I was mighty proud to have a horse like that but still some stupid because I hadn't tumbled to what you might call his speciality. He had to show me. It was during fall round-up. We had a bunch of steers in the home corral being culled for market and something spooked them and they started milling wild and pocketed me and Mark in a corner. They were slamming into the fence rails close on each side. I knew we'd have to do some fancy stepping to break through and get around them. I must have felt nervous on the reins because that Mark horse took charge himself. He swung away from those steers and leaped straight at the near fence and sailed over it. He swung in a short circle and stopped, looking back at those steers jamming into the corner where we'd been and I sat the saddle catching the breath he'd jolted out of me.

I should have known. He was a jumper. He was what people back east called a hunter. Maybe he'd been a timber horse, a steeplechaser. He'd cleared that four-foot fence with just about no take-off space like a kid skipping at hopscotch. I'm telling you, mister, I had me a time the next days jumping him over everything in sight. When I was sure of my seat I made him show me what he really could do and he played along with me for anything within reason, even stretching that reason considerable. The day I had nerve enough and he took me smack over an empty wagon I really began to strut. But there was one thing he wouldn't do. He wouldn't keep jumping the same thing over and over the same time out. Didn't see any sense in that. He'd clear whatever it was maybe twice, maybe three times, and if I tried to put him at it again he'd stop cold and swing his head to look at me and I'd shrivel down to size and feel ashamed . . .

So I had something new in these parts then, a jumping horse bred to it and built for it with the big frame to take the jolts and the power to do it right. I had me a horse could bring me some real money at the rodeos. I wouldn't have to try for prize money. I could put on exhibition stunts. I got together with some of the old show hands and we worked up an act that pleased the crowd. They'd lead Mark out so the people could see the size of him and he'd plunge around at the end of the shank, rolling his eyes and tossing his head. He'd paw at the sky and lash out behind like he was the worst mean-tempered mankiller ever caught.

It was all a joke because he was the safest horse any man ever handled and anyone who watched close could see those hooves never came near connecting with anything except air. But he knew what it was all about and he made it look good. The wranglers would get him over and into the outlaw chute with him pretending to fight all the way. They'd move around careful outside and reach through the bars to bridle and saddle him like they were scared green of him. I'd climb to the top rails and ease down on the saddle like I was scared too but determined to break my neck trying to ride one hell of a bucking brute. We'd burst out of the chute like a cannon going off and streak for the high fence on the opposite side of the arena. All the people who'd not

'. . . and I'd be standing in the stirrups waving my hat and yelling and the crowd'd go wild.'

seen it before would come up gasping on their seats expecting a collision that would shake the whole place. And at the last second that horse Mark would rise up and over the fence in a clean, sweet jump, and I'd be standing in the stirrups waving my hat and yelling and the crowd'd go wild.

After a time most people knew what to expect and the surprise part of that act was gone so we had to drop it. But we worked up another that got the crowds no matter how many times they saw it. I never liked it much but I blew too hard once how that horse would jump anything and someone suggested this and I was hot and said sure he'd do it and I was stuck with it. He never liked it much either but he did it for me. Maybe he knew I was getting expensive habits and needed the money coming in. Well, anyway, we did it and it took a lot of careful practice with a slow old steer before we tried the real thing. I'd be loafing around on Mark in the arena while the bull riding was on. I'd watch and pick a time when one of the bulls had thrown his rider and was hopping around in the clear or making a dash across the open. I'd nudge Mark with my heels and he'd be off in that forward flowing with full power in it. We'd streak for the bull angling in at the side and the last sliced second before a head-on smash we'd lift and go over in a clean sweep and wing to come up by the grandstand and take the applause.

Thinking of that since I've been plenty shamed. I've a notion the reason people kept wanting to see it wasn't just to watch a damned good horse do a damned difficult job. They were always hoping something would happen. Always a chance the bull might swerve and throw us off stride and make it a real smash. Always a chance the horns might toss too high and we'd tangle with them and come down in a messy scramble. But I didn't think about that then or how I was asking more than a man should expect in a tight spot that can't be avoided from a horse that's always played square with him. I was thinking of the money and the cheers and the pats on the back. And then it happened . . .

Not what maybe you're thinking, mister. Not that at all. That horse never failed in a jump and never would. We'd done our stint on the day, done it neat and clean, gone over a big head-tossing bull with space to spare and were just about ready to take the exit gate without

33

bothering to open it. Another bull was in the arena, a mean, tricky one that'd just thrown his rider after a tussle and was scattering dust real mad. The two tenders on their cagey little cow ponies had cut in to let the rider scramble to safety and were trying to hustle the bull into the closing out pen. They thought they had him going in and were starting to relax in their saddles when that brute broke away and tore out into the open again looking for someone on foot to take apart. While the tenders were still wheeling to go after him he saw something over by the side fence and head towards it fast. I saw too and sudden I was cold all over. Some damn fool woman had let a little boy get away from her, maybe three-four years old, too young to have sense, and that kid had crawled through the rails and was twenty-some feet out in the arena.

I heard people screaming at him and saw him standing there confused and the bull moving and the tenders too far away. I slammed my heels into Mark and we were moving too the way only that horse could move. I had to lunge forward along his neck or he'd have been right out from under me. There wasn't time to head the bull or try to pick up the kid. There wasn't time for anything fancy at all. There was only one thing could be done. We swept in angling straight to the big moving target of that bull and I slammed down on the reins with all my strength so Mark couldn't get his head up to jump and go over, and in the last split second all I could think of was my leg maybe getting caught between when they hit and I dived off Mark sidewise into the dust and he drove on alone and smashed into that bull just back of the big sweeping horns.

They picked me up half dazed with an aching head and assorted bruises and put me on some straw bales in the stable till a doctor could look me over. They led Mark into one of the stalls with a big gash from one of the horns along his side and a swelling shoulder so painful he dragged the leg without trying to step on it. They put ropes on the bull where he lay quiet with the fight knocked out of him and prodded him up and led him off. I never did know just what happened to the kid except that he was safe enough. I didn't care because when I pushed up off those bales without waiting for the doctor and went into the stall that Mark horse wouldn't look at me . . .

So that's it, mister. That's what happened. But I won't have you getting any wrong notions about it. I won't have you telling me the way some people do that horse is through with me because I made him smash into that bull. Nothing like that at all. He doesn't blame me for the pulled tendon in his shoulder that'll bother him long as he lives when the weather's bad. Not that horse. I've thought the whole business over again and again. I can remember every last detail of those hurrying seconds in the arena, things I wasn't even aware of at the time itself. That horse was flowing forward before I slammed my heels into him. There wasn't any attempt at lifting that big head or any gathering of those big muscles under me for a jump when I was slamming down on the reins. He'd seen. He knew. He knew what had to be done. That horse is through with me because at the last second I went yellow and I let him do it alone. He thinks I didn't measure up in the partnership. I pulled out and let him do it alone.

He'll let me ride him even now but I've quit that because it isn't the same. Even when he's really moving and the weather's warm and the shoulder feels good and he's reaching for distance and notching it up in the straight joy of eating the wind he's doing that alone too. I'm just something he carries on his back and he won't look at me . . .

SONG AND DANCE

Bess Leese

'I am sick of cars,' said Mr Christmas, giving his second-hand Ford a vindictive kick. 'Why can't we have a holiday without this thing? Why can't we leave it behind? Why can't we get away from it all? Think of it,' he said wistfully, 'a holiday entirely free of traffic jams, petrol fumes, parking problems and policemen saying, "Is this vehicle yours, sir?" and asking you to breathe into plastic bags. It would be idyllic.'

And that was why they found themselves in Ireland, travelling through the damp green lanes at about 2.7 m.p.h. in a hired red and yellow barrel-topped horse-drawn caravan.

It was Toby's idea. Toby never liked going away in summer, when there were so many interesting things like gymkhanas, pony club camp, the novice one-day event, on the calendar. Leaving Buttons, his pony, for a whole fortnight was bad enough. A holiday entirely without horses was unthinkable.

'A horse-drawn caravan? In Ireland? Just the job,' said Mr Christmas, and thought about Ireland's national drink, and the number of pints he would be able to consume without falling foul of the law.

'You must be *chef d'équipe*,' said Toby's mother, and thought about the long books she would at last have time to read: *War and Peace*, *The Bible* from cover to cover, the whole of Proust.

Toby thought about the horses.

'I suppose we couldn't take Buttons?' he said, and Mr Christmas said he supposed right.

'We'll hire a pony for you to ride,' he promised.

'Great,' said Toby, wondering how the horses would compare with Buttons.

They compared unfavourably. In fact, Toby had never clapped eyes on such a disreputable gang of rogues and paralytics, not even at pony club rallies. Some were expert at not being caught, some at refusing to go between the shafts. Some were expert at unarmed combat.

However, the horse which pulled Toby's caravan, a young skewbald mare called Kitty, seemed at first sight the pick of the bunch. And the little chestnut pony he was to ride, although green and unschooled, moved with a bright and willing stride that reminded him of Buttons. It was called Nijinsky.

'Doesn't look a bit like Nijinsky to me,' said Mr Christmas, thinking of the racehorse.

'The resemblance is fairly remote,' said Mrs Christmas, thinking of the ballet dancer.

'Never mind that,' said Toby. 'Let's go.'

'Lead on,' said Mr Christmas. He picked up the reins, and the wagon rumbled off after Toby and the chestnut pony. Mrs Christmas put on her spectacles, opened a paperback edition of *War and Peace* at page one and, wedging herself in the corner seat, started to read. The idyllic, carefree holiday had begun.

Mr Christmas's immediate goal was the nearest pub. In his mind's eye he pictured a pint of velvet-brown Guinness, topped with an inch or so of creamy froth, drawn from the barrel with consummate artistry by a comely Irish barmaid. It was the moment he had been looking forward to since he stepped off the ferry on to Irish soil. But the nearest pub was several miles away, and by the time they got there, Mr Christmas was beginning to think that there were, after all, certain virtues about motorized transport that the humble horse and cart lacked. Speed, for instance.

'I could have been here in five minutes in the car,' he complained when they arrived. 'Here, Toby. You look after the horses. We'll bring you a Coke out presently.'

Toby dismounted and loosened Nijinsky's girths. The horses were really quite hot. Perhaps they shouldn't have trotted along with quite such urgency. The sweat had gathered under Kitty's browband and her ears were quite sticky. She rubbed her nose on her foreleg, then peered longingly at the pub door.

'I could do with a pint myself,' she remarked.

Toby glanced round the yard. He looked at the sky, the ground, the road ahead, and underneath the caravan. Then he looked at Kitty again.

'Did you say that?' he said.

'Who else?' said the horse.

After considering this remark for a moment or two, Toby said, 'You're not supposed to talk.'

'Why not?'

'It's not usual. Not for horses, that is.'

'True, true. But not every horse has kissed the Blarney Stone. If you want to be blessed with the gift of the gab, let me recommend the Blarney Stone. It's done wonders for me.'

'Yes, I can tell.'

'What about my pint, then?'

Toby imagined himself going into the pub and saying, 'The horse wants a Guinness.' Then he imagined what his father would say. He said to the horse, 'Why don't you ask him yourself?'

'I'm particular who I speak to.'

'There's nothing wrong with my dad.'

'No,' Kitty agreed. 'Not yet . . . Did you notice this caravan has no brakes? A wagon with no brakes could easily get run away with. Easily. You've no idea. And the thirstier a horse gets, the more likely it is to run away.'

Toby didn't see why he should be blackmailed by a mere horse. He remembered his *Manual of Horse Injuries and Ailments*, which he had brought with him for reference, just in case; and he said, 'You shouldn't drink when you're hot. It'll do you lasting harm. And I shouldn't wonder if you get a hangover as well.'

'If I'm that hot, I shouldn't be kept hanging about here. What if I catch a chill? I can't afford to catch a chill, you know. It affects my voice.'

'A good thing, too,' said Toby.

Kitty laid back her ears. 'I'll have you know I've a very fine singing voice. You've heard of Ponselle, Schwarzkopf, Callas?'

'No,' said Toby.

'They are nothing beside me. The Irish Nightingale, they call me, the ones who've been privileged to hear me sing. I could have been the greatest Brünnhilde of them all. Listen to this.' She began to emit a strange lowing sound, reminiscent of somebody moaning into a jam-jar.

'What do you think of that?' she said.

'You sound just like Lee Marvin,' said Toby, and the horse looked gratified.

'I intend to perform one or two little arias at the Melody Fair in Avoca this week.'

'Over my dead body,' said Toby, aghast.

'What did you say?'

'We aren't thinking of going to Avoca.'

Kitty gave him a chilling stare. 'I'd advise you to reconsider that decision,' she said nastily, 'or it'll be the worse for you.'

'We'll see about that,' said Toby rashly.

Kitty made no reply, probably because Mr and Mrs Christmas appeared at that moment with Toby's Coke. But she gave him a very mean look.

'Onwards,' said Mr Christmas, climbing into the driving seat. 'The whole of green Ireland lies before us.' You could tell that the Guinness had done him good. 'Arklow, Avoca, Glendaloch . . .'

'We're not really going to Avoca, are we?' said Toby apprehensively.

'Not if you don't want to. Choose, my boy. Anywhere you like.'

'Cork,' said Toby at random.

'Cork it shall be,' said Mr Christmas, and they set off on the road again. Nobody knew exactly where Cork was, except that Toby thought it was bound to be a good safe distance from Avoca and its Melody Fair. The further away, the better.

That evening they camped on a farm with several other wagons. The horses were turned loose in the same field. Some of them came nosing round for titbits. Toby gave Nijinsky an apple and a handful of pony nuts. He was a nice little animal, really. He seemed especially taken with Mrs Christmas, and kept nuzzling her shoulder as she sat reading on the caravan shafts. Toby had enjoyed riding him, particularly because, unlike Kitty, he was silent. Nothing but an occasional friendly whicker passed his lips.

Nijinsky had one other virtue, which Toby discovered the next day. He was very easy to catch. Kitty, on the other hand, made off at a smart trot as soon as she saw the halter in Toby's hand. Toby mentioned that he had a carrot in his pocket, some pony nuts, and if she fancied them, a couple of fruit drops.

'Don't think you can bribe me,' said Kitty. 'I'm not slogging all the way to Cork. It's Avoca or nothing.'

Toby considered the situation. The field in which the horses grazed was the size of a smallish prairie, a paradise for the work-shy. Also, Kitty showed a horrid tendency to turn her quarters on him every time he approached.

'Okay, okay, we'll go to Avoca,' Toby agreed, playing for time.

'Good. Now, I plan to appear on Saturday,' said Kitty, lowering her nose into the halter. 'You shall be my dresser—clean the harness, polish up the brass, oil my hooves and so forth.'

'Thanks,' said Toby sourly.

It didn't look as if it was going to be much of a holiday for him. Kitty was very exacting, but if he objected to any of her demands, she blackmailed him with threats of running away, of wrecking the caravan, or of simply going on strike and refusing to pull the red and yellow wagon at all. When they camped by the seaside she demanded sea bathing for the good of her legs. She expected a thorough grooming morning and night, and ordered Toby to buy a stable rubber, body brush and curry comb so that he could get an extra bloom on her coat.

'You live out,' said Toby. 'You don't need body brushing. It'll take all the grease out of your coat, and then you'll get cold. You can't afford to catch cold. Think of your voice.'

Kitty thought of her voice, and warbled a simple tune.

'What's that dreadful noise?' said Mr Christmas, emerging from the caravan. 'Is the horse ill?'

'I think she's singing,' said Toby.

40

'Could be, could be,' said Mr Christmas. 'Sounds just like Lee Marvin.' And humming, rather tunelessly, 'I was born under a wandering star,' he went off to fetch the milk.

'Your father is obviously tone deaf,' said Kitty, 'as well as thoughtless. We did ten miles yesterday. Ten miles! I ask you! A horse of my exceptional ability should only be expected to do the lightest possible work. Anything else puts a considerable strain on the heart.'

'Yours goes like clockwork,' said Toby, pretending to listen.

'And the lungs.'

'There's nothing wrong with your wind.'

'Not to mention the legs.'

'What are you worried about? You've got plenty of bone.'

'All the same,' said Kitty, 'you could get the vet to give me the once-over.'

'The nearest vet is in Cork,' said Toby quickly. 'There's nothing wrong with a horse that eats like you do.'

'Look in your *Manual of Horse Injuries and Ailments*,' said Kitty; 'just to make sure.'

'See for yourself,' said Toby, flicking over the pages.

'I'm a horse, remember. You can't expect me to read.'

And that gave Toby an idea.

Mr Christmas let Toby have the job of leading the way. He said it was easier. He was not used to driving horses. He said that no matter what he did with the reins, Kitty wandered up grass verges, or down little by-lanes, or into farmyards and pig-sties. He said it was much easier to let her follow Toby and Nijinsky. So Toby trotted ahead, and the red and yellow caravan rumbled comfortably behind. Mr Christmas sat in the driving seat smoking his cigar and pointing out features of the landscape to his wife, who, without once looking up from her book, said 'Hum' or 'Ha' or 'Yes dear' or 'No dear' as the occasion demanded.

When they came to a signpost, the cavalcade halted. Toby read the signpost. 'Avoca,' it said to the right.

'This way,' said Toby, pointing to the left. 'Follow me.'

But Nijinsky, who was usually so obedient, refused to stir.

'You follow me, then,' said Mr Christmas, and shook the reins. Kitty took no notice. He slapped her rump with the end of the reins,

41

and at once she wheeled round and set off at a racking canter straight down the road to Avoca. The caravan lurched from side to side, shedding splinters of decorative woodwork as it went. The wheels looked as if they might come off. Forlorn cries came from Mr Christmas. Toby set off in pursuit, and once he had turned Nijinisky's head in the direction of Avoca, the pony leapt into action. But they couldn't overtake the caravan.

'You'll ruin your lungs,' shouted Toby, and Kitty stopped dead. There was a crashing inside the caravan, as if a lot of cups and saucers and teapots had fallen off the shelves.

'What was that noise?' said Mrs Christmas, turning over two pages at once.

'The horse bolted,' said Mr Christmas.

'I've lost my place,' said Mrs Christmas.

'And we're on the road to Avoca,' said Toby bitterly.

Kitty said nothing, but Toby could have sworn she was humming a victory song under her breath.

'Galloping along the hard road will make you lame,' said Toby;

'and serve you right.'

Kitty snapped at him spitefully, but Nijinsky jumped quickly out of the way. Toby patted him gratefully. 'Good job one of you is normal,' he said.

It was quite late when they reached Avoca; and when the horses were turned out for the night, Toby had a private word with Kitty.

'You said you couldn't read.'

'I can't.'

'What about that signpost?'

'I don't need to read signposts. I know the way to Avoca blindfold. Been here hundreds of times.'

'Not to sing?'

'No,' said Kitty. 'This is my debut. As a tribute to the Bard of Avoca, I shall sing "Believe me if all those endearing young charms," with, possibly, "How oft has the banshee cried" as an encore.'

Toby groaned.

'I shall expect an especially good grooming tomorrow. You could plait my mane if you like; and you could wash my tail and give me a

Kitty wheeled round and set off at a canter straight down the road to Avoca.

shampoo. I don't expect to do any work, of course. I must have a complete rest before my appearance on stage.'

'What if my dad wants to move on?' said Toby.

'I have ways of making him change his mind,' said Kitty.

Mr Christmas said: 'I don't know why you were so set against Avoca, Toby. Seems quite a jolly place to me. All those flags and bunting. Some kind of festival. I think there's going to be concerts, singing and dancing and so on. They're commemorating some poet or other.'

'Thomas Moore,' said Mrs Christmas without lifting her eyes from page 380 of *War and Peace*.

'We could stop on a day or two, join in the fun.'

Mr Christmas started enjoying the fun that evening. There was a band playing, and outside the pub, which was lit with coloured lights, there was a platform for music and dancing. A small drunken Irishman with no teeth reeled on to the stage and danced a jig, and a bosomy girl with a voice like a chainsaw sang nostalgically about Erin's Green Isle and the Lakes of Killarney. Mr Christmas, fortified by several pints of the national drink, tossed the paperback edition of *War and Peace* into the river, and waltzed Mrs Christmas up and down the streets.

But Toby went back to the caravan early and lay on his bunk plotting. He plotted putting carrots sliced the wrong way into Kitty's feed in the hopes that she would choke. He plotted watering after feeding so that she might get colic. Other dastardly ideas entered his head, but he had to reject them all, because he knew in his heart of hearts that he was not unscrupulous enough to carry them out. He didn't really want any harm to come to Kitty. He just didn't want her to sing. And he was fed up with taking orders from a horse.

The next day, before the celebrations began again, he decided to go for a ride on Nijinsky.

'You'd better groom me first,' said Kitty. 'I don't want any skimped last-minute jobs done on me.'

So Toby tied both horses to the caravan and began working on Kitty's coat. Kitty practised a few arpeggios as he brushed, interrupting herself occasionally to observe that he had left mud on her fetlocks, and directing him to examine her feet.

'I think my off-hind shoe is loose.'

'No it's not.'

'And I may have a gall where the collar rubs.'

'No you haven't.'

'None of that harness fits very well. Makes me itch.'

She rubbed her quarters against the caravan, and the flaking paint came off and dusted her rump with patches of lemony yellow.

'You've gone a funny colour,' said Toby.

'What do you mean?'

'On your backside. It's all yellow. You look like a buttercup.'

'The saints preserve us!' said Kitty in consternation. 'What is it? Is it spreading? It's some dreadful disease, I know it. Get the vet quickly, before it's too late.'

Toby fetched his *Manual of Horse Injuries and Ailments*, and leafed through the pages while Kitty peered anxiously over his shoulder.

'Hurry up,' she said. 'Every moment may be precious.'

'Just as I thought,' said Toby, pointing to a heading which said, quite plainly, 'Bog Spavin.' 'What you are suffering from is the Avoca Crunge, or Galloping Hypochondria. It starts as a discolouration on the hindquarters and spreads rapidly to the head, affecting the larynx and, in extreme cases, causing complete dumbness. There is no known cure, it says here'—Kitty rolled her eyes in despair—'but time and a complete rest of the vocal chords may alleviate the condition.'

'I shan't be able to sing,' Kitty whispered.

'What a shame,' said Toby, and led her back to the field. Then he saddled up Nijinsky. He had got very fond of Nijinsky. A nice ordinary pony that did as he was told, mostly, and kept his mouth shut.

'Have a sugar lump,' he said, pushing it under the pony's nose.

'Thanks,' said Nijinsky.

Toby sighed.

'Aren't you the biggest liar!' said Nijinsky, and his voice was tinged with admiration. 'The Avoca Crunge, indeed. She hasn't even got Bog Spavin.'

'The Blarney Stone has a lot to answer for,' said Toby. 'Don't tell me you can read as well.'

'Course I can read. Didn't care much for *War and Peace*, though. Could you lend me one of your comics after lunch?'

45

'Sure,' said Toby. 'On one condition. You're not to sing in this Melody Fair.'

'Sing?' said Nijinsky. He seemed quite affronted. 'I wouldn't dream of making such an exhibition of myself.' He gave a little pirouette as Toby climbed into the saddle.

'I'm going to dance,' he said.

ROYAL HUNT

Rosemary Sutcliff

Phaedrus the Gladiator rides north to the wilds of Caledonia on a strange mission. At the end of it he is no longer Phaedrus the Gladiator but Midir of the Dalriads and Lord of the Horse People, with the Mark of the Horse Lord tattooed on his forehead. Now the great Horse Lord must hunt and capture Princess Murna, daughter of the She-Wolf.

The next time Phaedrus woke, it was to the flicker of firelight through eyelids still half gummed together with sleep and the morning sky milk-silver beyond the smoke-hole in the crown of the King's Place roof. He lay for a few moments basking in the sense of well-being that lapped him round; the aching stiffness and the leaden weight of exhaustion all washed away by the black warm tide of sleep. Then gradually a weight of some other kind settled on him in its place as he remembered. Yesterday he had been crowned Horse Lord, but today was the day of his marriage to the Royal Woman.

He opened his eyes and came to one elbow with something between a groan and a curse; and a small rhythmic sound that had been going on all the while without his noticing it, stopped abruptly. The young warrior Brys, squatting by the great fire that glowed warmly in the centre of the big square hut, looked up alertly from the great war-spear with the black horsehair collar he had been burnishing across his knee.

Phaedrus scowled, startled for the moment at finding he was not alone. 'What in Typhon's name are you doing here?'

'I was burnishing your gear and weapons while you slept, Lord.

Gault bade me come to serve you.

'Gault!' Something in Phaedrus seemed to snap. 'Gault bids this thing—Gaults bids that thing—Gault will choose me my armour-bearer, *and* my wife——' He checked at sight of Brys's face, and quietened his tone somewhat. 'You have served me well; that spear blade looks as though it had this morning come fresh from the armourer's hands. Now go back to your own Lord, and if you should be seeing Gault on the way, tell him I thank him for his care of me, but I will choose my own armour-bearer.'

There was a moment's pause, and then Brys said, 'My own Lord is dead.'

And suddenly Phaedrus was remembering the place where the fortress stream dived through the outer wall, and Brys holding the torch that called that answering gleam from the silver apples under the water. Gault had said, 'Your Lord Gallgoid,' and the boy had said, 'My Lord Gallgoid is dead.' He rubbed the back of one hand across his forehead, trying to clear the confusion that still blurred all the edges of that night. 'Of course. You will be—you will have been Gallgoid's armour-bearer.'

'His armour-bearer and his charioteer.'

'It is in my mind that to suit Gallgoid, a charioteer would need to be good at his trade.'

'I am,' Brys said with conviction.

'*Sa*—and modest as well. And now you would be mine?'

'I am of the Kindred,' the boy said proudly, stating his claim. 'You would not be remembering; I was only in my first year in the Boys' House when you—when the Bad Thing happened. But I am of the Kindred.'

'Gallgoid had no one with him all that moon and more that he was with me in the Cave of the Hunter.'

'He left me behind in his Hall, until the time came to join him here in Dun Monaidh. There had to be those that he could trust, while he was supposed to be lying sick in his own place.'

'And you were one that he could trust.'

'Nobody found out that he was not there.'

Phaedrus looked at Brys with fresh eyes, noticing the good straight look of him, and the stubborn mouth. '*Sa, sa*—it may be that I shall

48

need someone to trust, one day . . . I will take Gallgoid's charioteer after him.'

'In spite of Gault the Strong?' Brys said slowly.

'In spite of Gault the Strong.' Suddenly Phaedrus laughed. 'If Gault had sent me Cuchulain himself this morning to be my armour-bearer and drive my team, I would have spat in Cuchulain's eye, if I could not be coming at Gault to spit in his.' Then as the slow smile broadened on Brys's face, 'Now leave that burnishing, and go and find me something to eat, for my belly's cleaving to my back-bone.'

The unpegged curtain of skins across the doorway had scarcely fallen behind Brys when voices sounded outside and the heavy folds were thrust back once more, and Conory, with Shân draped across his shoulders, strolled in. 'A fine and fortunate day to you,' he said pleasantly, and deposited on the low stool by the fire, a gaming board and a carved wooden box. 'Since there's no going out for the bridegroom until they summon him out to his marrying, it was in my mind that a game of Fox and Geese might serve to pass the time.'

Phaedrus flung off the bed-rugs with a sudden violence, and sat up. 'Conory, it's madness! I can't be going through with this marrying!'

Conory had settled on to his heels, and taken up the gaming box to open it. He said very softly, 'Midir, it is in my mind that you have no choice.'

'She will know!'

'Keep your voice down, you've a King's Guard outside. Here—let you put that cloak round you and come to the fire.'

'Friends and Furies!' Phaedrus swore, but he picked up the heavy saffron cloak that lay tumbled on the bed-place, and flung it round him over the light under-tunic which was all he had on, and came to squat beside the fire, facing Conory across the checkered board on which he had begun to set out the pieces of red amber and narwhal ivory. '*She will know!*' he repeated desperately.

'She will not. She was only ten—eleven summers old when it happened. A babe who would scarcely have begun her weapon training.' (To Phaedrus, it still seemed strange that the women of the Northern tribes shared the training of the young warriors, becoming as used to the throw-spear as to the distaff; and unconsciously, he frowned.) 'You have nothing to fear on that count. She will not know the balance of the blade.'

Phaedrus had just drawn breath for one more furious protest, for, indeed, it seemed to him a horrible thing, not only on his own account but on Midir's also, that he should take this She-Wolf's daughter for his woman; but at that moment Brys returned, with a beer-jar in one hand and a bowl piled with cold pig-meat and barley bannock in the other, and the protest must be left unmade. Instead, while they ate together—Brys had brought more than enough for two—he turned to the questions he had longed to ask yesterday. And Conory answered him as best he could, while Shân, springing down from his shoulder, pounced on and played with and tormented a lump of pig-fat that he had tossed for her beside the fire, until she wearied of the game and stalked out, tail erect, in search of better hunting elsewhere.

By the time they had finished eating, it was all told: the number of the dead, and how many women were among them, the success of the rising that had swept like heath fire through Earra-Ghyl, freeing the Dalriads of the dark bondage that had held them for seven years; the flight with Liadhan of the Earth Priests not killed in the fighting.

'Now it will be for the women once again to make the Mysteries of the Mother, as they have always done,' Conory said.

'Those furies!' Phaedrus gave a small shudder, thinking of the women with their knives and their rending claws, and Conory and himself fighting for life in the middle of them.

Conory flicked a faint, warning glance towards Brys, who was standing by to take up the bowl and beer-jar. 'Do you ever remember them like that before, save when a man intruded on the Women's Mysteries? And any man who does that has himself to blame for the thing that happens to him, as any woman would have only herself to blame, who spied on the boys' initiation ceremonies. Ach no, that night was Liadhan's doing, and the dancing in the Fire Hall, and the flute-magic of the priests.

When Brys had departed with the empty bowl, Phaedrus looking after him, with his mind full of the things that they had been talking of, found that his thoughts had slipped sideways for a moment, and he was discovering that the Princess Murna could not be more than a year older than Brys himself. For that one moment he was thinking of her as a person, wondering how it had been with her in the days since

Liadhan had fled, and where she was held captive, and if she also had woken to a weight on her heart this morning—supposing that she had slept at all.

Then Conory said, 'Shall we begin? Amber plays first.'

They played three games, and Conory won them all.

'Since you have my kingdom,' he said, when he had made the winning move for the third time, 'it is only fair that I should have the games.'

There was a laugh from the direction of the doorway and looking up, Phaedrus saw that several of the Companions had entered, and were standing just inside, watching the end of the game.

Yesterday they had been no more than strange faces and chance-heard names, these men who had been boys with Midir. But now, after the wild ride down from the Place of Life, that they had shared, and last night's feasting that they had shared also, names and faces had begun to join together. Lean, freckled Loarne, and Diamid of the sombre eyes and devil's-quirk eyebrows; Comgal and Domingart who were brothers and seldom apart; the little dark one, probably with Earthling blood in him, whom they called Baruch the Grass-Snake. And in a vague, tentative kind of way, they were beginning to take on a friendly look.

'The day be fortunate to you,' Diamid said, 'and may all the ill luck of it have gone into the gaming board.'

'Fox and Geese was never your game, my Lord Midir.' That was Domingart, shaking his head regretfully as he surveyed the board before Conory began to gather up the pieces. 'And still it would seem that it is not.'

'I am seven years out of practice,' Phaedrus returned. The excuse was unanswerable.

Brys had come in behind them, and began taking many-coloured garments from the big carved chest against the far wall, gravely proud to be the King's armour-bearer, so that Phaedrus thought if he had had a tail like a hound's, it would have been lashing slowly from side to side behind him.

Time to be moving, then. He flung off the saffron cloak and got to his feet and stood ready for them.

When he was once again clad in the ritual dress of the Horse Lord,

from the brogues on his feet to the great stallion head-dress that had
been brought from the hut where the priests kept the sacred objects,
he went out with the Companions, to the Horse Court beside the Court
of the Footprint, where the horses stood ready for them, and they
mounted and rode down into the great Forecourt.

The Forecourt was already alive with men, and growing more so
every moment, as others came in from all over Dun Monaidh. There
were few women among them, for the Women's Side were for the
most part gathering in the same way to the Royal Court. A shout
greeted Phaedrus, when he appeared with the Companions riding
about him, and they were caught up in the general movement and
swept across towards the gate gap which gave on to the Court of the
Footprint and from there into the Citadel.

'The King rides hunting!'

Somebody raised the shout and suddenly it was running through the
great gathering, taken up from end to end of the Dun.

'The King rides hunting!' And then, 'Who rides with the King?'

Conory and the Companions crashed out the answer: '*We* ride
hunting with the King!'

They were close before the inner gateway now, jostling and jostled;
the ponies stamped and snorted, puffing clouds of steam from their
nostrils; the colours of cloaks and fringed riding rugs and the glint of ·
bronze from brooch or bridle-bit were darkly brilliant in the grey
light of the winter's day that was already far past noon. 'What quarry
for the King's hunting? What quarry for the King's hunting?'

For a moment there was no answer, and the crowd fell silent,
watching the gate. Then from within that last inner circle of rock
walling rose the low wailing of the Women's Side, making the ritual
lament for a maiden carried off from among them against her will.
Phaedrus, on the red horse with the mealy mane, ignored Gault's
dark face among the nobles in the forefront of the crowd and glanced
aside under his red brows, at Conory; saw that Conory looked amused
and politely interested more than anything else, and could have hit
him. There was a little stir among the waiting tribesmen, and then the
dead thorn-bush that closed the inner gateway was dragged aside.
He could glimpse movement within, and the glint of colours, and the
Princess Murna came walking slowly through the gate, with the

women of the Kindred behind her and on either side. She walked looking neither to right nor left, down through the Court of the Footprint and out into the wide Forecourt. Her head was held very high and the soft, springing hair, loosed from its braids and drawn forward over her shoulders, hung in thick falls of dove-gold down over the breast of her many-coloured gown. The last time Phaedrus saw her she had been wearing the silver Moon Diadem; now she was crowned only with a narrow head-band of crimson stuff, strung about with shining wires and hung with discs of gold and coral; but under it her face was covered by a mask of red mare's-skin that gave her the look of something not belonging to the world of men, so that looking at her, Phaedrus felt the skin crawl and prickle at the back of his neck.

'What quarry for the King's hunting?' the men shouted again, and the women flung back the answer:

'A Royal quarry! A Royal quarry for the King's hunting!'

Down at the foot of the outer court, where the timbered gates stood open, two men had just flung a fringed riding rug across the back of a young black mare, which looked, as Phaedrus had thought when he first glanced down towards her past the Pillar Stone, to have been ridden already today. He had said as much to Conory, and Conory had smiled that gentle smile and said, 'A sad thing it would be if the quarry should outrun the hunter.'

The Princess was level with him now. She turned her head once in passing, and he caught the flicker of light behind the eye-slits of the mask. Then she passed on, the men parting to let her through, until she reached the gate and the black mare waiting there. She seemed to come to life then, and scooping up a great fold of her skirt, drew it through her belt and made the steed-leap as lightly as any boy.

A strange high cry like a sea-bird's floated back to them as she wheeled the mare towards the gate, and with a sharp jab of the horse-rod, urged from a stand into a canter.

She was out through the gate, and under the chanting of the Sun Priests invoking Lugh of the Shining Spear, they heard the hoof-beats trippling down to the outer gap, then burst into the drumming rhythm of full gallop. Phaedrus saw in his mind's eye that steep rocky track down to the marshes—and she was riding it as though it were a level practice field. His hand clenched on the horse-rod of green ash, and

53

unconsciously he must have tightened his knees. The red stallion
stirred and buckled forward under him, and instantly Conory's finger
flicked up, warningly, on his own bridle-rein. 'Not yet.'

There was a general laugh all about him. 'See how eager he is! This
will be a fine, fierce hunting!'

The drum of hoof-beats was very faint now, almost lost. The chanting of the Sun Priests died on a last long, glowing note, ane again the
finger flicked on Conory's bridle-rein. Phaedrus raised the small,
bronze-bound hunting-horn that hung from the stallion's pectoral
strap, and putting it to his mouth, set the echoes flying; then while the
notes still hung on the winter air, heeled the red horse from a stand to a
canter in his turn. The Companions were close behind him, Conory as
usual just to his right, as he bore down on the great gate. Behind him he
heard cries of, 'Good hunting!' Gault's bull-roar topping all the rest.
'Good hunting to you, Midir of the Dalriads!'

They were out through the gates and across the ditch causeway, the
track dropping before them towards the moss. For a moment there was
no sign of horse or rider. Then Conory pointed. 'There she goes!'
And away northward, Phaedrus saw the flying figure, already dimming
into the sear grey and tawny of the marshes.

'She's not going to be easy to follow, once the light begins to go.'

They took the plummeting track at breakneck speed, down from
the hill of Dun Monaidh, from the in-pastures where that year's colts
scattered, kicking up their heels as they drummed past, and out into
the great emptiness of Mhoin Mhor.

The Companions were stringing out like a skein of wild geese
threading the winter sky. The red horse snorted and stretched out
his neck, and the foam flew back from his muzzle to spatter against
Phaedrus's breast and thighs, the mealy silver of the mane flowed back
across his bridle wrist as the land fled by beneath the pounding hooves.
Excitement rose in them all: laughter and hunting cries began to break
from the men behind him. He guessed that in the ordinary way of things
the girl's flight would have been only a pretence, like the wailing of the
Women's Side. But this was different; if he wished to catch the Princess
Murna, then he would have to hunt her in good earnest; and pity
twinged in him, not for her, the She-Wolf's daughter, but for the
weary mare she rode.

The wild hunt swept after the She-Wolf's daughter, hooves drumming through the blackened heather . . .

55

The track was pulling up now, out of the great flats of Mhoin Mhor, and the quarry, striking away from it, was making north-eastward for the hills around Loch Abha head. And the wild hunt swept after her, hooves drumming through the blackened heather, skirting little tarns that reflected the sword-grey sky, startling the green plover from the pasture clearings. Far over to the west the clouds were breaking as they came up into the hills, and a bar of sodden daffodil light was broadening beyond the Island, casting an oily gleam over the wicked swirling water of the Old Woman, while away and away northward, the high snows of Cruachan caught the westering beams and shone out sour-white against the storm-clouds dark behind.

But now the chase was turning tail to the sunset, and all at once Conory let out a startled curse, and urging his horse level with Phaedrus's, shouted, 'By the Black Goddess! She's making for the Royal Water and Caledonia!'

And his words were caught up in a startled splurge of voices and echoed to and fro behind him.

'The vixen!' Phaedrus said, and laughed. 'You were saying it would be a sad thing if the quarry were to outrun the hunt. The Sun's warmth for ever on the shoulders of the man who rode that mare today!'

After that it was a hunt in deadly earnest, and shouting to the rest, Phaedrus crouched lower and dug in his heels and settled down to ride as he had never ridden in his life before. The ground began to be cut up, soon they were into a maze of shallow glens, wooded in their hollows, and tangled with stone-brambles and bilberry and sour juniper scrub along the ridges between; and once they thought they had lost her—until Baruch the Grass-Snake pointed across the glen, yelling, 'There she goes!' and on the crest of the far ridge the flying shape of horse and rider showed for an instant against the sky. They wheeled the horses and plunged downhill after her, fording the little burn between its snow-puddled edges, and stringing out in a bee-line up the opposite hillside. When they gained the crest, she was no-where to be seen, but a few moments later, she came into view again, heading up the glen towards the high moors; she had doubled north-ward, in an effort to throw them off her trail, relying maybe on the fading light to cover her. But there was just too much light left, and in turning north she had missed the ford a short way downstream, and was left with a tiring horse, and fast water running between her and her way of escape.

Conory was riding almost neck-to-neck with Phaedrus, a little in advance of the rest. He leaned towards him and said quickly, 'It is seven years since you were in these hills. Will you let me give the orders?'

Phaedrus nodded, and Conory fell back a little, shouting over his shoulder to the smother of horsemen that followed after, 'The mare is tiring fast, and if we can hold her in sight a while longer, she's ours! Baruch, Finn, Domingart, you three ride the lightest of us all—back to the ford with you, and come up the far side. If you can reach the glen head before her, you can turn her back, while we keep her from breaking away on this side, and we'll have her before the last light goes!'

The three young men wheeled their horses and plunged away, while the main chase swept on after their desperate, flagging quarry. But in a short while they appeared again, deliberately showing themselves on the skyline, and going like the Blue Riders of the West Wind. Phaedrus saw the black mare flinch sideways, flinging up her head, as though the hand on her bridle had involuntarily jerked at the bit; the rider snatched a glance over her shoulder; he could almost feel her despairing moment of indecision, then she wheeled about and took to the open hillside, swinging west again.

It was not quite a hunt now, more like rounding up a runaway colt. The Companions were not only behind her but creeping up on either side, heading her back the way she had come. The light was going fast as they dropped down from the hills on to lower ground. What still lingered of it lay over the wide levels of Mhoin Mhor stretching grey and dun and dreary-pale towards the sea; but on the left, behind the down-thrust tongue of the hills, the gathering twilight could not yet quench the one stretch of full colour in all that winter evening, the luminous, wicked green of bog between its islands of half-thawed snow.

The distance between them and the wild rider was lessening steadily, the mare, despite all her valiant efforts, rocking in her gallop and almost done. Then the girl snatched one more glance behind her, as though judging the distance that she still had in hand, and wrenching the mare round in her tracks, sent her plunging down into the hazel woods that sloped southward into those luminous green shadows.

Conory cried, 'Thunder of Tyr! She's heading straight for the bog!'

So she would take even that last hideous way out! Ahead of them as they crashed after her, heads low against the whipping hazel twigs, the bog lay smooth and deadly, and the girl was heading straight towards it, crouched over the mare's straining neck, drumming her heels into the poor labouring flanks. Her voice blew back to them, crying endearments and encouragement. Phaedrus, driving in his own heels, had somehow flung the red stallion out before the rest; he was circling to ride her off as the herd lads rode to turn a breakaway. The divots of soft black earth that spun from the mare's hooves flew past him like a flight of swallows; behind him the muffled hoof-drum of his Companions, ahead and to the right, the mare floundering and swaying in her stride; and the livid greenness of the bog rushing nearer—nearer, in the evening light. The cold rooty smell of it was all about them. A few moments more, and they would be into it . . .

Shouting would be no use. Desperately, Phaedrus flung the horse-rod point-over-butt as though it were a dagger and saw it arch spinning past the mare and plung into the bog myrtle just ahead of her and to the left. That was one useful trick learned in the Gladiators' School, anyway. Startled, she swerved aside, snorting, and plunged on, but no longer straight towards the fringe of the bog. Now the red horse's muzzle was almost level with the dark streaming tail, as the Princess struggled to head her mount back to the waiting greenness of the bog that was now so hideously close. But the mare was just about done, and Phaedrus clamped in his knees and hurled the stallion forward, and they were neck and neck. And with only a few strides to go and the ground softening at every hoof-fall, he wrenched round and deliberately took the black mare in the shoulder, all but bringing her down. She screamed with fear, and lashed out, but the crash had spun her in her tracks, away from the deadly verge. In the same instant Phaedrus felt his own mount side-slither under him, as one great round hoof slipped into the black quaking ooze beneath the green. For one long-drawn sickening moment the red horse lurched on the brink, and it seemed that in the next, they must be over into the bog, but his own speed carried him on, and the next flying stride found solid myrtle tussocks underfoot again.

The girl had turned with a cry of fury and lashed him across the face with her horse-rod, but he had her reins and they were racing along the flank of the bog, perilously locked together, floundering in and out of solid ground and sinking pocket, but drawing steadily away from the livid greenness of the hungry mire. Then with a sound between a laugh and a sob, Phaedrus had an arm round the Princess Murna and dragged her across the red horse's withers. The wild-eyed mare, lightened of her load, sprang away and went streaking back towards the hills, with a couple of the Companions in pursuit. And Phaedrus, still riding full gallop, was clamping the Royal Woman against him with his free arm, while she struggled to break free and fling herself off.

Then quite suddenly the fight seemed to go out of her as they slackened pace from that wild gallop to a canter. Phaedrus freed one hand—he was controlling the panting stallion with his knees now—and caught at the red mare's-skin mask.

Just for an instant, as his hand touched the hairiness of the hide, he wondered if it were the Moon Diadem trick over again, and the face beneath it would not be Murna's. Wondered, with a little shiver of cold between his shoulder-blades, whether it would be a human face at all, or something else, something that was not good to see . . . Then he pulled away the mask, and flung it behind him among the following horsemen. It was Murna's face looking up at him, grey-white and somehow ragged, as though in pulling off the bridal mask he had torn holes in something else, some inner defence that she was naked and terrified without. And for that one instant, despite the dusk, he could look into her face instead of only at the surface of it. Still feeling rather sick from the nearness of the bog, he laughed in sudden triumph, and bent his head and kissed her.

Surprisingly, she yielded against him and kissed him back. But as she did so, he felt her hand steal out, light as a leaf, but not quite light enough, towards the dagger in his belt.

His own hand flashed down and caught her wrist, twisting the weapon from her grasp before she well had hold of it, and sent it spinning into a furze bush. 'Softly, sweetheart! Maybe we shall do better if we are both unarmed,' he said, gently dangerous. She could have no other weapon about her, or she would not have gone for his dagger.

59

She gave a sharp cry of baffled fury, and became a thing as rigid and remote as one of the stocks of wood, charmed into human shape, that the People of the Hills left behind in its place when they stole a child of the Sun Folk. And yet the odd thing—Phaedrus knew it beyond all doubt, was that the kiss she had given him had been as real as her hand feeling for his dagger.

It was long past full dark by the time they came back to the Dun, and all down the steep track and massed in the gateways, the warriors were waiting, with pine-knot torches in their hands, so that they rode through a ragged avenue of light. Midir of the Dalriads, with the Royal Woman conquered and captive across his horse; and after them, the Companions, Conory triumphantly bearing aloft the red mare's-skin mask on the point of his spear, as though it were a trophy.

The King was home from his hunting.

THE OLD STAGE-COACH

Washington Irving

Washington Irving, a famous American writer and historian, once spent a Christmas in England, and his account of a ride in an old stage-coach is a reminder of how important horses were to the travellers in the nineteenth century. Travelling by stage-coach was often a test of endurance: the pace was slow—little more than ten miles an hour—and poor roads often made the journey a very uncomfortable one. Sometimes, on hills or over rough ground, coachman and passengers would have to plod alongside the struggling horses. But, for the most part, horses were well cared for and rested at scheduled stops.

In the course of a December tour in Yorkshire, I rode for a long distance in one of the public coaches, on the day preceding Christmas. The coach was crowded, both inside and out, with passengers who, by their talk, seemed to be principally bound to the mansions of relations or friends, to eat the Christmas dinner. It was loaded also with hampers of game, and baskets and boxes of delicacies; and hares hung dangling their long ears about the coachman's box, presents from distant friends for the impending feast.

I had three fine rosy-cheeked schoolboys for my fellow-passengers inside, full of the buxom health and manly spirit which I have observed in the children of this country. They were returning home for the holidays in high glee, and promising themselves a world of enjoyment. It was delightful to hear the gigantic plans of the little rogues, and the impracticable feats they were to perform during their six weeks' emancipation from the abhorred captivity of book, birch and pedagogue.

They were full of anticipations of the meeting with the family and household, down to the very cat and dog; and of the joy they were to give their little sisters by the presents with which their pockets were crammed. But the meeting to which they seemed to look forward with the greatest impatience was with Bantam, which I found to be a pony, and according to their talk, possessed of more virtues than any steed since the days of Bucephalus. How he could trot! How he could run! And then such leaps as he would take—there was not a hedge in the whole country that he could not clear.

They were under the particular guardianship of the coachman, to whom, whenever an opportunity presented, they addressed a host of questions, and pronounced him one of the best fellows in the world.

Indeed, I could not but notice the more than ordinary air of bustle and importance of the coachman, who wore his hat a little on one side, and had a large bunch of Christmas greens stuck in the buttonhole of his coat. He is always a personage full of mighty care and business, but he is particularly so during this season, having so many commissions to execute in consequence of the great interchange of presents.

And here, perhaps, it may not be unacceptable to my untravelled readers to have a sketch that may serve as a general representation of this very numerous and important class of functionaries, who have a dress, a manner, a language, an air, peculiar to themselves, and prevalent throughout the fraternity; so that, wherever an English stage-coachman may be seen, he cannot be mistaken for one of any other craft or mystery.

He has commonly a broad, full face, curiously mottled with red, as if the blood had been forced by hard feeding into every vessel of the skin. He is swelled into jolly dimensions by frequent consumptions of malt liquors, and his bulk is still further increased by a multiplicity of coats, in which he is buried like a cauliflower, the upper one reaching to his heels. He wears a broad-brimmed, low-crowned hat; a huge roll of coloured handkerchief about his neck, knowingly knotted and tucked in at the bosom; and has in summertime a large bouquet of flowers in his buttonhole—the present, most probably, of some enamoured country lass.

His waistcoat is commonly of some bright colour, striped, and his smallclothes extend far below the knees, to meet a pair of jockey-boots which reach about halfway up his legs. All this costume is maintained with much precision; he has a pride in having his clothes of excellent

Here the coachman is surrounded by those nameless hangers-on that infest inns.

materials. And, notwithstanding the seeming grossness of his appearance, there is still discernible that neatness and propriety of person which is almost inherent in an Englishman.

He enjoys great consequence and consideration along the road; he has frequent conferences with the village housewives, who look upon him as a man of great trust and dependence, and he seems to have a good understanding with every bright-eyed country lass. The moment he arrives where the horses are to be changed, he throws down the reins with something of an air and abandons the cattle to the care of the ostler; his duty being merely to drive from one stage to another.

When off the box his hands are thrust into the pockets of his great coat, and he rolls about the inn yard with an air of the most absolute lordliness. Here he is generally surrounded by an admiring throng of ostlers, stableboys, shoe-blacks and those nameless hangers-on that infest inns and taverns, and run errands, and do all kinds of odd jobs, for the privilege of battening on the drippings of the kitchen and the leakage of the tap-room. These all look up to him as to an oracle; treasure up his cant phrases; echo his opinions about horses and other topics of jockey lore; and above all, endeavour to imitate his air and carriage. Every ragamuffin that has a coat to his back thrusts his hands in the pockets, rolls in his gait, talks slang, and is an embryo 'coachey'.

Perhaps it might be owing to the pleasing serenity that reigned in my own mind, that I fancied I saw cheerfulness in every countenance throughout the journey. A stage-coach, however, carries animation always with it, and puts the world in motion as it whirls along. The horn, sounded at the entrance of a village, produces a general bustle. Some hasten forth to meet friends, some with bundles and bandboxes to secure places, and in the hurry of the moment can hardly take leave of the group that accompanies them.

In the meantime the coachman has a world of small commissions to execute. Sometimes he delivers a hare or pheasant; sometimes he jerks a small parcel or newspaper to the door of a public-house. And sometimes, with knowing leer and words of sly import, he hands to some half-blushing, half-laughing housemaid, an odd-shaped *billet-doux* from some rustic admirer.

As the coach rattles through the village, everyone runs to the window, and you have glances on every side of fresh country faces and blooming, giggling girls. At the corners are assembled groups of village idlers and wise men, who take their stations there for the important purpose of seeing company pass.

But the sagest knot is generally at the blacksmith's, to whom the passing of the coach is an event fruitful of much speculation. The smith, with the horse's heel in his lap, pauses as the vehicle whirls by; the cyclops round the anvil suspend their ringing hammers, and suffer the iron to grow cool. And the sooty spectre in brown paper cap, labouring at the bellows, leans on the handle for a moment, and permits the asthmatic engine to heave a long-drawn sigh while he glares through the murky smoke and sulphureous gleams of the smithy.

Perhaps the impending holiday might have given a more than usual animation to the country, for it seemed to me as if everybody was in good looks and good spirits. Game, poultry and other luxuries of the table were in brisk circulation in the villages; the grocers', butchers', and fruiterers' shops were thronged with customers. The housewives were stirring briskly about, putting their dwellings in order; and the glossy branches of holly, with their bright red berries, began to appear at the leaded windows.

The scene brought to mind an old writer's account of Christmas preparations:

'Now capons and hens, besides turkeys, geese, and ducks, with beef and mutton—must all die—for in twelve days a multitude of people will not be fed with a little. Now plums and spice, sugar and honey, square it among pies and broth. Now or never must music be in tube, for the youth must dance and sing to get them a heat, while the aged sit by the fire. The country maid leaves half her market, and must be sent again, if she forgets a pack of cards on Christmas Eve. Great is the contention of holly and ivy, whether master or dame wears the breeches. Dice and cards benefit the butler; and if the cook do not lack wit, he will sweetly lick his fingers.'

I was roused from this fit of luxurious meditation by a shout from my little travelling companions. They had been looking out of the coach windows for the last few miles, recognizing every tree and cottage as they approached home, and now there was a general burst of joy—'There's John! and there's old Carlo! and there's Bantam!' cried the happy little rogues, clapping their hands.

At the end of the lane there was an old sober-looking servant in livery, waiting for them. He was accompanied by a superannuated pointer, and by the redoubtable Bantam, a little old rat of a pony, with a shaggy mane and long rusty tail, who stood dozing quietly by the roadside, little dreaming of the bustling times that awaited him.

I was pleased to see the fondness with which the little fellows leaped about the steady old footman, and hugged the pointer, who wriggled his whole body for joy. But Bantam was the great object of interest! All wanted to mount at once, and it was with some difficulty that John arranged that they should ride by turns, and the eldest should ride first.

Off they set at last, one on the pony, with the dog bounding and barking before him, and the others holding John's hands; both talking at once, and over-powering him with questions about home, and with school anecdotes. I looked after them with a feeling in which I do not know whether pleasure or melancholy predominated. For I was reminded of those days when, like them, I had known neither care nor

65

sorrow, and a holiday was the summit of earthly joy.

We stopped a few moments afterwards to water the horses, and on resuming our route, a turn of the road brought us in sight of a neat country seat. I could just distinguish the forms of a lady and two young girls in the portico, and I saw my little comrades, with Bantam, Carlo, and old John, trooping along the carriage road. I leaned out of the coach window in the hopes of witnessing the happy meeting, but a grove of trees shut it from my sight.

In the evening we reached a village where I had determined to pass the night. As we drove into the great gateway of the inn, I saw on one side the light of a rousing kitchen fire beaming through a window.

I entered, and admired for the hundredth time, that picture of convenience, neatness, and broad, honest enjoyment, the kitchen of an English inn. It was of spacious dimensions, hung round with copper and tin vessels highly polished, and decorated here and there with a Christmas green. Hams, tongues, and flitches of bacon were suspended from the ceiling; a smoke-jack made its ceaseless clanking beside the fireplace, and a clock ticked in one corner. A well-scoured deal table extended along one side of the kitchen, with a cold round of beef and other hearty provisions upon it, over which two foaming tankards of ale seemed to be mounting guard.

Travellers of inferior order were preparing to attack this stout repast, while others sat smoking and gossiping over their ale on two high-backed oaken settles beside the fire. Trim housemaids were hurrying backwards and forwards under the directions of a fresh bustling landlady, but still seizing an occasional moment to exchange a flippant word, and have a rallying laugh with the group round the fire . . .

I had not been long at the inn when a post-chaise drove up to the door. A young gentleman stepped out, and by the light of the lamps, I caught a glimpse of a countenance which I thought I knew. I moved forward to get a nearer view, when his eye caught mine. I was not mistaken: it was Frank Bracebridge, a sprightly good-humoured young fellow with whom I had once travelled on the continent.

Our meeting was extremely cordial, for the countenance of an old fellow-traveller always brings up the recollection of a thousand pleasant scenes, odd adventures and excellent jokes. To discuss all these in a transient interview at an inn was impossible, and finding that I was not pressed for time, and was merely making a tour of observation, he insisted that I should give him a day or two at his father's country seat, to which he was going to pass the holidays, and which lay at a few miles' distance.

'It is better than eating a solitary Christmas dinner at an inn,' said he, 'and I can assure you of a hearty welcome in something of the old-fashioned style.'

His reasoning was cogent, and I must confess the preparation I had seen for universal festivity and social enjoyment had made me feel a little impatient of my loneliness. I closed, therefore, at once, with his invitation. The chaise drove up to the door, and in a few moments I was on my way to the family mansion of the Bracebridges.

THE PENSIONERS

James Herriot

This warm-hearted story is taken from the best-selling book It Shouldn't Happen to a Vet, *written by a vet practising in Yorkshire.*

As I sat at breakfast I looked out at the autumn mist dissolving in the early sunshine. It was going to be another fine day but there was a chill in the old house this morning, a shiveriness as though a cold hand had reached out to remind us that summer had gone and the hard months lay just ahead.

'It says here,' Siegfried said, adjusting his copy of the *Darrowby and Houlton Times* with care against the coffee-pot, 'that farmers have no feeling for their animals.'

I buttered a piece of toast and looked across at him.

'Cruel, you mean?'

'Well, not exactly, but this chap maintains that to a farmer, livestock are purely commercial—there's no sentiment in his attitude towards them, no affection.'

'Well, it wouldn't do if they were all like poor Kit Bilton, would it? They'd all go mad.'

Kit was a lorry driver who, like so many of the working men of Darrowby, kept a pig at the bottom of his garden for family consumption. The snag was that when killing time came, Kit wept for three days. I happened to go into his house on one of these occasions and found his wife and daughter hard at it cutting up the meat for pies and brawn while Kit huddled miserably by the kitchen fire, his eyes swimming with tears. He was a huge man who could throw a twelve-stone sack of meal on to his wagon with a jerk of his arms, but he seized my hand in his and sobbed at me 'I can't bear it,' Mr Herriot. He was like a Christian was that pig, just like a Christian.'

'No, I agree.' Siegfried leaned over and sawed off a slice of Mrs Hall's home-baked bread. 'But Kit isn't a real farmer. This article is about people who own large numbers of animals. The question is, is it possible for such men to become emotionally involved? Can the dairy farmer milking maybe fifty cows become really fond of any of them or are they just milk producing units?'

'It's an interesting point,' I said, 'and I think you've put your finger on it with the numbers. You know there are a lot of our farmers up in the high country who have only a few stock. They always have names for their cows—Daisy, Mabel, I even came across one called Kipperlugs the other day. I do think these small farmers have an affection for their animals but I don't see how the big men can possibly have.'

Siegfried rose from the table and stretched luxuriously. 'You're probably right. Anyway, I'm sending you to see a really big man this morning. John Skipton of Dennaby Close—he's got some tooth rasping to do. Couple of old horses losing condition. You'd better take all the instruments, it might be anything.'

I went through to the little room down the passage and surveyed the tooth instruments. I always felt at my most medieval when I was caught up in large animal dentistry and in the days of the draught horse it was a regular task. One of the commonest jobs was knocking the wolf teeth out of young horses. I have no idea how it got its name but you found the little wolf tooth just in front of the molars and if a young horse was doing badly it always got the blame.

It was no good the vets protesting that such a minute, vestigial object couldn't possibly have any effect on the horse's health and that the trouble was probably due to worms. The farmers were adamant; the tooth had to be removed.

We did this by having the horse backed into a corner, placing the forked end of a metal rod against the tooth and giving a sharp tap with an absurdly large wooden mallet. Since the tooth had no proper root the operation was not particularly painful, but the horse still didn't like it. We usually had a couple of fore-feet waving around our ears at each tap.

And the annoying part was that after we had done the job and pointed out to the farmer that we had only performed this bit of black magic to humour him, the horse would take an immediate turn for the better and thrive consistently from then on. Farmers are normally reticent about our successful efforts for fear we might put a bit more on the bill but in these cases they cast aside all caution. They would shout at us across the market place: 'Hey, remember that 'oss you knocked wolf teeth out of? Well he never looked back. It capped him.'

I looked again with distaste at the tooth instruments; the vicious forceps with two-feet-long arms, sharp-jawed shears, mouth gags, hammers and chisels, files and rasps; it was rather like a quiet corner in the Spanish Inquisition. We kept a long wooden box with a handle for carrying the things and I staggered out to the car with a fair selection.

Dennaby Close was not just a substantial farm; it was a monument to a man's endurance and skill. The fine old house, the extensive buildings, the great sweep of lush grassland along the lower slopes of the fell were all proof that old John Skipton had achieved the impossible; he had started as an uneducated farm labourer and he was now a wealthy landowner.

The miracle hadn't happened easily; old John had a lifetime of grinding toil behind him that would have killed most men, a lifetime with no room for a wife or family or creature comforts, but there was more to it than that; there was a brilliant acumen in agricultural matters that had made the old man a legend in the district. 'When all t'world goes one road, I go t'other' was one of his quoted sayings and it is true that the Skipton farms had made money in the hard times when others were going bankrupt. Dennaby was only one of John's farms; he had two large arable places of about four hundred acres each lower down the dale.

He had conquered, but to some people it seemed that he had himself been conquered in the process. He had battled against the odds for so many years and driven himself so fiercely that he couldn't stop. He could be enjoying all kinds of luxuries now but he just hadn't the time; they said that the poorest of his workers lived in better style than he did.

I paused as I got out of the car and stood gazing at the house as though I had never seen it before; and I marvelled again at the elegance which had withstood over three hundred years of the harsh climate. People came a long way to see Dennaby Close and take photographs of the graceful manor with its tall, leaded windows, the massive chimneys towering over the old moss-grown tiles; or to wander through the neglected garden and climb up the sweep of steps to the entrance with its wide stone arch over the great studded door.

There should have been a beautiful woman in one of those pointed hats peeping out from that mullioned casement or a cavalier in ruffles and hose pacing beneath the high wall with its pointed copings. But there was just old John stumping impatiently towards me, his tattered, buttonless coat secured only by a length of binder twine round his middle.

'Come in a minute, young man,' he cried. 'I've got a little bill to pay you.' He led the way round to the back of the house and I followed, pondering on the odd fact that it was always a 'little bill' in Yorkshire. We went in through a flagged kitchen to a room which was graceful and spacious but furnished only with a table, a few wooden chairs and a collapsed sofa.

The old man bustled over to the mantelpiece and fished out a bundle of papers from behind the clock. He leafed through them, threw an envelope on to the table then produced a cheque book and slapped it down in front of me. I did the usual—took out the bill, made out the amount on the cheque and pushed it over for him to sign. He wrote with a careful concentration, the small-featured, weathered face bent low, the peak of the old cloth cap almost touching the pen. His trousers had ridden up his legs as he sat down showing the skinny calves and bare ankles. There were no socks underneath the heavy boots.

When I had pocketed the cheque, John jumped to his feet. 'We'll have to walk down to t'river; 'osses are down there.' He left the house almost at a trot.

I eased my box of instruments from the car boot. It was a funny thing but whenever I had heavy equipment to lug about, my patients were

The two horses had been rubbing their chins gent

always a long way away. This box seemed to be filled with lead and it wasn't going to get any lighter on the journey down through the walled pastures.

The old man seized a pitchfork, stabbed it into a bale of hay and hoisted it effortlessly over his shoulder. He set off again at the same brisk pace. We made our way down from one gateway to another, often walking diagonally across the fields. John didn't reduce speed and I stumbled after him, puffing a little and trying to put away the thought that he was at least fifty years older than me.

About halfway down we came across a group of men at the age-old task of 'walling'—repairing a gap in one of the dry stone walls which trace their patterns everywhere on the green slopes of the Dales. One of the men looked up. 'Nice mornin', Mr Skipton,' he sang out cheerfully.

'Bugger t'mornin'. Get on wi' some work,' grunted old John in reply, and the man smiled contentedly as though he had received a compliment.

I was glad when we reached the flat land at the bottom. My arms

long each other's backs, unconscious of our approach.

seemed to have been stretched by several inches and I could feel a trickle of sweat on my brow. Old John appeared unaffected; he flicked the fork from his shoulder and the bale thudded on to the grass.

The two horses turned towards us at the sound. They were standing fetlock-deep in the pebbly shallows just beyond a little beach which merged into the green carpet of turf; nose to tail, they had been rubbing their chins gently along each other's backs, unconscious of our approach. A high cliff overhanging the far bank made a perfect wind break while on either side of us clumps of oak and beech blazed in the autumn sunshine.

'They're in a nice spot, Mr Skipton,' I said.

'Aye, they can keep cool in the hot weather and they've got the barn when winter comes.' John pointed to a low thick-walled building with a single door. 'They can come and go as they please.'

The sound of his voice brought the horses out of the river at a stiff trot and as they came near you could see they really were old. The mare was a chestnut and the gelding was a light bay but their coats were so flecked with grey that they almost looked like roans. This was most

73

pronounced on their faces, where the sprinkling of white hairs, the sunken eyes and the deep cavity above the eyes gave them a truly venerable appearance.

For all that, they capered around John with a fair attempt at skittishness, stamping their feet, throwing their heads about, pushing his cap over his eyes with their muzzles.

'Get by, leave off!' he shouted. 'Daft awd beggars.' But he tugged absently at the mare's forelock and ran his hand briefly along the neck of the gelding.

'When did they last do any work?' I asked.

'Oh, about twelve years ago, I reckon.'

I stared at John. 'Twelve years! And have they been down here all that time?'

'Aye, just lakin' about down here, retired like. They've earned it an' all.' For a few moments he stood silent, shoulders hunched, hands deep in the pockets of his coat, then he spoke quietly as if to himself. 'They were two slaves when I was a slave.' He turned and looked at me and for a revealing moment I read in the pale blue eyes something of the agony and struggle he had shared with the animals.

'But twelve years! How old are they, anyway?'

John's mouth twisted up at one corner. 'Well you're t'vet. You tell me.'

I stepped forward confidently, my mind buzzing with Galvayne's groove, shape of marks, degree of slope and the rest; I grasped the unprotesting upper lip of the mare and looked at her teeth.

'Good God!' I gasped, 'I've never seen anything like this.' The incisors were immensely long and projecting forward till they met at an angle of about forty-five degrees. There were no marks at all—they had long since gone.

I laughed and turned back to the old man. 'It's no good, I'd only be guessing. You'll have to tell me.'

'Well she's about thirty and gelding's a year or two younger. She's had fifteen grand foals and never ailed owt except a bit of teeth trouble. We've had them rasped a time or two and it's time they were done again, I reckon. They're both losing ground and dropping bits of half chewed hay from their mouths. Gelding's the worst—has a right job champin' his grub.'

I put my hand into the mare's mouth, grasped her tongue and pulled it out to one side. A quick exploration of the molars with my other hand revealed what I suspected; the outside edges of the upper teeth were overgrown and jagged and were irritating the cheeks while the inside edges of the lower molars were in a similar state and were slightly excoriating the tongue.

'I'll soon make her more comfortable, Mr Skipton. With those sharp edges rubbed off she'll be as good as new.' I got the rasp out of my vast box, held the tongue in one hand and worked the rough surface along the teeth, checking occasionally with my fingers till the points had been sufficiently reduced.

'That's about right,' I said after a few minutes. 'I don't want to make them too smooth or she won't be able to grind her food.'

John grunted. 'Good enough. Now have a look at t'other. There's summat far wrong with him.'

I had a feel at the gelding's teeth. 'Just the same as the mare. Soon put him right, too.'

But pushing at the rasp, I had an uncomfortable feeling that something was not quite right. The thing wouldn't go fully to the back of the month; something was stopping it. I stopped rasping and explored again, reaching with my fingers as far as I could. And I came upon something very strange, something which shouldn't have been there at all. It was like a great chunk of bone projecting down from the roof of the mouth.

It was time I had a proper look. I got out my pocket torch and shone it over the back of the tongue. It was easy to see the trouble now; the last upper molar was overlapping the lower one resulting in a gross overgrowth of the posterior border. The result was a sabre-like barb about three inches long stabbing down into the tender tissue of the gum.

That would have to come off—right now. My jauntiness vanished and I suppressed a shudder; it meant using the horrible shears—those great long-handled things with the screw operated by a cross bar. They gave me the willies because I am one of those people who can't bear to watch anybody blowing up a balloon and this was the same sort of thing only worse. You fastened the sharp blades of the shears on to the tooth and began to turn the bar slowly, slowly. Soon the tooth began to groan and creak under the tremendous leverage and you knew that any second it would break off and when it did it was like somebody letting off a rifle in your ear. That was when all hell usually broke loose, but mercifully this was a quiet old horse and I wouldn't expect him to start dancing around on his hind legs. There was no pain for the horse because the overgrown part had no nerve supply—it was the noise that caused the trouble.

Returning to my crate I produced the dreadful instrument and with it a Haussman's gag, which I inserted on the incisors and opened on its ratchet till the mouth gaped wide. Everything was easy to see then and, of course, there it was—a great prong at the other side of the mouth exactly like the first. Great, great, now I had two to chop off.

The old horse stood patiently, eyes almost closed, as though he had seen it all and nothing in the world was going to bother him. I went through the motions with my toes curling and when the sharp crack came, the white-bordered eyes opened wide, but only in mild surprise. He never ever moved. When I did the other side he paid no attention at all in fact, with the gag prising his jaws apart he looked exactly as though he was yawning with boredom.

As I bundled the tools away, John picked up the bony spicules from the grass and studied them with interest. 'Well, poor awd beggar. Good job I got you along, young man. Reckon he'll feel a lot better now.'

On the way back, old John, relieved of his bale, was able to go twice as fast and he stumped his way up the hill at a furious pace, using the fork as a staff. I panted along in the rear, changing the box from hand to hand every few minutes.

About halfway up, the thing slipped out of my grasp and it gave me a chance to stop for a breather. As the old man muttered impatiently I looked back and could just see the two horses; they had returned to the shallows and were playing together, chasing each other jerkily, their feet splashing in the water. The cliff made a dark backcloth to the picture—the shining river, the trees glowing bronze and gold and the sweet green of the grass.

Back in the farmyard, John paused awkwardly. He nodded once or twice, said 'Thank ye, young man,' then turned abruptly and walked away.

I was dumping the box thankfully into the boot when I saw the man who had spoken to us on the way down. He was sitting, cheerful as ever, in a sunny corner, back against a pile of sacks, pulling his dinner packet from an old army satchel.

'You've been down to see t'pensioners then? By gaw, awd John should know the way.'

'Regular visitor, is he?'

'Regular? Every day God sends you'll see t'awd feller ploddin' down there. Rain, snow or blow, never misses. And allus has summat with him—bag o' corn, straw for their bedding.'

'And he's done that for twelve years?'

The man unscrewed his Thermos flask and poured himself a cup of black tea. 'Aye, them 'osses haven't done a stroke o' work all that time and he could've got good money for them from the horse-flesh merchants. Rum 'un, isn't it?'

'You're right,' I said, 'it is a rum 'un.'

Just how rum it was occupied my thoughts on the way back to the surgery. I went back to my conversation with Siegfried that morning; we had just about decided that the man with a lot of animals couldn't be expected to feel affection for individuals among them. But those buildings back there were full of John Skipton's animals—he must have hundreds.

Yet what made him trail down that hillside every day in all weathers? Why had he filled the last years of those two old horses with peace and beauty? Why had he given them a final ease and comfort which he had withheld from himself?

It could only be love.

THE ENCHANTED HORSE

Anonymous

The Nooroze, or the new day, which is the first of the year and spring, is observed as a solemn festival throughout all Persia.

On one of these festival days, just as the Sultan of Shiraz was concluding his public audience, which had been conducted with unusual splendour, a Hindu appeared at the foot of the throne, with an artificial horse richly adorned, and so spiritedly modelled, that at first sight he was taken for a living animal.

The Hindu prostrated himself before the throne and, pointing to the horse, said to the sultan, 'This horse is a great wonder: whenever I mount him, be it where it may, if I wish to transport myself through the air to the most distant part of the world, I can do it in a very short time. This is a wonder which nobody ever heard speak of, and which I offer to show your majesty if you command me.'

The Emperor of Persia, who was fond of everything that was curious, and who, notwithstanding the many prodigies of art he had seen, had never beheld or heard of anything that came up to this, told the Hindu that he was ready to see him perform what he had promised.

The Hindu instantly put his foot into the stirrup, mounted his horse with admirable agility, and when he had fixed himself in the saddle, asked the emperor whither he pleased to command him.

'Do you see that mountain?' said the emperor, pointing to it. 'Ride your horse there, and bring me a branch of a palm tree that grows at the bottom of the hill.'

The Emperor of Persia had no sooner declared his will than the Hindu turned a peg, which was in the hollow of the horse's neck, just by the pommel of the saddle; and in an instant the horse rose off the ground and carried his rider into the air with the rapidity of lightning to a great height, to the admiration of the emperor and all the spectators. Within less than a quarter of an hour they saw him returning with the palm branch in his hand; but before he descended, he took two or three turns in the air over the spot, amid the acclamations of all the people, then alighted on the spot whence he had set off. He dismounted, and going up to the throne, prostrated himself, and laid the branch of the palm tree at the feet of the emperor.

The emperor, who had viewed with no less admiration than astonishment this unheard-of sight which the Hindu had exhibited, conceived a great desire to have the horse, and said to the Hindu, 'I will purchase him of you, if he is to be sold.'

'Sire,' replied the Hindu, 'there is only one condition on which I can part with my horse, and that is the gift of the hand of the princess your daughter as my wife; this is the only bargain I can make.'

The courtiers about the Emperor of Persia could not forbear laughing aloud at this extravagant proposal of the Hindu; but the Prince Feroze-shah, the eldest son of the emperor and presumptive heir to the crown, could not hear it without indignation. 'Sire,' he said, 'I hope you will not hesitate to refuse so insolent a demand, or allow this insignificant juggler to flatter himself for a moment with the idea of being allied to one of the most powerful monarchs in the world. I beg of you to consider what you owe to yourself, to your own blood, and the high rank of your ancestors.'

'Son,' replied the Emperor of Persia, 'I will not grant him what he asked—and perhaps he does not seriously make the proposal; and, putting my daughter the princess out of the question, I may make another agreement with him. But before I bargain with him, I should be glad that you would examine the horse, try him yourself, and give me your opinion.' On hearing this, the Hindu expressed much joy, and ran before the prince, to help him to mount, and show him how to guide and manage the horse.

The prince mounted without the Hindu's assisting him; and, as soon as he had got his feet in the stirrups, without staying for the artist's advice, he turned the peg he had seen him use, when instantly the horse darted into the air, quick as an arrow shot out of a bow by the most adroit archer; and in a few moments neither horse nor prince were to be seen. The Hindu, alarmed at what had happened, prostrated himself before the throne. The sultan, in a passion, asked why he did not call him the moment he ascended.

'Sire,' answered the Hindu, 'your majesty saw as well as I with what rapidity the horse flew away. The surprise I was then and still am in deprived me of the use of my speech; but if I could have spoken, he was gone too far to hear me. If he had heard me, he knew not the secret to bring him back, which, through his impatience, he would not stay to learn. But, sire,' added he, 'there is room to hope that the prince, when he finds himself at a loss, will perceive another peg, and as soon as he turns that the horse will cease to rise, and descend to the ground, when he may turn him to what place he pleases by guiding him with the bridle.'

Notwithstanding all these arguments of the Hindu, which carried great appearance of probability, the Emperor of Persia was much alarmed at the evident danger of his son. 'I suppose,' replied he, 'it is very uncertain whether my son may perceive the other peg, and make a right use of it. May not the horse, instead of lighting on the ground, fall upon some rock, or tumble into the sea with him?'

'Sire,' replied the Hindu, 'I can deliver you from this apprehension, by assuring you that the horse crosses seas without ever falling into them, and always carries his rider wherever he may wish to go. And your majesty may assure yourself that if the prince does but find out the other peg I mentioned, the horse will carry him where he pleases. It is not to be supposed that he will stop anywhere but where he can find assistance, and make himself known.'

'Your head shall answer for my son's life, if he does not return safe, or I should hear that he is alive.' He then ordered his officers to secure the Hindu, and keep him close prisoner; after which he retired to his

80

palace, dismayed that the festival of Noorooze should have proved so inauspicious.

In the meantime the prince was carried through the air with prodigious velocity. In less than an hour's time he ascended so high that he could not distinguish anything on the earth. It was then he began to think of returning, and conceived he might do this by turning the same peg the contrary way, and pulling the bridle at the same time. But when he found that the horse still continued to ascend, his alarm was great. He turned the peg several times in different ways, but all in vain. It was then he saw his fault, and apprehended the great danger he was in, from not having learnt the necessary precautions to guide the horse before he mounted. He examined the horse's head and neck with attention, and perceived behind the right ear another peg, smaller than the other. He turned that peg and presently realized that he descended in the same oblique manner as he had mounted, but not so swiftly.

Night had overshadowed that part of the earth over which the prince was when he discovered and turned the small peg; and as the horse descended, he by degrees lost sight of the sun, till it grew quite dark; insomuch that, instead of choosing what place he would go to, he was forced to let the bridle lie upon the horse's neck, and wait patiently till he alighted, though not without the dread lest it should be in the desert, a river or the sea.

At last the horse stopped upon some solid substance about midnight, and the prince dismounted very faint and hungry, having eaten nothing since the morning, when he came out of the palace with his father to assist at the festival. He found himself to be on the terrace of a magnificent palace, surrounded with a balustrade of white marble, breast high; and groping about reached a staircase, which led down into an apartment, the door of which was half open.

The prince stopped at the door, and listening, heard no other noise than the breathing of some people who were fast asleep. He advanced a little into the room, and by the light of a lamp saw that those persons were black mutes, with naked sabres laid by them: which was enough to inform him that this was the guard-chamber of some sultan or princess.

Prince Feroze-shah advanced on tiptoe, without waking the attendants. He drew aside the curtain, went in, and saw a magnificent chamber containing many beds, one alone being on a raised dais, and the others on the floor. The princess slept in the first and her women in the others. He crept softly towards the dais without waking either the princess or her women, and beheld a beauty so extraordinary that he was charmed at the first sight. He fell on his knees, and twitching gently the princess's sleeve, kneeling beside her, pulled it towards him. The princess opened her eyes, and seeing a handsome young man, was in great surprise, yet showed no sign of fear.

The prince availed himself of this favourable moment, bowed his head to the ground, and rising, said, 'Beautiful princess, by the most extraordinary and wonderful adventure, you see at your feet a suppliant prince, son of the Emperor of Persia; pray afford him your assistance and protection.'

The personage to whom Prince Feroze-shah so happily addressed himself was the Princess of Bengal, eldest daughter of the rajah of that kingdom, who had built this palace at a small distance from his capital, for the sake of the country air. She thus replied: 'Prince, you are not in a barbarous country—take courage; hospitality, humanity, and politeness are to be met with in the Kingdom of Bengal, as well as in that of Persia. I grant you the protection you ask—you may depend on what I say.'

The Prince of Persia would have thanked the princess, but she would not give him leave to speak. 'Notwithstanding I desire,' said she, 'to know by what miracle you have come hither from the capital of Persia in so short a time, and by what enchantment you have evaded the vigilance of my guards, yet as you must want some refreshment, I will postpone my curiosity, and give orders to my attendants to show you an apartment, that you may rest yourself after your fatigue, and be better able to answer my inquiries.'

The princess's attendants were much surprised to see the prince in the princess's chamber, but they at once prepared to obey her commands. They each took a wax candle, of which there were great numbers lighted up in the room; and after the prince had respectfully taken leave, went before and conducted him into a handsome hall; where, while some were preparing the bed, others went into the kitchen and prepared a supper; and when he had eaten as much as he chose, they removed the trays, and left him to taste the sweets of repose.

The next day the princess prepared to give the prince another interview, and in expectation of seeing him, she took more pains in dressing and adjusting herself at the glass than she had ever done before. She tried her women's patience, and made them do and undo the same thing several times. She adorned her head, neck, arms, and waist, with the finest and largest diamonds she possessed. The habit she put on was one of the richest stuffs of the Indies, of a most beautiful colour, and made only for kings, princes, and princesses. After she had consulted her glass, and asked her women, one after another, if anything was wanting to her attire, she sent to tell the Prince of Persia that she would make him a visit.

The Prince of Persia, who by the night's rest had recovered the fatigue he had undergone the day before, had just dressed himself when he received notice of the intention of the princess, and expressed himself to be fully sensible of the honour conferred on him. As soon as the princess understood that the Prince of Persia waited for her, she immediately went to pay him a visit.

After mutual compliments, the prince related to her the wonders of the magic horse, of his journey through the air, and of the means by which he had found an entrance into her chamber; and then, having thanked her for her kind reception, expressed a wish to return and relieve the anxiety of the sultan his father. When the prince had finished, the princess replied, 'I cannot approve, Prince, of your going so soon; grant me at least the favour I ask of a little longer acquaintance; and since I have had the happiness to have you alight in the Kingdom of Bengal, I desire you will stay long enough to enable you to give a better account of what you may see here at the court of Persia.'

The Prince of Persia could not well refuse the princess this favour, after the kindness she had shown him, and therefore politely complied with her request; and the princess's thoughts were directed to render his stay agreeable by all the amusements she could devise.

Nothing went forward for several days but concerts of music, accompanied with magnificent feasts and collations in the gardens, or hunting parties in the vicinity of the palace, which abounded with all sorts of game, stags, hinds, and fallow deer, and other beasts peculiar to the Kingdom of Bengal, which the princess could pursue without danger. After the chase, the prince and princess met in some beautiful spot, where a carpet was spread and cushions laid for their accommodation. There resting themselves, they conversed on various subjects.

Two whole months the Prince of Persia abandoned himself entirely to the will of the Princess of Bengal, yielding to all the amusements she contrived for him; for she neglected nothing to divert him, as if she thought he had nothing else to do but to pass his whole life with her in this manner. But he now declared seriously he could not stay longer, and begged of her to give him leave to return to his father.

'And, princess,' observed the Prince of Persia, 'that you may not doubt the truth of my affection, I would presume, were I not afraid you would be offended at my request, to ask the favour of taking you along with me.'

The princess returned no answer to this address of the Prince of Persia; but her silence, and eyes cast down, were sufficient to inform him that she had no reluctance to accompany him into Persia. The only difficulty she felt was, that the prince knew not well enough how to govern the horse, and she was apprehensive of being involved with him in the same difficulty as when he first made the experiment. But the prince soon removed her fear, by assuring her she might trust herself with him, for that after the experience he had acquired, he defied the Hindu himself to manage him better. She thought, therefore, only of concerting measures to get off with him so secretly, that nobody belonging to the palace should have the least suspicion of their design.

The next morning, a little before daybreak, when all the attendants were asleep, they went upon the terrace of the palace. The prince turned the horse towards Persia, and placed him where the princess could easily get up behind him, which she had no sooner done, and was well settled with her arms about his waist, for her better security, than he turned the peg, when the horse mounted into the air, and making his usual haste, under the guidance of the prince, in two hours the prince discovered the capital of Persia.

The prince would not alight in the palace of his father, but directed his course towards a kiosk at a little distance from the capital. He led the princess into a handsome apartment, where he told her, that to do her all the honour that was due to her, he would go and inform his

The prince turned the peg and the enchanted horse mounted into the air . . .

father of their arrival, and return to her immediately. He ordered the attendants of the palace, whom he summoned, to provide the princess with whatever she had occasion for.

After the prince had taken his leave of the princess, he ordered a horse to be brought, which he mounted, and set out for the palace. As he passed through the streets he was received with acclamation by the people, who were overjoyed to see him again. The emperor, his father, was holding his divan when he appeared before him in the midst of his council. He received him with tears of joy and tenderness, and asked him what was become of the Hindu's horse.

This question gave the prince an opportunity of describing the embarrassment and danger he was in when the horse ascended into the air, and how he had arrived at last at the Princess of Bengal's palace, the kind reception he had met with there, and that the motive which had induced him to stay so long with her was the mutual affection they entertained for each other; also, that after promising to marry her, he had persuaded her to accompany him into Persia. 'But, sire,' added the prince, 'I felt assured that you would not refuse your consent, and have brought her with me on the enchanted horse to your summer palace, and have left her there, till I could return and assure her that my promise was not in vain.'

After these words, the prince prostrated himself before the emperor to obtain his consent, when his father raised him up, embraced him a second time, and said to him, 'Son, I not only consent to your marriage with the Princess of Bengal, but will go myself and bring her to my palace, and celebrate your nuptials this day.'

The emperor now ordered that the Hindu should be fetched out of prison and brought before him. When the Hindu was admitted to his presence, he said to him, 'I secured thy person, that thy life might answer for that of the prince my son. Thanks be to God, he is returned again: go, take your horse, and never more let me see your face.'

As the Hindu had learned of those who brought him out of prison that Prince Feroze-shah was returned with a princess, and was also informed of the place where he had alighted and left her, and that the emperor was making preparations to go and bring her to his palace, as soon as he got out of the presence, he thought of being revenged upon the emperor and the prince. He mounted his horse, and without losing any time, went directly to the palace, and addressing himself to the captain of the guard, told him he came from the Prince of Persia for the Princess of Bengal, and to conduct her behind him through the air to the emperor, who waited in the great square of his palace to gratify the whole court and city of Shiraz with that wonderful sight.

The captain of the guard, who knew the Hindu, and that the emperor had imprisoned him, gave the more credit to what he said because he saw that he was at liberty. He presented him to the Princess of Bengal; who no sooner understood that he came from the Prince of Persia than she consented to what the prince, as she thought, had desired of her.

The Hindu, overjoyed at his success and the ease with which he had accomplished his villainy, mounted his horse, took the princess behind him, with the assistance of the captain of the guard, turned the peg, and instantly the horse mounted into the air.

At the same time the Emperor of Persia, attended by his court, was on the road to the palace where the Princess of Bengal had been left, and the Prince of Persia had gone ahead to prepare the princess to receive his father—when the Hindu, to revenge himself for the ill-treatment he had received, appeared over their heads with his prize.

When the Emperor of Persia saw the Hindu, he stopped. His surprise and affliction were the more terrible, because it was not in his power to punish so high an affront. He loaded him with a thousand threats, as did also all the courtiers, who were witnesses of so signal a piece of insolence and unparalleled artifice and treachery.

The Hindu, little moved with their threats, which just reached his ears, continued his way, while the emperor, extremely mortified at so great an insult, but more so that he could not punish the author, returned to his palace in rage and vexation.

But what was Prince Feroze-shah's grief at beholding the Hindu hurrying away with the Princess of Bengal, whom he loved so passionately! He returned to the summer palace, where he had last seen the princess, melancholy and broken-hearted.

When he arrived, the captain of the guard, who had learnt his fatal credulity in believing the artful Hindu, threw himself at his feet with tears in his eyes, accused himself of the crime which unintentionally he had committed, and condemned himself to die by his hand. 'Rise,' said the prince to him, 'I do not impute the loss of my princess to thee, but to my own want of precaution. But not to lose time, fetch me a holy man's habit, and take care you do not give the least hint that it is for me.'

The captain readily obtained such a habit and carried it to Prince Feroze-shah. The prince immediately pulled off his own dress, put the habit on, and being so disguised, and provided with a box of jewels which he had brought as a present to the princess, left the palace, uncertain which way to go, but resolved not to return till he had found out his princess, and brought her back again, or perished in the attempt.

In the meantime the Hindu, mounted on his enchanted horse with the princess behind him, arrived early next morning at the capital of the Kingdom of Kashmir. He did not enter the city, but alighted in a wood, and left the princess on a grassy spot, close to a rivulet of fresh water, while he went to seek for food. On his return, and after he and the princess had partaken of refreshment, he began to maltreat the princess because she refused to become his wife. As the princess cried out for help, the Sultan of Kashmir and his court passed through the

The sultan, addressing himself to the Hindu, demanded who he was and wherefore he ill-treated the lady.

wood on their return from hunting, and hearing a woman's voice calling for help, went to her rescue.

The sultan, addressing himself to the Hindu, demanded who he was and wherefore he ill-treated the lady. The Hindu, with great impudence, replied that she was his wife, and what had anyone to do with his quarrel with her?

The princess, who knew neither the rank nor quality of the person who came so seasonably to her relief, exclaimed, 'My lord, whoever you are whom heaven has sent to my assistance, have compassion on me. I am a princess. This Hindu is a wicked magician, who has forced me away from the Prince of Persia, to whom I was going to be married, and has brought me hither on the enchanted horse you behold there.'

The Princess of Bengal had no occasion to say more. Her beauty, majestic air, and tears, declared that she spoke the truth. Justly enraged at the insolence of the Hindu, the sultan ordered his guards to surround him, and strike off his head, which sentence was immediately executed.

The sultan then conducted the princess to his palace, where he lodged her in the most magnificent apartment, next to his own, and commanded a great number of women slaves to attend her.

The Princess of Bengal's joy was inexpressible at finding herself delivered from the Hindu, of whom she could not think without horror. She flattered herself that the Sultan of Kashmir would complete his generosity by sending her back to the Prince of Persia when she would have told him her story, and asked that favour of him. But she was much deceived in these hopes; for her deliverer had resolved to marry her himself the next day; and for that end had issued a proclamation, commanding the general rejoicing of the inhabitants of the capital. At the break of day the drums were beaten, the trumpets sounded, and shounds of joy echoed throughout the whole palace.

The Princess of Bengal was awakened by these tumultuous concerts, but attributed them to a very different cause from the true one. When the Sultan of Kashmir came to wait upon her, after he had inquired after her health, he acquainted her that all these rejoicings were to render her nuptials the more solemn, and at the same time desired her assent to the union. This declaration put her into such a state of agitation that she fainted away.

The women slaves who were present ran to her assistance, though it was a long time before they succeeded in bringing her to herself. But when she recovered, rather than break the promise she had made to Prince Feroze-shah, by consenting to marry the Sultan of Kashmir, who had proclaimed their nuptials before he had asked her consent, she resolved to feign madness. She began to utter the most extravagant expressions before the sultan, and even rose off her seat as if to attack him, insomuch that he was greatly alarmed and afflicted that he had made such a proposal so unreasonably.

When he found that her frenzy increased rather than abated, he left her with her women, charging them never to leave her alone, but to take great care of her. He sent often that day to inquire how she did, but received no other answer than that she was rather worse than better.

The Princess of Bengal continued to talk wildly, and showed other marks of a disordered mind next day and the following, so that the sultan was induced to send for all the physicians belonging to his court, to consult them upon her disease, and to ask if they could cure her.

When the Sultan of Kashmir saw that his court physicians could not cure her, he called in the most celebrated and experienced of the city, who had no better success. He then sent for the most famous in the kingdom, who prescribed without effect. Afterwards he despatched to the courts of neighbouring sultans, with promises of magnificent rewards to any who should devise a cure for her malady.

Various physicians arrived from all parts, and tried their skill, but none could boast of success.

During this interval, Feroze-shah, disguised in the habit of a holy man, travelled through many provinces and towns, involved in grief, and making diligent inquiry after his lost princess at every place he came to. At last, passing through a city of Hindustan, he heard the people talk much of a Princess of Bengal, who had become mad on the day of the intended celebration of her nuptials with the Sultan of Kashmir. At the name of the Princess of Bengal, and supposing that there could exist no other Princess of Bengal than her upon whose account he had undertaken his travels, he hastened towards the Kingdom of Kashmir, and, upon his arrival at the capital, took up his lodging at a khan, where, the same day, he was informed of the story of the princess and the fate of the Hindu. The prince was convinced that he had at last found the beloved object he had sought so long.

Being informed of all these particulars, he provided himself with a physician's habit, and his beard having grown long during his travels, he passed the more easily for the character he assumed. He went boldly to the palace, and announced his wish to be allowed to undertake the cure of the princess to the chief of the officers.

Some time had elapsed since any physician had offered himself, and the Sultan of Kashmir with great grief had begun to lose all hope of ever seeing the princess restored to health, though he still wished to marry her. He at once ordered the officer to introduce the physician he had announced. The Prince of Persia being admitted to an audience, the sultan told him the Princess of Bengal could not bear the sight of a physician without falling into most violent transports, which increased her malady; and conducted him into a closet, from whence, through a lattice, he might see her without being observed.

There Feroze-shah beheld his lovely princess sitting melancholily, with tears in her eyes, and singing an air in which she deplored her unhappy fate, which had deprived her, perhaps for ever, of the object she loved so tenderly: and the sight made him more resolute in his hope of effecting her cure. On his leaving the closet, he told the sultan that he had discovered the nature of the princess's complaint, and that she was not incurable; but added withal, that he must speak with her in private and alone, as, notwithstanding her violent agitation at the sight of physicians, he hoped she would hear and receive him favourably.

The sultan ordered the princess's chamber-door to be opened, and Feroze-shah went in. As soon as the princess saw him (taking him by his habit to be a physician), she resorted to her old practice of meeting her physicians with threats and indications of attacking them. He made directly towards her, and when he was nigh enough for her to hear him, and no one else, said to her, in a low voice, 'Princess, I am not a physician, but the Prince of Persia, and am come to procure you your liberty.'

The princess, who knew the sound of the voice, and recognized his face, notwithstanding he had let his beard grow so long, grew calm at once, and felt a secret joy in seeing so unexpectedly the prince she loved. Feroze-shah told her as briefly as possible his own travels and adventures, and his determination to find her at all risks. He then desired the princess to inform him of all that happened to her, from the time she was taken away till that happy moment, telling her that it was of the greatest importance to know this, that he might take the most proper measures to deliver her from the tyranny of the Sultan of Kashmir. The princess informed him of all that had happened, and that she had feigned to be mad that she might so preserve herself for a prince to whom she had given her heart and faith, and not marry the sultan, whom she neither loved nor could ever love.

The Prince of Persia then asked her if she knew what became of the horse, after the death of the Hindu magician. To which she answered, that she knew not what orders the sultan had given; but supposed, after the account she had given him of it, he would take care of it as a curiosity. As Feroze-shah never doubted but that the sultan had the horse, he communicated to the princess his design of making use of it to convey them both into Persia; and after they had consulted together on the measures they should take, they agreed that the princess should next day receive the sultan.

The Sultan of Kashmir was overjoyed when the Prince of Persia stated to him what effect his first visit had had towards the cure of the princess. On the following day, when the princess received him in such a manner as persuaded him her cure was far advanced, he regarded the prince as the greatest physician in the world, and exhorted the princess carefully to follow the directions of so skilful a physician, and then retired. The Prince of Persia, who attended the Sultan of Kashmir on his visit to the princess, inquired of him how the Princess of Bengal came into the dominions of Kashmir thus alone, since her own country was far distant.

The sultan at once informed him of what the princess had related, when he had delivered her from the Hindu magician: adding that he had ordered the enchanted horse to be kept safe in his treasury as a great curiosity, though he knew not the use of it.

'Sire,' replied the pretended physician, 'the information which your majesty has given your devoted slave affords me a means of curing the princess. As she was brought hither on this horse, and the horse is enchanted, she hath contracted something of the enchantment, which can be dissipated only by a certain incense which I am acquainted with. If your majesty would entertain yourself, your court, and the people of your capital, with the most surprising sight that ever was beheld, let the horse be brought tomorrow into the great square before the palace, and leave the rest to me. I promise to show you, and all that assembly, in a few moments' time, the Princess of Bengal completely restored in body and mind. But the better to effect what I propose, it will be requisite that the princess should be dressed as magnificently as possible, and adorned with the most valuable jewels in your treasury.' The sultan would have undertaken much more difficult things to have secured his marriage with the princess, which he expected soon to accomplish.

The next day, the enchanted horse was by his order taken out of the treasury, and placed early in the great square before the palace. A report was spread through the town that there was something extraordinary to be seen, and crowds of people flocked thither from all parts, insomuch that the sultan's guards were placed to prevent disorder, and to keep space enough round the horse.

The Sultan of Kashmir, surrounded by all his nobles and ministers of state, was placed in a gallery erected on purpose. The Princess of Bengal, attended by a number of ladies whom the sultan had assigned her, went up to the enchanted horse, and the women helped her to mount. When she was fixed in the saddle, and had the bridle in her hand, the pretended physician placed round the horse at a proper distance many vessels full of lighted charcoal, which he had ordered to be brought, and going round them with a solemn pace, cast in handfuls of incense; then, with downcast eyes, and his hands upon his breast, he ran three times about the horse, making as if he pronounced some mystical words.

The moment the pots sent forth a dark cloud of smoke—accompanied with a pleasant smell, which so surrounded the princess that neither she nor the horse could be discerned—watching his opportunity, the prince jumped nimbly up behind her, and reaching his hand to the peg, turned it; and just as the horse rose with them into the air, he pronounced these words, which the sultan heard distinctly, 'Sultan of Kashmir, when you would marry princesses who implore your protection, learn first to obtain their consent.'

Thus the prince delivered the Princess of Bengal, and carried her the same day to the capital of Persia, where he alighted in the square of the palace, before the emperor his father's apartment. The solemnization of the marriage took place as soon as the emperor had made certain the ceremony would be pompous and magnificent.

After the days appointed for the rejoicings were over, the Emperor of Persia's first care was to name and appoint an ambassador to go to the Rajah of Bengal with an account of what had passed, and to demand his approbation and ratification of the alliance contracted by this marriage; which the Rajah of Bengal took as an honour, and granted with great pleasure and satisfaction.

AND AS FOR PEDRO...

Ruby Ferguson

When Jill and her friend Bar go shopping, they return with a surprising new inmate for their hacking stable at the vicarage.

I don't know what you feel about it, but I always think that on days when anything terrific happens, something else terrific happens almost immediately after. I mean, you go on the same old round of school and eating meals and having a ride before you start your homework for days and days and even weeks and weeks, and all of a sudden something happens to you almost as though you were in a book and before you get your breath something else—if you see what I mean.

I mean, I think it was a pretty terrific thing for me to go and buy a horse for thirty-two pounds, but if anybody had told me that before the day was over—but I'd better get on with it.

When we got off the bus Bar said she'd better go to the cake shop and get some buns for tea, so I waited outside for her. And right opposite where I was standing at the kerb-side was the poorest, dirtiest pony I ever saw in my life. I couldn't help staring at him because he was so wretched, and it made a little cold feeling start in my middle and work right up to my neck. You couldn't see what colour he was, he was so dirty; and yet in spite of it all, and in spite of his miserable, downcast head, he had nice lines and good legs and I think it was partly

The man picked up the reins and lashed the pony across the face with them.

that which made me look at him and think what an awful pity it was he was so neglected.

He was harnessed with filthy, string-mended harness to a little cart with a few sticks of firewood on it, and on the side of the cart was painted in very dirty paint: *J. Biggs. Timber Merchant.*

Just then J. Biggs himself came out of the pub, and he was just as dirty as the cart and the pony, but they couldn't help it and he could.

The first thing he did was to say a horrible word, and then he picked up the reins which were trailing in the gutter—which was his fault—and lashed the pony across the face with them. Then he gave it a bang on the flank with his fist, and it staggered and slipped and he gave it another bang.

Well, I don't know what you would have done, but you can do all sorts of things when you lose your temper that you wouldn't dare to do in cold blood, and I rushed at the man and said, 'Don't do that, you beast.'

He looked very surprised, and I said, 'I've a jolly good mind to fetch a policeman.'

96

I think he would have said a few things to me then, but a man who was passing stopped and said, 'Good for you, little girl,' and a lady also stopped and said, 'Poor little pony! It looks half-starved. He ought to be reported. Take his name and address.'

Just then Bar came out of the cake shop and said, 'What on earth's going on?'

'Oh Bar!' I gasped. 'Did you ever see such a poor miserable pony? And he's sweet, too. And this horrible man——'

Seeing that everybody was against him, the horrible man thought it was time to change his tune, so he said in a wheeling voice, 'I'm sorry, Miss, I lost my temper a bit. You see, I'm a poor man and I've had a lot of trouble. I've got a sick wife and seven hungry kids at home, I have.'

'Well, you've no business to hit that pony——' I began, and Bar interrupted, 'You don't deserve to have a pony. People like you make my blood boil.'

'Well, it's like this, Miss,' said the man, 'I had to take this 'ere pony as part of a debt and he's been a bad bargain. No use to me in my business, he isn't. He's a dead loss, as you might say. Don't understand kindness, he don't. I have to nearly kill him to make him go at all, I do.' And he turned round as if he was going to hit the pony again, just to show us.

'Stop!' said Bar; and at the same time I heard myself saying, 'You won't take him away and beat him. I'll buy him from you. How much do you want for him?'

Bar and the man both stared at me, and the man found his tongue first and said, 'Well, I'd want a good lot for him, you know. I'm a poor man, I am. Five quid I'd want for him.'

'All right,' I said. 'Here's five pou—I mean, quid.' And I took my six pounds out of my pocket and peeled off one and held out the rest to him. This is the sort of thing you do when you're in a blazing temper.

The man looked absolutely thunderstruck, I suppose thinking he had suddenly come across a millionaire child, and said, 'Did I say only five quid? I meant seven——'

'Oh no, you didn't,' said Bar, and some people who were standing by said, 'You said five quid! Take the money and give the little girl the pony!'

'Well I'm blowed!' said the man, only he didn't say blowed.

97

'Get him unharnessed,' I said, 'and we'll make a halter out of that bit of dirty rope on the cart and take him with us.'

'But what am I going to do with the cart?' said the man, and some people in the crowd which had by now assembled said, 'It wouldn't hurt you to push it home yourself.'

Actually I think he was awfully glad to get the five pounds, and just at that moment a policeman came along and began to say, 'Pass along, please,' and believe me, in about two minutes everybody had melted away, including the man and his cart, and there stood Bar and I with the dirty pony between us and the end of his dirty rope in my hand.

'We're both absolutely mad,' said Bar. 'Here, butterfingers, let me make that into something like a halter.'

'I know it was mad,' I said as we walked towards home, rather slowly to accommodate the pony which seemed bewildered, poor little thing, 'but I simply had to do it. Something made me.'

'I'd probably have done the same, if I had five pounds,' said Bar. 'Gosh! Let's get home quick before we buy any more horses!'

It was only about a mile, and when we came in sight of St Mary's Vicarage we saw the boys in the garden on the look-out for us. As soon as they caught sight of us they came running, and if you had seen their faces when they beheld Bar and me, one on each side of that wretched pony! It dawned on us they must be thinking that was what we had bought at the sale!

'No, no!' shouted Bar, and I yelled, 'We didn't buy it, this isn't it; I mean, we did, but it isn't, I mean it's coming tomorrow, not this one, the proper one!'

We got into the yard at last, and the pony seemed thankful to stand still, shivering a little and looking miserable, his head hung down. The boys gathered round, and somehow between us Bar and I managed to tell the whole tale of the day's adventures.

'I think you did quite right, Jill,' said Mike, walking round and round the pony. 'And I think he's a nice pony—if he was clean and you could tell what colour he was. If I had a million pounds I'd do nothing but buy poor ponies like this one, and I think five pounds was jolly cheap. I bet the man stole him and was glad to get anything for him before he was caught.'

'He isn't small, either,' said Pat, 'fourteen hands if he wasn't so sort of wilted.' And he put his arm round the pony's neck and began to stroke his nose. The pony flinched as though he expected to be hit, but he stood still and seemed to be slightly enjoying it. He even turned his head and had a look at Pat out of what would have been a lovely eye if it hadn't been so bloodshot and messed up with flies. Pat found a lump of sugar in his pocket and held it out for the pony, but the poor thing didn't seem to know what to do with it, which we thought was awfully touching.

'What are you going to do with him now?' said Bar.

'Well, is it all right if I put him in the box stall at the end?' I said. 'I mean, it's your stable.'

'Why, of course!' said Bar. 'He's going to live here, isn't he, boys— as long as Jill wants him to?'

'You bet!' said Pat and Mike.

'Thanks most frightfully,' I said, because after all it *was* their stable and I had wished this poor pony on them. 'I'm going to put him in the stall with heaps of clean straw, and give him a bran mash and leave him to rest until tomorrow. He'll feel better by then.'

'Goody!' said Mike. 'I'll go and fetch the straw.'

So we made the stall very comfortable, and we put the pony in, and he looked more bewildered than ever but just a bit pleased, and I fed him. He only hesitated a minute, and then he began to eat. Eat! I got frightened, and tried to slow him down, but I hadn't the heart to stop him really though I was a bit afraid he would swell up and burst during the night.

'Well, that's that,' said Bar as we fastened the door and came back into the yard. 'And we've hardly talked about Begorra at all!'

'And how's business been today?' I asked.

'Quite good,' said Pat. 'Dot did children's rides for two hours this morning and went out for an hour this afternoon with the Burton kid and its nannie. And Bungie is out with that Irish girl who likes him because he's so quiet, and I've been schooling Mipsy all afternoon and he's booked for the day tomorrow. And Ballerina is still out with Brenda Prince. And there'll be an awful lot of competition for Begorra, because absolutely everybody's big brothers and sisters want to ride. Everything's mighty fine.'

Of course when I got to bed that night I couldn't sleep a wink for thinking of what I had done and all the money I had spent on buying horses that weren't a bit what I wanted or what my forty pounds was intended for. I mean, fancy having forty pounds given to you by your loving mother to be spent on a show jumper and then going and spending thirty-seven of them on a fifteen year old hack and a dirty neglected pony with grazed knees and harness galls, which I regret to say my latest pony had. I sat up in bed in the silent watches of the night and I'm sure my hair was standing on end. And yet I'd have done it all again! And I wasn't worrying over only having one pound left, as the stable was doing so well and we were just about to have a share-out.

I got up at seven and ate a hurried breakfast at the kitchen table, which my aunt now allowed me to do, and simply rushed round to the stable. The pony hadn't bust in the night; in fact he looked heaps better already and was holding his head up! I called Bar and Pat and they agreed that he looked heaps better, and then Mike turned up and the first thing he said was, 'I say! He looks heaps better, doesn't he?'

'First of all,' I said, 'I'm going to get the vet round to see him because I want to be sure he isn't dying of some frantic disease, and then if he isn't, we'll groom him, Bar.'

So we rang up the vet—who was Uncle Toots' locum—and he happened to be coming past our way to see a cow at one of the farms, so he called in about half an hour and saw the pony and said there wasn't a thing actually the matter with him except neglect and starvation and he thought he had the makings of a nice pony and we might be surprised some day, which was quite cheering.

So Bar and I got to work. We laid on with dandy brushes and water brushes but they didn't seem to make the slightest impression on the dirt which was simply clotted on like an overcoat. So I'll tell you what we did, though it isn't usually done in stables. We waited until Agatha went out of the kitchen and upstairs, and we pinched the soap-flakes out of the scullery. We got some hot water from the scullery tap and we read the instructions carefully, and we used the whole packet of soap-flakes, and the pony looked exactly like a film star in one of those foam baths. And the dirt came off in *chunks*. And underneath he was a lovely dark bay. And then we worked with the dandy brush, and we washed his feet and his nose and eyes and mane and tail, and we polished his hooves and rubbed him up with a rubber and finished him off with a

100

wisp, and then we just stood with out tongues hanging out, panting like dogs.

When Pat and Mike came along to look they didn't recognize him, which wasn't surprising, he looked so nice, though we couldn't disguise his thinness and the harness galls.

'And now I'm going to feed him up like anything,' I said. 'He knows me, don't you, darling?' And as I said it, to my amazement he turned his head and looked at me and then made a lovely little whiffling noise and nuzzled my shoulder. I loved him from that very minute.

'Look at that!' said Bar. 'I believe this pony's got a history. We'll never know, but I think at some time he's been cared for. And he's a *good* pony. Look how he stands—and he lifted his feet for me to wash them as if he'd once been used to it. What are you going to do with him now, Jill?'

'Well, I should think he's pretty exhausted after all that washing,' I said. 'Besides, he's weak. The vet said rest him, so he can go back in the stall and tomorrow we'll put him in the paddock while the other ponies are out. And'—I added —'I've just thought of it, I'm going to call him Pedro after Pedro the Fisherman which I think is a jolly good song!'

DICK TURPIN'S
RIDE TO YORK

W. Harrison Ainsworth

This thrilling account of the notorious highwayman's ride to York, retold here by Jason Carr, is described in William Harrison Ainsworth's novel Rookwood.

The place of refreshment for the cockneys of Kilburn in the year 1737 was a substantial looking tenement of the old stamp with great bay windows and a balcony in front, bearing as its ensign the jovial figure of that lusty knight, Jack Falstaff.

It was here, on a day in late summer that same year, that two of the most famous highwaymen of the decade resumed an old friendship.

'Ha, Dick!' said one of them presently. 'You are off, I understand, to Yorkshire tonight. Upon my soul, you are a wonderful fellow. Here and everywhere at the same time. No wonder you are called the Flying Highwayman. Today in town, tomorrow at York, the day after at Chester. The devil only knows where you will pitch your quarters a week hence.'

Dick Turpin fingered his exuberant red whiskers and his keen grey eyes were smiling as he looked at his elegant friend. 'Perhaps,' said he, 'if you paid less attention to your riding-dress and more to the business in hand . . .' His words, though slightly malicious, were spoken with such an air of good humour that Tom King, better known as the Gentleman Highwayman, dismissed them with a languid wave of a well-manicured hand. 'But thank you for the compliment,' Dick went on, 'though to be sure it's no merit of mine. Black Bess alone enables me to do it, and to her be all the credit.'

'A glass to the best mare in England then,' cried Tom.

'I'll not refuse such a toast,' said Dick complacently, 'and after it we'll be on our way.'

After the toast to Dick's famous mare the two friends summoned the innkeeper.

'Order my horse—the black mare,' said Dick. 'We'll be in the garden.'

'And mine,' said King, 'the sorrel colt. Dick, I'll ride with you a mile or two on the road.'

Scarcely had the ostler brought out the two highwaymen's steeds when a post-chaise, escorted by two or three horsemen, drove furiously up to the door. The sole occupant of the carriage was a lady, whose slight and pretty figure was all that could be distinguished, her face being closely veiled.

The landlord, who was busy casting up Turpin's account, rushed to the summons of the lady in the carriage; a few hurried words passed between them, and the landlord pointed in the direction of the garden, whereupon the horsemen instantly dismounted.

'We have him now, sure enough,' said one of them exultantly.

'By the powers, I begin to think so,' replied another. 'But don't spoil all, Mr Coates, by being too hasty.'

'Never fear that, Mr Tyrconnel,' said Coates. 'I'm not an attorney for nothing!' And turning to the third horseman, he continued, 'We'll catch him, eh, Mr Paterson? We've got *you* now, the Chief Constable of Westminster, to back us. And now we've sprung the trap. He'll not leave without his mare!'

'We'll take them both,' said the chief constable. 'Tom King as well! We've long had an eye upon him—yes, we'll land him this time.'

'I'd rather you helped *us*, Mr Paterson. It's Turpin we want. Never mind King. Another time will do for him.'

'I'll take King myself,' said Paterson stubbornly. 'Surely you two, with the landlord and ostler, can manage Turpin amongst you.'

'I don't know about that,' returned Coates doubtfully. 'He's a devil of a fellow to deal with.'

'Take him quietly,' advised Paterson. 'Draw the chaise out of the way—Tom's fancy lady has played her part and will get her reward for giving us him on a plate—and tell the ostler to place their nags near the door. And now gentlemen,' he added, 'let's step aside a little. Don't use your firearms too soon.'

As if conscious of what was passing around her, and of the danger that awaited her master, Black Bess exhibited so much impatience, and plunged so violently, that it was with difficulty the ostler could hold her. 'The devil's in the mare,' said he. 'What's the matter with her? She was quiet enough a few minutes since. Soho! lass, stand!'

Meantime, preceded by the innkeeper, who was almost visibly trembling, Turpin and King advanced towards the door. At the unexpected sight of the constable each man rushed swiftly to his horse. Dick was up on the saddle in an instant and, stamping her foot upon the ostler's leg, Black Bess compelled the man, yelling with pain, to quit his hold of the bridle.

Tom King, however, was not so fortunate. Before he could mount his horse a loud shout was raised, one which startled the animal and caused him to swerve so that Tom lost his footing in the stirrup and fell to the ground. He was instantly seized by Paterson and a struggle commenced, King endeavouring, but in vain, to draw a pistol.

'Shoot him, Dick! Fire, or I'm taken!' cried King. 'Fire, damn you, why don't you fire?' He went on struggling desperately with Paterson, who was a strong man and more than a match for the lightweight King.

'I can't,' cried Dick. 'I'll hit you if I fire now!'

'Take your chance,' shouted Tom. 'Is this your friendship? Fire, I tell you!'

Thus urged, Turpin fired. The ball ripped up the sleeve of Paterson's coat but did not wound him.

Dick fired again but it was impossible for him to take sure aim. The ball lodged itself in King's breast. He fell at once.

Aghast at the deed he had accidentally committed, Dick remained for a few moments irresolute. He saw that King was mortally wounded, and that all attempts at a rescue would be fruitless. He hesitated no longer. Turning his horse, he galloped slowly off, little heeding the pursuit with which he was threatened.

Arriving at the brow of the hill, Turpin turned for an instant to reconnoitre his pursuers. Coates and Titus Tyrconnel he utterly disregarded, but Paterson was a more formidable foe, and he well knew that he had to deal with a man of experience and resolution. It was then, for the first time, that the thought of executing his extraordinary ride to York first flashed across his mind. His heart throbbed and he involuntarily exclaimed aloud, as he raised himself in the saddle, 'We'll do it, Bess, we'll do it!'

Then, aroused by the approaching clatter of his pursuers, Dick struck into a lane which lay on the right of the road and set off at a good pace in the direction of Hampstead.

'Now,' cried Paterson, as he saw Dick's move. 'Press forward, my boys. We must not lose sight of him for a second in these lanes.'

As Turpin was by no means desirous of inconveniencing his mare at this early stage, the parties preserved their relative distances. At length, after various twistings and turnings in that deep and devious lane, after scaring one or two farmers, and riding over a brood or two of ducks, after dipping into the green valley of West End, and ascending another hill, Turpin burst upon the gorsy, sandy and beautiful heath of London's Hampstead.

As he made for the lower part, it was here that the chase first assumed interest. Being open ground, the pursued and the pursuers were now in full view of each other, and as Dick rode swiftly across the heath, with the shouting trio hard at his heels, the scene was lively indeed.

To avoid Highgate Town, Dick struck into a narrow path and rode easily down the hill, but his pursuers were now within a hundred yards, and shouted to him to stand. Pointing to a gate which seemed to bar their further progress, Dick unhesitatingly charged it, clearing it in beautiful style. Not so with Coates's party, and the time they lost in unfastening the gate, which none of them dared to leap, enabled Dick to put additional space between them.

By now the whole neighbourhood was alarmed, and the shouts of 'Stop him! Stop him!' came at Turpin from all sides. On he rode with a pistol in each hand, his bridle in his teeth, and his fierce looks, his furious steed, and the boldness with which he pressed forward, bore down all before him.

As Dick approached the old Hornsey toll-bar with its high spiked gate, Paterson shouted exultantly, 'Shut the gate, man! We have him!'

105

The custodian of the turnpike swung the gate into its lock and held himself in readiness to spring upon the runaway, but Dick kept steadily on. He coolly calculated the height of the spiked gate. He looked to the right and to the left and saw that nothing better offered itself. He spoke a few words of encouragement to Bess, gently patted her neck, struck spurs into her sides—and cleared the vicious spikes by an inch!

Taking advantage of the time gained whilst his pursuers waited for the gate to be opened, Turpin rested Black Bess for a minute, then cantered easily along in the direction of Tottenham.

Little respite, however, was allowed him. Yelling like a pack of hounds in full cry, his pursuers were again at his heels. Indeed the whole countryside was up in arms; people were shouting, screaming, running, dancing and hurling every possible kind of missile at Black Bess and her rider. Dick laughed aloud at the clamour as he flew past, for the brickbats that were showered, thick as hail at his flying figure, fell harmlessly to the ground.

Away they flew, Dick and his gallant mare, like eagles on the wing, along the highway, and after them came Paterson and his men. But while their horses were streaming like water-carts, Black Bess had scarcely turned a hair.

What a horse she was, this heroine of a thousand stories of daring-do! A true thoroughbred, her sire was a desert Arab, renowned in his day and brought to England by a wealthy traveller. Her dam was an English racer, coal-black as Bess herself. How Turpin came into possession of such a horse is of little consequence, but now no sum on earth would have induced him ever to part with her. In Bess was united all the fire and gentleness, the strength and hardiness and endurance of the Arab, and all the spirit and fleetness of the racer.

Her smooth skin was polished jet, and not a single white hair could be detected in her satin coat. In make she was magnificent, every point was perfect, beautiful, compact, modelled for strength and speed. In Dick's eyes at least there was no horse in the world to match her—with her elegant little head, thin tapering ears closely placed together, and broad, snorting nostrils which seemed to snuff the wind with disdain.

Dick Turpin himself was no mean judge of horseflesh. He was the crack rider of England of his time—perhaps of any time—riding

Dick spoke a few words of encouragement to Bess and cleared the vicious spikes by an inch.

wonderfully light, and distributing his weight so exquisitively that his horse scarcely felt his pressure. He yielded to every movement made by the animal and became, as it were, part and parcel of itself. Thus he rode now and would always ride, no matter how hard the chase.

Confident in his mare's ability to out-distance any horse set against her, Dick made no attempt to ride away from his pursuers. He liked the fun of the chase, and would have been sorry to put a stop to his own enjoyment at such an early stage in the proceedings.

By now it was grey twilight. The mists of the coming night were weaving a thin curtain over the rich surrounding landscape. All the sounds and hum of that quiet hour were heard, broken only by the regular clatter of the horses' hoofs. Tired of shouting, the chasers now kept on their way in deep silence. Each man held his breath and plunged his spurs rowel-deep into his horse, but the animals were already at the top of their speed and incapable of greater exertion. Paterson, who was a hard rider and perhaps a shade better mounted, kept the lead. The rest followed as they might.

As for Bess, as the hours wore on, some fifty miles lay behind her and yet she showed no signs of distress. If possible, it seemed to Dick, she appeared fresher than when she started. He was intoxicated by her swiftness and her spirit. He shouted aloud to the night sky as the flints sparkled beneath his mare's hooves, and there was no thought in his head other than the glorious excitement of the chase.

As they entered the county of Huntingdon, and rode by the banks of the River Ouse, and then passed the bridge, Turpin heard the eleventh hour given from the iron tongue of St Mary's spire. In four hours they had now accomplished more than sixty miles!

A few drunken locals in the streets saw the horseman flit past, and one or two windows were thrown open; but he was gone, like a meteor, almost as soon as he appeared.

Huntingdon was left behind and once more, Dick was surrounded by dew-gemmed hedges and silent, slumbering trees, broad meadows, or pasture land with drowsy cattle or low-bleating sheep. But he spared them never a glance; all his thoughts were with his mare. At that moment he was willing to throw away his life in the hope of earning immortality for himself and Black Bess with this ride to York. He trembled with excitement, and Bess trembled under him.

108

Meanwhile, with unabated enthusiasm, Paterson and his men had pressed forward. A tacit compact seemed to have been entered into between the highwayman and his pursuers, that he was to fly while they were to follow. Like bloodhounds they kept steadily upon his trail; nor were they so far behind as Dick imagined.

At each post-house they passed they obtained fresh horses and, while these were saddled, a postboy was despatched to order relays at the next station. In this manner they proceeded after the first stoppage without interruption.

Eighty-odd miles had been covered, and it was now midnight—yet Turpin and his gallant mare had enjoyed no rest. Now, as he crossed the boundary of Northampton, Dick sought out a small wayside inn where the lad, who was the ostler there, could be trusted.

Riding up to the door of the stable, he knocked in a certain manner. After peering through a broken window, the lad came out, his hair full of hay. He gave Dick a sleepy but welcome salutation.

'Glad to see you, Captain Turpin,' said he. 'Can I do anything for you?'

'Get me a couple of bottles of brandy and a beefsteak, Ralph,' said Dick. 'And if there's no beefsteak to hand, raw meat will serve.'

'Raw meat?' echoed Ralph in surprise.

'That's what I want,' said Dick, unsaddling his mare. 'Give me a scraper. There, I can get a wisp of straw from your hair. Now run and get the brandy. Better bring three bottles. Uncork 'em, and let me have half a pail of water to mix with the spirit.'

'A pail full of brandy and water to wash down a raw steak! My eyes!' exclaimed Ralph, opening wide his mouth. But he went away immediately.

The most skilful groom in the world could not have bestowed more attention upon the horse of his heart than Dick Turpin now paid to his mare. He scraped, chafed and dried her, sounded each muscle, traced each sinew, pulled her ears, examined the state of her feet, and then finally washed her from head to foot in the diluted spirit, taking a thimbleful of the brandy to ease his own parched throat as he worked. And while Ralph was engaged in rubbing Bess down after her bath, Dick occupied himself in rolling the raw steak round the bit of his bridle.

'She will go as long as there's breath in her body,' said he, putting the flesh-covered iron within the mare's mouth.

The saddle being once more replaced, after champing a moment or two at the bit, Bess began to snort and paw the ground, as if impatient of delay. Knowing her indomitable spirit and power, Dick was still surprised at her condition, for, as he led her into the open space, her step became as light and free as when she started on her ride, and her sense of sound as quick as ever. Suddenly she pricked her ears and uttered a low neigh. A dull tramp was audible.

'Ha!' exclaimed Dick, springing into his saddle. 'They come!'

'Who comes, captain?' asked Ralph.

'The road takes a turn here, don't it?' asked Dick. 'It sweeps round to the right by the plantations in the hollow?'

'Ay, ay, captain,' answered Ralph. 'You knows the place, then?'

'What lies beyond the shed?'

'A stiff fence, a regular rasper! Beyond that—a hillside steep as a house. No 'oss as was ever shoed can go down it!'

'Indeed!' laughed Dick.

A loud hallo told Dick he was discovered, and he saw that Paterson and his friends had now been joined by a formidable enemy. This was Major Mowbray, with whom he had only recently crossed swords. The major, a superb horseman, was in the lead of the party.

No tall timber intervened between Dick and his pursuers, so that the actions of both parties were visible to each other. Dick saw in an instant that if he now started he should come into collision with the major exactly at the angle of the road, and he was by no means anxious to hazard such an encounter. He looked wistfully back at the fence.

'Come into the stable. Quick, captain, quick!' exclaimed Ralph.

'The stable?' echoed Dick, hesitating.

'Ay, the stable; it's your only chance. Don't you see he's turning the corner, and they are all coming. Quick, sir, quick!'

Dick, lowering his head, rode into the tenement, the door of which was most unceremoniously slammed in the major's face, and bolted on the other side.

'Villain!' cried Major Mowbray, thundering at the door. 'Come out! You are now fairly cornered at last—caught, like the woodcock, in your own trap. We have you. Open the door, I say, and save us the trouble of forcing it. You cannot escape us. We will burn the building down but we will have you!'

'What do you want, master?' asked Ralph from the lintel, blinking up at the major but keeping the door fast. 'You're clean mistaken. There be no one here.'

'We'll soon see that,' said Paterson, who had now arrived. Leaping from his horse, the chief constable took a short run to give himself impetus, and with his foot burst open the door. This being accomplished, in dashed the major and Paterson, but the stable was empty. A door was open at the back, and they rushed to it. The sharply sloping sides of a hill slipped abruptly downwards, within a yard of the door. It was a perilous descent to the horseman, yet the print of a horse's hooves was visible in the dislodged turf and scattered soil.

'Confusion!' cried the major. 'He has escaped us.'

'He is yonder,' said Paterson, pointing out Turpin moving swiftly through the steaming meadow. 'See, he makes again for the road—he clears the fence . . .'

'Nobly done, by heaven!' exclaimed the major. 'With all his faults, I honour the fellow's courage. He's already ridden tonight as I believe no man rode before. I would not have ventured to slide down that wall, for it's nothing else, with the enemy at my heels. What say you, gentlemen, have you had enough? Shall we let him go, or——'

'What says Mr Coates?' asked Paterson. 'I look to him.'

'Then mount, and off,' cried Coates. 'Public duty requires that we should take him.'

'And private vengeance,' returned the major. 'No matter! The end is the same. Justice shall be satisfied. To your steeds, my merry men!'

Once more on the move even the weary Titus forgot his distress. Major Mowbray and Paterson took the lead, but Coates was not far behind. They spurred on their horses furiously. When they reached Selby, they changed them at the inn, and learnt from the postboy that a toilworn horseman, on a jaded steed, had ridden through the town about five minutes before them, and could not be more than a quarter of a mile in advance.

'His horse was so dead beat,' said the lad, 'that I'm sure he cannot have got far, and if you look sharp, I'll be bound you'll overtake him before he reaches Cawood Ferry.'

Mr Coates was jubilant. 'We'll lodge him snug in York Castle before an hour, Paterson,' cried he, rubbing his hands.

'I hope so, sir,' said the chief constable, 'but I begin to have some doubts.

'Now, gentlemen,' shouted the postboy, 'come along, I'll soon bring you to him.'

The sun had just topped the eastern hills when Turpin reached the ferry of Cawood, and its beams were reflected upon the deep and sluggish waters of the Ouse. Wearily had he dragged his course to that point—wearily and slow. The powers of his gallant steed were spent, and he could scarcely keep her from sinking. Nine miles only lay before him and York, and that thought alone revived him. He reached the water's edge, and hailed the ferry-boat, which was then on the other side of the river. At that moment a loud shout reached his ears. It was the cry of his pursuers.

Despair was in Dick's eyes as he shouted to the boatman, telling him to pull fast. The man obeyed, but he had to breast a strong stream, and the boat was slow and heavy. He had scarcely left the shore when another cry was raised from the pursuers. The tramp of their horses grew louder and louder.

The boat had only reached the middle of the stream, and his captors were at hand. Quietly Dick walked down the bank, and as quietly entered the water. There was a plunge and horse and rider were swimming the river.

Major Mowbray was at the brink of the stream. He hesitated an instant, then urged his horse into the water. Coates, too, braved the current, but not Paterson. Very calmly he took out his pistol and, with his eyes on Turpin, calculated the chances of shooting him as he was swimming. 'I could certainly hit him,' he told himself. 'But what of that? A dead highwayman is worth nothing; alive, he's worth his weight in gold. No, I won't shoot him, but I'll make a pretence.' And he fired accordingly.

The shot skimmed over the water, but did not, as it was intended, do much mischief. It did, however, prove nearly fatal to the attorney. Alarmed at the report of the pistol, Coates drew in his rein so tightly that his horse instantly sank. A moment or two afterwards it rose, shaking its ears, and floundering heavily towards the shore, and such was the chilling effect of its rider's sudden immersion that Mr Coates now thought much more of saving himself than of capturing Turpin.

Dick, meanwhile, had reached the opposite bank and, refreshed by her bath, Bess scrambled up the banks of the stream to regain the road.

'I shall do it, yet!' Dick shouted. 'That stream has saved her. Away, lass! Away!'

Bess heard the cheering cry and answered to the call. She roused her energies, strained every sinew, and put forth all her remaining strength. Once more, on wings of swiftness, she bore Turpin away from his pursuers. Major Mowbray, who had now gained the shore, and made certain of securing him, saw him spring, like a wounded hare, from beneath his very hand.

'She cannot hold out,' said the major. 'That gallant horse must soon drop.'

'She be regularly booked, that's certain,' said the postboy. 'We shall find her on the road.'

Contrary to all expectation, however, Bess held on, and set pursuit at defiance. Her pace was as swift as when she started. But it was unconscious and mechanical action. It wanted the ease, the lightness, the life of her former riding. She seemed screwed up to a task which she must execute. There was no flogging, no gory heel; but her heart was throbbing, tugging at the sides within. Her spirit spurred her onwards. Her eye was glazing; her chest heaving; her flank quivering; her crest again fallen. Yet she held on. 'She is dying, by God!' said Dick. 'I feel it——' No, she held on.

Fulford is past. The towers and pinnacles of York burst upon him in all the freshness, the beauty and the glory of a bright, clear, autumnal morn. The ancient city seemed to smile a welcome—a greeting. The noble minster and its serene and massive pinnacles, crocketed, lantern-like, and beautiful; St Mary's lofty spire, All-Hallows Tower, the massive mouldering walls of the adjacent postern, the grim castle, and Clifford's neighbouring keep—all beamed upon him 'like a bright-eyed face, that laughs out openly.'

'It is done—it is won,' cried Dick. 'Hurrah, hurrah!' And the sunny air was cleft with his shouts.

Bess was not insensible to her master's joy. She neighed feebly in

113

answer to his call, and reeled forward. It was a piteous sight to see her—
to mark her staring, protruding eyeballs—her shaking flanks. But,
while life and limb held together, she held on.

Another mile is past. York is near.

'Hurrah!' shouted Dick, but his voice was hushed. Bess tottered—
fell. There was a dreadful gasp—a parting moan—a snort; her eye
gazed, for an instant, upon her master, with a dying glare; then grew
glassy, rayless, fixed. A shiver ran through her frame. Her heart had
burst.

Dick's eyes were blinded, as with rain. His triumph, though achieved,
was forgotten—his own safety was disregarded. He stood weeping and
swearing, like one beside himself.

'And art thou gone, Bess!' cried he, in a voice of agony, lifting up his
mare's head, and kissing her lips, covered with blood-flecked foam.
'Gone, gone! And I have killed the best steed that was ever crossed!
And for what?' added Dick, beating his brow with his clenched hand—
'for what? for what?'

At that moment the deep bell of the minster clock tolled out the
hour of six.

'I am answered,' gasped Dick. *'It was to hear those strokes!'*

Turpin was roused from the state of stupefaction into which he had
fallen by a smart slap on the shoulder. Recalled to himself by the blow,
he started at once to his feet, while his hands sought his pistols; but he
was spared the necessity of using them by discovering in the intruder
the bearded face of his old acquaintance, the gypsy Balthazar. The
gypsy was dressed like a beggar and carried a large wallet upon his
shoulders.

'So it's all over with the best mare in England, I see,' said Balthazar;
'I can guess how it has happened—you are pursued?'

'I am,' said Dick, roughly.

'Your pursuers are at hand?'

'Within a few hundred yards.'

'Then why stay here? Fly while you can.'

'Never—never,' cried Turpin; 'I'll fight it out here by Bess's side.
Poor lass! I've killed her—but she has done it—ha! ha! We have won—
what?' And his utterance was again choked.

'I hear the tramp of horses, and shouts,' cried the gypsy. 'Take this

114

wallet. You will find a change of dress within it. Dart into that thick copse—save yourself.'

'But Bess—I cannot leave her,' exclaimed Dick, with an agonized look at his horse.

'And what did Bess die for, but to save you?' rejoined Balthazar.

'True, true,' said Dick, 'but take care of her. Don't let those dogs of hell meddle with her carcass.'

'Away,' cried his friend. 'Leave Bess to me.'

Possessing himself of the wallet, Dick disappeared into the adjoining copse.

He had not been gone many seconds when Major Mowbray rode up.

'Who is this?' exclaimed the major, flinging himself from his horse and seizing the gypsy. 'This is not Turpin.'

'Certainly not,' replied Balthazar, coolly. 'I am not exactly the figure for a highwayman.'

'Where is he? What has become of him?' asked Coates in despair, as he and Paterson joined the major.

'Escaped, I fear,' replied the major. 'Have you seen any one, fellow?' he added.

'I have seen no one,' replied Balthazar. 'I am only this instant arrived. This dead horse lying in the road attracted my attention.'

'Ha!' exclaimed Paterson, leaping from his mount. 'This may be Turpin after all. He has as many disguises as the devil himself, and may have carried that goat's hair in his pocket.' So saying, he seized the gypsy by the beard and shook it roughly.

'The devil! Hands off!' roared Balthazar. 'By Salmon I won't stand such usage. Do you think a beard like mine is the growth of a few minutes? Hands off, I say.'

'Regularly done!' said Paterson, removing his hold of Balthazar's chin, and looking as blank as a cartridge.

'Ay,' exclaimed Coates, 'all owing to this worthless piece of carrion. If it were not that I hope to see him dangling from those walls' (pointing towards the castle), 'I should wish her master were by her side now. To the dogs with her.' And he was about to spurn the breathless carcass of poor Bess, when a sudden blow, dealt by the gypsy's staff, felled him to the ground.

'I'll teach you to molest me,' said Balthazar, about to attack Paterson.

115

'Come, come,' said the discomfited chief constable, 'no more of this. It's plain we're in the wrong box. Every bone in my body aches sufficiently without the aid of your cudgel, old fellow. Come, Mr Coates, take my arm and let's be moving. We've had an infernal long ride for nothing.'

'Not so,' replied Coates, 'I've paid pretty dearly for it. However, let us see if we can get any breakfast at the bowling-green, yonder—though I've already had my morning draught,' added he, looking at his dripping apparel.

'Poor Black Bess!' said Major Mowbray, wistfully regarding the body of the mare as it lay stretched at his feet. 'You deserved a better fate and a better master. In you, Dick Turpin has lost his best friend. His exploits will, henceforth, lack the colouring of romance which your unfailing energies threw over them. Light lie the ground over you, matchless mare!'

To the bowling-green the party proceeded, leaving the gypsy in undisturbed possession of the lifeless body of Black Bess. Major Mowbray ordered a substantial repast to be prepared with all possible haste.

A countryman in a smock-frock was busily engaged at his morning's meal.

'To see that fellow bolt down his breakfast, one would think he had fasted for a month,' said Coates. 'I envy him his appetite—I should fall to with more zest were Dick Turpin in his place.'

The countryman looked up. He was an odd-looking fellow, with a terrible squint and a strange, contorted countenance.

'An ugly dog!' exclaimed Paterson. 'What a devil of a squint he has got!'

'What's that you says about Dick Taarpin, measter?' asked the countryman, his mouth half-full of bread.

'Have you seen aught of him?' asked Coates.

'Not I,' mumbled the rustic. 'But I hears aw the folk hereabouts talk on him. They say as how he sets all the lawyers and constables at defiance, and laughs in his sleeve at their efforts to cotch him—ha, ha! He gets over more ground in a day than they do in a week—ho, ho!'

'That's all over now,' said Coates, peevishly. 'He has cut his own throat—ridden his famous mare to death.'

116

The countryman almost choked himself, in the attempt to bolt a huge mouthful. 'Ay—indeed, measter! How happened that?' asked he, as soon as he recovered speech.

'The fool rode her from London to York last night,' returned Coates; 'such a feat was never performed before. What horse could be expected to live through such work as that?'

'Ah, he were a fool to attempt that,' observed the countryman. 'But you followed belike?'

'We did.'

'And took him arter all, I reckon?' asked the rustic, squinting more horribly than ever.

'No,' returned Coates, 'I can't say we did. But we'll have him yet. I'm pretty sure he can't be far off. We may be nearer him than we imagine.'

'May be so, measter,' returned the countryman. 'But might I be so bold as to ax how many horses you used i' the chase—some half-dozen, may be?'

'Half a dozen!' growled Paterson. 'We had twenty at the least.'

'And I *one*!' Turpin said to himself—for he was the countryman!

BILLY, THE COB

Roy Wirgman

Billy was a dark bay, a stocky little horse with a rugged coat that even after the most arduous grooming somehow always looked a little dusty. He had a coarse, thick mane, with tail to match, and tufts of shaggy hair festooned his fetlocks. Despite his appearance, however, he was the most prized possession of Mrs Harper and her thirteen-year-old daughter, Fiona.

In the spring Billy pulled a small plough and harrow to prepare the soil for planting. On market days he was backed into the pony-trap, loaded up with poultry, eggs, fresh vegetables and fruit produced on the farm's thirty acres. He could carry Fiona or her mother all day over the moors in search of stray sheep or cattle, though it needed a firm hand to hold him when following the local hunt.

Three years ago, a tragic accident had robbed Fiona of her father and Mrs Harper of a beloved bread-winner and husband, and times had been hard. They had taken the smallholding as a backing for Mr Harper's career as a market auctioneer. Now. Fiona soon came to realize, there was only a bare living to be made after paying the wages of Zacky Wilks, a grumpy old pensioner, whose knowledge of farming and animals made him indispensable.

In her spare time Fiona did all she could to help her mother. She looked after the hens, geese and turkeys; collected the eggs, washed and packed them ready for market; picked and bunched onions and radishes; cut lettuce and bagged potatoes and bent her back until it ached over the strawberry beds, and any other seasonal jobs that needed doing.

Her favourite task, however, was the care of Billy, the cob. When she had first begun to groom him she had had to stand on a box to reach his withers. Now, on tiptoe, she could reach easily. When she whistled he would come trotting across the paddock, knowing that he would get a piece of carrot or a sugar lump for his pains. She fed him, watered him, combed the tangles out of his mane and oiled his hooves until they gleamed. She had even taught him to back into the shafts of the trap while she held them up for him.

As the farm lay four miles from the nearest village, Fiona had no near neighbours of her own age out of school hours, so she had formed the habit of confiding in Billy as they worked together. 'With all this hard work Mummy will stop looking pretty,' she would say. 'That's why you and I must do all we can to help her.' Billy would nod his head as if he understood, but he was really just nuzzling his manger for a few grains of corn that he might have missed at feed-time.

The small thatched farmhouse was divided from its farm buildings by a private road which led through a water-splash, straight up a hill to the old manor house of Flaxton, hidden from view by a clump of trees that crowned the hill-crest. The manor had been empty for some years, but just recently it had been bought by a London businessman called Rammage. It was rumoured that he meant to do the place up and farm the land, which had long lain idle.

Fiona's first sight of Mr Rammage and his son was a fleeting one. His big, shiny car sped past the farm, plunged through the water-splash like a speedboat, spraying the grassy banks. 'One of these 'ere days,' Zacky remarked sourly to Fiona, after this had happened several times, 'that fine gentleman will come charging through 'ere just when I be wartering the cattle. And if 'e do, 'e is liable to 'ave a couple of cow-horns as a mascot on 'is radiator wot 'e didn't expect!'

It was Fiona's habit to take Billy to the water-splash for his evening drink before bedding him down for the night. She was chatting away to him as usual, the halter in her hand, when she heard a rumbling and then a loud shout. Glancing up, she saw a weird wooden contraption on wheels, mounted by a fair-haired boy, swooping down the hill at a reckless pace towards the water-splash.

Before Fiona could lead Billy out of danger, the boy and the go-cart were on them. As he hit the water, a shower of spray struck Fiona and Billy in the face. The cob attempted to rear up, but Fiona prevented him and he only succeeded in throwing her off balance. The go-cart ploughed through the water until its front axle struck the cob's foreleg with an ominous crack. Then it ran back into the deeper water and collapsed.

By the time Fiona had brushed the water from her eyes, Billy had backed up the bank. Shivering and snorting with fright, he stood on three legs, a streak of bright blood staining his injured foreleg. Horrified, Fiona scrambled to her feet and ran towards him; the boy, still gasping and spluttering, struggled upright in the brook and shouted at her furiously.

'Why couldn't you get that stupid animal out of my way?' he yelled. 'You must have seen me coming!'

'We had no chance. You shouted too late!' Fiona retorted, turning her back on him and stooping to examine her cob's injury.

Just then old Zacky came out of the yard to find out the meaning of the noise and shouting. 'Wot be goin' on then?' he demanded.

'That idiot of a boy came crashing down the hill out of control when I was watering Billy,' explained Fiona. 'I heard Billy's leg crack—like a stick breaking!' and she gave a little sob.

Zacky ran his hand gently down the cob's leg, then straightened up, shaking his head. 'The leg's broke,' he announced. 'There's nothin' can be done. Best call the vet to put 'im out of 'is misery.'

Fiona burst into tears. 'I won't have Billy put down. I won't! I won't!' And she glared at the boy.

'It be young Rammage,' muttered Zacky, staring at the boy in no friendly manner. 'Well, you'd best git off home and tell yer Dad to bring his cheque-book along, young feller,' he went on, as he started to lead the hobbling pony slowly back to the stable.

Michael Rammage looked at Fiona appealingly before, wet and

'The leg's broke,' announced Zacky. 'There's nothin' can be done. Best call
the vet to put 'im out of 'is misery.'

bedraggled, he set off up the hill, slowly pulling his wrecked go-cart behind him.

Fiona's mother, who had been on a shopping trip, was surprised and alarmed to see the car belonging to Mr Rider, the vet, standing in the lane when she returned home. She hurried over to the yard and found Fiona, Zacky and the vet standing by Billy in the loose-box. 'What has happened?' she asked anxiously.

'I'm afraid this cob of yours has broken his nearside foreleg, Mrs Harper,' explained Mr Rider, shaking his head.

'Mr Rider thinks Billy will have to be shot, Mummy,' Fiona burst out. 'But I won't have Billy shot!' she added with a kind of hopeless violence. 'You won't let them, will you?' And she flung herself into her mother's arms in a passion of fresh tears.

Over Fiona's head, Mrs Harper looked to Mr Rider for an answer, but he shook his head sadly. 'I'm sure you wouldn't want Billy to suffer, darling,' she murmured. 'After all, Mr Rider knows more than we do about——'

Fiona turned to Mr Rider. 'If they saved Mill Reef, the Derby winner, you can save my Billy,' she asserted fiercely.

'My dear child, Mill Reef was a thoroughbred worth hundreds of thousands of pounds,' the vet said patiently.

'And Billy is worth his weight in gold to us,' Fiona retorted. 'We need him desperately.'

'Is there nothing we can do?' asked Mrs Harper after a pause.

'The cut will soon heal,' said the vet, 'and the leg can be put in a splint, but I shall have to rig up a sling from these rafters to keep his forelegs off the ground. That's not the problem. In those conditions many horses go off their food and have to be put down anyway. You see Fiona, even if we can save him, the cob may never be able to work for you again.'

'He'll take his food from me!' Fiona cried, glimpsing a ray of hope. I know he will. As for the leg, it could mend perfectly—there's always a chance!'

'Well, its your decision,' said Mr Rider, unhappily.

Fiona turned to her mother. 'Please, Mummy!' she whispered urgently.

Mrs Harper sighed as she drew her daughter into her arms. They really could not afford to keep a sick animal. On the other hand, Fiona was so good and so hard-working, it was impossible to refuse her request.

'Very well, Mr Rider,' she said at last. 'Do all you can. I'm sure Fiona will do anything you say to help. Meanwhile, we shall have to look around for a replacement.'

'That boy's Dad will 'ave to pay,' put in Zacky. ''E ain't short of a pound or two. Wot we needs is a tractor, not another 'orse, m'am.'

'When you can find a tractor to do all the things Billy can do, Mummy will buy one!' Fiona interrupted indignantly.

Before he left, Mr Rider fixed Billy's leg in a splint, and gave him a pain-killing injection. 'I'll come tomorrow to see how he is doing, Zacky,' he said, as Fiona went off to make a warm bran mash, which was the cob's favourite supper.

Later that evening, two visitors arrived at the farmhouse—Mr Rammage and Michael. Mrs Harper invited them into the living-room.

'My boy has told me about his disaster at the water-splash,' Mr Rammage began. 'I understand your horse was hurt, Mrs Harper.'

'Rather badly, I'm afraid,' replied Fiona's mother, liking Mr Rammage in spite of herself. 'Mr Rider, our vet, is doing his best to save Billy, but his leg is broken and it is doubtful if he will be able to work again.'

'I'm sorry to hear that. Michael here had spent weeks building that go-cart. This was his first run. May I ask what the injured animal was worth?'

'More than all the money in the world,' maintained Fiona, who was preparing to work around the farm. 'I don't know what we are going to do without him!'

Mr Rammage gave her a startled glance. Fiona looked like a very ordinary girl, in her faded jeans, muddy Wellingtons and dusty old beret perched on her dark curly hair. It was her small brown face, with its large, blazing eyes—so like her mother's—that demanded his respect.

Michael broke the silence by stammering out how sorry he was to cause so much trouble.

'I'm sure you meant no harm,' said Mrs Harper, gently. 'Fiona,

123

why don't you take Michael out to the stables and show him what Mr Rider has done to make Billy comfortable?'

Fiona gave the boy a dubious glance, but by the look on his face he seemed genuinely sorry. 'Very well, then, come on!' she said, leading the way.

Michael examined the sling arrangement with interest, but he began to look embarrassed when Fiona told him how much they depended on Billy to keep the farm going. 'I'm sorry, old chap,' he murmured at last, patting Billy's neck. 'Hope you'll soon be better.'

'I shall miss him this winter,' Fiona sighed. 'He takes me to school if I miss the school bus. All I have to do to send him back is to knot the reins, slide the stirrup irons up the leathers and head him for home. You'd be surprised how many people ring up Mummy, thinking I've had a fall.'

'Dad is going to buy me a pony when we have settled in,' Michael told her. 'I shan't be able to use it much because I'm at boarding school. Perhaps your mother could have it in your stables, then you could exercise it for me.'

'You'll have to ask her. I don't expect she would mind,' replied Fiona, now beginning to like the boy, and thinking his pony would be another source of income.

When they returned to the house Mr Rammage was ready to leave. He shook hands gravely with Fiona and said he hoped the cob would soon recover, before getting into his big car and driving off.

'What did he say?' Fiona asked her mother when they were alone.

'I'm afraid its rather complicated,' sighed Mrs Harper. 'He is covered by some insurance which will pay eventually. He has to fill up a claim form and it may take some time.'

'You aren't going to buy a tractor, Mummy?'

'No, dear. They cost far more than Billy is worth. We will have to look around for a replacement. We can't possibly manage without a horse.'

A few days later, Mr Rammage's farm manager, Joe Barley, drove up to the farmhouse. He was a hard-faced fellow, with a gruff voice and cold eyes, and Fiona disliked him on sight.

'I'm here about that old cob of yours,' he announced. 'The boss will be away for a week or two and wants me to handle the matter. Can I see the animal?'

'Very well!' Mrs Harper led him out to Billy's loose-box.

'Not much sense in trying to patch up that kind of beast,' Barley exclaimed. 'He'll be worthless even if he survives. Even if he had four sound legs, he's not worth much. Will you take forty pounds for him?'

'He's worth more than that to us,' replied Mrs Harper. 'And I've got to find a replacement to do all the jobs Billy did.'

'Forty pounds is a good offer,' said Barley gruffly. 'What you buy with it isn't my business.'

'Mr Rammage thought we should have a proper valuation by an expert.'

'I *am* an expert!' declared the man.

'You could be biased . . .'

'I'm certainly not convinced that the boy was to blame.'

'Of course he was!' exclaimed Fiona, angrily, as she joined her mother. 'Michael admitted it, and I'm sure Mr Rammage won't like the way you are treating us when he gets back.' Barley went red in the face and muttered that he was not there to deal with cheeky kids.

'I think we will wait until Mr Rammage gets back,' said Mrs Harper, calmly. 'You'd better go.'

A little later, the vet called to see Billy. 'He doesn't seem to be fretting too much,' he told Fiona. 'Meanwhile, I hear old Mr Dance, over at Three Oaks Farm, has a nice little horse for sale. You should have a look at her.'

That afternoon Fiona and her mother called on Mr Dance. 'I was sorry to hear of your mishap,' said the old farmer after they had exchanged greetings. 'If you recall, your husband bought your cob from me some years back. Well, the one I have for sale is a sister to Billy. Her name's Princess. She's sound and she is handy. I'm offering her because I've just bought a pair of big shire horses and don't need her.'

'And what is the price, Mr Dance?' asked Fiona's mother.

'Have her on trial for a week or two first, Mrs Harper, and if she satisfies we'll see if we can have a deal.'

Fiona was delighted with this offer, and the kind old farmer lent her a saddle and bridle so that she could ride Princess home. The little mare went beautifully, and if she lacked the eagerness that was charac-

125

teristic of Billy, her manners were perfect.

Zacky was disappointed at not getting a tractor, but he had to admit that Princess was an excellent worker. She was a much lighter bay than Billy and her coat and mane were finer. She soon settled down in the box next to Billy. who seemed glad there was another horse in the yard.

When Mr Rammage and Michael came back to the manor the boy lost no time to calling to see Billy, and was glad to hear that they had found a replacement.

'She's only on trial,' Fiona explained as she introduced him to Princess. 'We won't be able to buy her unless your father's insurance comes through.'

'Didn't Mr Barley settle with you? I know Dad told him to.'

Fiona told him about Mr Barley's visit.

'Dad won't like it when I tell him,' said Michael with a frown. 'I'll tell him as soon as I get back.'

The result was that Mr Rammage came down immediately to apologize for his farm manager's behaviour. He insisted on paying for Princess, no matter how much she cost.

'It's very kind of you,' said Fiona's mother gratefully. 'Princess is a comfortable ride and would suit Michael, if you wanted a pony for him in the holidays. And if Billy recovers fully you could have Princess up at the manor.'

Michael was delighted with this idea, and it was all agreed.

Winter came and went before Billy could put foot to ground again. His long suspension had softened his leg muscles, and Fiona shed bitter tears as she watched his first shuffling steps.

'Lots of quiet exercise is what he needs,' advised the vet, and he gave Fiona a special embrocation to rub in.

Fiona gave every spare moment of her time to exercising the cob and doing all she could to restore his confidence. Although she had grown quite fond of Princess, the little mare could never replace Billy in her heart. Besides, she was determined to justify her faith in the full recovery of the cob. But although his muscles grew strong and the vet declared that there was nothing more that he could do, Billy continued to limp badly.

'I'm afraid he's lost confidence,' Mr Rider explained. 'It's difficult to say when he'll regain it—if ever.'

Billy was still limping when Michael came to see Fiona at Christmas. He was very anxious to ride Princess to the meet of the local foxhounds on Boxing Day, and Fiona would have loved to go with him, because all the local children turned out on this occasion, but there was no question of it. However, she decided to saddle Billy and walk him round the lanes and see as much of the hunt as she could.

She was about a mile from the farm, walking sedately between the low stone walls which lined the lane, when she heard the huntsman's horn and saw the hounds streaming down from the moor. The fox leapt into the lane and out again, and the hounds poured after him. Moments later, horses and riders came thundering towards her.

To Fiona's astonishment, Billy began to snort and prance and reach against the bit in the way he used to do before the accident. As the field went by, she felt his haunches gather under him and he broke into a canter. Then he turned and set off after the others at a gallop.

'Oh, Billy, you darling!' Fiona cried, as the wind streaked the happy tears across her cheeks. She flew past the amazed Michael and gave him the thumb's up sign. The fox went to earth shortly afterwards, and Fiona and Michael trotted back to the farm side by side.

'It's just great!' Michael kept repeating. 'And you deserve it, Fiona. You were the only one who really believed Billy would recover.'

'Perhaps I wanted it most because I loved him most,' Fiona replied happily.

THE TALKING HORSE

F. Anstey

The real name of the writer of this amusing story was Thomas Anstey Guthrie. Before his death in 1934 he had written a number of books and short stories which brought him fame—mainly because they were so full of humour.

It was on the way to Sandown Park that I met him first, on that horribly wet July afternoon when Bendigo won the Eclipse Stakes. He sat opposite to me in the train going down, and my attention was first attracted to him by the marked contrast between his appearance and his attire. I think I never saw a man who had made himself more aggressively horsey. He wore snaffle sleeve-links, a hard hunting-hat, a Newmarket coat, and extremely tight trousers. And with all this he fell as far short of the genuine sportsman as any stage super who ever wore his spurs upside down in a hunting chorus.

He puzzled and interested me so much that I did my best to enter into conversation with him, only to be baffled by the jerky embarrassment with which he met all advances, and when we got out at Esher, curiosity led me to keep him still in view.

Evidently he had not come with any intention of making money. He avoided the grandstand, with the bookmakers huddling in couples, like hoarse lovebirds, and he kept away from the members' enclosure. He drifted listlessly about the course in the rain till the clearing-bell rang and it seemed as if he was searching for someone whom he only wished to discover in order to avoid.

After the Ten Thousand was run, I looked round for my incongruous stranger, and saw him engaged in a well-meant attempt to press a currant bun on a carriage-horse tethered to one of the trees. After that I could no longer control my curiosity—I felt I must speak to him again, and I made an opportunity later, as we stood alone on a stand which commanded the finish of one of the shorter courses, by suggesting that he should share my umbrella.

Before accepting he glanced suspiciously at me through the rills that streamed from his unprotected hat-brim. 'I'm afraid,' I said, 'it is rather like shutting the stable door after the steed is stolen.'

He started. 'He *was* stolen, then,' he cried; 'so you have heard?'

I explained that I had only used an old proverb which I thought might appeal to him, and he sighed heavily.

'I was misled for the moment,' he said. 'You have guessed, then, that I have been accustomed to horses?'

'You have hardly made any great secret of it.'

'The fact is,' he said, instantly understanding this allusion to his costume, 'I—I put on these things so as not to lose the habit of riding altogether—I have not been on horseback lately. At one time I used to ride constantly—constantly. I was a regular attendant in Rotten Row—until something occurred which shook my nerve, and I am only waiting now for the shock to subside.'

I did not like to ask any questions, and we walked back to the station, and travelled up to Waterloo in company, without any further reference to the subject.

As we were parting, however, he said, 'I wonder if you would care to hear my full story some day? I cannot help thinking it would interest you, and it would be a relief to me.'

I was ready enough to hear whatever he chose to tell me; and persuaded him to dine with me at my rooms that evening and unbosom himself afterwards, which he did to an extent for which I confess I was unprepared.

I give the story, as far as possible, in the words of its author; and have only to add that it would never have been published here without his full consent and approval.

My name (said he), is Gustavus Pulvertoft. I have no occupation, and six hundred pounds a year. I lived a quiet and contented bachelor until I was twenty-eight, and then I met Diana Chetwynd for the first time. We were spending Christmas at the same county house, and it did not take me long to become the most devoted of her many adorers.

I don't think I have mentioned that, besides being exquisitely lovely, Diana was an heiress. Still, I was not absolutely penniless, and I had some cause, as I have said, for believing that she was, at least, not ill-disposed towards me. It seemed a favourable sign, for instance, when she asked me one day why it was I never rode. I replied that I had not ridden for years—though I did not add that the exact number of those years was twenty-eight.

'Oh, but you must take it up again!' she said, with the prettiest air of imperiousness. 'You ought to ride in the Row next season.'

'If I did,' I said, 'would you let me ride with you sometimes?'

'We should meet, of course,' she said; 'and it is such a pity not to keep up your riding—you lose so much by not doing so.'

And so, with this incentive, I overcame my private misgivings, and soon after my return to town attended a fashionable riding-school near Hyde Park, with the fixed determination to acquire the whole art and mystery of horsemanship.

That I found learning a pleasure I cannot conscientiously declare. I have passed happier hours than those I spent in cantering round four bare whitewashed walls on a snorting horse, with my stirrups crossed upon the saddle. The riding-master informed me from time to time that I was getting on, and I knew instinctively when I was coming off; but I must have made some progress. I persevered, inspired by the thought that each fresh horse I crossed (and some were very fresh indeed) represented one more barrier surmounted between myself and Diana.

I was perpetually questioning my riding-master as to when he considered I should be ripe enough for Rotten Row. He was dubious, but not actually dissuasive. 'It's like this, you see, sir,' he explained, 'if you get hold of a quiet, steady horse—why, you won't come to no harm; but if you go out on an animal that will take advantage of you, Mr Pulvertoft, why, you'll be all no-how on him, sir.'

They would have mounted me at the school; but I knew most of the stud there, and none of them quite came up to my ideal of a 'quiet, steady horse'; so I went to a neighbouring job-master, from whom I had occasionally hired a brougham, and asked to be shown an animal he could recommend to one who had not had much practice lately. He admitted candidly enough that most of his horses 'took a deal of riding', but added that it so happened that he had one just then which would suit me 'down to the ground'—a phrase which grated unpleasantly on my nerves, though I consented to see the horse. He was a chestnut of noble proportions, with a hogged mane; but what reassured me was the expression of his eye, indicating as it did self-respect and sagacity.

'You won't get a showier park 'ack than what he is, not to be so quiet,' said the owner. 'He's what you may call a kind 'oss, and as gentle—you could ride him on a packthread.'

I considered reins safer, but I was powerfully drawn towards the horse, and with hardly a second thought, I engaged him for the following afternoon.

I mounted at the stables, with just a passing qualm, perhaps, while my stirrup-leathers were being adjusted, and a little awkwardness in taking up my reins, which were more twisted than I could have wished; however, at length I found myself embarked on the stream of traffic on the back of the chestnut—whose name, by the way, was Brutus.

Shall I ever forget the pride and ecstasy of finding that I had my steed under perfect control, that we threaded the maze of carriages with absolute security? I turned him into the park, and clucked my tongue: he broke into a canter, and how shall I describe my delight at the discovery that it was not uncomfortable? I said, 'Whoa,' and he stopped, so gradually that my equilibrium was not seriously disturbed; he trotted, and still I accommodated myself to his movements without any positive inconvenience. I could have embraced him for gratitude: never before had I been upon a beast whose paces were so easy, whose behaviour was so considerate. I could ride at last!—or, which amounted to the same thing, I could ride the horse I was on, and I would 'use no other'. I was about to meet Diana Chetwynd, and need not fear even to encounter her critical eyes.

We had crossed the Serpentine Bridge, and were just turning in on the Ride, when—and here I am only too conscious that what I am

131

about to say may strike you as almost incredible—when I heard an unfamiliar voice addressing me with, 'I say—you!' and the moment afterwards realized that it proceeded from my own horse!

I am not ashamed to own that I was as nearly off as possible, but I was too much engaged in feeling for my left stirrup to make any reply, and presently the horse spoke once more. 'I say,' he inquired, and I failed to discern the slightest trace of respect in his tone—'do you think you can ride?' You can judge for yourself how disconcerting the inquiry must have been from such lips. I felt rooted to the saddle—a sensation which, with me, was sufficiently rare. I looked round in helpless bewilderment, at the shimmering Serpentine, and the white houses in Park Lane gleaming out of a lilac haze, at the cocoa-coloured Row, and the flash of distant carriage-wheels in the sunlight: all looked as usual—and yet, there was I on the back of a horse which had just inquired 'whether I thought I could ride'!

'I have had two dozen lessons at a riding-school,' I said at last, with rather a flabby dignity.

'I should hardly have suspected it,' was his brutal retort. 'You are

'I heard an unfamiliar voice addressing me with "I say—you!" and the moment afterwards realized that it proceeded from my own horse!'

evidently one of the hopeless cases.'

I was deeply hurt, the more so because I could not deny that he had some claim to be a judge. 'I—I thought we were getting on so nicely together,' I faltered, and all he said in reply to that was, '*Did* you?'

'Do you know,' I began, striving to be conversational, 'I never was on a horse that talked before.'

'You are enough to make any horse talk,' he answered; 'but I suppose I *am* an exception.'

'I think you must be,' said I. 'The only horses I ever heard of as possessing the gift of speech were the Houyhnhnms in *Gulliver's Travels*.'

'How do you know I am not one of them?' he replied.

'If you are, you will understand that I took the liberty of mounting you under a very pardonable mistake; and if you will have the goodness to stand still, I will no longer detain you.'

'Not so fast,' said he: 'I want to know something more about you first. I should say now you were a man with plenty of oats.'

'I am—well off,' I said. How I wished I was!

'I have long been looking out for a proprietor who would not over-work me: now, of course, I don't know, but you scarcely strike me as a *hard* rider.'

'I do not think I could be fairly accused of that,' I answered, with all the consciousness of innocence.

'Just so—then buy me.'

'No,' I gasped, 'after the extremely candid opinion you were good enough to express of my riding, I'm surprised that you should even suggest such a thing.'

'Oh, I will put up with that—you will suit me well enough, I dare say.'

'You must excuse me. I prefer to keep my spare cash for worthier objects; and, with your permission, I will spend the remainder of the afternoon on foot.'

'You will do nothing of the sort,' said he.

'If you won't stop, and let me get off properly,' I said, with firmness, 'I shall *roll* off.'

'You will only reduce me to the painful necessity of rolling on you,' he replied. 'You must see that you are to a certain extent in my power.

133

Suppose it occurred to me to leap those rails and take you into the Serpentine, or to run away and upset a mounted policeman with you—do you think you could offer much opposition?'

I could not honestly assert that I did. 'You were introduced to me,' I said reproachfully, 'as a *kind* horse!'

'And so I am—apart from matters of business. Come, will you buy, or be bolted with? I hate indecision!'

'Buy!' I said, with commercial promptness. 'If you will take me back, I will arrange about it at once.'

It is needless to say that my own idea was to get safely off his back: after which, neither honour nor law could require me to execute a contract extorted from me by threats. But, as we were going down the mews, he said reflectively, 'I've been thinking—it will be better for all parties if you make your offer to my proprietor *before* you dismount.' I was too vexed to speak. This animal's infernal intelligence had foreseen my manoeuvre—he meant to foil it, if he could.

And then we clattered in under the glass-roofed yard of the livery stables; and the job-master, who was alone there, cast his eyes up at the sickly-faced clock, as if he were comparing its pallor with my own. 'Why, you *are* home early, sir,' he said. 'You didn't find the 'orse too much for you, did you?' He said this without any suspicion of the real truth; and, indeed, I may say, once for all, that this weird horse—Houyhnhnm, or whatever else he might be—admitted no one but myself into the secret of his marvellous gifts, and in all his conversations with me, managed (though how, I cannot pretend to say) to avoid being overheard.

'Oh, dear no,' I protested, 'he carried me admirably—admirably!' and I made an attempt to slip off.

No such thing: Brutus instantly jogged my memory, and me, by the slightest suggestion of a 'buck'.

'He's a grand 'orse, sir, isn't he?' said the job-master complacently.

'M—magnificent!' I agreed, with a jerk. 'Will you go to his head, please?'

But the horse backed into the centre of the yard, where he plunged with a quiet obstinacy. 'I like him so much,' I called out, as I clung to the saddle, 'that I want to know if you're at all inclined to part with him?' Here Brutus became calm and attentive.

134

'Would you be inclined to make me a orfer for him, sir?'

'Yes,' I said faintly. 'About how much would he be?'

'You step into my orfice here, sir,' said he, 'and we'll talk it over.'

I should have been only too willing, for there was no room there for the horse, but the suspicious animal would not hear of it: he began to revolve immediately.

'Let us settle it now—here,' I said, 'I can't wait.'

The job-master stroked away a grin. 'Well, you *'ave* took a violent fancy to the 'orse and no mistake, sir,' he remarked. 'But I don't know, really, as I can do without him just at this time of year. I'm under 'orsed as it is for the work I've got to do.'

A sweet relief stole over me. I had done all that could be expected of me. 'I'm very sorry to hear that,' I said, preparing to dismount. 'That *is* a disappointment; but if you can't, there's an end of it.'

'Don't you be afraid,' said Brutus, *'he'll* sell me readily enough: make him an offer, quick!'

'I'll give you thirty guineas for him.' I said, knowing well enough that he would not take twice the money.

'I thought a gentleman like you would have had more insight into the value of a 'orse,' he said. 'Why, his action alone is worth that, sir.'

It is unnecessary to prolong this painful scene. Brutus ran me up steadily from sum to sum, until his owner said at last: 'Well, we won't 'aggle, sir, call it a hundred.'

So I found myself the involuntary possessor of a Houyhnhnm, or something even worse, and I walked back to my rooms in Park Street in a state of stupor. What was I to do with him? To ride an animal so brutally plainspoken would be a continual penance; and yet, I should have to keep him, for I knew he was cunning enough to outwit any attempt to dispose of him.

I had to provide Brutus with stabling in another part of the town, for he proved exceedingly difficult to please: he found fault with everything, and I only wonder he did not demand that his stable should be fitted up with blue china and mezzotints. In his new quarters I left him for some days to his own devices: a course which I was glad to find, on visiting him again, had considerably reduced his arrogance.

He wanted to go in the Row and see the other horses, and it did not at all meet his views to be exercised there by a stableman at unfashionable hours. So he proposed a compromise. If I would only consent to mount him, he engaged to treat me with forbearance, and pointed out that he could give me, as he expressed it, various 'tips' which would improve my seat. I was not blind to the advantages of such an arrangement. It is not everyone who secures a riding-master in the person of his own horse; the horse is essentially a generous animal, and I felt that I might trust to Brutus's honour. And to do him justice, he observed the compact with strict good faith. Some of his 'tips', it is true, very nearly tipped me off, but their result was to bring us closer together; our relations were less strained; it seemed to me that I gained more mastery over him every day, and was less stiff afterwards.

But I was not allowed to enjoy this illusion long. One day when I innocently asked him if he found my hands improving, he turned upon me his off sardonic eye. 'You'll *never* improve, old sack-of-beans' (for he had come to address me with a freedom I burned to resent); 'hands! why, you're sawing my mouth off all the time. And your feet "home", and tickling me under my shoulders at every stride—why, I'm half ashamed to be seen about with you.'

I was deeply hurt. 'I will spare you for the future,' I said coldly. 'This is my last appearance.'

'Nonsense,' he said, 'you needn't show temper over it. Surely, if I can put up with it, *you* can! But we will make a new compact.' (I never knew such a beast as he was for bargains!) 'You only worry me by interfering with the reins. Let 'em out, and leave everything to me. Just mention from time to time where you want to go, and I'll attend to it—if I've nothing better to do.'

I felt that such an understanding was destructive of all dignity, undermining, as it did, the natural relations between horse and rider; but I had hardly any self-respect left, and I consented, since I saw no way of refusing. And on the whole, I cannot say, even now, that I had any grave reason for finding fault with the use Brutus made of my concessions; he showed more tact than I could have expected in disguising the merely nominal nature of my authority.

I had only one serious complaint against him, which was that he had a habit of breaking suddenly away, with a merely formal apology, to exchange equine civilities with some cob or mare, to whose owner I was a perfect stranger, thus driving me to invent the most desperate excuses

136

to cover my seeming intrusion; but I managed to account for it in various ways, and even made a few acquaintances in this irregular and involuntary manner. I could have wished he had been a less susceptible animal, for, though his flirtations were merely Platonic, it is rather humiliating to have to play 'gooseberry' to one's own horse—a part which I was constantly being called upon to perform!

As it happened, Diana was away in Paris that Easter, and we had not met since my appearance in the Row; but I knew she would be in town again shortly, and I began to excite Brutus's curiosity by sundry careless, half-slighting allusions to Miss Chetwynd's little mare, Wild Rose. 'She's too frisky for my taste,' I said, 'but she's been a good deal admired, though I dare say you wouldn't be particularly struck by her.'

So that, on the first afternoon of Diana's return to the Row, I found it easy, under cover of giving Brutus an opportunity of forming an opinion, to prevail on him to carry me to her side. Diana, who was with a certain Lady Verney, her chaperon, welcomed me with a charming smile.

'I had no idea you could ride so well,' she said; 'you manage that beautiful horse of yours so very easily—with such light hands, too.'

This was not irony, for I could now give my whole mind to my seat; and, as I never interfered at all with the steering apparatus, my hands must have seemed the perfection of lightness.

'He wants delicate handling,' I answered carelessly, 'but he goes very well with *me*.'

'I wish you would let me try his paces some morning, Pulvertoft,' struck in a Colonel Cockshott, who was riding with them, and whom I knew slightly: 'I've a notion he would go better on the curb.'

'I shall be very happy,' I began, when, just in time, I noticed a warning depression in Brutus's ears. The Colonel rode about sixteen stone, and with spurs! 'I mean,' I added hastily, 'I should have been—only, to tell you the truth, I couldn't conscientiously trust anyone on him but myself.'

'My dear fellow!' said the Colonel, who I could see was offended, 'I've not met many horses in my time that I couldn't get upon terms with.'

'I think Mr Pulvertoft is *quite* right,' said Diana. 'When a horse gets accustomed to one he does so resent a strange hand; it spoils his temper for days. I never will lend Wild Rose to anybody for that very reason!'

The Colonel fell back in the rear in a decided sulk. 'Poor dear Colonel Cockshott!' said Diana, 'he is so proud of his riding, but *I* think he dragoons a horse. I don't call that *riding*, do you?'

'Well—hardly,' I agreed, with easy disparagement. 'I never believe in ruling a horse by fear.'

'I suppose you are very fond of yours?' she said.

'Fond is not the word!' I exclaimed—and it certainly was not.

As Brutus and I were going home, he observed that it was a good thing I had not agreed to lend him to the Colonel.

'Yes,' I said, determined to improve the occasion, 'you might not have found him as considerate as—well, as some people!'

'I meant it was a good thing for *you*!' he hinted darkly, and I did not care to ask for an explanation. 'What did you mean,' he resumed, 'by saying that I should not admire Wild Rose? Why, she is charming—charming!'

'In that case,' I said, 'I don't mind riding with her mistress occasionally—to oblige you.'

'You don't mind!' he said; 'you will *have* to, my boy—and every afternoon!'

I suppressed a chuckle: after all, man *is* the nobler animal. I could manage a horse—in my own way. My little ruse had succeeded: I should have no more forced introductions to mystified strangers.

For some weeks my life passed in a happy dream. I only lived for those hours in the Row, where Brutus turned as naturally to Wild Rose as the sunflower to the sun, and Diana and I grew more intimate every day.

And then, without warning, my riding was interrupted for a while. Brutus was discovered, much to his annoyance, to have a saddle-raw, and was even so unjust as to lay the blame on me, though, for my own part, I thought it a mark of apt, though tardy, retribution. I was not disposed to tempt fortune upon any other mount, but I could not keep away from the Row, nevertheless, and appeared there on foot. I saw Diana riding with the Colonel, who seemed to think his opportunity had come at last; but whenever she passed the railings on which I leaned, she would raise her eyebrows and draw her mouth down into a little curve of resigned boredom, which completely reassured me.

Still, I was very glad when Brutus was well again, and we were cantering down the Row once more, both in the highest spirits.

'I never heard the horses here *whinny* so much as they do this season,' I said, by way of making conversation. 'Can you account for it at all?' For he sometimes gave me pieces of information which enabled me to impress Diana afterwards by my intimate knowledge of horses.

'Whinnying?' he said. 'They're *laughing*, that's what they're doing—and no wonder!'

'Oh!' said I, 'and what's the joke?'

'Why, *you* are!' he replied. 'You don't suppose you take *them* in, do you?' They know all about you, bless your heart!'

'Oh, do they?' I said blankly. This brute took a positive pleasure, I believe, in reducing my self-esteem.

'I dare say it has got about through Wild Rose,' he continued. 'She was immensely tickled when I told her. I'm afraid she must have been feeling rather dull all these days, by the by.'

I felt an unworthy impulse to take his conceit down as he had lowered mine.

'Not so very, I think,' I said. 'She seemed to me to find that brown hunter of Colonel Cockshott's a very agreeable substitute.'

It was only a mean desire to retaliate, a petty and ignoble spite, that prompted me thus to poison Brutus's confidence, and I regretted the words as soon as I had uttered them.

'That beast!' he said, starting as if I had touched him with a whip—a thing I never used—'why, he hasn't two ideas in his great fiddle-head!'

'I grant he has not your personal advantages and charm of manner,' I said. 'No doubt I was wrong to say anything about it.'

'No,' he said, 'you—you have done me a service,' and he relapsed into a sombre silence.

I was riding with Diana as usual, and was about to express my delight at being able to resume our companionship, when her mare drew slightly ahead and lashed out suddenly, catching me on the left leg and causing intense agony for the moment.

Diana showed the sweetest concern, imploring me to go home in a cab at once, while her groom took charge of Brutus. I declined the cab; but, as my leg was really painful, and Brutus was showing an impatience I dared not disregard, I had to leave her side.

139

'Wild Rose drew slightly ahead and lashed out suddenly, catching me on the left leg and causing intense agony . . .'

On our way home, Brutus said moodily, 'It is all over between us—you saw that?'

'I felt it!' I replied. 'She nearly broke my leg.'

'It was intended for me,' he said. 'It was her way of signifying that we had better be strangers for the future. I taxed her with her faithlessness; she denied it, of course—every mare does; we had an explanation, and everything is at an end!'

I did not ride him again for some days, and when I did, I found him steeped in gloom. He even wanted at first to keep entirely on the Bayswater side of the park, though I succeeded in arguing him out of such weakness. 'Be a horse!' I said. 'Show her you don't care. You only flatter her by betraying your feelings.'

This was a subtlety that had evidently not occurred to him, but he was intelligent enough to feel the force of what I said. 'You are right,' he admitted; 'you are not quite a fool in some respects. She shall see how little I care!'

Naturally, after this, I expected to accompany Diana as usual, and it was a bitter disappointment to me to find that Brutus would not hear of doing so. He had an old acquaintance in the park, a dapple-grey, who, probably from some early disappointment, was a confirmed cynic, and whose society he thought would be congenial just then. The grey was ridden regularly by a certain Miss Gittens, whose appearance as she cantered laboriously up and down had often furnished Diana and myself with amusement.

And now, in spite of all my efforts, Brutus made straight to the grey. I was not in such difficulties as might have been expected, for I happened to know Miss Gittens slightly, as a lady no longer in the bloom of youth, who still retained a wiry form of girlishness. Though rather disliking her than not, I found it necessary just then to throw some slight effusion into my greetings. She, not unnaturally, perhaps, was flattered by my preference, and begged me to give her a little instruction in riding, which—heaven forgive me for it!—I took upon myself to do.

Even now I scarcely see how I could have acted otherwise: I could not leave her side until Brutus had exhausted the pleasures of cynicism with his grey friend, and the time had to be filled up somehow. But, oh, the torture of seeing Diana at a distance, and knowing that only a miserable misunderstanding between our respective steeds kept us apart, feeling constrained even to avoid looking in her direction, lest she should summon me to her side!

But, with a horse like mine, what was a man to do? What would you have done yourself? As soon as was prudent, I hinted to Brutus that his confidences had lasted long enough; and as he trotted away with me, he remarked, 'I thought you were never going.' Was he weary of the grey already? My heart leaped. 'Brutus,' I said thickly, 'are you strong enough to bear a great joy?'

'Speak out,' he said, 'and do try to keep those heels out of my ribs.'

'I cannot see you suffer,' I told him, with a sense of my own hypocrisy all the time. 'I must tell you—circumstances have come to my knowledge which lead me to believe that we have both judged Wild Rose too hastily. I am sure that her heart is yours still. She is only longing to tell you that she has never really swerved from her allegiance.'

'It is too late now,' he said, and the back of his head looked inflexibly obstinate; 'we have kept apart too long.'

'No,' I said, 'listen. I take more interest in you than you are, perhaps, aware of, and I have thought of a little plan for bringing you together again. What if I find an opportunity to see the lady she belongs to—we have not met lately, as you know, and I do not pretend that I desire a renewal of our intimacy——'

'You like the one on the grey best; I saw that long ago,' he said; and I left him in his error.

'In any case, for your sake, I will sacrifice myself,' I said magnanimously. 'I will begin tomorrow. Come, you will not let your lives be wrecked by a foolish lovers' quarrel?'

He made a little half-hearted opposition, but finally, as I knew he would, consented. I had gained my point: I was free from Miss Gittens at last!

That evening I met Diana in the hall of a house in Eaton Square. She was going downstairs as I was making my way to the ballroom, and greeted me with a rather cool little nod.

'You have quite deserted me lately,' she said, smiling, but I could read the reproach in her eyes, 'you never ride with us now.'

My throat was swelling with passionate eloquence—and I could not get any of it out.

'No, I never do,' was all my stupid tongue could find to say.

'You have discovered a more congenial companion,' said cruel Diana.

'Miss Chetwynd,' I said eagerly, 'you don't know how I have been wishing——! Will you let me ride with you tomorrow, as—as you used to do?'

'You are quite sure you won't be afraid of my naughty Wild Rose?' she said. 'I have given her such a scolding, that I think she is thoroughly ashamed of herself.'

'You thought it was *that* that kept me!' I cried. 'Oh, if I could tell you!'

She smiled: she was my dear, friendly Diana again.

How excited I was the following day: how fearful, when the morning broke grey and lowering: how grateful, when the benignant sun shone out later, and promised a brilliant afternoon: how careful I dressed, and what a price I paid for the flower for my buttonhole!

So we cantered on to the Row, as goodly a couple as any there; and by and by, I saw, with the quick eye of a lover, Diana's willowy form in the distance. She was not alone, but I knew that the Colonel would soon have to yield his place to me.

As soon as she saw me, she urged her mare to a trot, and came towards me with the loveliest faint blush and dawning smile of welcome, when, all at once, Brutus came to a dead stop, which nearly threw me on his neck, and stood quivering in every limb.

'Do you see that?' he said hoarsely. 'And I was about to forgive her!'

I saw: my insinuation, baseless enough at the beginning, was now but too well justified. Colonel Cockshott was on his raw-boned brown hunter, and even my brief acquaintance with horses enabled me to see that Wild Rose no longer regarded him with her former indifference.

Diana and the Colonel had reigned up and seemed waiting for me—would Brutus never move? 'Show your pride,' I said in an agonised whisper. 'Treat her with the contempt she deserves!'

'I will,' he said between his bit and clenched teeth.

And then Miss Gittens came bumping by on the grey, and, before I could interfere, my Houyhnhnm was off like a shot in pursuit. I saw Diana's sweet, surprised face: I heard the Colonel's jarring laugh as I passed, and I—I could only bow in mortified appeal, and long for a gulf to leap into like Curtius!

I don't know what I said to Miss Gittens. I believe I made myself recklessly amiable, and I remember she lingered over parting in a horrible emotional manner. I was too miserable to mind; all the time I was seeing Diana's astonished eyes, hearing Colonel Cockshott's heartless laugh. Brutus made a kind of explanation on our way home: 'You meant well,' he said, 'but you see you were wrong. Your proposed sacrifice, for which I am just as grateful to you as if it had been effected, was useless. All I could do in return was to take you where your true inclination lay. I, too, can be unselfish.'

I was too dejected to curse his unselfishness. I did not even trouble myself to explain what it had probably cost me. I only felt drearily that I had had my last ride; I had had enough horsemanship for ever!

That evening I went to the theatre. I wanted to deaden thought for the moment; and during one of the intervals I saw Lady Verney in the stalls, and went up to speak to her. 'Your niece is not with you?' I said; 'I thought I should have had a chance of—of saying goodbye to her before she left for the continent.'

I had a lingering hope that she might ask me to lunch, that I might have one more opportunity of explaining.

'Oh,' said Lady Verney, 'but that is all changed; we are not going— at least, not yet.'

'Not going!' I cried, incredulous for very joy.

'No, it is all very sudden; but—well, you are almost like an old friend, and you are sure to hear it sooner or later. I only knew myself this afternoon, when she came in from her ride. Colonel Cockshott has proposed and she has accepted him. We're *so* pleased about it.'

All that night my heart was slowly consumed by a dull rage that grew with every sleepless hour; but the object of my resentment was not Diana. She had only done what as a woman she was amply justified in doing after the pointed slight I had apparently inflicted upon her. Her punishment was sufficient already, for, of course, I guessed that she had only accepted the colonel under the first intolerable sting of desertion. No: I reserved all my wrath for Brutus, who had betrayed me at the moment of triumph. I planned revenge. Cost what it might I would ride him once more. In the eyes of the law I was his master. I would exercise my legal rights to the full.

The afternoon came at last. I was in a white heat of anger, though as

I ascended to the saddle there were bystanders who put a more un-charitable construction upon my complexion.

Brutus cast an uneasy eye at my heels as we started: 'What are those things you've got on?' he inquired.

'Spurs,' I replied curtly.

'You shouldn't wear them till you have learnt to turn your toes in,' he said. 'And a whip, too! May I ask what that is for?'

'We will discuss that presently,' I said very coldly; for I did not want to have a scene with my horse in the street.

When we came round by the statue of Achilles and on to the Ride, I shortened my reins, and got a better hold of the whip, while I found that, from some cause I cannot explain, the roof of my mouth grew uncomfortably dry.

'I shall be glad of a little quiet talk with you, if you've no objection,' I began.

'I am quite at your disposal,' he said, champing his bit with a touch of irony.

'First, let me tell you,' I said, 'that I have lost my only love for ever.'

'Well,' he retorted flippantly, 'you won't die of it. So have I. We must endeavour to console one another!'

I still maintained a deadly calm. 'You seem unaware that you are the sole cause of my calamity,' I said. 'Had you only consented to face Wild Rose yesterday, I should have been a happy man by this time!'

'How was I to know that, when you let me think all your affections were given to the elderly thing who is trotted out by my friend the grey?'

'We won't argue, please,' I said hastily. 'It is enough that your infernal egotism and self-will have ruined my happiness. I have allowed you to usurp the rule, to reverse our natural positions. I shall do so no more. I intend to teach you a lesson you will never forget.'

For a horse, he certainly had a keen sense of humour. I thought the girths would have snapped.

'And when do you intend to begin?' he asked, as soon as he could speak.

'I intend to begin *now*,' I said. 'Monster, demon, whatever you are that have held me in thrall so long, I have broken my chains! I have been a coward long enough. You may kill me if you like. I rather hope you will; but first I mean to pay you back some of the humiliation with which you have loaded me. I intend to thrash you as long as I remain in the saddle.'

I have been told by eye-witnesses that the chastisement was of brief duration, but while it lasted, I flatter myself, it was severe. I laid into him with a stout whip, of whose effectiveness I had assured myself by experiments upon my own legs. I dug my borrowed spurs into his flanks. I jerked his mouth. I dare say he was almost as much surprised as pained. But he *was* pained!

I was about to continue my practical rebuke, when my victim suddenly evaded my grasp; and for one vivid second I seemed to be gazing upon a bird's-eye view of his back; and then there was a crash, and I lay, buzzing like a bee, in an iridescent fog, and each colour meant a different pain, and they faded at last into darkness, and I remember no more.

'It was weeks,' concluded Mr Pulvertoft, 'before the darkness lifted and revealed me to myself as a strapped and bandaged invalid. But—and this is perhaps the most curious part of my narrative—almost the first sounds that reached my ears were those of wedding bells; and I knew, without requiring to be told, that they were ringing for Diana's marriage with the colonel. *That* showed there wasn't much the matter with me, didn't it? Why, I can hear them everywhere now. I don't think she ought to have had them rung at Sandown though: it was just a little ostentatious, so long after the ceremony; don't you think so?'

'Yes—yes,' I said; 'but you never told me what became of the horse.'

'Ah! the horse—yes. I am looking for him. I'm not so angry with him as I was, and I don't like to ask too many questions at the stables, for fear they may tell me one day that they had to shoot him while I was so ill. You knew I was ill, I dare say?' he broke off: 'there were bulletins about me in the papers. Look here.'

He handed me a cutting on which I read:

'THE RECENT ACCIDENT IN ROTTEN ROW—There is no change as yet in Mr Pulvertoft's condition. The unfortunate gentleman is still lying unconscious at his rooms in Park Street; and his medical attendants fear that, even if he recovers his physical strength, the brain will be permanently injured.'

'But that was all nonsense!' said Mr Pulvertoft, with a little nervous laugh, 'it wasn't injured a bit, or how could I remember everything so clearly as I do, you know?'

And this was an argument that was, of course, unanswerable.

RESCUE PARTY

O. M. Salter

If you are blessed with a surname like Ply you soon get used to being called 'Three'. Three's forbidden adventure with his Shetland pony and his friend, Formosa, nearly ends in disaster . . .

'Let's drive out in your pony trap and have a look at the sea,' suggested Formosa, almost as soon as she had arrived at the Ply's house.

'Three' Ply looked at her in doubt. Formosa Macfyffe had come over for the weekend to keep him company while his parents were away. She was a good friend, and as keen about Shetland ponies as Three himself, but being the only child of a very wealthy widowed father, and also a year older, on occasions Three found her difficult to deal with.

'I'm not supposed to drive on the road alone,' he said. 'Not on the main roads, anyway.'

'You won't be alone, you'll have me with you,' retorted Formosa, who always insisted Three called her 'Four' for short—just to remind them both that she was one whole year older. 'And besides,' she went on, 'we probably needn't go on any main roads. You've got a map, I suppose? It can't be many miles to the sea from here—we'll look out a byways route, explore a bit. That's the fun of a wee trap like yours, and a pony—you can go places where a car couldn't.

Three still felt doubtful about this forbidden adventure; but the summer was nearly over, there would not be many more days as perfect for a trip to the coast as this one.

'Deadman's Cove is the nearest,' he said. 'It's an old smuggling place—Dad goes there to swim sometimes. I think I could find a way to it without going on the by-pass, and there's a path goes down to it from the cliffs. But its pretty steep and rocky, we'd never get the trap down there.'

'Who wants to try? We'll unharness at the top, of course—couldn't your pony get down the path to the beach?'

Three considered. Polka, his Shetland mare, was surefooted like all her breed, and also adept at calmly carrying out almost any project that youthful minds could devise for her to attempt.

'I expect she can—if there is any beach. It disappears when the tide's high at Deadman's Cove, that's why we don't often go there.'

'Right—then we'd better take picnic lunch, make a day of it. Its going to be a gloriously hot afternoon—if we can get Polka on the beach we'll give her a paddle in the sea; she'll love that. I've brought my swimsuit—we can have a dip ourselves at the same time.'

'I'm not allowed to bathe at Deadman's Cove,' Three muttered. 'The current's too strong there.'

'There doesn't seem much you are allowed to do,' snapped Miss Macfyffe, and then relented. She knew that before they met, Three Ply had suffered a long illness. It had made him what she described in her own mind as scary. It had also left him with a weak back, but Three preferred this not to be mentioned in front of Formosa—and anyway the back was much better now.

'Okay, we'll just paddle, too,' conceded Four. 'I'll go to the kitchen now and ask for some food while you catch Polka.'

Mrs Dumby, the 'help', who was also staying the weekend at Ply Wood to take care of the children, had her mind on a bit of very late spring-cleaning round the kitchen department, and was quite pleased to supply sandwiches and lemondade in place of the hot lunch she would normally have to prepare.

'I didn't tell the Dumb we're driving to the sea in the trap,' said Four casually, joining Three in the stableyard a little later, over her shoulder a haversack stuffed with provisions.

'I think she thinks we're going there by bus. So we'd better get off without making too much noise, then she won't be worried.'

At that time on a Saturday morning fortunately there was no one about to see the old governess cart being dragged out of its shed, and Polka harnessed to it. But Nana, the bobtail sheepdog, nearly gave the trip away.

Three had reluctantly ordered her to stay put, realizing she could not be expected to accompany them on the mythical bus. Nana usually obeyed orders, but today for some reason she was determined not to be left behind. She ran round and round the children in mad circles, barking wildly, until even her great friend, Polka, became restive.

'We'll have to take her,' said Three. 'We never chain her up—my father doesn't think it's fair to dogs. I hope Mrs Dumby won't find out she's gone.'

He put her in the trap, where to the relief of everybody she immediately calmed down, and Three was able to get on with the harnessing.

'I hope that's all right,' he said as he buckled the last strap into place. 'When I drive Polka at the shows, my dad always looks the harness over for me, last thing.'

'We shall soon know if there's anything wrong,' said Formosa coolly. 'Come on, let's get away quietly now. I'll sit in the trap and hold your dog so she doesn't make a row, and you'd better lead Polka until we get out on the road.'

'Low tide!' Formosa exclaimed with delight as they stood on the cliff above Deadman's Cove and, looking down, saw waves breaking listlessly over a narrow spit of sand.

'There's a beach all right—hurry, let's get down to it!'

Three was thankful to be at Deadman's Cove whatever the state of the tide. Getting there by pony trap had not been easy. Perhaps the map was out of date, or perhaps Four, who held it and gave directions while he drove, had mistaken railway lines, rivers or even boundaries for the small roads they were trying to keep to. They had been lost and had to ask the way so many times that Three felt the whole county must know by now he and Formosa and Polka and Nana were taking a forbidden drive to the sea.

Then the thunderstorm had come without warning. They took shelter under a bridge, so they did not get very wet, but Formosa was frankly frightened, and Three would have been even more so if all his faculties had not been concentrated on stopping Polka from doing a bolt.

She had never bolted in her life; but the thunder echoed fiendishly under the bridge, and a passing train did not improve matters. Three got out of the trap and held the pony's head pressed close to his own chest. He felt her body shudder at each lightning flash and each clap of thunder. But she did not bolt.

So now Three sighed with relief as he walked back to the pony, left at some distance from the cliff edge to prevent her possibly taking the trap over it, and began to unharness her.

The storm had at least cleared Deadman's Cove of any other trippers, and the sun was shining again, hot and glorious as ever. The thought of lunch, then a paddle in the sea, was irresistible.

'Better take the driving reins down with us,' advised Four, 'we might want to tie the pony up while we have our food.'

'I don't suppose there's anything to tie her to,' said Three, but he hung the reins over his shoulder as they began the steep descent to the beach.

Polka had never seen the sea before. At first the waves now breaking nearer over the rocks and sand made her snort with astonishment, but after Nana had dashed into them several times and emerged unharmed, the Shetland obviously decided surf was beneath her notice.

There was no need to tie her up. Nana went off up the cliff rabbiting, and while the children ate, Polka slowly explored the tiny cove from end to end, sniffing at seaweed, pawing at the sand, sometimes testing a rock-pool with her foot almost as if she were a human on the lookout for crabs or shrimps.

'Three, look at Nana!' said Formosa suddenly.

Three turned to look at the cliff face above them.

'She's hunting,' he began to say easily, and stopped, realizing that Nana was *not* hunting. She was making unsuccessful efforts to scrabble up to the cliff top from a small ledge, some yards down, on which she had somehow alighted. The drop above and below the ledge was sheer and rocky, and her claws slipped at each attempt. Three remembered

151

only that morning he had trimmed them back because Mrs Dumby had complained of scratches on the hall floor.

Even as he spoke, the sheepdog stood motionless, uttering a series of sharp, short barks that to Three Ply plainly said: 'I'm in a jam.'

'She must have gone over the cliff after a rabbit, and that ledge brought her up short. I think she's stuck!' he exclaimed in horror. 'What can we do?'

'Get Polka and bring her up to the top,' ordered Formosa. 'Bring the reins with you—we'll strap them together to make a long line. Nana isn't too far down—I believe I could get her all right if I have a life-line to hang to.'

'I don't see any point in trying that,' said Three quickly. 'You couldn't carry Nana up—you couldn't even lift her. She weighs a ton!'

'I'll tell you what we can do, when you've got Polka. Hurry, now! I'm going to the trap to get her driving collar.'

'Four's got one of her crazy notions,' thought the boy in alarm. 'I wish we'd never come out on this trip.'

It was a crazy notion all right, as Three realized when he arrived at the cliff top with Polka and was given further orders.

'Put Polka's collar on and strap one end of the reins on to the traces. She's stronger and heavier than I am—she can hold me while I slither down to Nana on the rein. Then I'll fasten it on to Nana's collar, and when I give another pull on the line—that will be a signal for you to lead Polka slowly away from the cliff edge. That way she can haul the dog up.'

'Hang the dog, you mean!' exclaimed Three.

'We'll have to risk hanging her a little bit—its the only way to get her up. There's not more than three or four yards to go—it will only take few seconds—and I can push her from behind to start.'

'But you'll be left down the cliff—how are you going to get back?'

'The same way, of course.'

Four by now was lying on her stomach with her face over the cliff edge, examining the rocky face down which she proposed to slither.

'I can see lots of crevices I can put my toes into—its only because its hard and slippery Nana couldn't get up. And it'll be easier for me because I've got hands. I can hold on to the rein.'

152

Suddenly there was an enormous lop-sided wrench on Polka's collar which caused her to stagger and nearly go down on her knees.

'How do I know you won't pull Polka and me down the cliff on top of you?' thought Three, but he kept silent.

Four was now slipping the collar over Polka's patient head.

The next few minutes were some of the most alarming Three had ever known. From his stance with the pony, as far away from the cliff edge as the life-line would allow, he watched Four's feet, and finally her face, disappear from view. Suddenly there was an enormous lop-sided wrench on Polka's collar which caused her to stagger and nearly go down on her knees.

Three prayed she would be able to recover, and gallantly she did. He soothed her as well as he could, all the time waiting, sick with apprehension, for the next pull on the line, which should be Four's signal to begin hauling Nana up the cliff.

But the line remained slack. Instead there was a faint shout from down the cliff.

'Stand, Polka, stand!' begged Three, and line in hand rushed to the edge. It was his turn to lie on his stomach and peer over, and on the ledge below to his relief he saw Four sitting, one hand hooked into

153

Nana's collar, the other wrapped round her own ankle.

'What happened?' he shouted.

Formosa upturned a pale face.

'I slipped a bit of the way down—I've done something to my foot. I can't move, Three—you'll have to go for help.'

Three Ply would not forget for years his very first ride on Polka the Shetland, so named because of her dancing trot.

'Don't be long,' Four begged him in a voice that sounded weak and distinctly shaky. 'I feel pretty queer—I might faint, and then I might roll down the cliff. Has the tide stopped coming in yet? It sounds fearfully loud from here. It won't come up as far as where I am, will it?'

'Of course not,' Three replied, wishing he could remember how far it did come up the narrow, sucking funnel of the tiny cove.

His mind raced as he tried to think out the rescue possibilities. There was the farm where the track from Deadman's Cove joined the metalled road, but he could not remember if it had a telephone. Or there was the coastguard station along the cliffs. He could see it from here—a long dab of white on the headland, perhaps a mile away.

Coastguards would have everything necessary for rescuing Four and Nana. If he could get to them. There was a path along the cliffs; it must lead somewhere. He couldn't take the trap along it, though—too rough and too steep.

Perhaps it would be best to drive to the farm and bring back help from there. But suppose a doctor was needed? And to harness up Polka was such a lengthy, fiddling business. 'Don't be long . . .'

Formosa's voice again came up from the ledge, and met the thought forming in Three's mind. '. . . I've got a bit of cord in my pocket you can use for a rein on Polka. I'll tie it to the driving reins and you can pull it up.'

Four was taking it for granted he would ride for help. In his place she would have done so as a matter of course, and ridden like a mad thing too. All the time he had known her he had always managed to avoid telling her he could not ride a pony. It was easy to pretend he was not keen on riding, that he liked driving best, and he had done precisely that.

Years ago, before his illness, long before Polka, he had many times

154

been lifted on to the back of his father's hunter, his brothers' ponies. Vaguely now he could remember the awkward though thrilling jig-jog motion that ensued. Less vaguely, he could remember on one occasion falling off. It was funny then, with his father's strong arm to catch him. It might not be at all funny now, if he damaged his always suspect back.

No saddle, no stirrups, a piece of cord instead of reins. Polka had been ridden in the past, bareback, mostly wildly, and quite against parental orders, by 'One' and 'Two' Ply. It had made Three furious at the time, to see his brothers prancing about on his pony, when he was not allowed to ride her himself. But now he was grateful to them, as he fastened Formosa's bit of cord into the rings of Polka's bridle.

'I'll be as quick as I can,' he called down. 'I'm going to the coastguards —they'll have ropes and a phone and everything. They'll probably come by car and get here before I do because I'm going on Polka; it'll save time. So just sit tight, hang on to Nana and don't worry.'

To the Shetland he said, 'I've got to get up on your back and try to ride on you. I shan't be able to use the rein much, because I haven't got any saddle or irons and I expect I shall be mostly hanging on to your mane. So please don't gallop, and don't go off the path whatever you do. Gently now, Polka, *please* . . .'

'I needn't have worried about riding Polka,' Three confided to his mother when the worst was over—Nana safe in her kennel at home, Four recovering from a damaged ankle in the cottage hospital, and Three himself recovering from his father's sharp lecture on disobedience.

'She went so slowly and carefully when I was on her back, I could have run almost as fast really—though I'm glad I didn't have to, up that great headland.

'But when I had to drive her home, after they took Four to the hospital, Polka went like the wind—and she seemed to know the way too; I didn't get lost once. Honestly, it was just as if she knew something was up, and she was giving a hand all the time.'

'That's what Shetland ponies are for,' said Mrs Ply with a smile.

155

BATTLE WITH A MUSTANG

R. M. Ballantyne

R. M. Ballantyne was a master storyteller of the last century. Among the many exciting books he wrote was The Dog Crusoe, *in which young Dick Varley follows a trail which leads him into hair-raising adventures. With the help of his clever dog, Crusoe, Dick determines to capture a wild mustang.*

Dick had left his encampment a week ago, and was now advancing by rapid stages towards the Rocky Mountains, closely following the trail of his lost comrades, which he had no difficulty in finding and keeping now that Crusoe was with him. The skin of the buffalo that he had killed was now strapped to his shoulders, and the skin of another animal that he had shot a few days after was cut up into a long line and slung in a coil round his neck. Crusoe was also laden. He had a little bundle of meat slung on each side of him.

For some time past numerous herds of mustangs, or wild horses, had crossed their path, and Dick was now on the lookout for a chance to crease one of those magnificent creatures.

On one occasion a band of mustangs galloped close up to him before they were aware of his presence, and stopped short with a wild snort of surprise on beholding him; then, wheeling round, they dashed away at full gallop, their long tails and manes flying wildly in the air, and their hooves thundering on the plain. Dick did not attempt to crease one upon this occasion, fearing that his recent illness might have rendered his hand too unsteady for so extremely delicate an operation.

In order to crease a wild horse the hunter requires to be a perfect shot, and it is not every man of the West who carries a rifle that can do it successfully. Creasing consists in sending a bullet through the gristle of the mustang's neck, just above the bone, so as to stun the animal. If the ball enters a hair-breadth too low, the horse falls dead instantly. If it hits the exact spot, the horse falls as instantaneously, and dead to all appearance; but, in reality, he is only stunned, and if left for a few minutes will rise and gallop away nearly as well as ever. When hunters crease a horse successfully they put a rope, or halter, round his under jaw and hobbles round his feet, so that when he rises he is secured, and, after considerable trouble, reduced to obedience.

The mustangs which roam in wild freedom on the prairies of the West are descended from the noble Spanish steeds that were brought over by the wealthy cavaliers who accompanied Fernando Cortez, the conqueror of Mexico, in his expedition to the New World in 1518. These bold, and, we may add, lawless cavaliers were mounted on the finest horses that could be procured from Barbary and the deserts of the Old World.

The poor Indians of the New World were struck with amazement and terror at these awful beings, for, never having seen horses before, they believed that horse and rider were one animal. During the wars that followed many of the Spaniards were killed, and their steeds bounded into the wilds of the new country to enjoy a life of un-restrained freedom. These were the forefathers of the present race of magnificent creatures, which are found in immense droves all over the Western wilderness, from the Gulf of Mexico to the confines of the snowy regions of the far north.

At first the Indians beheld these horses with awe and terror, but gradually they became accustomed to them, and finally succeeded in capturing great numbers and reducing them to a state of servitude; not, however, to the service of the cultivated field, but to the service of the chase and war. The Indians soon acquired the method of captur-ing wild horses by means of the lasso—as the noose at the end of a long line of raw hide is termed—which they adroitly threw over the heads of the animals and secured them, having previously run them down. At the present day many of the tribes of the West almost live on horse-back, and without these useful creatures they could scarcely subsist,

157

as they are almost indispensable in the chase of the buffalo.

Mustangs are regularly taken by the Indians to the settlements of the white men for trade, but very poor specimens are these of the breed of wild horses. This arises from two causes. First, the Indian cannot overtake the finest of a drove of wild mustangs, because his own steed is inferior to the best among the wild ones, besides being weighted with a rider, so that only the weak and inferior animals are captured. And, secondly, when the Indian does succeed in lassoing a first-rate horse he keeps it for his own use. Thus, those who have not visited the far-off prairies and seen the mustang in all the glory of untrammelled freedom, can form no adequate idea of its beauty, fleetness, and strength.

The next drove of mustangs that Dick and Crusoe saw were feeding quietly and unsuspectingly in a rich green hollow in the plain. Dick's heart leaped up as his eyes suddenly fell on them, for he had almost discovered himself before he was aware of their presence.

'Down, pup!' he whispered, as he sank and disappeared among the grass, which was just long enough to cover him when lying quite flat.

Crusoe crouched immediately, and his master made his observations of the drove, and the dispositions of the ground that might favour his approach, for they were not within rifle range. Having done so he crept slowly back until the undulation of the prairie hid him from view; then he sprang to his feet, and ran a considerable distance along the bottom until he gained the extreme end of a belt of low bushes, which would effectually conceal him while he approached to within a hundred yards or less of the troop.

Here he made his arrangements. Throwing down his buffalo robe, he took the coil of line and cut off a piece of about three yards in length. On this he made a running noose. The longer line he also prepared with a running noose. These he threw in a coil over his arm.

He also made a pair of hobbles, and placed them in the breast of his coat, then, taking up his rifle, advanced cautiously through the bushes—Crusoe following close behind him. In a few minutes he was gazing in admiration at the mustangs, which were now within easy shot, and utterly ignorant of the presence of man, for Dick had taken care to approach in such a way that the wind did not carry the scent of him in their direction.

And well might he admire them. The wild horse of these regions is not very large, but it is exceedingly powerful, with prominent eye, sharp nose, distended nostril, small feet, and a delicate leg. Their beautiful manes hung at great length down their arched necks, and their thick tails swept the ground. One magnificent fellow in particular attracted Dick's attention. He was of a rich dark-brown colour, with black mane and tail, and seemed to be the leader of the drove.

Although not the nearest to him, he resolved to crease this horse. It is said that creasing generally destroys or damages the spirit of the horse, so Dick determined to try whether his powers of close shooting would not serve him on this occasion. Going down on one knee he aimed at the creature's neck, just a hairbreadth above the spot where he had been told that hunters usually hit them, and fired. The effect upon the group was absolutely tremendous. With wild cries and snorting terror they tossed their proud heads in the air, uncertain for one moment in which direction to fly; then there was a rush as if a hurricane swept over the place, and they were gone.

But the brown horse was down. Dick did not wait until the others had fled. He dropped his rifle, and with the speed of a deer sprang towards the fallen horse, and affixed the hobbles to his legs. His aim had been true. Although scarcely half a minute elapsed between the shot and the fixing of the hobbles, the animal recovered, and with a frantic exertion rose on his haunches, just as Dick had fastened the noose of the short line in his under jaw. But this was not enough. If the horse had gained his feet before the longer line was placed round his neck, he would have escaped. As the mustang made the second violent plunge that placed it on its legs, Dick flung the noose hastily; it caught on one ear, and would have fallen off, had not the horse suddenly shaken its head, and unwittingly sealed its own fate by bringing the noose round its neck.

And now the struggle began. Dick knew well enough, from hearsay, the method of 'breaking down' a wild horse. He knew that the Indians choke them with the noose round the neck until they fall down exhausted and covered with foam, when they creep up, fix the hobbles, and the line in the lower jaw, and then loosen the lasso to let the horse breathe, and resume its plungings till it is almost subdued, when they gradually draw near and breathe into its nostrils. But the violence and strength of this animal rendered this an apparently hopeless task. We

159

Dick threw all his weight on the long line . . .

have already seen that the hobbles and noose in the lower jaw had been fixed, so that Dick had nothing now to do but to choke his captive, and tire him out, while Crusoe remained a quiet though excited spectator of the scene.

But there seemed to be no possibility of choking this horse. Either the muscles of his neck were too strong, or there was something wrong with the noose which prevented it from acting, for the furious creature dashed and bounded backwards and sideways in its terror for nearly an hour, dragging Dick after it, till he was almost exhausted; and yet, at the end of that time, although flecked with foam and panting with terror, it seemed as strong as ever. Dick held both lines, for the short one attached to its lower jaw gave him great power over it. At last he thought of seeking assistance from his dog.

'Crusoe!' he cried. 'Lay hold, pup!'

The dog seized the long line in his teeth and pulled with all his might. At the same moment Dick let go the short line and threw all his weight on the long one. The noose tightened suddenly under the strain and the mustang, with a gasp, fell choking to the ground.

160

mustang, with a gasp, fell choking to the ground.

Dick had often heard of the manner in which the Mexicans 'break' their horses, so he determined to abandon the method which had already almost worn him out, and adopt the other, as far as the means in his power rendered it possible. Instead, therefore, of loosening the lasso and recommencing the struggle, he tore a branch from a neighbouring bush, cut the hobbles, strode with his legs across the fallen steed, seized the end of the short line or bridle, and then, ordering Crusoe to quit his hold, he loosened the noose which compressed the horse's neck and had already well-nigh terminated its existence.

One or two deep sobs restored it, and in a moment it leaped to its feet with Dick firmly on its back. To say that the animal leaped and kicked in its frantic efforts to throw this intolerable burden would be a tame manner of expressing what took place. Words cannot adequately describe the scene. It reared, plunged, shrieked, vaulted into the air, stood straight up on its hind legs, and then almost as straight upon its fore ones; but its rider held on like a burr. Then the mustang raced wildly forward a few paces, then as wildly back, and then stood still and trembled violently. But this was only a brief lull in the storm, so

161

Dick saw that the time was now come to assert the superiority of his race.

'Stay back, Crusoe, and watch my rifle, pup,' he cried, and raising his heavy switch he brought it down with a sharp cut across the horse's flank, at the same time loosening the rein which hitherto he had held tight.

The wild horse uttered a passionate cry, and sprang forward like the bolt from a crossbow.

And now commenced a race which, if not so prolonged, was at least as furious as that of the far-famed Mazeppa. Dick was a splendid rider, however—at least as far as 'sticking-on' goes. He might not have come up to the precise pitch desiderated by a riding-master in regard to carriage, etc., but he rode that wild horse of the prairie with as much ease as he had formerly ridden his own good steed, whose bones had been picked by the wolves not long ago.

The pace was tremendous, for the youth's weight was nothing to that muscular frame, which bounded with cat-like agility from wave to wave of the undulating plain in ungovernable terror. In a few minutes the clump of willows where Crusoe and his rifle lay were out of sight behind; but it mattered not, for Dick had looked up at the sky and noted the position of the sun at the moment of starting. Away they went on the wings of the wind, mile after mile over the ocean-like waste—curving slightly aside now and then to avoid the bluffs that occasionally appeared on the scene for a few minutes and then swept out of sight behind them. Then they came to a little rivulet. It was a mere brook of a few feet wide, and two or three yards, perhaps, from bank to bank. Over this they flew so easily that the spring was scarcel felt, and continued the headlong course. And now a more barren country was around them. Sandy ridges and scrubby grass appeared everywhere, reminding Dick of the place where he had been so ill.

Rocks, too, were scattered about, and at one place the horse dashed with clattering hooves between a couple of rocky sandhills which for a few seconds hid the prairie from view. Here the mustang suddenly shied with such violence that his rider was nearly thrown, while a rattlesnake darted from the path. Soon they emerged from this pass, and again the plains became green and verdant. Presently a distant line of trees showed that they were approaching water, and in a few minutes they were close on it. For the first time Dick felt alarm. He sought to check his steed, but no force he could exert had any influence on it.

Trees and bushes flew past in bewildering confusion. The river was before him; what width he could not tell, but he was reckless now, like his charger, which he struck with the willow rod with all his force as they came up. One tremendous bound, and they were across, but Dick had to lie flat on the mustang's back as it crashed through the bushes to avoid being scraped off by the trees. Again they were on the open plain, and the wild horse began to show signs of exhaustion.

Now was its rider's opportunity to assert his dominion. He plied the willow rod and urged the panting horse on, until it was white with foam and laboured a little in its gait. Then Dick gently drew the halter, and it broke into a trot; still tighter, and it walked, and in another minute stood still, trembling in every limb. Dick now quietly rubbed its neck, and spoke to it in soothing tones; then he wheeled it gently round, and urged it forward. It was quite subdued and docile. In a little time they came to the river and forded it, after which they went through the belt of woodland at a walk. By the time they reached the open prairie the mustang was recovered sufficiently to feel its spirit returning, so Dick gave it a gentle touch with the switch, and away they went on their return journey.

But it amazed Dick not a little to find how long that journey was. Very different was the pace, too, from the previous mad gallop, and often would the poor horse have stopped had Dick allowed him. But this might not be. The shades of night were approaching, and the camp lay a long way ahead.

At last it was reached, and Crusoe came out with great demonstrations of joy, but was sent back lest he should alarm the horse. Then Dick jumped off his back, stroked his head, put his cheek close to his mouth and whispered softly to him, after which he fastened him to a tree and rubbed him down slightly with a bunch of grass. Having done this, he left him to graze as far as his tether would permit; and, after supping with Crusoe, lay down to rest, not a little elated with his success in this first attempt at 'creasing' and 'breaking' a mustang.

Poor Dick spent that night in misery, and the greater part of the following day in sleep to make up for it.

163

When he got up to breakfast in the afternoon he felt much better, but shaky.

'Now, pup,' he said, stretching himself, 'we'll go and see our horse. *Ours*, pup; yours and mine: didn't you help to catch him, eh, pup?'

Crusoe acknowledged the fact with a wag and a playful 'Bow-wow —wow-oo-ow!' and followed his master to the place where the horse had been picketed. It was standing there quite quiet, but looking a little timid.

Dick went boldly up to it, and patted its head and stroked its nose, for nothing is so likely to alarm either a tame or a wild horse as any appearance of timidity or hesitation on the part of those who approach them.

After treating it thus for a short time, he stroked down its neck, and then its shoulders—the horse eyeing him all the time nervously. Gradually he stroked its back and limbs gently, and walked quietly round and round it once or twice, sometimes approaching and sometimes going away, but never either hesitating or doing anything abruptly. This done, he went down to the stream and filled his cap with water and carried it to the horse, which snuffed suspiciously and backed a little; so he laid the cap down and went up and patted him again. Presently, he took up the cap and carried it to his nose. The poor creature was almost choking with thirst, so that the moment he understood what was in the cap he buried his lips in it and sucked it up.

This was a great point gained: he had accepted a benefit at the hands of his new master; he had become a debtor to man, and no doubt he felt the obligation. Dick filled the cap and the horse emptied it again, and again, and again, until its burning thirst was slaked. Then Dick went up to his shoulder, patted him, undid the line that fastened him, and vaulted lightly on his back!

We say *lightly*, for it was so, but it wasn't *easily*, as Dick could have told you! However, he was determined not to forego the training of his steed on account of what *he* would have called a 'little bit pain'.

At this unexpected act the horse plunged and reared a good deal, and seemed inclined to go through the performance of the day before over again; but Dick patted and stroked him into quiescence, and having done so, urged him into a gallop over the plains, causing the dog to gambol round in order that he might get accustomed to him.

This tried his nerves a good deal, and no wonder, for if he took Crusoe for a wolf, which no doubt he did, he must have thought him a very giant of the pack.

By degrees they broke into a furious gallop and after breathing him well, Dick returned and tied him to the tree. Then he rubbed him down again, and gave him another drink. This time the horse smelt his new master all over, and Dick felt that he had conquered him by kindness. No doubt the tremendous run of the day before could scarcely be called kindness, but without this subduing run he never could have brought the offices of kindness to bear on so wild a steed.

During all these operations Crusoe sat looking on with demure sagacity—drinking in wisdom and taking notes. We know not whether any notes made by the canine race have ever been given to the world, but certain are we that, if the notes and observations made by Crusoe on that journey were published, they would, to say the least, surprise us!

Next day Dick gave the wild horse his second lesson and his name. He called him 'Charlie', after a much-loved companion in the Mustang Valley. And long and heartily did Dick Varley laugh as he told the horse his future designation in the presence of Crusoe, for it struck him as somewhat ludicrous that a mustang which, two days ago, pawed the earth in all the pride of independent freedom, should suddenly come down so low as to carry a hunter on his back and be named Charlie.

The next piece of instruction began by Crusoe being led up under Charlie's nose, and while Dick patted the dog with his right hand he patted the horse with his left. It backed a good deal at first and snorted, but Crusoe walked slowly and quietly in front of him several times, each time coming nearer, until he again stood under his nose; then the horse smelt him nervously, and gave a sigh of relief when he found that Crusoe paid no attention to him whatever. Dick then ordered the dog to lie down at Charlie's feet, and went to the camp to fetch his rifle, and buffalo robe, and pack of meat. These and all the other things belonging to him were presented for inspection, one by one, to the horse, who arched his neck, and put forward his ears, and eyed them at first, but smelt them all over, and seemed to feel more easy in his mind.

Next the buffalo robe was rubbed over his nose, then over his eyes and head, then down his neck and shoulder, and lastly was placed on his back. Then it was taken off and *flung* on; after that it was strapped on, and the various little items of the camp were attached to it. This done, Dick took up his rifle and let him smell it; then he put his hand on Charlie's shoulder, vaulted on to his back, and rode away.

Charlie's education was completed. And now our hero's journey began again in earnest, and with some prospect of its speedy termination.

In this course of training through which Dick put his wild horse, he had been at much greater pains and had taken far longer time than is usually the case among the Indians, who will catch, and 'break', and ride a wild horse into camp in less than *three hours*. But Dick wanted to do the thing well, which the Indians are not careful to do; besides, it must be borne in mind that this was his first attempt, and that his horse was one of the best and most high-spirited, while those caught by the Indians, as we have said, we are generally the poorest of a drove.

Dick now followed the trail of his lost companions at a rapid pace, yet not so rapidly as he might have done, being averse to exhausting his good dog and his new companion. Each night he encamped under the shade of a tree or a bush when he could find one, or in the open prairie when there were none, and, picketing his horse to a short stake or pin which he carried with him for the purpose, lit his fire, had supper, and lay down to rest. In a few days Charlie became so tame and so accustomed to his master's voice that he seemed quite reconciled to his new life. There can be no doubt whatever that he had a great dislike for solitude; for on one occasion, when Dick and Crusoe went off a mile or so from the camp, where Charlie was tied, and disappeared from his view, he was heard to neigh so loudly that Dick ran back, thinking the wolves must have attacked him. He was all right, however, and exhibited evident tokens of satisfaction when they returned.

On another occasion his fear of being left alone was more clearly demonstrated.

Dick had been unable to find wood or water that day, so he was obliged to encamp upon the open plain. The want of water was not seriously felt, however, for he had prepared a bladder in which he always carried enough to give him one pannikin of hot syrup, and leave a mouthful for Crusoe and Charlie. Dried buffalo dung formed a substitute for fuel. Spreading his buffalo robe, he lit his fire, put on his pannikin to boil, and stuck up a piece of meat to roast, to the great delight of Crusoe, who sat looking on with much interest.

Suddenly Charlie, who was picketed a few hundred yards off in a grassy spot, broke his halter close by the headpiece, and with a snort of delight bounded away, prancing and kicking up his heels!

Dick heaved a deep sigh, for he felt sure that his horse was gone. However, in a little Charlie stopped, and raised his nose high in the air, as if to look for his old equine companions. But they were gone; no answering neigh replied to his; and he felt, probably for the first time, that he was really alone in the world. Having no power of smell, whereby he might have traced them out as the dog would have done, he looked in a bewildered and excited state all round the horizon. Then his eye fell on Dick and Crusoe sitting by their little fire. Charlie looked hard at them, and then again at the horizon; and then, coming to the conclusion, no doubt, that the matter was quite beyond his comprehension, he quietly took to feeding.

Dick availed himself of the chance, and tried to catch him; but he spent an hour with Crusoe in the vain attempt, and at last they gave it up in disgust and returned to the fire, where they finished their supper and went to bed.

Next morning they saw Charlie feeding close at hand, so they took breakfast, and tried to catch him again. But it was of no use; he was evidently coquetting with them, and dodged about and defied their utmost efforts, for there were only a few inches of line hanging to his head. At last it occurred to Dick that he would try the experiment of forsaking him. So he packed up his things, rolled up the buffalo robe, threw it and the rifle on his shoulder, and walked deliberately away.

'Come along, Crusoe!' he cried, after walking a few paces.

But Crusoe stood by the fire with his head up, and an expression on his face that said, 'Hello, man! what's wrong? You've forgot Charlie! Hold on! Are you mad?'

'Come here, Crusoe!' cried his master in a decided tone.

Crusoe obeyed at once. Whatever mistake there might be, there was evidently none in that command; so he lowered his head and tail humbly, and trotted on with his master, but he perpetually turned his head as he went, first on this side and then on that, to look and wonder at Charlie.

When they were far away on the plain, Charlie suddenly became aware that something was wrong. He trotted to the brow of a slope, with his head and tail very high up indeed, and looked after them; then he looked at the fire, and neighed; then he trotted quickly up to it, and seeing that everything was gone he began to neigh violently, and at last started off at full speed and overtook his friends, passing within a few feet of them, and, wheeling round a few yards off, stood trembling like an aspen leaf.

Dick called him by his name and advanced, while Charlie met him halfway, and allowed himself to be saddled, bridled, and mounted forthwith.

After this Dick had no further trouble with his wild horse.

THE WHITE KNIGHT

Lewis Carroll

Of all the strange things that Alice saw in her journey Through the Looking-glass, *her meeting with the gentle, foolish White Knight was the one she always remembered most clearly. He came, as he said, to rescue her from the Red Knight, who galloped down on her as she sat alone in the woods, thinking some very confused thoughts . . .*

Alice's thoughts were interrupted by a loud shouting of 'Ahoy! Ahoy! Check!' and a Knight, dressed in crimson armour, came galloping down upon her, brandishing a great club. Just as he reached her, the horse stopped suddenly: 'You're my prisoner!' the Knight cried, as he tumbled off his horse.

Startled as she was, Alice was more frightened for him than for herself at the moment, and watched him with some anxiety as he mounted again. As soon as he was comfortably in the saddle, he began once more, 'You're my——' but here another voice broke in, 'Ahoy! Ahoy! Check!' and Alice looked round in some surprise for the new enemy.

This time it was a White Knight. He drew up at Alice's side, and tumbled off his horse just as the Red Knight had done: then he got on again, and the two Knights sat and looked at each other without speaking. Alice looked from one to the other in some bewilderment.

'She's *my* prisoner, you know!' the Red Knight said at last.

'Yes, but then *I* came and rescued her!' the White Knight replied.

'Well, we must fight for her, then,' said the Red Knight, as he took up his helmet (which hung from the saddle, and was something the

169

shape of a horse's head), and put it on.

'You will observe the Rules of Battle, of course?' the White Knight remarked, putting on his helmet too.

'I always do,' said the Red Knight, and they began banging away at each other with such fury that Alice got behind a tree to be out of the way of the blows.

'I wonder, now, what the Rules of Battle are,' she said to herself as she watched the fight, timidly peeping out from her hiding-place: 'one Rule seems to be that, if one Knight hits the other, he knocks him off his horse, and if he misses, he tumbles off himself—and another Rule seems to be that they hold their clubs in their arms, as if they were Punch and Judy. What a noise they make when they tumble. Just like fire-irons falling into the fender! And how quiet the horses are! They let them get on and off them just as if they were tables!'

Another Rule of Battle, that Alice had not noticed, seemed to be that they always fell on their heads, and the battle ended with their both falling off in this way, side by side: when they got up again, they shook hands, and then the Red Knight mounted and galloped off.

'It was a glorious victory, wasn't it?' said the White Knight, as he came up panting.

'I don't know,' Alice said doubtfully. 'I don't want to be anybody's prisoner. I want to be a Queen.'

'So you will, when you've crossed the next brook,' said the White Knight. 'I'll see you safe to the end of the wood—and then I must go back, you know. That's the end of my move.'

'Thank you very much,' said Alice. 'May I help you off with your helmet?' It was evidently more than he could manage by himself; however, she managed to shake him out of it at last.

'Now one can breathe more easily,' said the Knight, putting back his shaggy hair with both hands, and turning his gentle face and large mild eyes to Alice. She thought she had never seen such a strange-looking soldier in all her life.

He was dressed in tin armour, which seemed to fit him very badly, and he had a queer little deal box fastened across his shoulders upside-down, and with the lid hanging open. Alice looked at it with great curiosity.

'I see you're admiring my little box,' the Knight said in a friendly tone. 'It's my own invention—to keep clothes and sandwiches in. You see I carry it upside-down, so that the rain can't get in.'

'But the things can get *out*,' Alice gently remarked. 'Do you know the lid's open?'

'I didn't know it,' the Knight said, a shade of vexation passing over his face. 'Then all the things must have fallen out! And the box is no use without them.' He unfastened it as he spoke, and was just going to throw it into the bushes, when a sudden thought seemed to strike him, and he hung it carefully on a tree. 'Can you guess why I did that?' he said to Alice.

Alice shook her head.

'In hopes some bees may make a nest in it—then I should get the honey.'

'But you've got a beehive—or something like one—fastened to the saddle,' said Alice.

'Yes, it's a very good beehive,' the Knight said in a discontented tone, 'one of the best kind. But not a single bee has come near it yet. And the other thing is a mouse-trap. I suppose the mice keep the bees out—or the bees keep the mice out, I don't know which.'

'I was wondering what the mouse-trap was for,' said Alice. 'It isn't very likely there would be any mice on the horse's back.'

'Not very likely, perhaps,' said the Knight; 'but, if they *do* come, I don't choose to have them running all about.'

'You see,' he went on after a pause, 'it's as well to be provided for *everything*. That's the reason the horse has anklets round his feet.'

'But what are they for?' Alice asked in a tone of great curiosity.

'To guard against the bites of sharks,' the Knight replied. 'It's an invention of my own. And now help me on. I'll go with you to the end of the wood. What's that dish for?'

'It's meant for plum cake,' said Alice.

'We'd better take it with us,' the Knight said. 'It'll come in handy if we find any plum cake. Help me to get it into this bag.'

This took a long time to manage, though Alice held the bag open very carefully, because the Knight was so *very* awkward in putting in the dish: the first two or three times that he tried he fell in himself instead. 'It's rather a tight fit, you see,' he said, as they got it in at last; 'there are so many candlesticks in the bag.' And he hung it to the saddle, which was already loaded with bunches of carrots, and fire-irons, and many other things.

'I hope you've got your hair well fastened on?' he continued, as they set off.

'Only in the usual way,' Alice said, smiling.

'That's hardly enough,' he said anxiously. 'You see the wind is so *very* strong here. It's as strong as soup.'

'Have you invented a plan for keeping one's hair from being blown off?' Alice inquired.

'Not yet,' said the Knight. 'But I've got a plan for keeping it from *falling* off.'

'I should like to hear it very much.'

'First you take an upright stick,' said the Knight. 'Then you make your hair creep up it, like a fruit tree. Now the reason hair falls off is because it hangs *down*—things never fall *upwards*, you know. It's my own invention. You may try it if you like.'

It didn't sound a comfotable plan, Alice thought, and for a few minutes she walked on in silence, puzzling over the idea, and every now and then stopping to help the poor Knight, who certainly was *not* a good ridcr.

Whenever the horse stopped (which it did very often), he fell off in front; and whenever it went on again (which it generally did rather suddenly), he fell off behind. Otherwise he kept on pretty well, except that he had a habit of now and then falling off sideways; and as he generally did this on the side on which Alice was walking, she soon found that it was the best plan not to walk *quite* close to the horse.

'I'm afraid you've not had much practice in riding,' she ventured to say, as she was helping him up from his fifth tumble.

The Knight looked very much surprised, and a little offended at the remark. 'What makes you say that?' he asked, as he scrambled back into the saddle, keeping hold of Alice's hair with one hand, to save himself from falling over on the other side.

'Because people don't fall off quite so often, when they've had much practice.'

'I've had plenty of practice,' the Knight said very gravely, 'plenty of practice.'

Alice could think of nothing better to say than, 'Indeed?' but she

'The great art of riding,' said the White Knight, 'is to keep your balance.
Like this, you know——'

173

said it as heartily as she could. They went on a little way in silence after this, the Knight with his eyes shut, muttering to himself, and Alice watching anxiously for the next tumble.

'The great art of riding,' the Knight suddenly began in a loud voice, waving his right arm as he spoke, 'is to keep——' Here the sentence ended as suddenly as it had begun, as the Knight fell heavily on the top of his head exactly in the path where Alice was walking. She was quite frightened this time, and said in an anxious tone, as she picked him up, 'I hope no bones are broken?'

'None to speak of,' the Knight said, as if he didn't mind breaking two or three of them. 'The great art of riding, as I was saying, is—to keep your balance. Like this, you know——'

He let go the bridle, and stretched out both his arms to show Alice what he meant, and this time he fell flat on his back, right under the horse's feet.

'Plenty of practice!' he went on repeating, all the time that Alice was getting him on his feet again. 'Plenty of practice!'

'It's too ridiculous!' cried Alice, getting quite out of patience. 'You ought to have a wooden horse on wheels, that you ought!'

'Does that kind go smoothly?' the Knight asked in a tone of great interest, clasping his arms round the horse's neck as he spoke, just in time to save himself from tumbling off again.

'Much more smoothly than a live horse,' Alice said, with a little scream of laughter, in spite of all she could do to prevent it.

'I'll get one,' the Knight said thoughtfully to himself. 'One or two— several.'

There was a short silence after this; then the Knight went on again: 'I'm a great hand at inventing things. Now, I dare say you noticed, the last time you picked me up, that I was looking thoughtful?'

'You *were* a little grave,' said Alice.

'Well, just then I was inventing a new way of getting over a gate— would you like to hear it?.

'Very much indeed,' Alice said politely.

'I'll tell you how I came to think of it,' said the Knight. 'You see, I said to myself, "The only difficulty is with the feet: the *head* is high enough already." Now, first I put my head on the top of the gate— then the head's high enough—then I stand on my head—then the feet

174

are high enough, you see—then I'm over, you see.'

'Yes, I suppose you'd be over when that was done,' Alice said thoughtfully: 'but don't you think it would be rather hard?'

'I haven't tried it yet,' the Knight said gravely: 'so I can't tell for certain—but I'm afraid it *would* be a little hard.'

He looked so vexed at the idea that Alice changed the subject hastily. 'What a curious helmet you've got!' she said cheerfully. 'Is that your invention too?'

The Knight looked down proudly at his helmet, which hung from the saddle. 'Yes,' he said, 'but I've invented a better one than that—like a sugar-loaf. When I used to wear it, if I fell off the horse, it always touched the ground directly. So I had a *very* little way to fall, you see. But there *was* the danger of falling *into* it, to be sure. That happened to me once—and the worst of it was, before I could get out again, the other White Knight came and put it on. He thought it was his own helmet.'

The Knight looked so solemn about it that Alice did not dare to laugh. 'I'm afraid you must have hurt him,' she said in a trembling voice, 'being on the top of his head.'

'I had to kick him, of course,' the Knight said, very seriously. 'And then he took the helmet off again—but it took hours and hours to get me out. I was as fast as—as lightning, you know.'

'But that's a different kind of fastness,' Alice objected.

The Knight shook his head. 'It was all kinds of fastness with me, I can assure you!' he said. He raised his hands in some excitement as he said this, and instantly rolled out of the saddle, and fell headlong into a deep ditch.

Alice ran to the side of the ditch to look for him. She was rather startled by the fall, as for some time he had kept on very well, and she was afraid that he really *was* hurt this time. However, though she could see nothing but the soles of his feet, she was much relieved to hear that he was talking on in his usual tone. 'All kinds of fastness,' he repeated: 'but it was careless of him to put another man's helmet on—with the man in it, too.'

'How *can* you go on talking so quietly, head downwards?' Alice asked, as she dragged him out by the feet, and laid him in a heap on the bank.

175

The Knight looked surprised at the question. 'What does it matter where my body happens to be?' he said. 'My mind goes on working all the same. In fact, the more head downwards I am, the more I keep inventing new things.'

Alice spent some time with the friendly White Knight, who was so adept at tumbling off his horse. At last, however, after he had sung her a melancholy ballad to cheer her up, he turned his horse's head along the road by which they had come and rode slowly away into the forest.

THE UNICORN-STONE

Caroline Baxter

This haunting story, written by Caroline while still at school, was judged to be among the best stories submitted to The Times *Newspaper Competition in 1973. She has now written a thriller for older children.*

Lucy shut her eyes.

The unicorn was there, waiting. He stood at the end of the avenue of trees: a bright white shape at the end of the dark green tunnel. His head was up, looking at her, his nostrils flared and quivering. He began to move towards her, stepping proudly, disdainfully; and the golden shafts of sunlight dappled and slid on the white silk of his body.

'Lucy Grey!' Miss Acidulation's voice cut into her dream, and Lucy was jerked into wakefulness. 'What have I just been saying, Lucy?'

Lucy felt the familiar feeling of rising helplessness and misery. She bent over the untidy scrawl of lines and circles, smeared with rubbings-out, aware of everyone looking at her—not friendly or hostile, but pleased at the interruption to the lesson.

'Yes, Miss Acidulation, but . . .' Lucy's voice trailed off. How could she explain: she had really meant to concentrate, she had bent over her geometry book clenching her teeth with the effort, but her mind had slid away for one moment, and she had lost the train of reasoning.

She scowled over her book, biting back the tears and afraid to look at the hard, angular figure of Miss Acidulation. 'I did try—I really did

177

. . . it's just . . . I'm not any good at maths . . .'

The undercurrent of suppressed giggles and exchanged glances rose until it was almost audible as the class waited in fearful delight for the full force of Miss Acidulation's wrath. It was not long in coming.

'Lucy Grey, nobody would be "any good at maths" if they gave the amount of attention you give to me.' Miss Acidulation's voice grew hard with anger. 'You spend your entire day daydreaming: you hardly seem even to know where you are or what you are doing. In all my years of teaching at this school, I have never known anyone as scatter-brained, apathetic and idle as you. You have the mental application of a sparrow. Most girls in this school would, at any rate, do me the courtesy of listening in my lessons: and there is all the more reason for you to do so since you find mathematics difficult . . .' Miss Acidulation's voice stormed on.

Lucy choked back the hard knot of tears in her throat and stared at the radiator beside her. The mustard-yellow paint was flaking off, showing the dull grey metal underneath. The grey patch nearest Lucy looked like an eagle with its wings spread in flight. She picked at it with her fingernail to give the eagle a beak. Miss Acidulation's voice faded to an angry drone. Lucy heard it but did not listen to it.

The strident shrill of the bell, mercifully sounding the end of the lesson, made Lucy jump. Miss Acidulation held up her hand to stop the class moving, and they shifted restlessly, eager to get away.

'One moment, please. Girls, how often do I have to tell you that the lesson ends when *I* say it does and not just when the bell goes? Wait until I tell you that you can go. Lucy, did you hear what I said? Unless you hand in those three exercises by tomorrow, without fail, there will be trouble. As it is, I shall report your slackness to Miss Battersby. You can go.'

Miss Acidulation marched out with a vindictive sniff and a twitch at the pince-nez that had bitten a deep furrow in the sides of her bony nose. The rest of the class clattered after her, banging their desk-lids and chattering and laughing. Some looked sympathetically at Lucy as she sat there, but Lucy was too miserable to grin back.

She heard their shoes clatter away down the bare, school-green corridors that always smelled of chalk and carbolic soap. Lucy sat alone in the classroom, not wanting company or to have to listen to everyone else's cheerful noise over tea. It would be bread-and-marge and the prunes left over from lunch with cold custard, Lucy knew.

After two months at this school, Lucy was still bewildered and unhappy. She hated the grim, cold, ugly Victorian building, the hard dormitory beds, the repressive regulations. Awkward and unsociable, Lucy felt an outsider. Nobody took much notice of the tense, silent girl in the corner: except the staff when she did her work badly.

The classroom was empty and bleak now; and the rows of empty desks emphasized her loneliness. Lucy got up, not sure where to go. The cleaner was coming with her blue turban over her curlers, rattling her bucket angrily and groaning about her knees.

Lucy slipped into the cloakroom. She grabbed her school raincoat and ran out of the back entrance, her footsteps sounding unnaturally loud in the silent rows of coats.

Outside, she set off down the gravel drive, trying not to run. She strained her ears to listen to the barely audible clatter of plates and hum of voices, her heart thumping guiltily. She felt horribly noticeable walking all alone out of the massive iron gates. Out on the winding country road, Lucy began to run, with no clear idea except to forget for a time the horror she would have to face when she had not managed to do the exercises.

The beeches in the woods on either side of the road had just come out, very green and soft. Lucy swung off the road into the woods, slowing to a walk as she grew tired running through the deep leaves. This was the place for her unicorn, she thought, and she tried to recapture her daydream, but the picture had slid away.

Lucy had been here before, on a nature-walk with the shrill, ineffective Miss Soames. There was a broken-down cottage near by, and she made her way towards this.

It stood in a dank and gloomy part of the woods, where the leaves smelt of decay and the water dripped in green streaks down the beech-trunks. Thick rhododendron bushes, with leaves like dark green polished leather, pushed up close to the crumbling walls. The girls at school told horrific stories about it: stories which Lucy, listening to the seniors, had overheard; and although she did not exactly believe them, remembered fragments sent shivers of apprehension down her spine as she approached the hut.

Until a few weeks ago, old Mrs Bedlam had lived in the hut. Lucy had met her once: a weird bundle of dingy rags and matted grey hair, shambling through the woods in the dusk and muttering to herself. 'Eccentric, of course, but harmless, poor thing' was how the staff termed her. She had given Lucy a long, malevolent stare from flint-black eyes, undimmed by age; and Lucy, backing away, had felt the terror of a mouse watched by a stoat. That night, Lucy had fallen ill with a fever, and old Mrs Bedlam had haunted her feverish dreams with some nameless dread. The dreams had quickly gone when she recovered, but they left a cold taint of fear in the back of Lucy's mind as she approached the hut. Mrs. Bedlam, she knew, had been taken away to some old people's home: but Lucy still felt nervous.

'Over-imaginative' she told herself firmly, and walked up to the window. It was encrusted with pale green dirt, and almost impossible to see through. Lucy cupped her hands against the glass, and peered in. It was too dark to see much, but the hut seemed empty. Lucy's tight knot of nervousness relaxed slightly.

'There's no one there,' she said out loud, to calm her thudding heart; and she pushed at the door. It was warped with damp, but, pushing hard, Lucy made a crack large enough to squeeze through.

For a moment, Lucy could see nothing in the gloom. The hut smelled of damp and decaying leaves. It was almost empty. Dead leaves had piled in a corner, and straggling grass had started to grow through the earthen floor, sickly yellow-white from lack of sunlight. There was a heap of old rubbish under the window. Lucy went over to have a look. There were scraps of rotting rags and piles of dirty glass jars—like jam-jars, only Lucy did not think that their contents looked as if they could ever have been jam. There were parts of tattered old books, with black writing written very close and crabbed on the yellowed pages. Lucy tried to read one, but the writing was too spiky and had run with the damp. There were bits of old iron eaten away by rust, rust-corroded saucepans, a bottle with a dark liquid in it which shone violet when Lucy rubbed the dirt off it and held it up to the greenish light from the window; and, near the bottom, a sheep's skull with huge eye-sockets and a few foolishly protruding teeth.

Lucy began to feel cold in the chill damp of the cottage. She shivered, and was about to turn away when something gleaming caught her eye at the edge of the pile.

It was a pale, shining stone shaped like a pendant with a hole at one end, flat and very smooth. In the gloom of the cottage it seemed to be shining with a queer pearly whiteness. Lucy picked it up. It was cold and strangely heavy. A curious tingling ran up her fingers as she touched it; and for a second she felt as if a shadow had just flickered past the door. Her heart twisted with fear and she spun round to look before she became too terrified to turn; but there was no one there. Only the tall clump of nettles outside the door was swaying as if someone had just passed. Lucy ran out of the hut, clutching the stone. Outside, her panic died down. It was starting to get dark under the trees now, and Lucy knew she must go back before she was missed at bed-time.

She paused to look at the stone. It was still gleaming, but more faintly now: with a pale ethereal glimmer, hardly visible. It was like a moonstone should be, thought Lucy, a unicorn-stone.

She started to hurry, anxious not to get into more trouble by being discovered missing. She remembered the mathematical exercises she had to do again, now, but somehow they did not seem too terrible and insurmountable a problem any more. The shadows under the beech-trees were deepening now. Darkness was crowding in on her.

Lucy broke into an anxious jog-trot, rustling noisily through the dry leaves. For a moment, she thought she heard something rustling behind her. She stopped to listen, but the only sound was her own heavy breathing.

'Don't be so silly,' Lucy told herself. 'Stop frightening yourself. That's all it is. You've done this often before.' She set off again, outwardly calm, but nervously taut so that a twig snapping underfoot sounded like a pistol-shot and made her shy like a frightened horse. She seemed to hear rustlings, whisperings, stealthy movements all around her, as if the forest were coming to life and crouching to spring.

'Don't run,' Lucy commanded herself, but she found herself running blindly, tripping over roots and torn at by branches. Through the racing thud of her heart she thought she heard something snuffling and panting at her heels, and she fled on almost sobbing with terror.

She stumbled on to the road by chance, and with a gasp of relief she saw the school lights through the trees, and knew she was almost back. With a last burst of energy she sped up the drive, the gravel spurting

181

from under her flying feet, and collapsed inside the cloakroom. For some time she sat there, propped against the lockers, feeling the reassuring solidity of the wood and the hard knobbles of the brass handles pressed into her back; while she listened to the tearing gasps of her breathing and the sickening pounding of her heart. It was almost dark in the cloakroom. Lucy could only just see the lines of hanging coats as darker densities in the gloom, and she became aware that the stone seemed to be giving out light, throbbing through her clenched fingers. She opened out her hand, and the stone was lying on her palm: but the light, if there was any, was fading quickly, until Lucy was not sure if she had seen it or not; and the stone seemed to shrink and grow colder as she looked at it.

She got to her feet, feeling weak and trembly with exhaustion, and groped her way to where the door showed as a hair-thin line of golden light.

The light from the passage flooded in on her as she opened the door, seeming unnaturally cheerful and welcoming although it was only the usual bare bulb hanging from a thin flex. Lucy listened anxiously, wondering what the time was, and where everyone else was. How long had she been out there? She had a sudden, horrible idea that she might find the whole school lit but empty, with the naked bulbs blazing on deserted rooms, before she heard the faint clatter of plates and the noise of distant talking. For a moment she wondered stupidly if it was still tea, if she had been away for any time at all; and then she realized that it must now be supper. Lucy realized suddenly how hungry she was, and how tired. She went towards the dining-hall, feeling isolated and lonely as she listened to the noises within, and longing to be back with the usual herd of girls in a comfortable routine. There was a scraping of chairs as she approached, and the school poured out. Lucy managed to slip unnoticed into the crowd and was carried with them up to the dormitories. Later, lying awake in the darkness, Lucy looked again at the stone. Someone beside her was breathing deeply, and she could just see the rows of beds and sense the security of all the other sleepers. The stone now had almost no light: it was no more than a pale shape in the gloom. Lucy padded across the cold linoleum and rummaged in her drawer to find a bootlace. She threaded the stone on to it by the light of the half-moon, holding it up against the semi-circle of silver to find the hole, and slipped the bootlace around her neck. The stone lay icy-cold against her shrinking flesh. Outside, the woods were quiet and full of shadows in the moonlight.

Lucy went back to bed.

She awoke the next morning before the others, with the feeling there was something unpleasant ahead of her although she could not remember what it was: like waking up on the first day back to school or the morning of a visit to the dentist. It took a few minutes before she remembered: the exercises had to be in today. The cold shock cleared the last warm clouds of sleep, and she was fully awakened. She got quickly out of bed and crept out of the dormitory in her dressing-gown, the stone bumping unfamiliarly against her chest and reminding her of its presence. She ran quickly downstairs and along the icy tiled corridors to her classroom, where the pale gold early morning sun was pouring in over the empty desks. She grabbed her books and scurried back upstairs on cold bare feet.

Tucking her chilled feet under her, Lucy sat up in bed and spread out her maths books. She had half an hour before the first bell went, Lucy calculated quickly: a maximum of fifty free minutes before the first lesson, mathematics. She couldn't possibly finish the work by then. She twitched back the curtain to let a bar of sunlight flood her bed with a bright strip, and bent over the books with the sun warm upon her back. The stone round her neck fell forward as she bent, and the sunlight made it shine like mother-of-pearl as it swung gently. Lucy suddenly felt an upsurge of confidence: she felt light and unreal as if filled with some strange power. She found the page; and the answers seemed to spring into her mind, although she could not say how she knew them. It was almost as if she were watching somebody else's hands, a long way off and nothing to do with her, writing out the answers: the page very white and bright in the sunlight and the ink showing very black against it.

Lucy was jolted back into consciousness, and the rest of the room seemed to jerk back into focus around her. In the rows of beds, the others were turning over and stretching, grumbling as they awoke. Lucy wondered if she had slipped back into sleep, and she looked at the books. The answers were still there, set out neatly in her exercise book; and one of her feet was developing pins-and-needles from being sat

183

on too long. Hastily, Lucy tucked the stone back inside her pyjama-top neck and swung her legs out of bed.

Eating her breakfast later, ravenously hungry, Lucy remembered her terror in the woods the night before: the cold panic that had fluttered inside her in the broken-down hut and her blind fear as she bolted through the clawing branches. The scratches were still there; but her fear seemed a long way away. With the sunlight slanting in at the high windows, although the hall had not yet lost the chill of the night-time, and with the jostling and hubbub all around her, last night seemed far away and almost unreal.

She filed into the classroom, with none of the usual sickening dread of Miss Acidulation's sharp anger over work messily done or unfinished. She hugged her contentment to her as she waited in her seat, staring out at the sun on the young green of the beeches. She rose to her feet with a start as the scrape of chairs and sudden hush announced Miss Acidulation's entrance.

'Still daydreaming, Lucy, I see,' she remarked scathingly. She had had bad indigestion this morning, the class noted. 'I suppose,' she went on disagreeably, 'that you have not managed to complete the task I set you.'

With a certain quiet satisfaction, Lucy came forward and handed over her book.

'Hmmm,' sniffed Miss Acidulation, although slightly mollified, 'wait there just a moment, Lucy, while I mark your work. And the rest of you', she added, glancing up sharply over her gold-rimmed pince-nez, 'keep quiet. You can start on exercise forty-nine in your classwork books.'

Lucy leant against the blackboard in a patch of the spring sunlight. She stared out through the French windows, level with Miss Acidulation's desk, at the wood beyond the strip of grass. A thrush was making short runs on fast-moving legs, head slightly tilted, stabbing at the ground periodically with a greedy beak. Lucy watched it idly, pleasantly aware, out of the corner of her eye, of the movement of Miss Acidulation's hand repeating rapidly scratched ticks down the page of her book. Unconsciously, she fingered the smooth, flat bump of the stone under her school shirt, lying next to her skin, as she dreamily gazed out of the window.

It came as no surprise when she saw the unicorn. It was as if she had known it would be there, white against the beech trees; but she caught her breath in joy and recognition. It seemed smaller than she had imagined, more solid and animal-like, but more fiercely beautiful. The sunlight falling through the half-transparent spring leaves dappled its pure, sleek skin with green shadows, sliding over its muscles as it shifted its feet restlessly in the dead leaves. Its head was up, the whole animal poised and nervously alert like a coiled spring, its strange horn, slender and lethal-looking, gleaming dangerously with the blue-white light of Lucy's unicorn-stone.

This was no gentle beast: it was wild and watchfully alive, with fierce vitality barely suppressed. Lucy stared motionless, caught by a light, breathless joy tinged with fear.

The unicorn seemed to relax slightly. It turned to pull at the soft, young beech leaves, jerking and tossing its head impatiently as it tugged at them; and through the tumbled strands of mane the white rim of a wary eye glinted dangerously.

'You! Child, stop gawping out of the window at nothing in that aimless fashion!' Miss Acidulation's voice rapped out the words harshly. Lucy whipped round, started, her hand flying guiltily from the stone. 'I . . . I . . .' she stammered, as the sea of faces turned to her, all full of suppressed laughter.

They could see nothing.

Desperately, Lucy turned back, but already the unicorn was going, moving back into the wood, and seeming to dissolve into the shifting shadows as it went.

The stone felt hot and heavy round Lucy's neck, feeling as if it were pulsating gently with waves of heat.

Lucy flung herself at the French windows, pressing herself against the cold glass; straining her eyes after the fading shape, and rattling at the handle of the locked door. She could hear the stifled giggles behind her starting to burst out.

The stone seemed to be pulling her down to the ground, intolerably heavy. She clutched at it through her shirt, feeling its heat through the thin cotton.

The unicorn was there again, stepping lightly and proudly out of the shadows. It paused on the edge of the trees, head high, listening intently, its horn showing like a needle-keen stiletto, white against green. Hastily, Lucy rubbed away the mist of her condensed breath from the glass, and held her breath so as not to cloud her view.

The unicorn came forward, high-stepping, each movement proudly graceful with the vigour of controlled energy; and its coat blazed white as it stepped out into the sunlight. Its crest hard-arched, it came towards Lucy with its ears pricked to listen; until she could see its flared nostrils, distended with fear and quivering with its snorted breaths, and its rolling eyes ringed with wild white.

Lucy was seized from behind by Miss Acidulation's bony hands gripping her shoulders, with Miss Acidulation's strident voice shrieking in her ear against a rising gale of smothered laughter. She was wrenched violently round, and the stone, swinging round, broke the flimsy bootlace, flew through the air in a shining arc and skidded, blazing white fire, across the ink-stained floor into the corner. Lucy, held tightly a few inches from Miss Acidulation's face, saw a sudden change come over it. For a moment her features froze, still puckered with anger, then her jaw slowly dropped, and she loosed her hold on Lucy, staring out over her head with bulging eyes. There was a sudden silence. Miss Acidulation clumsily took off her deeply-embedded pince-nez, looking blank and blinded without it, rubbed the glasses with trembling hands and fixed it back on the furrows in her nose.

Lucy turned round. The unicorn was still there, crouching on bunched hocks with forelegs taut and quivering. She could still see it: and so, apparently, could everyone else.

Miss Acidulation screamed: a high, quavering shriek.

The unicorn reared, flailing hooves black against the sky, in a flurry of mane and glinting teeth and eyes, its belly streaked and darkened with fear-sweat. It dropped on to all four feet again, with a spatter of gravel sent flying under crashing fore-feet. Its ears flattened wickedly into its tangled mane, its neck snaked out in fury: then it dropped its head and charged.

There was a wild rush for the door, a shrieking, pushing, stumbling mob of girls, sending the chairs flying, a thunder of hooves as Lucy dived for the stone, then the crash of splintering glass, and the unicorn was in the classroom. Lucy was sent flying, the breath knocked out of her by a hurtling mass of muscle and sweat-streaked flesh bowling her

There was a thunder of hooves as Lucy dived for the stone, then the crash of splintering glass, and the unicorn was in the classroom.

over, and she had a brief glimpse of thrashing legs, a great body that blacked out her vision and streaming horsehair as it knocked into her. It plunged for the door after the screaming girls: there was a slam and a noise of rending wood as the unicorn's horn drove deeply into the door.

Lucy scrambled on hands and knees for the stone, cutting her palms on a sliver of broken glass, as the unicorn plunged back on its hocks, wrenching its horn out of the door.

Maddened, it wheeled to turn on her, lashing out in frenzied fury at the desks that crowded around it, splintering the wood and trampling it underfoot, magnificent and savage. Blood was running down its flanks from the broken glass it had leapt through; its eyes reddened and crazy, nostrils cracking at the scent of blood as it circled and plunged.

As it gathered itself to charge, Lucy's wildly scrabbling fingers found the stone, searing hot now and blazing out blinding white fire. She saw it reflected in the unicorn's rolling eyes, and in the long moment as it leapt, all hooves and foam and deadly horn, her arm went back and sent the stone streaking to meet it in its own perfect curve, streaming blue-white sparks.

Then there was nothing.

A stunning stillness and silence. The classroom looked as if a whirlwind had hit it: but it was empty. Outside the door, someone was having noisy hysterics. Lucy's legs trembled and gave way: she felt suddenly weak and thought she was going to be sick.

Outside, the sun was still shining as if nothing had happened.

A ROUGH RIDE

R. D. Blackmore

*John Ridd is the hero of this story and of the classic book of high
adventure,* Lorna Doone, *from which it is taken.*

It happened upon a November evening (when I was about fifteen years
old, and out-growing my strength very rapidly, my sister Annie being
turned thirteen, and a deal of rain having fallen, and all the troughs in
the yard being flooded, and the bark from the wood-ricks washed down
the gutters, and even our water-shoot going brown) that the ducks in
the court made a terrible quacking, instead of marching off to their
pen, one behind another. Thereupon Annie and I ran out, to see what
might be the sense of it. There were thirteen ducks, and ten lily-white
(as the fashion then of ducks was), not I mean twenty-three in all, but
ten white and three brown-striped ones; and without being nice
about their colour, they all quacked very movingly. They pushed their
gold-coloured bills here and there (yet dirty, as gold is apt to be), and
they jumped on the triangles of their feet, and sounded out of their
nostrils; and some of the over-excited ones ran along low on the
ground, quacking grievously, with their bills snapping and bending,
and the roofs of their mouths exhibited.

Annie began to cry 'dilly, dilly, einy, einy, ducksey', according to
the burden of a tune they seem to have accepted as the national ducks'

189

anthem; but instead of being soothed by it, they only quacked three times as hard, and ran round, till we were giddy. And then they shook their tails all together, and looked grave, and went round and round again.

Now I am uncommonly fond of ducks, whether roystering, roosting, or roasted; and it is a fine sight to behold them walk, plodding one after other, with their toes out, like soldiers drilling, and their little eyes cocked all ways at once, and the way that they dib with their bills, and dabble, and throw up their heads and enjoy something, and then tell the others about it. Therefore I knew at once, by the way they were carrying on, that there must be something or other gone wholly amiss in the duck world. Sister Annie perceived it too, but with a greater quickness; for she counted them like a good duck-wife, and could only tell thirteen of them, when she knew there ought to be fourteen.

And so we began to search about, and the ducks ran to lead us aright, having come that far to fetch us; and when we got down to the foot of the courtyard where the two great ash trees stand by the side of the little water, we found good reason for the urgence and melancholy of the duck-birds. Lo! the old white drake, the father of all, a bird of high manners and chivalry, always the last to help himself from the pan of barley-meal, and the first to show fight to a dog or cock intruding upon his family, this fine fellow, and pillar of the state, was now in a sad predicament, yet quacking very stoutly. For the brook, wherewith he had been familiar from his callow childhood, and wherein he was wont to quest for water-newts, and tadpoles and caddis-worms, and other game, this brook, which afforded him very often scanty space to dabble in, and sometimes starved the cresses, was now coming down in a great brown flood, as if the banks never belonged to it. The foaming of it, and the noise, and the cresting of the corners, and the up and down, like a wave of the sea, were enough to frighten any duck, though bred upon stormy waters, which our ducks had never been.

There is always a hurdle, nine feet long, and four and a half in depth, swung by a chain at either end from an oak laid across the channel. And the use of this hurdle is to keep our kine at milking time from straying away there drinking (for in truth they are very dainty) and to fence strange cattle, or Farmer Snowe's horses, from coming along the bed of the brook unknown, to steal our substance. But now this hurdle, which hung in the summer a foot above the trickle, would have been dipped more than two feet deep, but for the power against it. For the torrent came down so vehemently that the chains at full stretch when creaking, and the hurdle, buffeted almost flat, and thatched (so to say) with the drift-stuff, was going see-saw with a sulky splash on the dirty red comb of the waters. But saddest to see was between two bars, where a fog was of rushes, and floodwood, and wild celery-haulm, and dead crowsfoot, who but our venerable mallard, jammed in by the joint of his shoulder, speaking aloud as he rose and fell, with his top knot full of water, unable to comprehend it, with his tail washed far away from him, but often compelled to be silent, being ducked very harshly against his will by the choking fall-to of the hurdle.

For a moment I could scarce help laughing; because, being borne up high and dry by a tumult of the torrent, he gave me a look from his one little eye (having lost one in fight with the turkey-cock), a gaze of appealing sorrow, and then a loud quack to second it. But the quack came out of time, I suppose, for his throat got filled with water, as the hurdle carried him back again. And then there was scarcely the screw of his tail to be seen until he swung up again, and left small doubt by the way he spluttered, and failed to quack, and hung down his poor crest, but that drown he must in another minute, and frogs triumph over his body.

Annie was crying, and wringing her hands, and I was about to rush into the water, although I liked not the look of it, but hoped to hold on by the hurdle, when a man on horseback came suddenly round the corner of the great ash-hedge on the other side of the stream, and his horse's feet were in the water.

'Ho, there,' he cried; 'get thee back, boy. The flood will carry thee down like a straw. I will do it for thee, and no trouble.'

With that he leaned forward, and spoke to his mare—she was just of the tint of a strawberry, a young thing, very beautiful—and she arched up her neck, as disliking the job; yet, trusting him, would attempt it. She entered the flood, with her dainty forelegs sloped further and further in front of her, and her delicate ears pricked forward, and the size of her great eyes increasing; but he kept her straight in the turbid rush, by the pressure of his knee on her. Then she looked back, and wondered at him, as the force of the torrent grew stronger, but he bade

191

'He leaned from his saddle, in a manner which I never could have thought possible, and caught up old Tom with his right hand . . .'

her go on; and on she went, and it foamed up over her shoulders; and she tossed up her lip and scorned it, for now her courage was waking. Then as the rush of it swept her away, and she struck with her forefeet down the stream, he leaned from his saddle, in a manner which I never could have thought possible, and caught up old Tom with his right hand, and set him between his holsters, and smiled at his faint quack of gratitude. In a moment all three were carried downstream, and the rider lay flat on his horse, and tossed the hurdle clear from him, and made for the bend of smooth water.

They landed, some thirty or forty yards lower, in the midst of our kitchen-garden, where the winter cabbage was; but though Annie and I crept in through the hedge, and were full of our thanks, and admiring him, he would answer us never a word, until he had spoken in full to the mare, as if explaining the whole to her.

'Sweetheart, I know thou couldst have leaped it,' he said, as he patted her cheek, being on the ground by this time, and she was nudging up to him, with the water pattering off from her; 'but I had good reason, Winnie dear, for making thee go through it.'

She answered him kindly with her soft eyes, and sniffed at him very lovingly, and they understood one another. Then he took from his waistcoat two peppercorns, and made the old drake swallow them, and tried him softly upon his legs, where the leading gap in the hedge was. Old Tom stood up quite bravely, and clapped his wings, and shook off the wet from his tail-feathers; and then away into the court-yard, and his family gathered around him, and they all made a noise in their throats, and stood up, and put their bills together, to thank God for this great deliverance.

Having taken all this trouble, and watched the end of that adventure, the gentleman turned round to us, with a pleasant smile on his face, as if he were lightly amused with himself; and we came up and looked at him. He was rather short, about John Fry's height, or maybe a little taller, but very strongly built and springy, as his gait at every step showed plainly, although his legs were bowed with much riding, and he looked as if he lived on horseback. To a boy like me he seemed very old, being over twenty, and well-found in beard; but he was not more than four-and-twenty, fresh and ruddy-looking, with a short nose, and keen blue eyes, and a merry waggish jerk about him, as if the world were not in earnest. Yet he had a sharp, stern way, like the crack of a pistol, if anything disliked him; and we knew (for children see such things) that it was safer to tickle than tackle him.

'Well, young 'uns, what be gaping at?' He gave pretty Annie a chuck on the chin, and took me all in without winking.

'Your mare,' said I, standing stoutly up, being a tall boy now; 'I never saw such a beauty, sir. Will you let me have a ride of her?'

'Think thou couldst ride her, lad? She will have no burden but mine. Thou couldst never ride her. Tut! I would be loth to kill thee.'

'Ride her!' I cried with the bravest scorn, for she looked so kind and gentle; 'there never was horse upon Exmoor foaled but I could tackle in half an hour. Only I never ride upon saddle. Take them leathers off of her.'

He looked at me, with a dry little whistle, and thrust his hands into his breeches-pockets, and so grinned that I could not stand it. And Annie laid hold of me in such a way that I was almost mad with her. And he laughed, and approved her for doing so. And the worst of all was—he said nothing.

'Get away, Annie, will you? Do you think I am a fool, good sir? Only trust me with her, and I will not override her.'

'For that I will go bail, my son. She is liker to override thee. But the ground is soft to fall upon, after all this rain. Now come out into the yard, young man, for the sake of your mother's cabbages. And the mellow straw-bed will be softer for thee, since pride must have its fall. I am thy mother's cousin, boy, and am going up to house. Tom Faggus is my name, as everybody knows; and this is my young mare, Winnie.'

What a fool I must have been not to know it at once! Tom Faggus, the great highwayman, and his young blood-mare, the strawberry! Already her fame was noised abroad, nearly as much as her master's; and my longing to ride her grew tenfold, but fear came at the back of it. Not that I had the smallest fear of what the mare could do to me, by fair play and horse-trickery; but that the glory of sitting upon her seemed to be too great for me; especially as there were rumours abroad that she was not a mare after all, but a witch. However, she looked like a filly all over, and wonderfully beautiful, with her supple stride, and soft slope of shoulder, and glossy coat, beaded with water, and prominent eyes, full of love or of fire. Whether this came from her eastern blood of the Arabs newly imported, and whether the cream colour, mixed with our bay, led to that bright strawberry tint, is certainly more than I can decide, being chiefly acquainted with farm-horses. And these come of any colour and form; you never can count what they will be, and are lucky to get four legs to them.

Mr Faggus gave his mare a wink, and she walked demurely after him, a bright young thing, flowing over with life, yet dropping her soul to a higher one, and led by love to anything; as the manner is of females, when they know what is the best for them. Then Winnie trod lightly upon the straw, because it had soft muck under it, and her delicate feet came back again.

'Up for it still, boy, be ye?' Tom Faggus stopped, and the mare stopped there; and they looked at me provokingly.

'Is she able to leap, sir? There is good take-off on this side of the brook.'

Mr Faggus laughed very quietly, turning round to Winnie, so that she might enter into it. And she, for her part, seemed to know exactly where the joke was.

'Good tumble-off, you mean, my boy. Well, there can be small harm to thee. I am akin to thy family, and know the substance of their skulls.'

'Let me get up,' said I, waxing wrath, for reasons I cannot tell you, because they are too manifold; 'take off your saddlebag things. I will try not to squeeze her ribs in, unless she plays nonsense with me.'

Then Mr Faggus was up on his mettle, at this proud speech of mine; and John Fry was running up all the while, and Bill Dadds, and half a dozen. Tom Faggus gave one glance around, and then dropped all regard for me. The high repute of his mare was at stake, and what was my life compared to it? Through my defiance, and stupid ways, here was I in a duello, and my legs not come to their strength yet, and my arms as limp as a herring.

Something of this occurred to him, even in his wrath with me, for he spoke very softly to the filly, who now could scarce subdue herself; but she drew in her nostrils, and breathed to his breath, and did all she could to answer him.

'Not too hard, my dear,' he said; 'let him gently down on the mixen. That will be quite enough.' Then he turned the saddle off, and I was up in a moment. She began at first so easily, and pricked her ears so lovingly, and minced about as if pleased to find so light a weight on her, that I thought she knew I could ride a little, and feared to show any capers. 'Gee wugg, Polly!' cried I, for all the men were now looking on, being then at the leaving-off time; 'Gee wugg, Polly, and show what thou be'est made of.' With that I plugged my heels into her, and Billy Dadds flung his hat up.

Nevertheless she outraged not, though her eyes were frightening Annie, and John Fry took a pick to keep him safe; but she curbed to and fro, with her strong forearms rising, like springs in-gathered, waiting and quivering grievously, and beginning to sweat about it. Then her master gave a shrill clear whistle, when her ears were bent towards him, and I felt her form beneath me gathering up like whalebone, and her hind legs coming under her, and I knew that I was in for it.

First she reared upright in the air, and struck me full on the nose with her comb, till I bled worse than Robin Snell made me; and then down with her forefeet deep in the straw, and her hind feet going to heaven.

Finding me stick to her still like wax (for my mettle was up as hers was), away she flew with me, swifter than ever I went before, or since, I trow. She drove full-head at the cob-wall—'oh, Jack, slip off,' screamed Annie—then she turned like light, when I thought to crush her, and ground my left knee against it. 'Mux me,' I cried, for my breeches were broken, and short words went the furthest—'if you kill me, you shall die with me.' Then she took the courtyard gate at a leap, knocking my words between my teeth, and then right over a quickset hedge, as if the sky were a breath to her; and away for the water-meadows, while I lay on her neck like a child at the breast, and wished I had never been born. Straight away, all in the front of the wind, and scattering clouds around her, all I knew of the speed we made was the frightful flash of her shoulders, and her mane like trees in a tempest. I felt the earth under us rushing away, and the air left far behind us, and my breath came and went, and I prayed to God, and was sorry to be so late of it.

All the long swift while, without power of thought, I clung to her crest and shoulders, and dug my nails into her creases, and my toes into her flank-part, and was proud of holding on so long, though sure of being beaten. Then in her fury at feeling me still, she rushed at another device for it, and leaped the wide water-trough sideways across, to and fro, till no breath was left in me. The hazel-boughs took me too hard in the face, and the tall dog-briars got hold of me, and the ache of my back was like crimping a fish; till I longed to give up, and lay thoroughly beaten, and lie there and die in the cresses.

But there came a shrill whistle from up the home-hill, where the people had hurried to watch us; and the mare stopped as if with a bullet; then set off for home with the speed of a swallow, and going as smoothly and silently. I never had dreamed of such delicate motion, fluent, and graceful, and ambient, soft as the breeze flitting over the flowers, but swift as the summer lightning. I sat up again, but my strength was all spent, and no time left to recover it; and at last, as she rose at our gate like a bird, I tumbled off into the mixen.

'Well done, lad,' Mr Faggus said, good-naturedly; for all were now gathered round me, as I rose from the ground somewhat tottering, and miry, and crestfallen, but otherwise none the worse (having fallen upon my head, which is of uncommon substance); nevertheless John Fry was laughing so that I longed to clout his ears for him; 'Not at all bad work, my boy; we may teach you to ride by and by, I see; I thought not to see you stick on so long——'

'I should have stuck on much longer, sir, if her sides had not been wet. She was so slippery——'

'Boy, thou art right. She hath given many the slip. Ha, ha! Vex not, Jack, that I laugh at thee. She is like a sweetheart to me, and better than any of them be. It would have gone to my heart, if thou hadst conquered. None but I can ride my Winnie mare.'

IN PURSUIT OF
A WILD STALLION
Joseph E. Chipperfield

Dark Fury, the last of the great wild stallions, has been captured and forced to work in a circus. His friends, Indians of the Coeur D'Alenes tribe, succeed in setting him free. Hot on his trail ride the ruthless horse thieves. But young Kirk Merrett has promised the Indians that he will watch over Dark Fury, and he too sets out after the stallion, heading for the secret canyon where the last of the great wild horse herds run free.

Full of the confidence of youth, and sure that he was again close on the track of Dark Fury, Kirk Merrett came riding through the gorge between the Deep Creek Mountains and the impressive upthrust of Bannock Peak. The horse's hooves clattered merrily on the loose stones and debris. He tossed his head as he paced evenly along the rutted trail. Like his master, he too had achieved a new confidence which showed clearly in his gait. Every now and again he half turned his head as if trying to get a glimpse of Kirk in the saddle. Since the night of the attack by the band of the coyotes, the animal had developed a strong liking for his master as if he knew that, but for Kirk's timely intervention with the stick that spat fire, he might have joined his late companion in the dark valley of silence.

The trail began to rise and Kirk, swaying in the saddle, suddenly realized that the gorge was opening out into a clearing where aspens made a glow of whiteness against the red walls of the surrounding cliffs. Striking through the small wood of aspens was a trail of vivid green.

'This is a dandy place to set up camp,' Kirk remarked aloud. 'An early rest'll do me a power of good fer sure. We've travelled some . . . the hoss an' me . . .'

He swung himself around and looked back along the trail. All he could see was the grim outline of the mountains that terminated in Deep Creek Peak. Beyond it stretched the endless trail back to Black Pine Peak.

Yep, he thought. He sure had travelled some since coming down off Kelton Pass. He wondered how much farther he would have to go before striking the watershed of the Bannock Range and the foothills marking the course of Snake River.

He straightened himself in the saddle and coaxed the horse to quicken his pace in order to reach the grove of aspens the more quickly. The place seemed tempting, and he sure felt saddle weary.

Acting instinctively, Kirk gave the horse his head, and the animal went off at a swinging trot. Straight towards the trees he went, watching closely the track and fixing every small rise as something he must remember.

He trotted without hesitation to the most likely glade and, without being spoken to, halted and waited for Kirk to dismount. He was growing very wise for a mustang of unknown ancestry, and was learning to interpret his master's wishes.

Kirk's tent was soon erected and the usual fire of dead wood sent its plume of blue smoke unfurling through the trees. Quite near to the camp, a mocking-bird imitated the cry of a solan goose it had heard in the winter. Hidden deep in the wood, a bluebird twittered gaily, and for a long time after he had finished his supper, Kirk lay on his back listening to it, while the darkness crept along the gorge and finally invaded the clearing and the aspen grove.

Not long afterwards, it was another night, as still as had been the countless other nights the clearing had known. The only difference lay in the flickering of the camp-fire and the slow movement of the horse which grazed under the trees and the man who slept close beside the fire instead of in the tent.

It was the flickering of the camp-fire and the scent of woodsmoke carried to them on the breeze that attracted Luke Unwin and his companions.

For many days now, they had followed close on Kirk's trail, and whilst they had no idea as to how near, or far, they were, they knew they were at least travelling in the right direction. In places, hoof-prints were more than merely indicated on the track. They were heavily scored, particularly where the ground was moist. The only hoof-marks missing were those of Dark Fury. Even so, like Kirk, Unwin's gang felt they were on the right trail. It was the very route they had followed when bringing the animal down from the desolation of Snake River Plain.

They rode into Kirk's camp a little after midnight, and roused the young fellow by their ribald shouting.

As Kirk sat up, his eyes still heavy with sleep, he heard Unwin remark mockingly: 'Well, if it ain't ole man Burke's buddy . . . Bet he's after the stallion too.'

The others laughed.

Kirk then saw that all four men were sitting in a half-circle around the fire while their horses stood quietly under the trees.

'Ain't very entertainin' is 'e?' Maitland remarked, with a vein of sarcasm sharpening the conclusion of the sentence.

'Perhaps ole man Burke told 'im we wuz rustlers or sumthin',' Enos Wills suggested on a wheezing note of laughter.

'Mebbe 'e ain't got a tongue in 'is 'ead anymore,' said Corson, speaking his little piece with obvious relish.

'Cut it out!' Unwin interjected harshly. 'We ain't here for fun.' Then to Kirk, he said slowly, putting a special emphasis on each word: 'Mebbe you can tell us jest where the black stallion is hidin', eh?'

By this time, Kirk had all his wits about him; to save Dark Fury from possible capture by Unwin's gang, he would have to play for time.

He forced a smile to his lips.

'Uh,' he said quickly, 'if I knew jest where the stallion was, I'd hardly be here at me ease in camp. I'd be with him some place back o' the Bannock Range.'

He nodded in a direction well away from the trail he sensed the stallion was following.

'Oh, is that so?' Unwin remarked with a sneer. 'Well, you ain't back o' the Bannock Range, an' never will be. You're right here, kiddo! Mebbe Dark Fury ain't so far either. What 'eve you to say to that?'

He thrust his unshaven chin towards Kirk. In a way, he was experiencing a sardonic satisfaction in sitting there, leering at the young fellow. All that was brutal in his nature rejoiced in the present situation. He laughed in Kirk's face. Then bending forward, he shook him violently.

'You've no answer to that question, 'eve yeh? We know the hoss is somewhere hereabouts. More'n that, we gotta idea you're all set to meet one of them Indians some place. 'Ow about tellin' jest where, eh?'

Kirk turned his head away from the unshaven chin and beetling brows thrust so close to his face.

Enraged, Unwin caught hold of his hair and forced him to look once again in his direction.

'Quit the stallin' . . . Where you meetin' that Indian? We know where the redskin is, the stallion won't be far away. Now get talkin' . . .'

Maitland, Corson and Wills sat motionless, letting Unwin do all the talking. They too were enjoying the situation, each harbouring vivid remembrances of their own unhappy circumstances beside another camp-fire.

'I ain't meetin' no Indian,' Kirk managed to gasp.

'What about the hoss?' Unwin probed.

'I ain't seen him since comin' down off the divide from Utah,' he answered.

Unwin's face flushed with increasing rage.

'That's a lie, an' you know it,' he shouted.

'It's the truth,' Kirk reiterated, resolving at all costs not to let Unwin and his gang of ruffians know how well set they were on the stallion's trail.

Unwin's next words, however, confounded him.

'We know the hoss is on this trail, an' hidin' some place near. We brought him along this very trail when we wuz travellin' south to join up with ole man Burke's circus.'

'Then you find him!'

Kirk spat the words out viciously.

Unwin started to laugh again.

'We will! Yeh can be sure of thet. One other thing is certain sure . . . you won't! Mebbe we'll leave you here . . . tied up, an' easy pickin' fer the coyotes . . .'

He continued to laugh loudly, the others joining in. Unwin then thrust Kirk away from the fire and sat for a while, staring into the flames.

After a few moments of silence, Wills nudged Unwin.

'What we do now, boss?' he asked.

Luke spat into the fire.

'Wait till morning' . . . that's what. We'll settle with this bucko then. Tie 'im up meantime . . .'

Soon afterwards, Kirk, tied hand and foot, lay under the trees, and Unwin and his companions, having eaten their supper, stretched themselves out before the fast-dying fire and dozed.

Kirk knew that it was useless to try and free himself from the bonds. The men were professionals in the making of knots, and they had tied him much too securely to allow for any attempt at escaping. In his despair he was aware of one consolation. His horse had come up from out of the gloom and stood over him, as if on guard. This seemed to strengthen the feeling of kinship between them, the one attempting to succour the other by nuzzling him. Not till the dawn began to make pink the sky did the animal move off into the trees, and even then, not until he glimpsed the first of Unwin's gang rising to stretch.

Corson cooked breakfast, then all four jested as they ate. They seemed to be in no great hurry to hit the trail.

At last Unwin strolled carelessly over to where Kirk lay.

'Do yeh still say yeh don't know where thet hoss is?' he asked.

Kirk did not answer, but merely glared at his tormenter.

'Oh well, there's only one way to settle with yeh, me bold kiddo . . .' He looked towards the camp. 'Wills!' he shouted.

Enos Wills was about to obey Unwin's command when Maitland, starting to his feet, pointed upwards.

'Look!' he screamed.

Luke gazed in the direction indicated. His face flushed with excitement.

Way up on a ridge of high ground overlooking the grove of aspens stood Dark Fury. The horse was clearly defined against the red colouring of the cliffs that enclosed the gorge on its eastern limits.

'The stallion!' Unwin shouted hoarsely. 'The black devil himself . . .'

He ran over to his companions and with them stood staring up at

Unwin's face flushed with excitement. 'The stallion!' he shouted hoarsely. 'The black devil himself.'

the ledge, mentally debating how best to reach it and drive the stallion into some broken gorge from which he could not escape.

It dawned on him then that the ledge could not be reached from this side of the valley. A steady focusing of his eyes on the cliff disclosed the fact that the ledge was part of a seam in the rock which began where a break in the mountain showed clearly where a divide led down to the opposite side of the range.

All four men had completely forgotten Kirk. They continued to stare unfalteringly at the motionless shape of the horse that seemed so near and yet so far away.

'We'll heve to make fer the divide,' Unwin began.

His voice died in his throat as a sharp cry came echoing down from the ridge. It went on and on in what seemed a rising note of excitement.

Willis had ceased to stare up at the stallion. Something in the stallion's stance caused him to glance up at the head of the gorge.

He gave a shout of warning.

'The Indians . . . They're headin' this way . . .'

The others reached for their guns as they took in the scene at a glance. Wills was right. The band of Coeur D'Alenes had indeed entered the gorge, and although still more than a mile away, were riding towards the aspen grove.

'We'll fight it out,' Unwin cried.

Wills shook his head.

'We'd better make a getaway while the goin's good. There's too many of them. They'd finish us off sure. If we get out of the gorge, we might yet get the hoss. 'E ain't thet far away!'

Unwin, for all his blustering, was not slow in agreeing with Wills' observations. There was no time now to decide what to do with their captive as the Indians were approaching very rapidly. They resolved to leave him where he was.

'Let his pals see to him,' was Unwin's comment as he and the others hastily saddled their horses.

'How about this?' Maitland said, indicating his gun.

Unwin shook his head.

'Them Indians 'ud 'eve another score to settle with us then, an' we might never get the hoss . . .'

He jumped up into the saddle as he spoke.

The gang rode off just as the Coeur D'Alenes entered the first of the timber and headed direct for the camp.

Kirk, unable to suppress the excitement he felt, lay waiting for the help he knew now was approaching. He swore to get even with Unwin, whatever the cost. He struggled into a sitting posture, stirred by the violent surging of emotion in his breast, and saw the Indians riding up the grassy trail between the aspens.

What he did not see was the shape of Dark Fury still up on the ridge watching every movement of both friends and enemies.

The stallion remained unmoving until the Coeur D'Alenes halted before the remains of Kirk's camp-fire while two of their number, dismounting, hastened to release the young man from his bonds.

Then, and only then, did Dark Fury leave this vantage point so high above the valley, making with unerring instinct for the divide from which a well-defined trail led down to Silver Creek and the tributary that flowed direct to the distant Snake River.

The ground in silver creek had dried up, and despite the heavy rain of a few days before, the river was running quite low. A woodpecker drummed loudly on a decayed oak tree that still continued to grow gnarled and twisted close to the track Dark Fury was following. The bird ceased when it beheld the stallion, and stood clinging precariously to the bark of the trunk with head turned to one side so that it could better observe the approach of the animal who had suddenly invaded this hitherto undisturbed hinterland of the mountains.

Dark Fury paused close to the old tree and then went slowly to the river to drink.

The woodpecker continued to watch him, and only fluttered to a higher position when a porcupine moved swiftly across the trail to the security of a boulder. But for the movement of the porcupine, and that of the stallion, there was nothing else in the entire wood to cause the woodpecker alarm.

Dark Fury was conscious of the quietness as he dipped his muzzle into the river to drink. It reminded him of many another such quietness that he had known in other remote places. Here, not even the murmuring of the tumbling currents seemed to touch his hearing. He only knew that the river was flowing endlessly on, moving in one long silver gleam that broke into arrow-heads of light where shallows marked the watercourse.

Then again the drumming of the woodpecker on the old tree trunk went echoing up into the still air. The sound and the gleaming flow of the river seemed to be one. Dark Fury was no more aware of one than he was of the other.

Nature, in Silver Creek, was a kindly thing, so different from the dangers he had known since his escape from the showground. The stallion was almost inclined to stay awhile beside the river.

Already he had made a distinct classification of events. He knew that danger such as he had experienced in the past existed for the most part only in the nearness of the four men who had originally taken him captive. For those others, the Indians and Kirk, he had no feeling of fear. He was beginning to accept them as followers habitual to the trail. If anything, he sensed a special affinity with Kirk, born out of what the young fellow had done for him, and strengthened by his persistence in keeping so close to him on the trail.

Even as these vague glimmerings of what was instinctive reasoning passed through his brain, Dark Fury experienced once more the more urgent growth of curiosity taking possession of him. As a result, when glancing back along the trail, he half expected to see Kirk riding towards him.

At last, moved by the intensity of the reactions he began to experience, the stallion moved from the river to stand for some minutes beside the old tree where, once again, the woodpecker clung very quiet and very still, watching him.

Dark Fury was conscious of a strange disappointment when, after some little while, no sign of Kirk was visible on the distant approaches of the trail.

By this time, the afternoon sun was deepening in shade and on one peak where snow lay in heavy drifts, the colour slowly expired like a flame dwindling and dying in a place where winds held constant play. Mauve-blue contours marked the division between earth and sky. Lower down, the contours merged into one like hands folded across a breast of snowy whiteness. They did, however, but serve to foreshorten the serrated outline of the unnamed peak that rose in the east, lost in a halo of cloud.

Whilst Dark Fury continued to stand gazing up the trail, he did not observe the constant change of colour on the mountains, but did see the shadows lengthening across the river; and a wind coming from off the unnamed peak blew over him in a steady stream, and fanned his long black tail until it waved slowly like a silken banner.

It was then, perhaps, more than at any time since his escape from Burke's corral, that Dark Fury seemed again to be in his full prime. Despite his journeying, and the hardships he had undergone, the leanness had gone from his frame and his hide had taken on a new lustre that was the lustre of good health. He had assuredly recovered from his desert ordeal. His intelligence too had sharpened in that he was able to assess more quickly the dangers that might threaten him from the approach of those who, in the past, had betrayed him. He possessed also a more reactionary method of reasoning, closely allied to a new courage that was born of new experience rather than of the wild. Moreover, he was thrilled with the sense of well-being that moved through him like the surging of a warmer blood through his veins.

With his head set high on his sturdy neck, and his black tail being gently fanned by the rising breeze, he might have been in very truth the black talisman of the Coeur D'Alenes waiting for the great chieftain to come and sit astride his gleaming back.

For ten minutes, maybe fifteen, he stood thus under the shadow of the decaying oak tree, while less discernible shadows continued to lengthen across the river, and the mauve-blue contours of the hills far up the valley became misted over with a scarf of cloud that had unfurled from off the unnamed peak.

Then, the stallion was no longer there. He had departed suddenly, travelling swiftly westwards; and only the woodpecker saw him depart. It seemed that the lengthening shadows pursued him like transient range followers who sought quickly to reach that strange country beyond the Snake River Plain.

By the time the woodpecker had resumed its monotonous drumming, light was departing from the river and the westering sun sinking behind the ramparts of the hills that kept the Oregon State Line.

Dark Fury, in crossing over the hill track that led away from the valley of the aspens, did not follow the main trail leading down to the

207

river basin. Instead, he turned into a small creek that struck northwards and was concealed by the walls of the main mountain ridge that followed the watercourse that shaped the valley west of the Bannock Range.

This unexpected move by the stallion had thrown Luke Unwin and his gang completely off his track. Unsuspecting his change in tactics, they had followed the main trail which they had used when they had captured Dark Fury.

Kirk Merrett was more fortunate inasmuch that after he had been released by the Indians, they had agreed to accompany him as far as the Snake River Basin. Thus when the young man and the Coeur D'Alenes came out on to the mountain trail, and saw the small northward creek, one of the Indians investigated the ground very carefully, finally remarking with calm assurance that Dark Fury had, at this point, deserted the main track and had gone due north.

This caused the leader of the Coeur D'Alenes to reconsider his previous decision to accompany Kirk as far as the Snake River. His task was to keep in close touch with Luke Unwin and his companions who had clearly kept to the main trail.

He consulted the remainder of the band.

It was well past noon when the Coeur D'Alenes indicated that because of Dark Fury's deviation, Kirk would have to travel alone up the creek in search of the stallion. As the leader explained, Dark Fury was Kirk's responsibility whereas Luke Unwin and his disreputable friends were his.

'We keep bad men on move,' the leader said.

Kirk understood, and while thankful for what the Coeur D'Alenes had already done for him, was secretly overjoyed to know that he was to journey on alone. He had long since discovered that he preferred his own company to that of others. There was, he often confessed to himself, a strange delight in travelling alone, for it gave one much time for thinking and searching out the secret places of the heart. Moreover, alone, one got to savour the atmosphere of a place and to know that it was not merely an expanse of country made up of just so many hills and valleys.

Kirk, like many another man before him, was not long in discerning that there were sermons a-plenty to be read in stones, and the whole history of the world in the shape of a mountain or in the burrowing of a watercourse. What was more, one learnt these things quickly when one

His smile of assent satisfied the Coeur D'Alenes who, raising their hands in token of farewell, spurred their horses forward. They went down the mountain trail at a steady trot, leaving Kirk free to pursue his solitary way along the creek that, within a few miles, opened out on to the fair prospect of Silver Creek.

Like Dark Fury, Kirk too was feeling exceedingly fit. His brief encounter with Luke Unwin's gang had done little more than rouse in him the desire to get even at some future date. For the rest, he was happy to be in the saddle, listening to his horse's feet clip-clopping along the trail, and knowing that no matter what happened now, there must come the day when he would be safely across the Snake River and in the great plain itself; and then, in a month, maybe two, would be in the land of the lost rivers and at not too great a distance from Lost Canyon.

Kirk thought a lot about Lost Canyon that afternoon. Indeed, it occupied most of his conscious thinking from the very moment he left the Coeur D'Alenes. It was not, after all, entirely in a spirit of adventure that he wanted to visit the hidden canyon, nor was it altogether because it was Dark Fury's legendary home. He really wanted to discover if the old tales about it were true . . . whether, as was so often said by old timers, it was a valley rich in gold desposits. Also—and despite Dark Fury, this it was that thrilled him the most—whether it was indeed the last stronghold of the great wild horse bands.

With the night already heavy on the hills, he entered the approaches of Silver Creek. The silence was unbroken; not even the woodpecker drummed where the old oak tree was like a crooked shadow down on the trail.

Reining his horse, Kirk sat hunched in the saddle, trying to catch some faint movement or sound.

He drew in his breath as he felt a wild elation rising up in him. Once more he realized that this was truly the life all men should live. The faint gleam of the river that was like a silken thread slipped quietly away to the unending plain of Snake River. Suddenly, he heard a night bird call out clear and strong, and the sound was like music in his ears, reaching up and entwining itself about his heart.

209

Some little time later, when he rode down towards the twisted shape of the ancient oak, he knew from some very recent droppings that here it was Dark Fury had been but a few hours before.

In spite of the old familiar thrill he experienced at the discovery, it was important that he should set up camp and rest his horse awhile. The animal had been constantly on the move since leaving the aspen grove early that morning.

One consolation Kirk had, however. Even as he and his own horse must rest, so indeed must the stallion take rest, and the miles that separated them would not be materially lengthened by the night that must pass before he again broke camp and hit the trail.

It was as he dismounted and prepared to erect his tent by the oak tree that Kirk heard the first frail shiver of the river. It crept up to him from out of the gloom, a sharp musical murmur where the currents eddied over some broken shallows.

The sound was, for all the world, like a complaint in rhythm—a complaint, moreover, that rose and fell, reached a sharp-edged note of pain, then subsided. It might have been the old eternal cry of the river for the warmth and light that evening had taken away. There might have been a mild resentment in it too, a resentment of the loneliness that night brought when the wind blew chill from off the mountains, and only the stars quivered like drowned things in the deep pools where the rainbow trout were wont to lie.

Because of it, Kirk had the feeling that Silver Creek in being so intimate had accepted him, and that he could rest the night in peace without fear of being overtaken by those who, the previous night, had come upon him unawares.

Even as the river predicted, only the wind stirred as he slept, the chill wind the river had always known. At daybreak, the woodpecker was back at its drumming in the oak trunk, and out in the river, a trout leaped, and way above the mountain peaks, a wide-pinioned eagle came gliding down the uncharted airlines of the sky . . .

Yes, indeed! Life was truly a thing of never-ending surprises and beauty to one travelling alone!

WHERE'S THE SADDLE?

George Borrow

*Born in Norfolk in 1803, George Henry Borrow was both a writer and a great traveller. His wanderings and deep interest in gypsy-lore provided material for two of his most famous books—*Lavengro, *from which this story comes, and* Romany Rye. *His young hero is a soldier's son, stationed for a time in barracks in Ireland. It is not long before he is persuaded to take his first, unforgettable ride . . .*

And it came to pass that, as I was standing by the door of the barrack stable, one of the grooms came out to me, saying, 'I say, young gentleman, I wish you would give the cob a breathing this fine morning.'

'Why do you wish me to mount him?' said I; 'you know he is dangerous. I saw him fling you off his back only a few days ago.'

'Why, that's the very thing, master. I'd rather see anybody on his back than myself; he does not like me; but, to them he does, he can be as gentle as a lamb.'

'But suppose,' said I, 'that he should not like me?'

'We shall soon see that, master,' said the groom; 'and if so be he shows temper, I will be the first to tell you to get down. But there's no fear of that; you have never angered or insulted him, and to such as you, I say again, he'll be as gentle as a lamb.'

'And how came you to insult him,' said I, 'knowing his temper as you do?'

'Merely through forgetfulness, master: I was riding him about a month ago, and having a stick in my hand, I struck him, thinking I was on another horse, or rather thinking of nothing at all. He has never

211

forgiven me, though before that time he was the only friend I had in the world; I should like to see you on him, master.'

'I should soon be off him: I can't ride.'

'Then you are all right, master; there's no fear. Trust him for not hurting a young gentleman, an officer's son, who can't ride. If you were a blackguard dragoon, indeed, with long spurs, 'twere another thing; as it is, he'll treat you as if he were the elder brother that loves you. Ride! he'll soon teach you to ride, if you leave the matter with him. He's the best riding master in all Ireland, and the gentlest.'

The cob was led forth; what a tremendous creature! I had frequently seen him before, and wondered at him; he was barely fifteen hands, but he had the girth of a metropolitan dray-horse; his head was small in comparison with his immense neck, which curved down nobly to his wide back: his chest was broad and fine, and his shoulders models of symmetry and strength; he stood well and powerfully upon his legs, which were somewhat short. In a word, he was a gallant specimen of the genuine Irish cob, a species at one time not uncommon, but at the present day nearly extinct.

'There!' said the groom, as he looked at him, half admiringly, half sorrowfully, 'with sixteen stone on his back, he'll trot fourteen miles in one hour, with your nine stone, some two and a half more, ay, and clear a six-foot wall at the end of it.'

'I'm half afraid,' said I; 'I had rather you would ride him.'

'I'd rather so, too, if he would let me; but he remembers the blow. Now, don't be afraid, young master, he's longing to go out himself. He's been trampling with his feet these three days, and I know what that means; he'll let anybody ride him but myself, and thank them; but to me he says, "No! you struck me".'

'But,' said I, 'where's the saddle?'

'Never mind the saddle; if you are ever to be a frank rider, you must begin without a saddle; besides, if he felt a saddle, he would think you don't trust him, and leave you to yourself. Now, before you mount, make his acquaintance—see there, how he kisses you and licks your face, and see how he lifts his foot; that's to shake hands. You may trust him—now you are on his back at last; mind how you hold the bridle— gently, gently! It's not four pair of hands like yours can hold him if he wishes to be off. Mind what I tell you—leave it all to him.'

Off went the cob at a slow and gentle trot—too fast, however, for so inexperienced a rider. I soon felt myself sliding off, the animal perceived it too, and instantly stood stone still till I had righted myself; and now the groom came up: 'When you feel yourself going,' said he, 'don't lay hold of the mane, that's no use; mane never yet saved man from falling, no more than straw from drowning; it's his sides you must cling to with your calves and feet, till you learn to balance yourself. That's it, now abroad with you; I'll bet my comrade a pot of beer that you'll be a regular rough rider by the time you come back.'

And so it proved; I followed the directions of the groom, and the cob gave me every assistance. How easy is riding, after the first timidity is got over, to supple and youthful limbs; and there is no second fear. The creature soon found that the nerves of his rider were in proper tone. Turning his head half round he made a kind of whining noise, flung out a little foam, and set off.

In less than two hours I had made the circuit of the Devil's Mountain, and was returning along the road, bathed with perspiration, but screaming with delight; the cob laughing in his equine way, scattering foam and pebbles to the left and right, and trotting at the rate of sixteen miles an hour.

Oh, that ride! that first ride!—most truly it was an epoch in my existence; and I still look back to it with feelings of longing and regret. People may talk of first love—it is a very agreeable event, I dare say— but give me the flush, and triumph, and glorious sweat of a first ride, like mine of the mighty cob! My whole frame was shaken, it is true; and during one long week I could hardly move foot or hand; but what of that? By that one trial I had become free, as I may say, of the whole equine species. No more fatigue, no more stiffness of joints, after that first ride round the Devil's Hill on the cob.

Oh, that cob; that Irish cob!—may the sod lie lightly over the bones of the strongest, speediest, and most gallant of its kind! Oh! the days when, issuing from the barrack-gate of Templemore, we commenced our hurry-skurry just as inclination led—now across the fields—direct over stone walls and running brooks—mere pastime for the cob!— sometimes along the road to Thurles and Holy Cross, even to distant Cahir!—what was distance to the cob?

It was thus that the passion for the equine race as first awakened

213

within me—a passion which, up to the present time, had been rather on the increase than diminishing. It is no blind passion; the horse being a noble and generous creature, intended by the All-Wise to be the helper and friend of man, to whom he stands next in the order of creation. On many occasions of my life I have been much indebted to the horse, and have found in him a friend and coadjutor, when human help and sympathy were not to be obtained. It is therefore natural enough that I should love the horse; but the love which I entertain for him has always been blended with respect; for I soon perceived that, though disposed to be the friend and helper of man, he is by no means inclined to be his slave; in which respect he differs from the dog, who will crouch when beaten; whereas the horse spurns, for he is aware of his own worth, and that he carries death within the horn of his heel. If, therefore, I found it easy to love the horse, I found it equally natural to respect him.

I much question whether philology, or the passion for languages, requires so little of an apology as the love for horses. It has been said, I believe, that the more languages a man speaks, the more a man is he; which is very true, provided he acquires languages as a medium for becoming acquainted with the thoughts and feelings of the various sections into which the human race is divided; but, in that case, he should rather be termed a philosopher than a philologist—between which two the difference is wise indeed! An individual may speak and read a dozen languages, and yet be an exceedingly poor creature, scarcely half a man; and the pursuit of tongues for their own sake, and the mere satisfaction of acquiring them, surely argues an intellect of a very low order; a mind disposed to be satisfied with mean and grovelling things; taking more pleasure in the trumpery casket than in the precious treasure which it contains, in the pursuit of words, than in the acquisition of ideas.

I cannot help thinking that it was fortunate for myself, who am, to a certain extent, a philogist, that with me the pursuit of languages has been always modified by the love of horses; for scarcely had I turned my mind to the former, when I also mounted the wild cob, and hurried forth in the direction of the Devil's Hill, scattering dust and flint-stones on every side; that ride, amongst other things, taught me that a lad with thews and sinews was intended by nature for something better

than mere word-culling; and if I have accomplished anything in after-
life worthy of mentioning, I believe it may partly be attributed to
the ideas which that ride, by setting my blood in a glow, infused into
my brain. I might, otherwise, have become a mere philologist; one of
those beings who toil night and day in culling useless words for some
opus magnum which Murray will never publish, and nobody ever read;
beings without enthusiasm, who, having never mounted a generous
steed, cannot detect a good point in Pegasus himself; like a certain
philologist, who, though acquainted with the exact value of every
word in the Greek and Latin languages, could observe no particular
beauty in one of the most glorious of Homer's rhapsodies. What knew
he of Pegasus? He had never mounted a generous steed; the merest
jockey, had the strain been interpreted to him, would have called it a
brave song!—I return to the brave cob.

On a certain day I had been out on an excursion. In a crossroad, at
some distance from the satanic hill, the animal which I rode cast a shoe.
By good luck a small village was at hand, at the entrance of which was
a large shed, from which proceeded a most furious noise of hammering.
Leading the cob by the bridle, I entered boldly. 'Shoe this horse, and
do it quickly, a gough,' said I to a wild, grimy figure of a man, whom
I found alone, fashioning a piece of iron.

'Arrigod yuit?' said the fellow, desisting from his work, and staring
at me.

'Oh, yes, I have money,' said I, 'and of the best;' and I pulled out an
English shilling.

'Tabhair chugam?' said the smith, stretching out his grimy hand.

'No, I shan't,' said I; 'some people are glad to get their money when
their work is done.'

The fellow hammered a little longer, and then proceeded to shoe
the cob, after having first surveyed it with attention. He performed his
job rather roughly, and more than once appeared to give the animal
unnecessary pain, frequently making use of loud and boisterous words.
By the time the work was done the creature was in a state of high excitement, and plunged and tore. The smith stood at a short distance,
seeming to enjoy the irritation of the animal and showing, in a remarkable manner, a huge fang, which projected from the under jaw of a
very wry mouth.

215

The smith performed his job rather roughly . . .

'You deserve better handling,' said I, as I went up to the cob and fondled it; whereupon it whinnied, and attempted to touch my face with its nose.

'Are ye not afraid of that beast?' said the smith, showing his fang. 'Arrah, it's vicious that he looks!'

'It's at you, then!—I don't fear him'; and thereupon I passed under the horse, between his hind legs.

'And is that all you can do, agrah?' said the smith.

'No,' said I, 'I can ride him.'

'Ye can ride him, and what else, agrah?'

'I can leap him over a six-foot wall,' said I.

'Over a wall, and what more, agrah?'

'Nothing more,' said I; 'what more would you have?'

'Can you do this, agrah?' said the smith; and he uttered a word which I had never heard before, in a sharp, pungent tone. The effect upon myself was somewhat extraordinary, a strange thrill ran through me; but with regard to the cob it was terrible; the animal forthwith became like one mad, and reared and kicked with the utmost desperation.

216

'Can you do that, agrah?' said the smith.

'What is it?' said I, retreating, 'I never saw the horse so before.'

'Go between his legs, agrah,' said the smith, 'his hinder legs;' and he again showed his fang.

'I dare not,' said I, 'he would kill me.'

'He would kill ye! and how do ye know that, agrah?'

'I feel he would,' said I, 'something tells me so.'

'And it tells ye truth, agrah; but it's a fine beast, and it's a pity to see him in such a state: Is agam an't leigeas'—and here he uttered another word in a voice singularly modified, but sweet and almost plaintive; the effect of it was as instantaneous as that of the other, but how different!—the animal lost all its fury, and became at once calm and gentle. The smith went up to it, coaxed and patted it, making use of various sounds of equal endearment, then turning to me, and holding out once more the grimy hand, he said, 'And now ye will be giving me the Sassanach ten pence, agrah?'

217

JODY AND THE
RED PONY
John Steinbeck

Jody never waited for the triangle to get him out of bed after the coming of the pony. It became his habit to creep out of bed even before his mother was awake, to slip into his clothes and to go quietly down to the barn to see Gabilan. In the grey quiet mornings when the land and the brush and the houses and the trees were silver-grey and black like a photograph negative, he stole toward the barn, past the sleeping stones and the sleeping cypress trees. The turkeys, roosting in the tree out of coyotes' reach, clicked drowsily. The fields glowed with a grey frost-like light and in the dew the tracks of rabbits and of fieldmice stood out sharply. The good dogs came stiffly out of their little houses, hackles up and deep growls in their throats. Then they caught Jody's scent, and their stiff tails rose up and waved a greeting—Doubletree Mutt with the big thick tail, and Smasher, the incipient shepherd—then went lazily back to their warm beds.

It was a strange time and a mysterious journey, to Jody—an extension of a dream. When he first had the pony he liked to torture himself during the trip by thinking Gabilan would not be in his stall, and worse, would never have been there. And he had other delicious little self-induced pains. He thought how the rats had gnawed ragged holes in the red saddle, and how the mice had nibbled Gabilan's tail until it was stringy and thin. He usually ran the last little way to the barn. He un-latched the rusty hasp of the barn door and stepped in, and, no matter how quietly he opened the door, Gabilan was always looking at him over the barrier of the box stall and Gabilan whinnied softly and stamp-ed his front foot, and his eyes had big sparks of red fire in them like oak-wood embers.

Sometimes, if the work-horses were to be used that day, Jody found Billy Buck in the barn harnessing and currying. Billy stood with him and looked long at Gabilan and he told Jody a great many things about horses. He explained that they were terribly afraid for their feet, so that one must make a practice of lifting the legs and patting the hooves and ankles to remove their terror. He told Jody how horses love con-versation. He must talk to the pony all the time, and tell him the reasons for everything. Billy wasn't sure a horse could understand everything that was said to him, but it was impossible to say how much was understood. A horse never kicked up a fuss if someone he liked explained things to him. Billy could give examples, too. He had known, for instance, a horse nearly dead-beat with fatigue to perk up when told it was only a little farther to his destination. And he had known a horse paralysed with fright to come out of it when his rider told him what it was that was frightening him. While he talked in the mornings, Billy Buck cut twenty or thirty straws into neat three-inch lengths and stuck them into his hat-band. Then, during the whole day, if he wanted to pick his teeth or merely to chew on something, he had only to reach up for one of them.

Jody listened carefully, for he knew and the whole country knew that Billy Buck was a fine hand with horses. Billy's own horse was a stringy cayuse with a hammer head, but he nearly always won the first prizes at the stock trials. Billy could rope a steer, take a double half-hitch about the horn with his riata, and dismount, and his horse would play the steer as an angler plays a fish, keeping a tight rope until the steer was down or beaten.

Every morning, after Jody had curried and brushed the pony, he let down the barrier of the stall, and Gabilan thrust past him and raced down the barn and into the corral. Around and around he galloped, and sometimes he jumped forward and landed on stiff legs. He stood quivering, stiff ears forward, eyes rolling so that the whites showed, pretending to be frightened. At last he walked snorting to the water-trough and buried his nose in the water up to the nostrils. Jody was proud then, for he knew that was the way to judge a horse. Poor horses only touched their lips to the water, but a fine spirited beast put his whole nose and mouth under, and only left room to breathe.

Then Jody stood and watched the pony, and he saw things he had never noticed about any other horse, the sleek, sliding flank muscles and the cords of the buttocks, which flexed like a closing fist, and the shine the sun put on the red coat. Having seen horses all his life, Jody had never looked at them very closely before. But now he noticed the moving ears, which gave expression and even inflection of expression to the face. The pony talked with his ears. You could tell exactly how he felt about everything by the way his ears pointed. Sometimes they were stiff and upright and sometimes lax and sagging. They went back when he was angry or fearful, and forward when he was anxious and curious and pleased; and their exact position indicated which emotion he had.

Billy Buck kept his word. In the early fall the training began. First there was the halter-breaking, and that was the hardest because it was the first thing. Jody held a carrot and coaxed and promised and pulled on the rope. The pony set his feet like a burro when he felt the strain. But before long he learned. Jody walked all over the ranch leading him. Gradually he took to dropping the rope until the pony followed him unled wherever he went.

And then came the training on the long halter. That was slower work. Jody stood in the middle of the circle, holding the long halter. He clucked with his tongue and the pony started to walk in a big circle, held in by the long rope. He clucked again to make the pony trot, and again to make him gallop. Around and around Gabilan went thundering and enjoying it immensely. Then he called 'Whoa', and the pony stopped. It was not long until Gabilan was perfect at it. But in many ways he was a bad pony. He bit Jody in the legs and stomped on Jody's feet. Now and then his ears went back and he aimed a tremendous kick at the boy. Every time he did one of these bad things, Gabilan settled back and seemed to laugh to himself.

Billy Buck worked at the hair rope in the evenings before the fire-place. Jody collected tail hair in a bag, and he sat and watched Billy slowly constructing the rope, twisting a few hairs to make a string and rolling two strings together for a cord, and then braiding a number of cords to make the rope. Billy rolled the finished rope on the floor under his foot to make it round and hard.

The long halter work rapidly approached perfection. Jody's father, watching the pony stop and start and trot and gallop, was a little bothered by it.

'He's getting to be almost a trick pony,' he complained. 'I don't like trick horses. It takes all the—dignity out of a horse to make him do tricks. Why, a trick horse is kind of like an actor—no dignity, no character of his own.' And his father said, 'I guess you better be getting him used to the saddle pretty soon.'

Jody rushed for the harness-room. For some time he had been riding the saddle on a saw-horse. He changed the stirrup length over and over, and could never get it just right. Sometimes, mounted on the saw-horse in the harness-room, with collars and hames and tugs hung all about him, Jody rode out beyond the room. He carried his rifle across the pommel. He saw the fields go flying by, and he heard the beat of the galloping hooves.

It was a ticklish job, saddling the pony the first time. Gabilan hunched and reared and threw the saddle off before the cinch could be tightened. It had to be replaced again and again until at last the pony let it stay. And the cinching was difficult, too. Day by day Jody tightened the girth a little more until at last the pony didn't mind the saddle at all.

Then there was the bridle. Billy explained how to use a stick of liquorice for a bit until Gabilan was used to having something in his mouth. Billy explained, 'Of course we could force-break him to everything, but he wouldn't be as good a horse if we did. He'd always be a little bit afraid, and he wouldn't mind because he wanted to.'

The first time the pony wore the bridle he whipped his head about and worked his tongue against the bit until the blood oozed from the corners of his mouth. He tried to rub the headstall off on the manger. His ears pivoted about and his eyes turned red with fear and with general devilishness. Jody rejoiced, for he knew that only a mean-souled horse does not resent training.

And Jody trembled when he thought of the time when he would first sit in the saddle. The pony would probably throw him off. There was no disgrace in that. The disgrace would come if he did not get right up and mount again. Sometimes he dreamed that he lay in the dirt and cried and couldn't make himself mount again. The shame of the dream lasted until the middle of the day.

Gabilan was growing fast. Already he had lost the long-leggedness of the colt; his mane was getting longer and blacker. Under the constant currying and brushing his coat lay as smooth and gleaming as orange-red lacquer. Jody oiled the hooves and kept them carefully trimmed so they would not crack.

The hair rope was nearly finished. Jody's father gave him an old pair of spurs and bent in the side bars and cut down the strap and took up the chainlets until they fitted. And then one day Carl Tiflin said:

'The pony's growing faster than I thought. I guess you can ride him by Thanksgiving. Think you can stick on?'

'I don't know,' said Jody shyly. Thanksgiving was only three weeks off. He hoped it wouldn't rain, for rain would spot the red saddle.

Gabilan knew and liked Jody by now. He nickered when Jody came across the stubble-field, and in the pasture he came running when his master whistled for him. There was always a carrot for him every time.

Billy Buck gave him riding instructions over and over. 'Now when you get up there, just grab tight with your knees and keep your hands away from the saddle, and if you get throwed, don't let that stop you. No matter how good a man is, there's always some horse can pitch him. You just climb up again before he gets to feeling smart about it. Pretty soon, he won't throw you no more, and pretty soon he can't throw you no more. That's the way to do it.'

'I hope it don't rain before,' Jody said.

'Why not? Don't want to get throwed in the mud?'

That was partly it, and also he was afraid that in the flurry of bucking Gabilan might slip and fall on him and break his leg or his hip. He had seen that happen to men before, had seen how they writhed on the ground like squashed bugs, and he was afraid of it.

He practised on the saw-horse how he would hold the reins in his left hand and a hat in his right hand. If he kept his hands thus busy, he couldn't grab the horn if he felt himself going off. He didn't like to think of what would happen if he did grab the horn. Perhaps his father and Billy Buck would never speak to him again, they would be so ashamed. The news would get about and his mother would be ashamed too. And in the schoolyard—it was too awful to contemplate.

He began putting his weight in a stirrup when Gabilan was saddled, but he didn't throw his leg over the pony's back. That was forbidden until Thanksgiving.

Every afternoon he put the red saddle on the pony and cinced it tight. The pony was learning already to fill his stomach out unnaturally large while the cinching was going on, and then to let it down when the straps were fixed. Sometimes Jody led him up to the brush line and let him drink from the round green tub, and sometimes he led him up through the stubble-field to the hilltop from which it was possible to see the white town of Salinas and the geometric fields of the great valley, and the oak trees clipped by the sheep. Now and then they broke through the brush and came to little cleared circles so hedged in that the world was gone and only the sky and circle of brush were left from the old life. Gabilan liked these trips and showed it by keeping his head very high and by quivering his nostrils with interest. When the two came back from an expedition they smelled of the sweet sage they had forced through.

LANTERN LIGHT TO MOONLIGHT

Monica Edwards

Tamzin and Rissa with their friends, Meryon and Roger, set out to kidnap a cargo of horses destined for slaughter. They enlist the help of Jimmy Decks and old Jim, his father, both fishermen, and some of their friends. Using a powerful motor launch they board the slaughter ship and overpower the crew—all except Jonah, a surly youngster, who grudgingly agrees to help them save the horses.

The slaughter ship, *Daisy Holman*, moved slowly up the river in the night. Her engine silenced, she was sailing under all her canvas and was towing the quiet motor launch behind her. Straight on through the little harbour the white ship sailed, a barge by name but very different from the barges of the inland waterways. She was essentially a sea-going vessel, capable of making long passages, and she was a lovely ship to look at under sail.

Had there been a watcher on the moonlit saltings beyond the village, he would have seen first the mainsail being brailed to the mast, the tall sprit remaining aloft and raking at the stars, then the mizzen, the topsail and the headsails. The *Daisy Holman* was drawing slowly in to the bank where a disused mooring was awaiting her.

Everyone was on deck; everyone that is except Jonah, and he remained below to guard the horses. Old Jim was at the tiller now, no one knowing the river so well as he did. Meryon and Roger, having first blindfolded the prisoners to Jim's orders, were now on guard beside them. Tamzin and Rissa were adding their weight on halliards and inhaul. Young Jimmy stood with Hookey Galley crouching on the

224

gunwale, the mooring warps in their hands, and Walter was slinging out the fenders. The slaughter ship was moving slower, slower to the bank. Now she was less than a yard from the broken wharfside and Jimmy and Hookey crouched lower, then jumped for the bank. In a second the warps were thrown over the old bollards and made fast. The *Daisy Holman* had come to rest, but not where she was expected.

Rissa said, 'How in thunder are we going to land them?' looking from the hatches to the bulwarks, the saltings and the broken-down wharf. Jim Decks had left the tiller and was squinting up at the main sprit. 'That's what *they* used to load 'em,' he said, 'so I'll lay we can play at that game ourselves. Use it fer a derrick, gal, the spritty merchants do. An' as fer these yur horses, I heard it guv out as how they lifted 'em in slings. The thing is, whur to find the slings.'

Tamzin said, 'I've got a notion, Jim. Can you come with Rissa and me?'

'Surelye. Do me best, leastways,' he added cautiously.

Tamzin said to Rissa in a whisper, 'Jonah will know,' her eyes flicking uneasily towards the bound and blindfolded prisoners. Meryon, seeing her, jerked his thumbs upward and Roger executed a victory dance across the prostrate legs of Taffy.

Down into the hold Jim followed Tamzin and Rissa, but nobody was there. Tamzin said, 'Jonah! It's all right, we want to talk to you.'

From the thickest of the shadows Jonah came, looking, Tamzin thought, wilder and harder even than she had remembered him. Seeing Jim he hesitated, unfriendly and suspicious of all men. Jim Decks poked his little beard forwards, stared with his faded blue eyes and said, 'Jumpin' gin bottles! Another of 'em. Rissa, fetch Hookey an' a rope.'

'Oh no, Jim! Not to tie up Jonah. He's on our side. He's going to help us. Tell him, Jonah!' she said anxiously.

Jonah had a stone-wall look again. 'It don't make no difference to me. But I'd sorter like to see the horses outer this. I'll help you if you want.'

Jim thrust his beard farther out at Jonah. 'More likely tell your barge-rats all we tell you,' he said sardonically.

'I won't talk,' said Jonah. 'Why should I? Wouldn't make no difference to me. I don't care nothin' fer folks,' he added in a hard flat

225

voice. 'I only thought to help the horses. Not you, partickler.' His eyes were as hard and bright and cold as grey glass, Tamzin noticed, thinking how strange it must be to have no one in all the whole world for whom one cared a single rap.

'Right, me boy. Then tell us where your slings are.'

Jonah said, 'I'll get them. We've got two, a big and a small one.' He went back into the shadows in the fore part of the hold, returning a minute later with a great rolled-up bundle of thick canvas and ropes. 'I'll show you how to use 'em if you won't let Bogle and them know you found me. Only I can't help you any more when they know I helped you once.'

Jim said, 'I'll get 'em stowed in the cabin.' He climbed the ladder and leaned his elbows on the deck. 'Hey! Hookey, Charlie! Shove those dogs' meats down below, will yer, and stand a proper guard still.' Then, 'Now,' he said, looking down at Jonah.

'Hatches off first,' said Jonah.

'Coulda guessed that,' said Jim dryly. 'Wally, hatches off!'

Jonah was unrolling the slings. 'If we do the foals first you can see how it works. That's the small sling. I'll go aloft and fix the sprit ready. Donkey engine's just abaft the mainmast.' He was up on deck in a moment, moving as easily about the boat as a monkey in a tree. Swiftly and efficiently the sprit was rigged for slinging, the donkey engine examined, the landing wharf approved and Jonah came swinging down the hatchway once again. Going to the smallest foal he unshackled the slender pasterns, untied the rope halter and led her out beneath the open hatchway, her long legs straddling the laid-out sling. Tamzin was there at once to hold the halter while Jonah and Rissa lifted up the sides of the sling, each with its large iron ring to fit over the hook on the derrick rope.

Down from above the long rope dangled, straight from the high pointing peak of the sprit. Jonah reached up and caught it, hooked it through the sling-rings then signalled to Walter on deck that all was ready for action. The donkey engine spluttered.

Jonah said, 'You two'll have to go ashore and see to the little 'un when she's landed.'

Tamzin and Rissa raced up on deck as the engine began to pull properly, stepped on to the gunwale and jumped down upon the grass-grown wharf. Turning, they stood together staring at the slaughter ship. She was not white now, but black with the yellow moon behind her. Her bare mainmast pointed like a long bony finger, and down at its base the donkey engine chugged and laboured.

Suddenly, from the yawning mouth of the hold, a dark shape rose and dangled, circling slowly on the end of the derrick rope like a giant spider on a thread. Slowly, slowly it ascended, revolving as it rose, then, the tall sprit moving outwards, the spider on its thread swung out above the deck, across the bulwarks, then clear above the wharf where Tamzin, Rissa, and now Meryon and Roger, stood beneath it, heads tilted, staring upwards.

The four long legs of the foal hung dangling, pathetically helpless. Her small head poked from the canvas like a tortoise's head from its shell. She was coming down. Hands were reaching up to help her. She was ringed with a bright aura from the clear moon behind her, and she might have been a legendary sky-horse floating earthwards for a charm.

Meryon's hands were on the sling, then Rissa's, pulling against the revolving movement of the weight, steadying it. Tamzin and Roger had reached it too. Down, down, down, and the small hooves were scraping and scrabbling on the ground, hands were on the halter and the first of the landings was accomplished. Quick fingers lifted the big rings off the hook.

'Want any help?' Jim called from the deck.

'No, we're all right,' Meryon called back.

'With this one, anyway,' Rissa added. 'She's being a proper angel.'

'Ah, flew high enough,' Jim remarked, spitting into the river. Then, to young Jimmy, who was looking for his tobacco tin in the cabin of the speedboat, 'Fetch us them bottles, son. I got a thirst fit ter float a battleship and reckon the most of us got the same affliction.'

'All of 'em?'

'All of 'em. Some's only fizz what I fetched along fer the young 'uns.'

Roger said, helping to lower the sling to the ground, 'If there isn't one for Jonah he can have half of mine.'

'Bet you he drinks rum or something,' Rissa said, and then the sling was lying on the wharf. Tamzin led the foal a few steps clear of it, talking softly all the time and patting and stroking the stiffly-arched

227

The four long legs of the foal hung dangling, pathetically helpless.

neck and trembling flank as the first refugee turned her woolly brown back upon the slaughter ship.

Jim was calling softly from the bulwarks, 'Pub's open, come and wet yer whistles afore we get right down to the job.'

Rissa said, 'I'll go and fetch ours and we can stay with the foal.'

Meryon and Roger went back on board, Roger saying, 'Is there one for Jonah, Jim?'

Jonah looked up from the donkey engine, then down at the ginger-beer bottles in Meryon's and Roger's hands. 'I don't drink that stuff, thanks.'

'Told you so!' Rissa grinned to Tamzin, back on the wharf with their bottles frothing at the neck.

'Th'a right, old young 'un,' said Jim approvingly. 'Hookey, give 'im grog.'

Hookey passed a dark brown bottle to the ship's boy. Jim was lifting his own with a flourish and the moon made a long bright streak upon it. 'Down the hatches!' he said, and tipped it down his throat, his knobby Adam's apple leaping with each swallow.

Jonah's had gone nearly as quickly. Meryon and Roger, drinking ginger-beer, felt childish because of this distinction. Hookey Galley was reaching for a second bottle but the ferryman's hand shot out to move it from his reach. They glowered at each other for a moment. 'Work first,' said Jim. 'Drink after.' Then, staring sadly into the dark depths of his own empty bottle, 'Ah, I knew a pub once. Folkstone, that were. Never was such drink. Now the landlord, 'e were good. Not religious, mind you, don't mistake me, 'e were *good*. Sunday nights, come church time, he would set down afore th'ole piana and we would down us mugs. Then up he strikes with a right proper hymn chune— I'm tellin' you no lies—an' all us chaps'd middling raise the roof. Come round with a plate, he did arterwards. Never knew what he rightly did wi' that.'

Young Jimmy gathered up the empty bottles.

' 'Sright, son,' said the old man. 'Fine words don't butter no parsnips. Us'd better be getting on.'

Rissa brought back her bottle and Tamzin's, and she, Meryon, Jonah and Roger swung down the ladder into the hold again. Jimmy started up the donkey engine and the empty sling came lightly up, up, over the *Daisy Holman*'s deck and disappeared down the lit-up hatch-way after them.

Tamzin watched from the wharf, beginning to realize that holding one subdued and frightened foal was one thing, but holding seven heavy carthorses, three cobs and two foals would be quite another. Looking about her in the clear moonlight she saw the long post-and-rail fence that ran across the saltings from the river to the road. That would do. When the next landing was accomplished she would take them both and tie them to the rails. She hoped it would be the second foal, the chestnut, and that all the horses would take kindly to being tied up in the open. It was awful when a horse pulled back and either broke the fence or the halter.

The derrick rope was winding up again, the canvas sling soared steadily out from lantern light to moonlight and the long thin legs that dangled from it told Tamzin that it was the chestnut foal. The first foal jerked back and snorted fearfully at the sight of this approaching menace in the sky, and Tamzin turned her round again to face the silver-dark saltings.

Walter Goddard and Charlie Briggs came vaulting over the gunwale to the wharf and reached up hands to steady the sling, rotating slowly downwards. 'Then Meryon and them can stay below and do the loading,' Jimmy said.

Tamzin watched them bring the foal to earth and unhook the rings. 'Who's guarding the prisoners?' she asked, with sudden misgiving.

They were lowering the canvas to the ground. 'Ol' Snowey,' said Walter. 'Nice cushy job; he only got to look at 'em and sing out iffen there's any trouble.'

'Take yer liddle horse, now,' said Charlie, holding out the halter rope and Tamzin, grasping it, led the babies of her team towards the fence.

Down in the hold they had the help of Hookey Galley for the slinging of the heavier horses. He was a dour and unfriendly person at the best of times and could be downright hostile. This was probably one of his rather better moments because he never spoke at all. All the same, it was a relief to have his huge muscular strength at the halters of the horses which left the boys and Rissa free to fit the slings and hook the iron rings.

230

They sent up the Welsh cob next, after endless delay and difficulty in getting the sling anywhere near at all. The cob was so nervous he was sweating and steaming like a plough horse and he jumped and reared at every touch. Rissa was terrified lest Hookey should lose all patience and hit him over the head with his enormous fist, but Hookey just held on, as grimly taciturn as ever, and finally the grey cob swung away up through the dark starlit square of the hatch and out to Tamzin's mercies.

One after the other they came, as the moon swam westwards over the sky. Some quiet, some frightened, some difficult, some apathetic, nearly all nervous. Of all the twelve, the three great percherons were the easiest to handle and the grey Welsh cob the worst.

'Lucky,' said Jim afterwards, 'you didn't get a wusser one nor he. Easy might've. Some you hear of is proper killers. Don't want none er them a–dangling over yur head, choose how.'

Tamzin had a lot of trouble with the Clydesdale, who proved to be the one kind of horse she had hoped she wouldn't have to deal with. The kind that won't tie up. He seemed all right when first she took him into her temporary horse line about halfway through the un-loading and tied his halter rope to the rail. Then suddenly he reared and swung back hard upon his haunches without a second's warning. The rope creaked as the hitches tightened and the big grey next to him threw up his head and edged sideways. Tamzin was at the Clydesdale's head at once, but her small wrists were like feathers pulling against so much power. The halter broke with a loud rending noise and the big horse galloped away, the broken halter falling at Tamzin's feet. 'At least,' she thought, 'I did remember to knot the rope at the noseband so that it couldn't pull tight round his muzzle.'

She was having trouble with some of the others now, excited by the Clydesdale's escape. The cob especially was working himself into a frenzy and Tamzin stayed with him until he quietened. It was fortunate that Charlie heard and saw the trouble and came across to help her because his slow deep voice was a useful one for calming horses. Snowey Peplow's squeak, now, or Hookey's menacing growl—they would be quite another matter.

But the Clydesdale had gone. There was no sign of him anywhere on the moon-drenched levels.

'Never mind,' said Charlie. 'What will be, will be. Happen he'll come back. And anyways we got to get on with the unloading or the morning will be here.'

They got on with it with no more real trouble. Snowey Peplow squeaked out once from the cabin that someone was getting his ropes off, but the two Jims soon put that right and the last of the horses left the whited sepulchre.

'Even her name!' said Tamzin disgustedly. '*Daisy Holman!* Did you ever hear anything so innocent?'

Charlie and Walter were handing her the halter of the last horse of the cargo, one of the two black carthorses from the fore part of the hold. She took it to the horse line before going aboard again to see what was to happen next.

'This is what,' said old Jim to the assembled rescue party, which included ship's boy, Jonah. 'Wally and young Jimmy here is to take the spritty back to sea, towing the speedboat behind 'em. Then, after Dungeness is rounded, they undo Taffy's hands—he's the smallest, see—and take to the speedboat immediate. Take some time afore Taffy's got the rest undone and made sail and got under way. They'll never know whur they bin to, all this blessed night.'

Tamzin said, 'But can't we keep them prisoners till the morning and then hand them over to the police? They're breaking the law, after all, and once they get in jail the whole beastly business will stop.'

Jim shook his head. 'Sounds fine, I dessay. Only a reckon you dis-remember we're breaking the law hem definite ourselves. We ain't got no right to take these horses.'

'An' another thing,' said Snowey, sounding like an old pram wheel, 'we got other reasons fer not wanting ter git too familiar with the coppers. There was that set-up two summers back when they reckoned we was smuggling.'

'The idea!' said Walter, grinning widely.

'Ah, better we don't parley with no coppers,' Charlie agreed.

'What about Jonah?' said Meryon.

'They can find me in the hold when you've gone,' said Jonah. 'Or I could go and help untie them, that'd look better. I'll say I was in hiding when you went down there—well, I was. And I won't forget I said I'd send a message.'

Jim Decks thumped him on the shoulder-blade. 'And happen things gets over warm, me lad, I got a corner in me hut whur I could doss you down, see.'

Jonah said it made no difference to him.

'And the horses?' said Rissa.

'Cor, darn take it, gal, them's your cup er tea. Take 'em out to Willy Merrow, doncher?'

'What, all twelve? And only four of us?'

'One got away,' Tamzin reminded her. 'There's only eleven. Three each and two for Roger. We ought to manage.'

'What if we see the Clydesdale on the way?' Roger asked.

'Oh well, someone else'll have to hold six while one of us goes and tries to catch it. Don't make difficulties before they happen. It's bad enough losing the Clydesdale without wondering what we'll do when we find it. Think what'll happen if the police or someone get hold of it.'

'Well, doddle along and git your fine horses,' said Jim, 'or there'll be hem little shut-eye fer any of you this night.'

'And some of us,' remarked Hookey sourly, 'has got to work come morning'.'

Tamzin took no notice of this. They had plenty to do themselves in the morning but Hookey wouldn't have called it work. Meryon was over the gunwale and Roger after him. Tamzin and Rissa said good-bye to Jim and the others, cocked a snook towards the cabin where the prisoners lay and jumped down after the boys. The moon was thinly clouded now and it was not so easy to see one's way about, though still far too bright to need a lantern.

'If Roger only takes two,' Rissa said, 'he's jolly well got to have two big ones. He's about as old as we are, and much stronger.'

'That isn't what counts, is it?' Tamzin said. 'We've had much more to do with horses, and I should've thought you'd be the last one to say brute strength was what was needed in handling them.'

'It does help, I suppose,' said Meryon reasonably. 'I don't know much about horses myself, but I dare say I shall have to manage three, and if that isn't because I'm hefty I'd like to know the reason.'

'Oh well,' Rissa said, 'will you take two of the percherons then, Roger? They may be huge but they're much the quietest of the lot.'

'It makes no difference to me!' grinned Roger, quoting Jonah.

'Meryon can have three big ones,' Tamzin said. 'The two black carthorses and one of the vanners?'

Meryon bowed.

'We can take a foal each,' Rissa said, 'and who's taking that so-and-so grey cob? I think Meryon really ought to have that!'

Tamzin frowned. 'That would be silly. The grey cob's only frightened. One of us two ought to have him really, because we've had ponies for so long, and nothing but experience is the least possible use with frightened horses. Strength just isn't anywhere if they've really got the wind up.'

'Well, in that case he's all yours,' said Rissa thankfully. 'You've had a lot more experience than I have. That's a foal and the cob for you; a foal and one of the vanners for me. There's the big roan and one percheron left.'

'Then bags I the percheron,' said Tamzin, 'if I've got the Welsh cob to put up with.'

'The roan's mine,' said Rissa. 'Let's snap into it.'

In bunches of two and three the eleven horses moved away from the horse line, Rissa leading with the big chestnut foal, the roan and a vanner, Roger following with his towering greys, Meryon with the blacks and the broken-kneed vanner, and Tamzin with the smallest foal, the third big grey and the snorting, staring Welshman.

Eleven horses snatched away from the slaughter. Somewhere a twelfth was roaming, but here were eleven good horses, young and strong and with a lifetime of useful work stored up in each of them. Their hooves bit into the soft ground of the saltings, their heads swung and tossed and nodded against the clouding midnight sky, and the Walland Marsh swallowed them from the sight of the old man on the deck of the *Daisy Holman*.

PANCHO

Dorian Williams

It was one of those soft March days. There was no sun, but it was slightly hazy and there was a soft wind from the west; ideal for a point-to-point, quite different from the bitterly cold day that one so often gets.

The Members' Race is always the first on the card. There were eight runners. The handsome trophy was on view on a table at the edge of the paddock. There was a fair crowd, and it was quite a struggle to force one's way through from the weighing-tent to the paddock.

Pancho had just been led in by Sara, and after being greeted by my wife in the middle, by the number board, had started to parade round with the others. We had arranged for the box to bring Pancho as late as possible, and for him to be brought into the paddock at the last possible moment so that he had little time to get excited.

I watched him going round, looking wonderfully fit, and as lithe and lean as a greyhound. I compared him with the others, and had to admit to myself that he was really in a different class, though there were some good horses—our Members' Race always being considered the best in the neighbourhood. My opinion seemed to be shared by the

public, as we were informed that the bookies had made him favourite.
I could hear the shouting now.

'Four to one, bar! Four to one, bar!' 'Five to two, Pancho. Five to
two, Pancho.' 'Threes the field!'

Pancho heard them too, and I could see he was restless. After a few
minutes Sara suddenly and unexpectedly brought him into the middle.

'Do you think he's all right, Mr Garrard? He's like he was that time
on Boxing Day—all shaking and sweating. Look how he's trembling.'

'It's just excitement being on a racecourse again.' I pulled at his ears.
They were very cold. 'He's all right,' I said, just a little doubtful. 'Keep
him walking.'

Sara looked anxious. This was the first time she had led a horse
round a parade ring.

'You're doing well,' I said encouragingly. 'Keep him walking.'

Another five minutes and the clerk of the course rang his bell.

'Jockeys up, please!'

I beckoned Sara. She brought him to the middle. My wife pulled
his rug off. I tested his girths. I slipped off my mohair coat and waited
until my wife was ready to give me a leg up.

Pancho was certainly sweating, and quivering all over. He gave a
little anxious snort. I patted him. A deft lift and I was in the saddle.
Suddenly in my thin colours—a lightweight jersey of royal blue with
black sleeves—I felt a slight chill. But I knew that it was apprehension
more than anything else; apprehension partly reflecting that of my
wife—I had given up point-to-pointing after Margot had been born,
and my wife had doubts as to whether I was really up to it now—and
partly due to my anxiety for Pancho. He just *had* to win, or at any rate
acquit himself honourably.

The huntsman, Will, one of the Hunt staff patrolling the course,
blew a note on his horn, and led the way out of the paddock.

'Off we go,' I said with a rather forced light-heartedness.

'Good luck then,' my wife said quietly, lightly pressing my knee
with her hand. She knew how much this race meant to me.

Sara led Pancho towards the exit. Once through she let him go.

'Do your best, Pancho,' she muttered, gulping with excitement.
'You've *got* to win.' And she gave him a pat.

We filed through the crowd, past the bookies, down to the course.

Pancho was certainly in a great state, jigging sideways, plunging, snatching at his bit.

So much so in fact that I realized that I was going to have a proper handful taking him down to the start. More than once I had seen some wretched jockey carted all round the course, being unable to stop when reaching the start.

But that problem was delayed. We arrived at the opening on to the course, and Pancho flatly refused to go through it. I coaxed him; I urged him; I tapped him down the shoulder with my whip. But he stood there, his head up, his eyes dilated, shaking.

'Come on, silly,' I said, but I was getting anxious. People started shouting and waving behind him. That, I knew, would upset him the more. I asked them to stop. Pancho still would not move.

Out of the crowd, from nowhere, Sara suddenly appeared. She took hold of his bridle, quietly but firmly.

'Come on, old boy.'

He hesitated for a moment or two more, then allowed himself to be led through. Once on the course he gave a great bound, and before I was properly composed he was off.

Before he had got into top gear or his head down, however, I managed to steady him; even brought him back to a half-trot, half-canter, and decided to maintain that pace all the way to the start.

Strange, I thought. Could there be something wrong after all?

And then at the start, contrary to all that I had feared, he stood like a statue, never moving a muscle.

The starter called out our numbers, and walked across to the side of the course.

'I shall just say "Ready? Go!" and then drop the flag,' he said. 'So good luck to you.'

The other seven, who had been walking round, shortening leathers, tightening girths, exchanging badinage—I was far too occupied with my own thoughts to join in—now straightened into a line and moved forward towards the flag. I urged Pancho towards them. He responded a little reluctantly. We were still two or three lengths behind them and almost flat-footed as the starter called out: 'Ready?'

I was about to say 'Just a moment!' when he said, 'Go!'—and we were off!

As soon as Pancho saw the others gallop away from him he took hold of the bit and charged after them.

There was not a long run to the first fence, and I had Pancho steady and well in hand. I could feel the tremor through his body as he saw the fence in front of him. Less than half a dozen strides away the horse on our left, and two lengths ahead, started swerving to the right. I had to swing Pancho to make sure I would avoid him. In fact the other horse swung even more, crashed through the fence and, although he did not actually fall, deposited his jockey right in our path. I snatched Pancho up to miss him, but although this interference caused him to jump a little stickily we were safely over and away.

He was quickly into his stride, about last but one of the field. Again he jumped the next fence paukily. 'It's upset him,' I thought, and drove him on towards the open ditch. He jumped this a little better—the guard-rail in front of an open ditch so often encourages boldness in a horse.

Between fences he was galloping really well, and I found that by fiddling him a little I was just able to keep him steady. He was going well within himself, which was just what I wanted. I had been afraid that he might dash off in his usual low-head tearaway style and take too much out of himself.

But he was still anything but fluent over his fences; so unlike the way he flew them out hunting. As we approached each fence I could feel this tremor of anticipation, and then he would hesitate, losing all his momentum and shortening his stride. We must have lost at least six lengths at every fence. Between the fences he made up most of it, but if he went on like this he would take too much out of himself.

We had completed three-quarters of the first circuit of the course and were just turning left-handed down to the second open ditch, which would be the third fence from home on the second circuit. It may have been the arrival at our side of the loose horse that had lost its jockey at the first fence—I don't know—but I had to drive Pancho forward to make sure that the loose horse did not cross us as we were about to take off. Suddenly Pancho took hold of the bit, swept forward, flew the open ditch like a bird, and raced on towards the straight and the next fence, which was the original first fence again.

Approaching it he properly took hold of the bit and hurled himself at it, clearing it with effortless ease and fluency. It was as though his confidence had suddenly been restored. It was as though now, suddenly, he was loving it, whereas before he had been apprehensive about it, even frightened.

A cheer went up from the great crowd as a mighty leap at the next fence in the straight took us within three lengths of the leaders. By the time we reached the open ditch we had passed them, and I was aware that I was riding an outstandingly brilliant fencer.

He had settled into a rhythm by this time, and I felt it better just to sit still and let him go, rather than to interfere, trying to adjust his pace. There was a little over a mile to go and he felt as if he could last for ever. He was gaining lengths at each fence, and a quick glance round showed me that only two of the five still standing were keeping with us at all, and they were having their work cut out to do so.

The three fences across the top of the course came and went in a series of lightning, devouring strides, and I experienced a feeling of incredible exhilaration. 'He has only to stand up to win,' I thought.

'*A mighty leap took us within three lengths of the leaders.*'

'They'll never catch us now.'

We jumped the fence at the corner and turned down towards the second open ditch, just over half a mile to go, only three more fences—and then it happened! I could mark the exact spot—I remember the very stride even. Perhaps I had instinctively half feared it.

It was as though someone at that moment had switched off the engine. The surging, forward drive in Pancho stopped dead. He was still galloping, but with no momentum. He was just an automaton.

For a moment I thought that he was injured, or wrong, that he had broken a blood-vessel. And then the truth dawned on me—it was so obvious—everything seemed to fit in. *He could only stay two and a half miles*—two, probably, if the going was not good. I remembered that gallop at the Hicksons'. Of course—he was the two-mile chaser type, rather than the hunter-chaser type, or the National type. And two and a half miles was his limit, his absolute limit. But a point-to-point is *three* miles. All the stuffing had now gone out of him; he was cooked, he was blown; I even felt him stagger under me. Perhaps I should have pulled up, but we were still such a long way ahead. I believed that I could nurse him home.

With courage and an instinctive reflex action he was over the open ditch, and turning for the straight. Somehow he kept going—somehow he was still galloping. I nursed him, cajoled him, talked to him. There was less than half a mile to go. Perhaps if I gave him a breather he would come again. I eased him round the corner, hugging the rails, desperately trying to help him maintain his rhythm.

We were barely cantering as we approached the last but one fence. Somehow he screwed over it, almost stopped, but got going again. What courage!

It was then that I could hear the approaching hooves of one of our rivals. I glanced round. He was still some way back. I shook up Pancho again and he responded. Somehow he found a stride and drove himself on towards the last. I sat as still as I was able, giving him all the support that I could with the strength of my seat and legs, fussing him as little as possible lest I might unbalance him.

The thud of hooves behind came closer, but I knew that we still had enough lead to hold off that challenge; as long as we could clear the last fence—the last barrier between us and the Lady Gordon Cup.

'You *must* make it, Pancho,' I breathed at him. 'Oh, Pancho, you must, you must! This will vindicate you for ever. Just one more fence. Come on, boy!'

The roar of the crowd, cheering desperately to get the favourite home, penetrated my ears—the hooves behind echoed mockingly—the last fence came closer, and closer, and closer.

Pancho laboured towards it. Only his great heart was carrying him forward. He bore relentlessly, courageously, determinedly onward. If we could meet the last fence right then I knew we would be home. But could we? He was beginning to weave slightly from left to right. I held him together, with all my physical strength, forcing my knees into the saddle-flaps, every muscle in my body taut as catgut.

Six strides to go! Five! Four! Three! *We were wrong.* He tried to put in a short one. With all his mighty strength he attempted to lift his racked body over the last fence. But he was too close, much too close; much, much, much too close.

It was obvious that he must crash into it.

I remember no more.

I have a vague recollection of my wife gently unknotting my silk scarf. I have a blurred picture of Sara's white face and the white blaze of a horse's head haloed in steam—and big long black ears. I can still see, or more accurately smell, the antiseptic white interior of an ambulance; hear faraway voices, feel a frantic, searing pain in my head.

I had fractured my skull, but it could have been worse. The first two or three days in hospital are a hazy merging of a split head, the apparently constant presence of my wife, starchy figures floating by, sometimes far, sometimes near, and an awareness of carnations.

There were increasingly lucid moments. In one of them I asked my wife: 'Is he all right?'

'Trust him,' she replied softly. 'Just got up and jogged off down the straight till he met Sara running down the course from where she had been watching by the winning-post. *He's* all right.'

Another time I asked: 'What happened?'

'He hit the fence and turned over. He can't have risen any higher than the guard-rail.'

'Poor old chap,' I muttered.

241

'He was cooked. He had taken too much out of himself when he pulled right away from the others going up the hill on the second circuit.'

I was too tired to try to explain.

She wouldn't understand anyway. He couldn't stay more than two miles. It was only his courage that had got him to the last fence. However much he had been nursed he would never have got three miles. Never. He was not bred that way—that's what counts. Poor old chap. I ought to have pulled him up. But I had so wanted him to vindicate himself. That cup. He did his best. It had nearly come off. The spirit had been willing enough. It was no fault of his that the flesh was weak. My head was splitting. I drifted off.

DON QUIXOTE AND ROZINANTE

Miguel Cervantes

The wildly magnificent adventures of Don Quixote and his poor old horse, Rozinante, were first set down about four hundred years ago by a Spanish writer, a man who was also a soldier and an adventurer. Some of Don Quixote's fantastic experiences are to be found in The Red Romance Book, *edited by Andrew Lang.*

Everybody knows that in the old times, when Arthur was king or Charles the Great emperor, no gentleman ever rested content until he had received the honour of knighthood. When once he was made a knight, he left his home and the court and rode off in search of adventures, seeking to help people in distress.

After a while, however, the knights grew selfish and lazy. They liked better to hunt the deer through the forest than wicked robbers who had carried off beautiful ladies. 'It is the king's business,' they said, 'to take care of his subjects, not ours,' so they dwelt in their own castles, and many of them became great lords almost as powerful as the king himself.

But though the knights no longer went in search of noble adventures, as knights of earlier days had been wont to do, there were plenty of books in which they could read if they chose of the wonderful deeds of their forefathers. Lancelot and Roland, Bernardo del Carpio, the Cid, Amadis de Gaule, and many more, were as well known to them as their own brothers, and if we will only take the trouble they may be known to us too.

Now, several hundreds of years after Lancelot and Roland and all the rest had been laid in their graves, a baby belonging to the family of Quixada was born in that part of Spain called La Mancha. We are not told anything of his boyhood, or even of his manhood till he reached the age of fifty, but we know that he was poor; that he lived with a housekeeper and a niece to take care of him, and that he passed all his days in company with these old books until the courts and forests which were the scenes of the adventures of those knights of bygone years were more real to him than any of his own doings.

'I wish all those books could be burned,' said the noble gentleman's housekeeper one day to his niece. 'My poor master's wits are surely going, for he never understands one word you say to him. Indeed, if you speak, he hardly seems to see you, much less to hear you!'

What the housekeeper said was true. The things that belonged to her master's everyday life vanished completely bit by bit. If his niece related to him some scrap of news which a neighbour had run in to tell her, he would answer her with a story of the giant Morgante, who alone among his ill-bred race had manners that befitted a Spanish knight. If the housekeeper lamented that the flour in her storehouse would not last out the winter, he turned a deaf ear to all her complaints, and declared that he would give her and his niece into the bargain for the pleasure of bestowing one kick on Ganelon the traitor.

At last one day things came to a climax. When the hour of dinner came round, Don Quixada was nowhere to be found. His niece sought him in his bedroom, in the little tower where his books were kept, and even in the stable, where lay the old horse who had served him for more years than one could count. He was in none of these; but just as she was leaving the stable a strange noise seemed to come from over the girl's head, and on looking up she beheld her uncle rubbing a rusty sword that had lain there long before anybody could remember, while by his side were a steel cap and other pieces of armour.

From that moment Don Quixada became deaf and blind to the things of this world. He was in despair because the steel cap was not a proper helmet, but only a morion without a vizor to let down. Perhaps a smith might have made him what he wanted, but the Don was too proud to ask him and, getting some cardboard, cut and painted it like a vizor, and then fastened it to the morion. Nothing could look—at a

244

little distance—more like the helmet the Cid might have worn, but Don Quixada knew well that no knight ever went forth in search of adventures without first proving the goodness of his armour, so, fixing the helmet against the wall, he made a slash at it with his sword. He only dealt two strpkes, whereas his enemy might give him twenty, but those two swept clean through the vizor, and destroyed in three minutes a whole week's work. So there was nothing for it but to begin over again, and this time the Don took the precaution of lining the vizor with iron.

'It looks beautiful,' he cried when it was finished; but he took care not to try his blade upon it.

His next act was to go into the stable and rub down his horse's coat, and to give it a feed of corn, vainly hoping that in a few days its ribs might become less plainly visible.

'It is not right,' he said to himself, one morning, as he stood watching the animal that was greedily eating out of its manger—'it is not right that a knight's good horse should go forth without a name. Even the heathen Alexander bestowed a high-sounding title on his own steed; and so, likewise, did those Christian warriors, Roland and the Cid!' But, try as he might, no name would come to him except such as were unworthy of the horse and his rider, and for four nights and days he pondered the question.

Suddenly, at the moment he had least expected it, when he was eating the plain broth his housekeeper had set before him, the inspiration came.

'Rozinante!' he cried triumphantly, laying down his spoon— 'Rozinante! Neither the Cid's horse nor Roland's bore a finer name than that!'

This weighty matter being settled, the Don now began to think of himself, and, not being satisfied with the name his fathers had handed down to him resolved to take one that was more noble, and better suited to a knight who was destined to do deeds that would keep him alive in the memory of men. For eight days he took heed of nothing save this one thing, and on the ninth he found what he had sought.

'The world shall know me as Don Quixote,' he said; 'and as the noble Amadis himself was not content to bear this sole title, but added to it the name of his own country, so I, in like manner, will add the name of mine, and henceforth will appear to all, as the good knight Don Quixote de la Mancha!'

Now Don Quixote de la Mancha had read far too many books about the customs of chivalry not to be aware that every knight worshipped some lady of whose beauty he boasted upon all occasions and whose token he wore upon his helmet in battle. It was not very easy for Don Quixote to find such a lady, for all his life long, the company which he met in his books had been dearer to him than that which he could have had outside his home.

'A knight without a liege lady is a tree without fruit, a body without soul,' he thought. 'Of what use will it be if I meet with some giant such as always crosses the path of a wandering knight, and disarm him in our first encounter, unless I have a lady at whose feet he can kneel?' So without losing more time he began to search the neighbouring villages for such a damsel, whose token he might wear, and at length found one with enough beauty for him to fall in love with, whose humble name of Aldonza he changed for that of Dulcinea del Toboso.

The sun had hardly risen on the following morning when Don Quixote laced on his helmet, braced on his shield, took his lance in hand, and mounted Rozinante.

Never during his fifty years had he felt his heart so light, and he rode forth into the wide plain, expecting to find a giant or a distressed lady behind every bush. But his joy was short-lived, for suddenly it came to his mind that in the days of chivalry it never was known that any man went in quest of adventures without being first made a knight, and that no such good fortune had happened to him. This thought was so terrible that he reeled in his saddle, and was near turning the head of Rozinante towards his own stable; but Don Quixote was a man of good courage, and in a short while he remembered on how many knights Sir Lancelot had conferred the honour of knighthood, and he determined to claim his spurs from the first that he managed to conquer in fight. Till then, he must, as soon as might be, make his armour white, in token that as yet he had had no adventures. In this manner he took heart again.

All that day he rode, without either bite or sup, and, of the two, Rozinante fared the better, for he at least found a tuft of coarse grass

246

Master and horse discovered that the light came from a small inn, which Don Quixote's fancy instantly changed into a castle . . .

to eat. At nightfall a light as big as a faint star was seen gleaming in the distance, and both master and horse plucked up courage once more. They hastened towards it, and discovered that the light came from a small inn, which Don Quixote's fancy instantly changed into a castle with four towers and pinnacles of shining silver, surrounded by a moat. He paused a moment, expecting a dwarf to appear on the battlements and announce by the blasts of his trumpet that a knight was approaching, but, as no dwarf could be seen, he dismounted at the door, where he was received with courtesy by the landlord, or the governor of the castle, as Don Quixote took him to be.

At the sight of this strange figure, which looked as if it had gone to sleep a thousand years ago, and had only just woke up again, the landlord had as much ado to keep from laughter as the muleteers and some women who were standing before the door. But being a civil man, and somewhat puzzled, he held the stirrup for Don Quixote to alight, offering to give him everything that would make him comfortable except a bed, which was not to be had. The Don made little of this, as became a good knight, and bade the landlord look well after Rozinante, for no better horse would ever stand in his stable. The man, who had seen many beasts in his day, did not rate him quite so highly, but said nothing, and after placing the horse in the stable returned to the house to see after the master.

As it happened, it was easier to provide for the wants of Rozinante than for those of Don Quixote, for the muleteers had eaten up everything in the kitchen, and nothing was left save a little dried fish and black bread. Don Quixote, however, was quite content; indeed, he imagined it the most splendid supper in the world, and when he had finished he fell on his knees before the landlord.

'Never will I rise again, noble sir,' said he, 'until you grant my prayer, which shall be an occasion of glory to you and of gain to all men.'

The landlord, not being used to such conduct on the part of his guests, tried to lift Don Quixote on to his feet, but the knight vowed that he would not move till his prayer was granted.

'The gift I would ask of you,' continued the Don, now rising to his feet, 'is that tonight I may watch my arms in the chapel of your castle, and at sunrise I shall kneel before you to be made a knight. Then I shall bid you farewell, and set forth on my journey through the world, righting wrongs and helping the oppressed, after the manner of the knights of old.'

'I am honoured indeed,' replied the landlord, who by this time saw very clearly that the poor gentleman was weak in his wits, and had a mind to divert himself. 'As a youth, I myself wandered through the land, and my name, the champion of all who needed it, was known to every court in Spain, till a deadly thrust in my side, from a false knight, forced me to lay down my arms, and to return to this my castle, giving shelter and welcome to any knights that ask it. But as to the chapel, it is but a week since it was made level with the ground, being but a poor place, and in no way worthy of the service of noble knights; but keep your watch in the courtyard of my castle, as your books will have told you that others have done in case of need. Afterwards, I will admit you into the Order of Chivalry, but before you take up your vigil tell me, I pray you, what money you have brought with you?'

This question surprised the Don very much.

'I have brought none,' he answered presently, 'for never did I hear that either Roland or Percival or any of the great knight-errants whose example I fain would follow, carried any money with them.'

'That is because they thought it no more needful to say that they carried money or clean shirts than that they carried a sword or a box of ointment to cure the wounds of themselves or their foes, in case no maiden or enchanter with a flask of water was on the spot,' replied the landlord; and he spoke so long and so earnestly on the subject that the Don promised never again to start on a quest without money and a box of ointment, besides at least three clean shirts.

It was now high time for his watch to begin, and the landlord led the way to a great yard at the side of the inn. Here the Don took his arms, and piled them on a trough of stone that stood near a well. Then bearing his lance he walked up and down beside his trough.

For an hour or two he paced the yard, watched, though he knew it not, by many eyes from the inn windows, which, with the aid of a bright moon, could see all that happened as clearly as if it were day. At length a muleteer who had a long journey before him drove up his team to the trough, which was fed by the neighbouring well, and in order to let his cattle drink, stretched out his arms to remove the sword and helmet which lay there. The Don perceived his aim, and cried in a voice of thunder: 'What man are you, ignorant of the laws of chivalry, who dares to touch the arms of the bravest knight who ever wore a sword? Take heed lest you lay a finger upon them, for if you do your life shall pay the forfeit.'

It might have been as well for the muleteer if he had listened, and had led his cattle to water elsewhere, but, looking at the Don's lean figure and his own stout fists, he only laughed rudely, and, seizing both sword and helmet, threw them across the yard. The Don paused a moment, wondering if he saw aright; then raising his eyes to heaven he exclaimed: 'O Lady Dulcinea, peerless in thy beauty, help me to avenge this insult that has been put upon me'; and, lifting high his lance, he brought it down with such a force on the man that he fell to the ground without a word, and the Don began his walk afresh.

He had not been pacing the yard above half an hour when another man, not knowing what had befallen his friend, drove his beasts up to the trough, and was stooping to move the Don's arms, so that the cattle could get at the water, when a mighty blow fell on *his* head, splitting it nearly into pieces.

At this noise the people from the inn ran out, and seeing the two muleteers stretched wounded on the ground picked up stones where-with to stone the knight. The Don, however, fronted them with such courage that they did not dare to venture near him, and the landlord, making use of their fears, called on them to leave him alone, for that he was a madman, and the law would not touch him, even though he should kill them all. Then, wishing to be done with the business and with his guest, he made excuses for the rude fellows, who had only got what they deserved, and said that, as there was no chapel to his castle, he could dub him knight where he stood, for, the watch of arms having been completed, all that was needful was a slap on the neck with a palm of the hand and the touch of the sword on the shoulder.

So Don Quixada was turned into Don Quixote de la Mancha, and, mounting Rozinante, he left the inn, and with a joyful heart started to seek his first adventure.

In time Don Quixote acquired a faithful squire called Sancho Panza who followed after his new master riding upon an ass. One of their first adventures together took place in the following circumstances . . .

They had been riding for some hours across a wide plain without seeing anything which would enable them to prove their valour. At length Don Quixote reined up Rozinante with a jerk and, turning to his squire, he said: 'Fortune is on our side, friend Sancho. Look there, what huge giants are standing in a row! Thirty of them at least! It is a glorious chance for a new-made knight to give battle to these giants, and to rid the country of this wretched horde.'

'What giants?' asked Sancho, staring about him. 'I see none.'

'Those drawn up over there,' replied the Don. 'Never did I behold such arms! Those nearest us must be two miles long.'

'Go not within reach of them, good master,' answered Sancho anxiously, 'for they are no giants, but windmills, and what you take for arms are the sails by which the wind turns the millstones.

'How little do you know, friend Sancho, of these sorts of adventures!' replied Don Quixote. 'I tell you, those are no windmills, but giants. Know, however, that I will have no man with me who shivers with fear at the sight of a foe, so if you are afraid you had better fall to praying, and I will fight them alone.'

And with that he put spurs to Rozinante and galloped towards the windmills, heedless of the shouts of Sancho Panza, which indeed he never heard. Bending his body and holding his lance in rest, like all the pictures of knights when charging, he rushed on, crying as he went, 'Do not fly from me, cowards that you are! It is but a single knight with whom you must do battle!' And calling on the Lady Dulcinea to come to his aid, he thrust his lance through the sail of the nearest windmill, which happened to be turned by a sharp gust of wind.

The sail struck Rozinante so violently on the side that he and his master rolled over together, while the lance broke into small pieces.

When Sancho Panza saw what had befallen the Don—though indeed it was no more than he had expected—he rode up hastily to give him help. Both man and horse were half stunned with the blow; but though Don Quixote's body was bruised, his spirit was unconquered and to Sancho's complaint that no one could have doubted that the windmills were giants save those who had other windmills in their brains, he only answered: 'Be silent, my friend, and do not talk of things of which you know nothing. For of this I am sure, that the enchanter Friston, who robbed me of my books, has changed these knights into windmills to rob me of my glory also. But in the end, his black arts will have little power against my keen blade!'

'I pray that it may be so,' said Sancho, as he still held the stirrup for his master, when he struggled, not without pain, to mount Rozinante.

'Sit straighter in your saddle,' went on the worthy man. 'You lean too much on one side, but that doubtless comes from the fall you have had.'

'You speak truly,' replied Don Quixote, 'and if I do not complain of my hurt, it is because it was never heard that any knight complained of a wound, however sore!'

'If that is so, I am thankful that I am only a squire,' answered Sancho, 'For this I can say, that I shall cry as loud as I please for any pain, however little it may be—unless squires are forbidden to cry out as well as knights-errant.'

At this Don Quixote laughed, in spite of his hurts, and bade him complain whenever he pleased, for squires might lawfully do what was forbidden to knighthood. And with that the conversation ended, as Sancho declared it was their hour for dinner.

THE RACING GAME

Berwyn Jones

If, like Michael Manners, trainer at a racing stable, you talk, think and dream about horses, then you'll enjoy this fascinating insight into a trainer's day.

Michael Manners yawned and stretched, and automatically reached over to the side-table on which lay a copy of the *Racing Calendar*. Before going to sleep he had been reading this to study how best to place and run those horses under his care that were being 'readied'.

Now thoroughly roused from his afternoon nap, he dressed, had some tea and then walked outside to his little runabout car. He drove to the nearby village where he saw his blacksmith, Jack Goody—a mountain of a man, nice-natured, full of smiling fun, and an artist at his job. To him nothing mattered about a horse except that feet were in proper trim, with a bold, clean frog, and so cunningly shod as to correct any fault of movement.

He and Michael Manners were at one in this matter for they both held strong views that many a race was lost by a lamentable general lack of knowledge of the horse's feet and the art of shoeing.

'Now, Jack,' said Michael Manners, 'Old Secundus goes racing tomorrow again, and I hope you've got some of those seated-out plates for him. On this hard going, with his flat soles he'll not go a yard unless the pressure's off them . . .'

253

Then the trainer went through the other jobs in hand before returning home to greet the owners of the stable, whom he knew would be arriving that evening. He disliked this side of the business for he knew he would never brook any interference in the management of his charges. They were his life. He talked and thought and dreamed of little but his horses.

Not that his owners ever did interfere. Indeed, they would not dare even to suggest any alterations in the stable management; for they well knew that there was no better man at his job.

When the owner of the racing stables, Franklyn Masterman, arrived with his daughter, Leonora, Michael said, 'It's six o'clock. We'll postpone a drink until after stables, if you please.'

His guests knew better than to argue with him, for the hour of six was sacred to Evening Stables.

They all walked down to the yard, where stood Pat, the head lad, in large checked cap. A brown holland overall, belted with an old stirrup leather, covered his studded shirt and green neckcloth.

He was a little wizened man, with spindly, bowed, gaitered legs, topping tiny feet in extra high ankle-boots. His high-coloured creased face wreathed in what he considered to be a smile of decorous greeting, as he showed his two remaining yellowed fangs in the tight-lipped grin he reserved for visitors.

'Evenin' Pat,' greeted Michael.

'Evenin' sorr, evenin' lady, evenin' gintlemin,' returned Pat, touching his cap with a gnarled and crooked forefinger.

He turned and went toward the nearest range of stabling and opened the door of the box, which had, on a plate with a horseshoe surround, the inscription, 'Meanwell by Manifold ex Poverty'.

Here stood a slender-limbed, bay filly in a well-soaped leather head-stall, racked up by a short T-hooked chain to a ring set high in the smooth grey-cast walls. Set on the ground in a corner was a manger with a smoothly rounded overhung rim. High in the wall was a louvre window. In another corner, from a back-bent hook hung a wooden bucket, painted blue and initialled 'M.M.' in white.

Behind the mare was a neatly stacked, squared heap of bedding, on which had been spread, as if for a military inspection, the contents of the lad's tack-basket; his grooming kit, body brush, curry comb and dandy, water brush and hoof-pick. Right up to the walls and the mare-pot, on the cement floor, was a sprinkling of gleaming wheat straw.

As the party approached, the lad, who had been wisping the mare's loins and quarters with a plaited coil of hay, ceased his work. No stable-hand can groom, or, after his apprenticeship, do any work requiring exertion without breathing in through clenched teeth and exhaling through puffed lips, thus making the extraordinary hissing and bubbling noise that seems to form an undertone and accompaniment to all their work.

'Stand to her head while I strip her,' said Pat to the lad, as Michael went into the box. 'She's a bit light of her heels,' explained Pat, as he removed the linen rubber that was laid on the mare's loins, and slid off the folded rug that had been protecting her shoulders from chill.

After patting the mare's neck, Michael ran his hand down her legs in turn, feeling for any heat or swelling or soreness that might have arisen since the morning. Then he stood back and took a whole view of the mare; noting her full bright eye, quiver of nostril, gleaming coat, hardening neck and well-let-down belly; and moving behind her noted the muscling quarters and thighs before telling the lad to 'stand her over'.

The lad slipped under her head, and with a hand on the head-stall put her over so that her off-side could be viewed. To keep her from fidgeting he let her pull at a wisp of grass in his hand.

Satisfied, Michael lifted a foot to be sure that they had been picked out clean, and that shoe and foot were in order. Then, with an affectionate slap on the mare's quarter, he went to the doorway and stood with his guests.

'Nice mare,' said Michael. 'She's coming on well, and has been no trouble yet. I said *yet*, Franklyn. I've only just started to school her over fences, but she's taking to it as if she likes it.'

'Cover her up, Tucker, before you slip on to your next,' Pat ordered the lad.

The party went on to the next box. Here stood old Secundus, a gallant old warrior still with the bloom of health and condition that characterized all Michael's horses, though the old horse's legs showed signs of his races.

'He's going tomorrow, Franklyn,' commented Michael. 'I hope it

255

rains tonight, for his old legs will not stand too much jarring. How long did he blow?' he asked, turning to Pat.

'Five minutes, sorr,' answered Pat, 'and he ate up clean! Wunnerful "doer", he is.'

Michael merely grunted. Never did he hint to his staff any of his hopes and plans. As far as his staff were concerned, even including his trusted head lad, all the horses were there to be cared for equally well. Their races were his own concern.

In practice, of course, this was not the case,. for his staff followed their charge's careers in their races, and their fortunes and misfortunes with the utmost interest. Such interest was fostered by the present that was traditionally made to the lad that 'did' a winner, to the smith that plated a winner and to the head lad, quite apart from that given to the jockey on top of the scale fee he earned.

Through each box went Michael, and to each occupant he gave the same careful attention; issuing orders and instructions to Pat about feeding, dosing, dressing and 'work'.

When he had finished, he said, 'Come up to the house after dinner and I'll give you orders for tomorrow.'

'Very good, sorr,' replied Pat as he touched his cap, and turned to the feed-room to issue the sieved oats and chop, the bran or the linseed, the boiled corn-feed or mash that his employer had directed should be given to each of his horses.

Five-thirty next morning, Michael Manners shrugged into his dressing-gown. Then, with greatcoat and muffler, and goloshes over his slippered feet, he went quietly down to the stables. He opened each box and looked around, saw which horses had fed-up; what droppings there were; whether hay nets were cleared, buckets dry, rugs and rollers maladjusted. He often made this early morning inspection; saying that he learnt more about his horses than he'd know in a week otherwise.

Back in the house he swallowed a cup of chocolate as he pulled on jodhpurs and jersey ready to mount his hack to go up to the gallops to meet his first string.

This October dawn was one of those stilly dawns of pastel-strewn cloud, with dewdrops hanging heavily on the bushes. It was no hunting

day, thought Michael, as he rode his hackamore-bridled old polo pony
to near a clump of firs that seemed to stand starkly black and still
asleep against the dayrise beyond.

Here, walking round in a large circle, were the dozen horses com-
prising the first lot; amongst them the runners for this day.

It was a sight that always thrilled him. The horses, chestnut, brown,
bay and grey; each night-capped and quarter-sheeted from wither to
loin, covering the saddle. The lads—some young, some elderly though
still active enough to 'do their two' and 'ride work'—mostly in polo
sweaters of various colours, and in grey bags tucked into their socks,
with caps twisted back to front so as not to be blown off by the wind of
their going.

Michael watched the horses pacing round the circle with a quick-
flung toe, with a grounding of the feet so dainty that hardly a footfall
could be heard. All showed a rhythmic grace of action seen only in a
'blood 'un'.

'Morning, Pat,' Michael called finally. 'Strip the runners.'

Pat signalled to three lads to leave the ring.

The lads pulled their mounts away from the 'walking string'; and,
in the manner of all racing lads whether they are riding half-broken
two-year-old colts or old chasers, with thumping heels and up-
swinging elbows they trotted over. They loosed the surcingles (the
band round the horse's body), and, standing up in their irons, flicked
off the quarter-sheets and leant forward to untape the night caps. This
done, they dropped them together in a heap on the ground to await
their orders.

'Now,' ordered Michael, 'go down to the "seven furlong doll" and
break off together, come four furlongs at half speed and then a nice
pace-gallop held well together. Watch me to see if I wave on or slow
you. Sit still and don't "do a Fred Archer"—I want no fancy finishes.
I shall break in on the last furlong and give individual orders then. Have
you got it? All right, then jog on down.'

The little cavalcade faded into a blur as Michael turned his pony
and trotted off to place himself at the last furlong. Here he waited with
unslung glasses ready to view them as they came along.

He watched them with critical eye. Then, ramming his glasses into
their case, he prepared to 'jump in' with the gallop the last furlong and

257

'go' with them. In this way he could better judge their speed and mark their action; and as they were pulling up he could listen to their blowing.

'Right,' called Michael, 'now get their sheets on and walk 'em down to the stables. I'll be there inside half-an-hour.'

He turned and went back to see his horses working; fast or slow, short sprint or long canter, according to their forwardness or the proximity of their races.

Back at the stables, Jim the yardman took the pony, and Michael walked out to the paddock where his first lot were grazing in a picksome way. 'Picking' they called it—nibbling a bit, walking on and grabbing an extra toothsome tuft, and then abruptly stopping.

When the horses came into their boxes, Michael said, 'I want to have a look at Gauntlet.'

He had seen the horse 'quid'. In other words, he had seen Gauntlet drop a little wad of grass from his mouth, and had noticed a little bulge in his cheek.

Calling for the gag, he opened Gauntlet's mouth wide, and with Jim holding the tongue, he felt along the molar teeth.

'Thought so,' he observed. 'The vet should have done all their teeth a fortnight ago, but he's been laid up with a kick and I'll have no one else. He's the only man I know to have a "French plane" and know how to use it. It knocks all these sharp points off the grinders in no time, and doesn't upset the horses like a long rasping.'

'You're right, sir,' replied Jim. 'They can grind up their oats real proper next feed. I was going to report that I'd seen oats in his droppings.'

'Going to! Going to!' grumbled Michael. 'Half the horses in the country are ruined for lack of attention to teeth, and t'other half with their feet.'

Jim thought it wiser to keep quiet.

'Now get me the gamgee tissue, my crepe bandages, and some tape,' Michael instructed. 'I'll do old Secundus before he leaves at eleven.'

Secundus had returned from his 'pipe-opener'—the short gallop that is always given on the morning of a race to loosen the muscles and open the lungs.

With a stool to save bending his back, Michael most carefully shaped and cut strips of wool for the forelegs. He then bandaged over so that no wrinkle should gall, pulling it tight enough to be a support and protection, yet not so firmly that the circulation or action should be impeded. Finishing off neatly with a circlet of tape, he stood up.

'Run on a set of stable bandages to keep all clean, and then, when he's fed, see that he's properly "done",' he told the lad. 'I'll be down after breakfast before Trimble arrives with the horse-box. Pat will plait him up with the others.'

After a final look round, Michael went up to the house to eat his belated breakfast.

When he had glanced through the paper, Michael opened his correspondence and sat down at his desk to answer the more urgent letters, and to sign and complete the entries to Wetherby's that, after consultation with the owners, he had decided upon the night before.

This done, he went back to the stables, where the lads had returned from their Mess Room and were 'doing over' the horses that had 'done work' early that day.

The runners, due to leave within the hour for their journey to the down-country course at Applebury, were shining. The neat plaits of the mane and skilful overplaiting of the tails gave a finish that no self-respecting stable would omit. A smart braided and initialled day-rug, in contrasting colours with roller to match, completed the picture.

'Pat,' called Michael, 'send up the second string. I'll follow soon, and I want a word with Trimble as soon as he comes.'

The big white five-horse box arrived.

'G'day Trimble,' said Michael, 'three go today, get 'em there quietly. I'll be there in time to declare my runners. Oh! and take a pair of blinkers for Perfectus, he don't like "going-sides" with another—tries to bite 'em. That's all, you've got everything else? A drink for Secundus?'

'I'll see to it, sir,' said Joe Trimble, a most trustworthy man. He had been a good jockey in his day, but now, after several crashing falls, he could ride no longer.

Back from working his second lot, Michael Manners went up to the house and quickly bathed, shaved and changed before setting out for the racecourse.

Approaching Applebury, he could see the racecourse buildings and the tiered stands, with—just beyond—the circled red sign of the winning post, backed by the white-painted judge's box. And over a low fence he could glimpse the gleam of water and, out in the country, the black and forbidding birched fences.

Driving into the car park reserved for owners and trainers, he locked his car and passed through a wicket opened for him by a uniformed official, whose duty it was to give admittance only to those whom he knew to have business on the course.

Michael Manners greeted and nodded to friends and acquaintances.

'How-do, John,' he called to another trainer. 'Well, Michael, but I've not got a moment. Everything's wrong! Why I train I can't think. Perhaps see you later.'

Michael knew his ways. 'Only time he looks happy,' he thought, 'is when his horses are not "having a go". His face gives him away when he's "busy", and when he thinks he's going to saddle a winner it stands out a mile.'

Walking over to the grandstand he entered the office of the clerk of the course, and to him he delivered his declarations, the names of his runners and their jockeys, and the colours they would wear. By the rules, this information had to be put in forty-five minutes before the advertised time of the race.

His declarations in, he walked over to the jockey's changing-room. Picking out Nat Child from the gossiping, leg-pulling, ragging crowd of jockeys who were changing into their kit, he told him to hurry to the trying-scales.

Nat pulled on his paper-thin racing top-boots, and, adjusting his neck-scarf, went to the scales. Grabbing his gear from his valet—silk colours, crash helmet, saddle, weight-cloth and rings—he held them on his lap while he sat on the seat. Michael added lead slips to make up the weight, and then buckled them into small leather compartments stitched on the weight-cloth.

'That'll do,' he approved. 'Now go and weigh out.'

In an adjoining room were placed formidable circus-like scales, with a shining brass tripod and a swinging seat on which Nat perched with his tack.

'You're not drawing the weight,' reproved the clerk of the scales.

Nat's valet passed over a pocket-bit; a small slip of lead. This tiny addition put down the scales so that Nat drew the weight.

'Now give me your tack,' said Trimble, who had joined them, 'for I've not too much time.'

In the racecourse stables, the lads had been busy with rubber and brush; had sponged out nostrils and dock; removed the tail bandages and completed their plaiting; and done the quarter-marking—the cunningly brushed 'diamonding' of the hairs of the quarters which enhanced the trim, well-groomed coats.

When the finishing touches had been put on Perfectus, he was led by his lad to the saddling enclosure, in which Trimble had reserved a stall and carried the tack after Nat had weighed out.

In the stall, the lad stood at his horse's head with a rein in each hand. With Trimble's help, Michael proceeded to saddle his first runner. He smoothly adjusted the number-cloth before putting on, well forward, the weight-cloth with its pocketed leads; inserted a wool-knitted wither-pad under the saddle; loosing the breast-girth before snugly pulling up the girth.

Then, with a ritual air he inserted two fingers between the girths and the skin, and ran them down to be sure of no wrinkle or pinch; put surcingle overall to complete; tied a loose tape on the blinkers; checked off the lay of the bit in the mouth.

Satisfied, he turned away and followed his horse to the paddock. In the centre the jockeys had gathered, wearing their owners' colours in silk or jersey, with gaily-coloured caps tied tight with bowed-ribbon in front. Each held a leather-flapped whip—some nervously, some with an air of bravado—and slapped their boots while taking instructions from their trainers.

'Now, Nat,' instructed Michael Manners, 'you've ridden Perfectus at work, and this might be his day, for he couldn't be better. I want you to ride a waiting race. Get nicely over the first with a clear run, then take him slowly back to the middle of the field and "sit and suffer". You've got your work cut out, for you know he pulls like a train and you've got to hold him up for one run. You can move up the last time round coming into the straight. He'll jump his way to the front, and he'll do his best. But remember, they pay off at the winning post, not the second last!'

There was a flash of the tapes as the gate went up.

Nat nodded his head vigorously in agreement.

'I don't want you to poke your nose in front, and to see daylight until you've jumped the last,' Michael went on. 'In no circumstances come up on the inside, for you know he doesn't like being bumped or squeezed, and he won't stand interference. If there are three or four "sides" battling when going into the last, pull wide to have a clear run; then sit down and ride as if the fence wasn't there. Ride with your hands and heels only. Don't, at any price, "pull out your bat". Keep your whip still! Understand?'

'Yes, sir,' replied Nat.

'Very well,' said Michael. 'I'm putting a fiver on for you.'

'Thank you, sir.'

All the jockeys were mounting and filing off to the starting gate on the far side of the course, and Michael gave Nat a leg up on Perfectus. Then he walked over to where a line of bookmakers were standing on stools by their blackboards, which displayed runners and prices. Each bookmaker had a brass-bound satchel slung round his shoulders; and their clerks keeping the book of the bets taken stood by their side.

''Ere you are now! 'Ere you are! Evens the field! I'll lay two to one Rapscallion! Two to one Rapscallion. Evens the favourite!' raucously bellowed one bookie as Michael approached.

'What price Perfectus?' asked Michael. 'He's not on your board.'

'What price can we do Perfectus?' whispered the bookie in a husky voice to his clerk, and they conferred for a moment.

'Say twenty to one to you, Mr Manners.'

'Right, I'll take you for two ponies.'

'Fifty parns to a tharsand, Perfectus,' confirmed the bookie to his clerk.

His bet laid, Michael walked over to the trainers' stand, and unslung his glasses to focus them where, in the distance, could be seen the starter, with his hack held in the infield by a groom. He was lining up the runners, now weaving and wavering behind the starting-gate.

There was a flash of the tapes as the gate went up. Well together, the runners got away, as a bell by the big board displaying the numbered runners and jockeys sounded the 'off'.

'A good start,' thought Michael, 'and Perfectus safely over the first;

but it looks as if he's "swallowed the poker". I hope Nat's man enough to take him back—Perfectus is so hard-mouthed.'

Coming into the third fence Nat was nicely blanked-out, according to orders. Round to the stands for the first time, the field was a little strung out, with a couple of horses who had already parted company with their jockeys jostling the others and taking the lead.

Perfectus had stopped his raking and had a nice hold. He had settled down and was going easily, well within himself. Jumping like a book-full of pictures, he lay about sixth.

'Curse those loose horses,' Michael said to himself. 'If one refuses the next and runs down the fence, there'll be grief.'

To his relief, on the bend the loose horses galloped straight on and were clear of the rest, who, now getting close to the water-jump, kicked on a bit. But for some splashes from those that dropped short, all got over safely.

Starting the second time round, they maintained their positions and much the same placing.

Michael noted that Nat had got some ground to make up, and hoped that he didn't get anxious. But as he watched, he saw that Nat was drawing up slowly.

As the runners came pounding nearer the leaders began to drop back a bit. Rathmore had blown his cork, but Gamechick would take some beating. At the penultimate fence, however, he pecked on landing.

Michael heaved a sigh of relief, now of the firm opinion that Nat would do it with something in hand. For he was moving up nicely, and had only two to beat; and these two were both tired and merely plodding on.

But Michael's relief was short-lived. On the inside, coming into the last fence with a great burst of speed, flashed a bay horse—Flying Winsom by name.

'If Nat looks round,' muttered Michael, 'I'll skin him alive, for it'll lose him the race.'

As they came up the straight, bookies excitedly shouted the odds: 'Two to one, Perfectus! Lay fives, Flyin' Winsom!'

Stride by stride they raced on; shoulder to shoulder, neck to neck. Then Flying Winsom faltered and, with winding tail, lurched a stride. But the jockey, with flapping whip and urging hands, and heels and legs working, tried to rally Flying Winsom as they went past the post, greeted by a roar from the crowd of 'Good old Winsom!'

But it was old Perfectus who had won—beating Flying Winsom by half a length.

'A good race,' thought Michael. 'We were lucky to win.'

In the ring the bookie who had laid him the odds turned sadly to his clerk. 'Marcus,' he said in lugubrious tones, 'Marcus, that old Perfectus fooled us all . . .'

Win or lose, to Michael Manners it was all in a trainer's day. He knew how to play the racing game.

THE MALTESE CAT

Rudyard Kipling

They had good reason to be proud, and better reason to be afraid, all twelve of them; for thought they had fought their way, game by game, up the teams entered for the polo tournament, they were meeting the Archangels that afternoon in the final match; and the Archangels men were playing with half a dozen ponies apiece. As the game was divided into six quarters of eight minutes each, that meant a fresh pony after every halt. The Skidars' team, even supposing there were no accidents, could only supply one pony for every other change; and two to one is heavy odds. Again, as Shiraz, the grey Syrian, pointed out, they were meeting the pink and pick of the polo ponies of Upper India, ponies that had cost from a thousand rupees each, while they themselves were a cheap lot gathered, often from country-carts, by their masters, who belonged to a poor but honest native infantry regiment.

'Money means pace and weight,' said Shiraz, rubbing his black-silk nose dolefully along his neat-fitting boot, 'and by the maxims of the game as I know it——'

'Ah, but we aren't playing the maxims,' said The Maltese Cat. 'We're playing the game; and we've the great advantage of knowing the game. Just think a stride, Shiraz! We've pulled up from bottom to second place in two weeks against all those fellows on the ground here. That's because we play with our heads as well as our feet.'

'It makes me feel undersized and unhappy all the same,' said Kittiwynk, a mouse-coloured mare with a red brow-band and the cleanest pair of legs that ever an aged pony owned. 'They've twice our style, these others.'

Kittiwynk looked at the gathering and sighed. The hard, dusty polo ground was lined with thousands of soldiers, black and white, not counting hundreds and hundreds of carriages and drags and dog-carts, and ladies with brilliant-coloured parasols, and officers in uniform and out of it, and crowds of natives behind them; and orderlies on camels, who had halted to watch the game, instead of carrying letters up and down the station; and native horse-dealers running about on thin-eared Biluchi mares, looking for a chance to sell a few first-class polo ponies. Then there were the ponies of thirty teams that had entered for the Upper India Free-for-All Cup—nearly every pony of worth and dignity, from Mhow to Peshawar, from Allahabad to Multan; prize ponies, Arabs, Syrian, Barb, countrybred, Deccanee, Waziri, and Kabul ponies of every colour and shape and temper that you could imagine. Some of them were in mat-roofed stables, close to the polo ground, but most were under saddle, while their masters, who had been defeated in the earlier games, trotted in and out and told the world exactly how the game should be played.

It was a glorious sight, and the come and go of the little, quick hooves, and the incessant salutations of ponies that had met before on other polo grounds or racecourses were enough to drive a four-footed thing wild.

But the Skidars' team were careful not to know their neighbours, though half the ponies on the ground were anxious to scrape acquaintance with the little fellows that had come from the north and, so far, had swept the board.

'Let's see,' said a soft gold-coloured Arab, who had been playing very badly the day before, to The Maltese Cat; 'didn't we meet in Abdul Rahman's stable in Bombay, four seasons ago? I won the Paikpattan Cup next season, you may remember?'

267

'Not me,' said The Maltese Cat, politely. 'I was at Malta then, pulling a vegetable cart. I don't race. I play the game.'

'Oh!' said the Arab, cocking his tail and swaggering off.

'Keep yourselves to yourselves,' said The Maltese Cat to his companions. 'We don't want to rub noses with all those goose-rumped half-breeds of Upper India. When we've won this cup they'll give their shoes to know *us*.'

'We shan't win the cup,' said Shiraz. 'How do you feel?'

'Stale as last night's feed when a musk-rat has run over it,' said Polaris, a rather heavy-shouldered grey; and the rest of the team agreed with him.

'The sooner you forget that the better,' said The Maltese Cat, cheerfully. 'They've finished tiffin in the big tent. We shall be wanted now. If your saddles are not comfy, kick. If your bits aren't easy, rear, and let the *saises* know whether your boots are tight.'

Each pony had his *sais*, his groom, who lived and ate and slept with the animal, and had bet a good deal more than he could afford on the result of the game. There was no chance of anything going wrong, but to make sure, each *sais* was shampooing the legs of his pony to the last minute. Behind the *saises* sat as many of the Skidars' regiment as had leave to attend the match—about half the native officers, and a hundred or two dark, black-bearded men with the regimental pipers nervously fingering the big, beribboned bagpipes. The Skidars were what they call a Pioneer regiment, and the bagpipes made the national music of half their men. The native officers held bundles of polo sticks, long cane-handled mallets, and as the grandstand filled after lunch they arranged themselves by ones and twos at different points round the ground, so that if a stick were broken the player would not have far to ride for a new one. An impatient British cavalry band struck up 'If you want to know the time, ask a p'leeceman!' and the two umpires in light dustcoats danced out on two little excited ponies. The four players of the Archangels' team followed, and the sight of their beautiful mounts made Shiraz groan again.

'Wait till we know,' said The Maltese Cat. 'Two of 'em are playing in blinkers, and that means they can't see to get out of the way of their own side, or they *may* shy at the umpires' ponies. They've *all* got white web-reins that are sure to stretch or slip!'

'And,' said Kittiwynk, dancing to take the stiffness out of her, 'they carry their whips in their hands instead of on their wrists. Hah!'

'True enough. No man can manage his stick and his reins and his whip that way,' said The Maltese Cat. 'I've fallen over every square yard of the Malta ground, and I ought to know.'

He quivered his little, flea-bitten withers just to show how satisfied he felt; but his heart was not so light. Ever since he had drifted into India on a troopship, taken, with an old rifle, as part payment for a racing debt, The Maltese Cat had played and preached polo to the Skidars' team on the Skidars' stony polo ground. Now a polo pony is like a poet. If he is born with a love for the game, he can be made. The Maltese Cat knew that bamboos grew solely in order that polo balls might be turned from their roots, that grain was given to ponies to keep them in hard condition, and that ponies were shod to prevent them slipping on a turn. But, besides all these things, he knew every trick and device of the finest game in the world, and for two seasons had been teaching the others all he knew or guessed.

'Remember,' he said for the hundredth time, as the riders came up, 'you *must* play together, and you *must* play with your heads. Whatever happens, follow the ball. Who goes out first?'

Kittiwynk, Shiraz, Polaris, and a short high little bay fellow with tremendous hocks and no withers worth speaking of (he was called Corks) were being girthed up, and the soldiers in the background stared with all their eyes.

'I want you men to keep quiet,' said Lutyens, the captain of the team, 'and especially not to blow your pipes.'

'Not if we win, captain *sahib*?' asked the piper.

'If we win you can do what you please,' said Lutyens, with a smile, as he slipped the loop of his stick over his wrist, and wheeled to canter to his place. The Archangels' ponies were a little bit above themselves on account of the many-coloured crowd so close to the ground. Their riders were excellent players, but they were a team of crack players instead of a crack team; and that made all the difference in the world. They honestly meant to play together, but it is very hard for four men, each the best of the team he is picked from, to remember that in polo no brilliancy in hitting or riding makes up for playing alone. Their captain shouted his orders to them by name, and it is a curious thing that if you call his name aloud in public after an English-man you make him hot and fretty. Lutyens said nothing to his men, because it had all been said before. He pulled up Shiraz, for he was playing 'back', to guard the goal. Powell on Polaris was half-back, and Macnamara and Hughes on Corks and Kittiwynk were forwards. The tough, bamboo ball was set in the middle of the ground, one hundred and fifty yards from the ends, and Hughes crossed sticks, heads up, with the captain of the Archangels, who saw fit to play forward; that is a place from which you cannot easily control your team. The little click as the cane-shafts met was heard all over the ground, and then Hughes made some sort of quick wrist-stroke that just dribbled the ball a few yards. Kittiwynk knew that stroke of old, and followed as a cat follows a mouse. While the captain of the Arch-angels was wrenching his pony round, Hughes struck with all his strength, and next instant Kittiwynk was away, Corks following close behind her, their little feet pattering like raindrops on glass.

'Pull out to the left,' said Kittiwynk between her teeth; 'it's coming your way, Corks!'

The back and half-back of the Archangels were tearing down on her just as she was within reach of the ball. Hughes leaned forward with a loose rein, and cut it away to the left almost under Kittiwynk's foot, and it hopped and skipped off to Corks, who saw that, if he was not quick, it would run beyond the boundaries. That long bouncing drive gave the Archangels time to wheel and send three men across the ground to head off Corks. Kittiwynk stayed where she was; for she knew the game. Corks was on the ball half a fraction of a second before the others came up, and Macnamara, with a backhanded stroke, sent it back across the ground to Hughes, who saw the way clear to the Archangels' goal, and smacked the ball in before any one quite knew what had happened.

'That's luck,' said Corks, as they changed ends. 'A goal in three minutes for three hits, and no riding to speak of.'

''Don't know,' said Polaris. 'We've made 'em angry too soon. Shouldn't wonder if they tried to rush us off our feet next time.'

'Keep the ball hanging, then,' said Shiraz. 'That wears out every pony that's not used to it.'

Next time there was no easy galloping across the ground. All the

Archangels closed up as one man, but there they stayed, for Corks, Kittiwynk, and Polaris were somewhere on the top of the ball, marking time among the rattling sticks, while Shiraz circled about outside, waiting for a chance.

'We can do this all day,' said Polaris, ramming his quarters into the side of another pony. 'Where do you think you're shoving to?'

'I'll—I'll be driven in an *ekka* if I know,' was the gasping reply, 'and I'd give a week's feed to get my blinkers off. I can't see anything.'

'The dust is rather bad. Whew! That was one for my off-hock. Where's the ball, Corks?'

'Under my tail. At least, the man's looking for it there! This is beautiful. They can't use their sticks, and it's driving 'em wild. Give old Blinkers a push and then he'll go over.'

'Here, don't touch me! I can't see. I'll—I'll back out, I think,' said the pony in blinkers, who knew that if you can't see all round your head, you cannot prop yourself against the shock.

Corks was watching the ball where it lay in the dust, close to his near foreleg, with Macnamara's shortened stick tap-tapping it from time to time. Kittiwynk was edging her way out of the scrimmage, whisking her stump of a tail with nervous excitement.

'Ho! They've got it,' she snorted. 'Let me out!' and she galloped like a rifle bullet just behind a tall lanky pony of the Archangels, whose rider was swinging up his stick for a stroke.

'Not today, thank you,' said Hughes, as the blow slid off his raised stick, and Kittiwynk laid her shoulder to the tall pony's quarters, and shoved him aside just as Lutyens on Shiraz sent the ball where it had come from, and the tall pony went skating and slipping away to the left. Kittiwynk, seeing that Polaris had joined Corks in the chase for the ball up the ground, dropped into Polaris' place, and then 'time' was called.

The Skidars' ponies wasted no time in kicking or fuming. They knew that each minute's rest meant so much gain, and trotted off to the rails, and their *saises* began to scrape and blanket and rub them at once.

'Whew!' said Corks, stiffening up to get all the tickle of the big vulcanite scraper. 'If we were playing pony for pony, we would bend those Archangels double in half an hour. But they'll bring up fresh ones and fresh ones and fresh ones after that—you see.'

'Who cares?' said Polaris. 'We've drawn first blood. Is my hock swelling?'

'Looks puffy,' said Corks. 'You must have had rather a swipe. Don't let it stiffen. You'll be wanted again in half an hour.'

'What's the game like?' said The Maltese Cat.

''Ground's like your shoe, except where they put too much water on it,' said Kittiwynk. 'Then it's slippery. Don't play in the centre. There's a bog there. I don't know how their next four are going to behave, but we kept the ball hanging, and made 'em lather for nothing. Who goes out? Two Arabs and a couple of country-breds! That's bad. What a comfort it is to wash your mouth out!'

Kitty was talking with a neck of a lather-covered soda-water bottle between her teeth, and trying to look over her withers at the same time. This gave her a very coquettish air.

'What's bad?' said Grey Dawn, giving to the girth and admiring his well-set shoulders.

'You Arabs can't gallop fast enough to keep yourselves warm— that's what Kitty means,' said Polaris, limping to show that his hock needed attention. 'Are you playing back, Grey Dawn?'

'Looks like it,' said Grey Dawn, as Lutyens swung himself up. Powell mounted The Rabbit, a plain bay country-bred much like Corks, but with mulish ears. Macnamara took Faiz-Ullah, a handy, short-backed little red Arab with a long tail, and Hughes mounted Benami, an old and sullen brown beast, who stood over in front more than a polo pony should.

'Benami looks like business,' said Shiraz. 'How's your temper, Ben?' The old campaigner hobbled off without answering, and The Maltese Cat looked at the new Archangel ponies prancing about on the ground. They were four beautiful blacks, and they saddled big enough and strong enough to eat the Skidars' team and gallop away with the meal inside them.

'Blinkers again,' said The Maltese Cat. 'Good enough!'

'They're chargers—cavalry chargers!' said Kittiwynk, indignantly. '*They'll* never see thirteen-three again.'

'They've all been fairly measured, and they've all got their certificates,' said The Maltese Cat, 'or they wouldn't be here. We must take things as they come along, and keep your eyes on the ball.'

272

The game began, but this time the Skidars were penned to their own end of the ground, and the watching ponies did not approve of that.

'Faiz-Ullah is shirking—as usual,' said Polaris, with a scornful grunt.

'Faiz-Ullah is eating whip,' said Corks. They could hear the leather-thonged polo-quirt lacing the little fellow's well-rounded barrel. Then The Rabbit's shrill neigh came across the ground.

'I can't do all the work,' he cried, desperately.

'Play the game—don't talk,' The Maltese Cat whickered; and all the ponies wriggled with excitement, and the soldiers and the grooms gripped the railings and shouted. A black pony with blinkers had singled out old Benami, and was interfering with him in every possible way. They could see Benami shaking his head up and down, and flapping his under lip.

'There'll be a fall in a minute,' said Polaris. 'Benami is getting stuffy.'

The game flickered up and down between goalpost and goalpost, and the black ponies were getting more confident as they felt they had the legs of the others. The ball was hit out of a little scrimmage, and Benami and The Rabbit followed it, Faiz-Ullah only too glad to be quiet for an instant.

The blinkered black pony came up like a hawk, with two of his own side behind him, and Benami's eye glittered as he raced. The question was which pony should make way for the other, for each rider was perfectly willing to risk a fall in a good cause. The black, who had been driven nearly crazy by his blinkers, trusted to his weight and his temper; but Benami knew how to apply his weight and how to keep his temper. They met, and there was a cloud of dust. The black was lying on his side, all the breath knocked out of his body. The Rabbit was a hundred yards up the ground with the ball, and Benami was sitting down. He had slid nearly ten yards on his tail, but he had had his revenge, and sat cracking his nostrils till the black pony rose.

'That's what you get for interfering. Do you want any more?' said Benami, and he plunged into the game. Nothing was done that quarter, because Faiz-Ullah would not gallop, though Macnamara beat him whenever he could spare a second. The fall of the black pony had impressed his companions tremendously, and so the Archangels could not profit by Faiz-Ullah's bad behaviour.

But as The Maltese Cat said when 'time' was called, and the four

He took his stick in both hands and, standing up in his stirrups, swiped at the ball in the air . . .

came back blowing and dripping, Faiz-Ullah ought to have been kicked all round Umballa. If he did not behave better next time The Maltese Cat promised to pull out his Arab tail by the roots and—eat it.

There was no time to talk, for the third four were ordered out.

The third quarter of a game is generally the hottest, for each side thinks that the others must be pumped; and most of the winning play in a game is made about that time.

Lutyens took over The Maltese Cat with a pat and a hug, for Lutyens valued him more than anything else in the world; Powell had Shikast, a little grey rat with no pedigree and no manners outside polo; Macnamara mounted Bamboo, the largest of the team; and Hughes Who's Who, alias The Animal. He was supposed to have Australian blood in his veins, but he looked like a clothes-horse, and you could whack his legs with an iron crowbar without hurting him.

They went out to meet the very flower of the Archangels' team; and when Who's Who saw their elegantly booted legs and their beautiful satin skins, he grinned a grin through his light, well-worn bridle.

'My word!' said Who's Who. 'We must give 'em a little football. These gentlemen need a rubbing down.'

'No biting,' said The Maltese Cat, warningly; for once or twice in his career Who's Who had been known to forget himself in that way.

'Who said anything about biting? I'm not playing tiddlywinks. I'm playing the game.'

The Archangels came down like a wolf on the fold, for they were tired of football, and they wanted polo. They got it more and more. Just after the game began, Lutyens hit a ball that was coming towards him rapidly, and it rolled in the air, as a ball sometimes will, with the whirl of a frightened partridge. Shikast heard, but could not see it for the minute, though he looked everywhere and up into the air as The Maltese Cat had taught him. When he saw it ahead and overhead he went forward with Powell as fast as he could put foot to ground. It was then that Powell, a quiet and level-headed man as a rule, became inspired, and played a stroke that sometimes comes off successfully after long practice. He took his stick in both hands and, standing up in his stirrups, swiped at the ball in the air, Munipore fashion. There was one second of paralysed astonishment, and then all four sides of the ground went up in a yell of applause and delight as the ball flew true (you could see the amazed Archangels ducking in their saddles to dodge the line of flight, and looking at it with open mouths), and the regimental pipes of the Skidars squealed from the railings as long as the pipers had breath.

Shikast heard the stroke; but he heard the head of the stick fly off at the same time. Nine hundred and ninety-nine ponies out of a thousand would have gone tearing on after the ball with a useless player pulling at their heads; but Powell knew him, and he knew Powell; and the instant he felt Powell's right leg shift a trifle on the saddle-flap, he headed to the boundary, where a native officer was frantically waving a new stick. Before the shouts had ended, Powell was armed again.

Once before in his life The Maltese Cat had heard that very same stroke played off his own back, and had profited by the confusion it wrought. This time he acted on experience, and leaving Bamboo to guard the goal in case of accidents, came through the others like a flash, head and tail low—Lutyens standing up to ease him—swept on and on before the other side knew what was the matter, and nearly pitched on his head between the Archangels' goalpost as Lutyens kicked the ball in after a straight scurry of a hundred and fifty yards. If there was one thing more than another upon which The Maltese Cat prided himself, it was on this quick, streaking kind of run half across the ground. He did not believe in taking balls round the field unless you were clearly overmatched. After this they gave the Archangels five-minuted football; and an expensive fast pony hates football because it rumples his temper.

Who's Who showed himself even better than Polaris in this game. He did not permit any wriggling away, but bored joyfully into the scrimmage as if he had his nose in a feed-box and was looking for something nice. Little Shikast jumped on the ball the minute it got clear, and every time an Archangel pony followed it, he found Shikast standing over it, asking what was the matter.

'If we can live through this quarter,' said The Maltese Cat, 'I shan't care. Don't take it out of yourselves. Let them do the lathering.'

So the ponies, as their riders explained afterwards, 'shut-up'. The Archangels kept them tied fast in front of their goal, but it cost the Archangels' ponies all that was left of their tempers; and ponies began to kick, and men began to repeat compliments, and they chopped at the legs of Who's Who, and he set his teeth and stayed where he was, and the dust stood up like a tree over the scrimmage until that hot quarter ended.

They found the ponies very excited and confident when they went to their *saises*; and The Maltese Cat had to warn them that the worst of the game was coming.

'Now *we* are all going in for the second time,' said he, 'and *they* are trotting out fresh ponies. You think you can gallop, but you'll find you can't; and then you'll be sorry.'

'But two goals to nothing is a halter-long lead,' said Kittiwynk, prancing.

'How long does it take to get a goal?' The Maltese Cat answered. 'For pity's sake, don't run away with a notion that the game is half-won just because we happen to be in luck *now*! They'll ride you into the grandstand, if they can; you must not give 'em a chance. Follow the ball.'

'Football, as usual?' said Polaris. 'My hock's half as big as a nosebag.'

'Don't let them have a look at the ball, if you can help it. Now leave me alone. I must get all the rest I can before the last quarter.'

He hung down his head and let all his muscles go slack, Shikast, Bamboo, and Who's Who copying his example.

'Better not watch the game,' he said. 'We aren't playing, and we shall only take it out of ourselves if we grow anxious. Look at the ground and pretend it's fly-time.'

They did their best, but it was hard advice to follow. The hooves were drumming and the sticks were rattling all up and down the ground and yells of applause from the English troops told that the Archangels were pressing the Skidars hard. The native soldiers behind the ponies groaned and grunted, and said things in undertones, and presently they heard a long-drawn shout and a clatter of hurrahs!

'One to the Archangels,' said Shikast, without raising his head. 'Time's nearly up. Oh, my sire—and *dam*!'

'Faiz-Ullah,' said The Maltese Cat, 'if you don't play to the last nail in your shoes this time, I'll kick you on the ground before all the other ponies.'

'I'll do my best when my time comes,' said the little Arab, sturdily.

277

The *saises* looked at each other gravely as they rubbed their ponies' legs. This was the time when long purses began to tell, and everybody knew it. Kittiwynk and the others came back, the sweat dripping over their hooves and their tails telling sad stories.

'They're better than we are,' said Shiraz. 'I knew how it would be.'

'Shut your big head,' said The Maltese Cat; 'we've one goal to the good yet.'

'Yes; but it's two Arabs and two country-breds to play now,' said Corks. 'Faiz-Ullah, remember!' He spoke in a biting voice.

As Lutyens mounted Grey Dawn he looked at his men, and they did not look pretty. They were covered with dust and sweat in streaks. Their yellow boots were almost black, their wrists were red and lumpy, and their eyes seemed two inches deep in their heads; but the expression in the eyes was satisfactory.

'Did you take anything at tiffin?' said Lutyens; and the team shook their heads. They were too dry to talk.

'All right. The Archangels did. They are worse pumped than we are.'

'They've got the better ponies,' said Powell. 'I shan't be sorry when this business is over.'

That fifth quarter was a painful one in every way. Faiz-Ullah played like a little red demon, and The Rabbit seemed to be everywhere at once, and Benami rode straight at anything and everything that came in his way; while the umpires on their ponies wheeled like gulls outside the shifting game. But the Archangels had the better mounts—they had kept their racers till late in the game—and never allowed the Skidars to play football. They hit the ball up and down the width of the ground till Benami and the rest were outpaced. Then they went forward, and time and again Lutyens and Grey Dawn were just, and only just, able to send the ball away with a long, spitting backhander.

Grey Dawn forgot that he was an Arab; and turned from grey to blue as he galloped. Indeed, he forgot too well, for he did not keep his eyes on the ground as an Arab should, but stuck out his nose and scuttled for the dear honour of the game. They had watered the ground once or twice between the quarters, and a careless waterman had emptied the last of his skinful all in one place near the Skidars' goal. It was close to the end of the play, and for the tenth time Grey Dawn was bolting after the ball, when his near hind-foot slipped on the greasy mud, and he rolled over and over, pitching Lutyens just clear of the goalpost; and the triumphant Archangels made their goal. Then 'time' was called—two goals all; but Lutyens had to be helped up, and Grey Dawn rose with his near hind leg strained somewhere.

'What's the damage?' said Powell, his arm around Lutyens.

'Collar-bone, *of course*,' said Lutyens, between his teeth. It was the third time he had broken it in two years, and it hurt him.

Powell and the others whistled.

'Game's up,' said Hughes.

'Hold on. We've five good minutes yet, and it isn't my right hand. We'll stick it out.'

'I say,' said the captain of the Archangels, trotting up, 'are you hurt, Lutyens? We'll wait if you care to put in a substitute. I wish—I mean—the fact is, you fellows deserve this game if any team does. 'Wish we could give you a man, or some of our ponies—or something.'

'You're awfully good, but we'll play it to a finish I think.'

The captain of the Archangels stared for a little. 'That's not half bad,' he said, and went back to his own side, while Lutyens borrowed a scarf from one of his native officers and made a sling of it. Then an Archangel galloped up with a big bath-sponge, and advised Lutyens to put it under his armpit to ease his shoulder, and between them they tied up his left arm scientifically; and one of the native officers leaped forward with four long glasses that fizzed and bubbled.

The team looked at Lutyens piteously, and he nodded. It was the last quarter, and nothing would matter after that. They drank out the dark golden drink, and wiped their moustaches, and things looked more hopeful.

The Maltese Cat had put his nose into the front of Lutyens' shirt and was trying to say how sorry he was.

'He knows,' said Lutyens, proudly. 'The beggar knows. I've played him without a bridle before now—for fun.'

'It's no fun now,' said Powell. 'But we haven't a decent substitute.'

'No,' said Lutyens. 'It's the last quarter, and we've got to make our goal and win. I'll trust The Cat.'

'If you fall this time, you'll suffer a little,' said Macnamara.

'I'll trust The Cat,' said Lutyens.

'You hear that?' said The Maltese Cat, proudly, to the others. 'It's worthwhile playing polo for ten years to have that said of you. Now then, my sons, come along. We'll kick up a little bit, just to show the Archangels this team haven't suffered.'

And, sure enough, as they went on to the ground, The Maltese Cat, after satisfying himself that Lutyens was home in the saddle, kicked out three or four times, and Lutyens laughed. The reins were caught up anyhow in the tips of his strapped left hand, and he never pretended to rely on them. He knew The Cat would answer to the least pressure of the leg, and by way of showing off—for his shoulder hurt him very much—he bent the little fellow in a close figure-of-eight in and out between the goalposts. There was a roar from the native officers and men, who dearly loved a piece of *dugabashi* (horse-trick work), as they called it, and the pipes very quietly and scornfully droned out the first bars of a common bazaar tune called 'Freshly fresh and newly new', just as a warning to the other regiments that the Skidars were fit. All the natives laughed.

'And now,' said The Maltese Cat, as they took their place, 'remember that this is the last quarter, and follow the ball!'

'Don't need to be told,' said Who's Who.

'Let me go on. All those people on all four sides will begin to crowd in—just as they did at Malta. You'll hear people calling out, and moving forward and being pushed back; and that is going to make the Archangel ponies very unhappy. But if a ball is struck to the boundary, you go after it, and let the people get out of your way. I went over the pole of a four-in-hand once, and picked a game out of the dust by it. Back me up when I run, and follow the ball.'

There was a sort of an all-round sound of sympathy and wonder as the last quarter opened, and then there began exactly what The Maltese Cat had foreseen. People crowded in close to the boundaries, and the Archangels' ponies kept looking sideways at the narrowing space. If you know how a man feels to be cramped at tennis—not because he wants to run out of the court, but because he likes to know that he can at a pinch—you will guess how ponies must feel when they are playing in a box of human beings.

'I'll bend some of those men if I can get away,' said Who's Who, as he rocketed behind the ball; and Bamboo nodded without speaking.

They were playing the last ounce in them, and The Maltese Cat had left the goal undefended to join them. Lutyens gave him every order that he could to bring him back, but this was the first time in his career that the little wise grey had ever played polo on his own responsibility, and he was going to make the most of it.

'What are you doing here?' said Hughes, as The Cat crossed in front of him and rode off an Archangel.

'The Cat's in charge—mind the goal!' shouted Lutyens, and bowing forward hit the ball full, and followed on, forcing the Archangels towards their own goal.

'No football,' said The Maltese Cat. 'Keep the ball by the boundaries and cramp 'em. Play open order, and drive 'em to the boundaries.'

Across and across the ground in big diagonals flew the ball, and whenever it came to a flying rush and a stroke close to the boundaries the Archangel ponies moved stiffly. They did not care to go headlong at a wall of men and carriages, though if the ground had been open they could have turned on a sixpence.

'Wriggle her up the sides,' said The Cat. 'Keep her close to the crowd. They hate the carriages. Shikast, keep her up this side.'

Shikast and Powell lay left and right behind the uneasy scuffle of an open scrimmage, and every time the ball was hit away Shikast galloped on it at such an angle that Powell was forced to hit it towards the boundary; and when the crowd had been driven away from that side, Lutyens would send the ball over to the other, and Shikast would slide desperately after it till his friends came down to help. It was billiards, and no football, this time—billiards in a corner pocket; and the cues were not well chalked.

'If they get us out in the middle of the ground they'll walk away from us. Dribble her along the sides,' cried The Maltese Cat.

So they dribbled all along the boundary, where a pony could not come on their right-hand side; and the Archangels were furious, and the umpires had to neglect the game to shout at the people to get back, and several blundering mounted policemen tried to restore order, all close to the scrimmage, and the nerves of the Archangels' ponies stretched and broke like cobwebs.

Five or six times an Archangel hit the ball up into the middle of the ground, and each time the watchful Shikast gave Powell his chance to send it back, and after each return, when the dust had settled, men could see that the Skidars had gained a few yards.

Every now and again there were shouts of 'Side! Off-side!' from the spectators; but the teams were too busy to care, and the umpires had all they could do to keep their maddened ponies clear of the scuffle.

At last Lutyens missed a short easy stroke, and the Skidars had to fly back helter-skelter to protect their own goal, Shikast leading. Powell stopped the ball with a backhander when it was not fifty yards from the goalposts, and Shikast spun round with a wrench that nearly hoisted Powell out of his saddle.

'Now's our last chance,' said The Cat, wheeling like a cockchafer on a pin. 'We've got to ride it out. Come along.'

Lutyens felt the little chap take a deep breath, and, as it were, crouch under his rider. The ball was hopping towards the right-hand boundary, an Archangel riding for it with both spurs and a whip; but neither spur nor whip would make his pony stretch himself as he neared the crowd. The Maltese Cat glided under his very nose, picking up his hind legs sharp, for there was not a foot to spare between his quarters and the other pony's bit. It was as neat an exhibition as fancy figure-skating. Lutyens hit with all the strength he had left, but the stick slipped a little in his hand, and the ball flew off to the left instead of keeping close to the boundary. Who's Who was far across the ground, thinking hard as he galloped. He repeated stride for stride The Cat's manoeuvres with another Archangel pony, nipping the ball away from under his bridle, and clearing his opponent by half a fraction of an inch, for Who's Who was clumsy behind. Then he drove away towards the right as The Maltese Cat came up from the left; and Bamboo held a middle course exactly between them. The three were making a sort of Government broad-arrow-shaped attack; and there was only the Archangels' back to guard the goal; but immediately behind them were three Archangels racing all they knew, and mixed up with them was Powell sending Shikast along on what he felt was their last hope. It takes a very good man to stand up to the rush of seven crazy ponies in the last quarters of a cup game, when men are riding with their necks for sale, and the ponies are delirious. The Archangels' back missed his stroke and pulled aside just in time to let the rush go by. Bamboo and Who's Who shortened stride to give The

Cat room, and Lutyens got the goal with a clean, smooth, smacking stroke that was heard all over the field. But there was no stopping the ponies. They poured through the goalposts in one mixed mob, winners and losers together, for the pace had been terrific. The Maltese Cat knew by experience what would happen and, to save Lutyens, turned to the right with one last effort that strained a back-sinew beyond hope of repair. As he did so he heard the right-hand goalpost crack as a pony cannoned into it—crack, splinter and fall like a mast. It had been sawed three parts through in case of accidents, but it upset the pony nevertheless, and he blundered into another, who blundered into the left-hand post, and then there was confusion and dust and wood. Bamboo was lying on the ground, seeing stars; an Archangel pony rolled beside him, breathless and angry; Shikast had sat down dog-fashion to avoid falling over the others, and was sliding along on his little bobtail in a cloud of dust; and Powell was sitting on the ground, hammering with his stick and trying to cheer. All the others were shouting at the top of what was left of their voices, and the men who had been spilt were shouting too.

As soon as the people saw no one was hurt, ten thousand native and English shouted and clapped and yelled, and before anyone could stop them the pipers of the Skidars broke on to the ground, with all the native officers and men behind them, and marched up and down, playing a wild northern tune called 'Zakhme Bagan', and through the insolent blaring of the pipes and the high-pitched native yells you could hear the Archangels' band hammering, 'For they're all jolly good fellows', and then reproachfully to the losing team, 'Ooh, Kafoozalum! Kafoozalum! Kafoozalum!'

Besides all these things and many more, there was a commander-in-chief, and an inspector-general of cavalry, and the principal veterinary officer of all India standing on the top of a regimental coach, yelling like schoolboys; and brigadiers and colonels and commissioners, and hundreds of pretty ladies joined the chorus. But The Maltese Cat stood with his head down, wondering how many legs were left to him; and Lutyens watched the men and ponies pick themselves out of the wreck of the two goalposts, and he patted The Maltese Cat very tenderly.

'I say,' said the captain of the Archangels, spitting a pebble out of his mouth, 'will you take three thousand for that pony—as he stands?'

283

'No thank you. I've an idea he's saved my life,' said Lutyens, getting off and lying down at full length. Both teams were on the ground too, waving their boots in the air, and coughing and drawing deep breaths, as the *saises* ran up to take away the ponies, and an officious water-carrier sprinkled the players with dirty water till they sat up.

'My aunt!' said Powell, rubbing his back, and looking at the stumps of the goalposts, 'That was a game!'

They played it over again, every stroke of it, that night at the big dinner, when the Free-for-All Cup was filled and passed down the table, and emptied and filled again, and everybody made most eloquent speeches. About two in the morning, when there might have been some singing, a wise little, plain little, grey little head looked in through the open door.

'Hurrah! Bring him in,' said the Archangels; and his *sais*, who was very happy indeed, patted The Maltese Cat on the flank, and he limped in to the blaze of light and the glittering uniforms, looking for Lutyens. He was used to messes, and men's bedrooms, and places where ponies are not usually encouraged, and in his youth had jumped on and off a mess table for a bet. So he behaved himself very politely, and ate bread dipped in salt, and was petted all round the table, moving gingerly; and they drank his health, because he had done more to win the cup than any man or horse on the ground.

That was glory and honour enough for the rest of his days, and The Maltese Cat did not complain much when the veterinary surgeon said that he would be no good for polo any more. When Lutyens married, his wife did not allow him to play, so he was forced to be an umpire; and his pony on these occasions was a flea-bitten grey with a neat polo-tail, lame all round, but desperately quick on his feet, and, as everybody knew, Past Pluperfect Prestissimo Player of the Game.

A HORSE CALLED GEORGE

Michael Williams

I have been asked to give some advice to a small boy on a pony. This is very difficult, because I have never been a small boy on a pony. Furthermore, I have sharp memories of the last time advice was sought in my presence. It happened many years ago on a certain day at White City, when a lady came breezing into the press box and asked a very crusty and very peppery old journalist if he would give her 'some advice to pass on to the kiddies.'

'Madam,' said the very crusty and very peppery old journalist, fixing her with a bloodshot eye, 'you can tell them they all deserve a sound thrashing.'

Now I wouldn't like any of you to get the wrong idea. It wasn't that the very crusty and very peppery old journalist disliked children. He loved them, specially at a distance. But he did not like lady journalists, and even less did he like lady journalists who were nearly as old as he was, particularly if they were writing for papers called *The Nursery* something or other.

I don't think there is any moral to this story. Except, perhaps, for me. From that day to this, I have neither sought advice nor given it. And I don't propose to break with this long tradition now.

So I have decided, instead, to tell you about a horse I used to know. A horse called George. George was a working horse, and in those days my job was to work with him; or, more precisely, to see that George did the work he was appointed to do.

I dare say this sounds easy to you, and that you are already thinking of some dear old dobbin with plenty of feather. George had feather all right. He was that sort of horse. But he also had a great deal of character, which gave him a decided will of his own.

In other words, he was a remarkably awkward customer to handle. I suspect now, looking back on my days with George, that he had never been properly broken.

George and I used to hoe Brussels sprouts together. Well, George did the hoeing and I held the reins, and we flew up and down those rows of Brussels like nobody's business. The householders on either side of the big field where we worked used to look out of their windows with wonder. You would have thought they were at the circus.

And there were some horrible little boys who used to stand around and shout rude remarks, such as, ' 'Ang on to 'im, Mister, he might take off!'

But by and large the two of us got on pretty well together, as long as I remembered, when I was having my sandwiches, to tie George to a tree. Left to his own devices he would eat half the field. He was a great eater, was George, and he never could resist Brussels-tops.

I was happy with George in the Brussels field. We understood each other. Unfortunately, there were other things we had to do besides hoeing Brussels, and one of them was carting large and heavy bags of fertilizer about the place. Inevitably, there came a day when George decided to wander off as I was in the act of loading the cart.

I wasn't worried at first, because there was plenty of space in which to move, and there seemed plenty of time for me to catch him. But before I could he had lumbered across the field and taken to the open road; and the nearest bit of open road on this occasion was the top of an immensely steep hill.

As George reached the hill I felt a shiver go up and down my spine; and there was good reason for it, because the weight of the cart and its load was certainly not acting as a brake. In fact, when I got to the top

George went clean through the garden fence . . .

of the hill myself, George and the cart were already making the descent, and in no time at all they were thundering down the hill on their own, and I was belting helplessly after them.

All I had time to do was to shout a warning to three small boys coming up the hill, causing them to dive headlong into the ditch as George shot past them.

At the bottom of the hill was another road. This didn't stop George, of course. He went straight across it. But beyond this road was a house and a garden. George was not stopped by the garden fence. He went clean through it, with the cart.

But he was stopped by the house, and when I arrived on the scene he was calmly eating somebody's rose bushes. Beside him was a policeman who had miraculously appeared from nowhere. I didn't like the look of this at all, and the policeman didn't appear to like the look of me. 'I shall have to take your particulars, son,' he said, fishing out a large notebook.

'You can take what you like, officer,' I said, 'so long as you get my horse on to the road again.'

The policeman went up to George and gave a mild tug at his bridle. George took no notice at all. Quite clearly he was finding roses a nice change from Brussels-tops. The policeman gave a harder tug. George went on eating roses.

It was pretty puzzling, I can tell you. But policemen are not policemen for nothing. Looking carefully to one side and then to the other, this one furtively plucked a rose, and holding it out temptingly in front of him, began to walk slowly backwards.

George turned his head round and very soon was lumbering after the rose. When I reached the road, and the cart was safely on it, the policeman graciously handed George his prize.

Well, when I told my boss the story afterwards, he said kindly, 'I shall give you one more chance.'

You see, he knew George was a great character and, though he was naturally very fond of him, he didn't fancy working with him.

So George and I went on hoeing Brussels, and carting fertilizer. It was the fertilizer that brought about our downfall. We were taking a load of it to another field some distance away. On this particular day we were working with some land girls, as they were called at the time, so I had on the cart with me ten bags of fertilizer and three girl passengers.

It was, I recall, a beautifully sunny day. A day to remember, I thought, as we jogged peacefully along the road. George was on his best behaviour. I felt very proud of him, and also just a bit proud of myself.

Just the same, when we came to the brink of the steepest hills in the district, I thought it prudent to warn the girls that there was a chance—only a small one, of course—that I might not be able to stop George from taking over the controls, and perhaps they would like to dismount.

At this the girls laughed merrily and said they were all right where they were. I think they were really rather lazy girls. So we all began the descent together. Well, it wasn't long before I was pulling on the reins as hard as I could. But the more I pulled the faster George went. It was by no means an ideal situation, and as I gave a last despairing tug George swerved violently.

In a matter of seconds the wheels of the cart were halfway up the bank at the side of the road. There was a sickening lurch and the cart overturned, and with it went the fertilizer, the girls and myself. George remained on his feet. The traces had snapped.

The girls, I am glad to say, were almost unhurt. I think they had one broken elbow between them.

It was the end of my association with George. My boss was very good about coming to see me in hospital. But by this time he had heard of a boy who was getting too big for his pony and wanted a dear old horse; and what was even more important, the boy had a kind father and mother who could afford to buy him one.

A RIDE WITH A MAD HORSE IN A FREIGHT CAR

W. H. H. Murray

The American Civil War is the background to this vivid story (slightly abridged here) of a fighting man's love for a horse that adopted him on the battlefield. W. H. H. Murray was an American who lived through the Civil War, and wrote a great deal about horses.

It was at the battle of Malvern Hill—a battle where the carnage was more frightful, as it seems to me, than in any this side of the Alleghanies during the whole war—that my story must begin. I was then serving as major in Massachusetts Regiment.

About 2 p.m. we had been sent out to skirmish along the edge of the wood in which, as our generals suspected, the Rebs lay massing for a charge across the slope, upon the crest of which our army was posted. We had barely entered the underbrush when we met the heavy formations of Magruder in the very act of charging. Of course, our thin line of skirmishers was no impediment to those on-rushing masses. They were on us and over us before we could get out of the way. I do not think that half of those running, screaming masses of men ever knew that they had passed over the remnants of as plucky a regiment as ever came out of the old Bay State.

But many of the boys had good reason to remember that afternoon at the base of Malvern Hill, and I among the number; for when the last line of Rebs had passed over me, I was left among the bushes with the breath nearly trampled out of me and an ugly bayonet-gash through my thigh; and mighty little consolation was it for me at that moment to see the fellow who ran me through lying stark dead at my side, with a bullet-hole in his head, his shock of coarse black hair matted with blood, and his stony eyes looking into mine.

Well, I bandaged up my limb the best I might, and started to crawl away, for our batteries had opened, and the grape and canister that came hurtling down the slope passed but a few feet over my head. It was slow and painful work, as you can imagine, but at last, by dint of perseverance, I had dragged myself away to the left of the direct range of the batteries, and, creeping to the verge of the wood, looked off over the green slope. I understood by the crash and roar of the guns, the yells and cheers of the men, and that hoarse murmur which those who have been in battle know, but which I cannot describe in words, that there was hot work going on out there; but never have I seen, no, not in that three days' desperate *mêlée* at the Wilderness, nor at that terrific repulse we had at Cold Harbour, such absolute slaughter as I saw that afternoon on the green slope of Malvern Hill.

The guns of the entire army were massed on the crest, and thirty thousand of our infantry lay, musket in hand, in front. For eight hundred yards the hill sank in easy declension to the wood, and across this smooth expanse the Rebs must charge to reach our lines. It was nothing short of downright insanity to order men to charge that hill; and so his generals told Lee, but he would not listen to reason that day, and so he sent regiment after regiment, and brigade after brigade, and division after division, to certain death.

It was at the close of the second charge, when the yelling mass reeled back from before the blaze of those sixty guns and thirty thousand rifles, even as they began to break and fly backward toward the wood, that I saw from the spot where I lay a riderless horse break out of the confused and flying mass, and, with mane and tail erect and spreading nostril, come dashing obliquely down the slope. Over fallen steeds and heaps of the dead she leaped with a motion as airy as that of the flying fox when, fresh and unjaded, he leads away from the hounds, whose sudden cry has broken him off from hunting mice amid the bogs of the meadow. So this riderless horse came vaulting along.

Now from my earliest boyhood I have had what horsemen call a 'weakness' for horses. Only give me a colt of wild irregular temper and fierce blood to tame, and I am perfectly happy. The wild, unmannerly, and unmanageable colt, the fear of horsemen the country round, finding in you not an enemy but a friend, receiving his daily food from you, and all those little 'nothings' which go as far with a horse as a woman to win and retain affection, grows to look upon you as his protector and friend, and testifies in countless ways his fondness for you. So when I saw this horse, with action so free and motion so graceful, amid that storm of bullets, my heart involuntarily went out to her, and my feelings rose higher and higher at every leap she took from amid the whirlwind of fire and lead. And as she plunged at last over a little hillock out of range and came careering toward me as only a riderless horse might come, her head flung wildly from side to side, her nostrils widely spread, her flank and shoulders flecked with foam, her eye dilating, I forgot my wound and all the wild roar of battle, and, lifting myself involuntarily to a sitting posture as she swept grandly by, gave her a ringing cheer.

Perhaps in the sound of a human voice of happy mood amid the awful din she recognized a resemblance to the voice of him whose blood moistened her shoulders and was even yet dripping from saddle and housings. Be that as it may, no sooner had my voice sounded than she flung her head with a proud upward movement into the air, swerved sharply to the left, neighed as she might to a master at morning from her stall, and came trotting directly up to where I lay, and, pausing, looked down upon me as it were in compassion. I spoke again, and stretched out my hand caressingly. She pricked her ears, took a step forward, and lowered her nose until it came in contact with my palm. Never did I fondle anything more tenderly, never did I see an animal which seemed to so court and appreciate human tenderness as that beautiful mare. I say 'beautiful'. No other word might describe her. Never will her image fade from my memory while memory lasts.

In weight she might have turned, when well conditioned, nine hundred and fifty pounds. In colour she was a dark chestnut, with a velvety depth and soft look about the hair indescribably rich and elegant. Many a time have I heard ladies dispute the shade and hue of her plush-like coat as they ran their white, jewelled fingers through her silken hair.

Her body was round in the barrel and perfectly symmetrical. She was wide in the haunches, without projection of the hip-bones, upon which the shorter ribs seemed to lap. High in the withers as she was, the line of her back and neck perfectly curved, while her deep, oblique shoulders and long, thick forearm, ridgy with swelling sinews, suggested the perfection of stride and power. Her knees across the pan were wide, the cannon-bone below them short and thin; the pasterns long and sloping; her hooves round, dark, shiny, and well set on. Her mane was a shade darker than her coat, fine and thin, as a thoroughbred's always is whose blood is without taint or cross. Her ear was thin, sharply pointed, delicately curved, nearly black around the borders, and as tremulous as the leaves of an aspen. Her neck rose from the withers to the head in perfect curvature, hard, devoid of fat, and well cut up under the chops. Her nostrils were full, very full, and thin almost as parchment. The eyes, from which tears might fall or fire flash, were well brought out, soft as a gazelle's, almost human in their intelligence, while over the small bony head, over neck and shoulders, yea, over the whole body and clean down to the hooves, the veins stood out as if the skin were but tissue-paper against which the warm blood pressed, and which it might at any moment burst asunder.

'A perfect animal,' I said to myself as I lay looking her over—'an animal which might have been born from the wind and the sunshine, so cheerful and so swift she seems.'

All that afternoon the beautiful mare stood over me, while away to the right of us the hoarse tide of battle flowed and ebbed. What charm, what delusion of memory held her there? Was my face to her as the face of her dead master, sleeping a sleep from which not even the wildest roar of battle, no, nor her cheerful neigh at morning, would ever wake him? Or is there in animals some instinct, answering to our intuition, only more potent, which tells them whom to trust and whom to avoid? I know not, and yet some such sense they may have, they must have; or else why should this mare so fearlessly attach herself to me? By what process of reason or instinct I know not, but there she chose me for her master; for when some of my men at dusk came searching, and found me, and, laying me on a stretcher, started toward our lines, the mare, uncompelled, of her own free will, followed at my side; and all through that stormy night of wind and rain, as my men struggled along through the mud and mire toward Harrison's Landing,

293

the mare followed, and ever after, until she died, was with me, and was mine, and I, so far as man might be, was hers. I named her Gulnare.

As quickly as my wound permitted, I was transported to Washington, whither I took the mare with me. Her fondness for me grew daily, and soon became so marked as to cause universal comment. I had her boarded while in Washington. The groom had instructions to lead her around to the window against which was my bed, at the hospital, twice every day, so that by opening the sash I might reach out my hand and pet her. But the second day, no sooner had she reached the street that she broke suddenly from the groom and dashed away at full speed.

I was lying, bolstered up in bed, reading, when I heard the rush of flying feet, and in an instant, with a loud, joyful neigh, she checked herself in front of my window. And when the nurse lifted the sash, the beautiful creature thrust her head through the aperture, and rubbed her nose against my shoulder like a dog. I am not ashamed to say that I put both my arms around her neck, and, burying my face in her silken mane, kissed her again and again.

Wounded, weak, and away from home, with only strangers to wait upon me, and scant service at that, the affection of this lovely creature for me, so tender and touching, seemed almost human, and my heart went out to her beyond any power of expression, as to the only being, of all the thousands around me, who thought of me and loved me. Shortly after her appearance at my window, the groom, who had divined where he should find her, came into the yard. But she would not allow him to come near her, much less touch her. If he tried to approach she would lash out at him with her heels most spitefully, and then, laying back her ears and opening her mouth savagely, would make a short dash at him, and, as the terrified groom disappeared around the corner of the hospital, she would wheel, and, with a face bright as a happy child's, come trotting to the window for me to pet her.

I shouted to the groom to go back to the stable, for I had no doubt but that she would return to her stall when I closed the window. Rejoiced at the permission, he departed. After some thirty minutes, the last ten of which she was standing with her slim, delicate head in my lap, while I braided her foretop and combed out her silken mane, I lifted her head, and, patting her softly on either cheek, told her that she must 'go'. I gently pushed her head out of the window and closed it, and then, holding up my hand, with the palm turned toward her, charged her, making the appropriate motion, to 'go away right straight back to her stable'. For a moment she stood looking steadily at me, with an indescribable expression of hesitation and surprise in her clear, liquid eyes, and then, turning lingeringly, walked slowly out of the yard.

Twice a day for nearly a month, while I lay in the hospital, did Gulnare visit me. At the appointed hour the groom would slip her headstall, and, without a word of command, she would dart out of the stable, and, with her long, leopard-like lope, go sweeping down the street and come dashing into the hospital yard, checking herself with the same glad neigh at my window; nor did she ever once fail, at the closing of the sash, to return directly to her stall. The groom informed me that every morning and evening, when the hour of her visit drew near, she would begin to chafe and worry, and, by pawing and pulling at the halter, advertise him that it was time for her to be released.

But of all exhibitions of happiness, either by beast or man, hers was the most positive on that afternoon when, racing into the yard, she found me leaning on a crutch outside the hospital building. The whole corps of nurses came to the doors, and all the poor fellows that could move themselves—for Gulnare had become a universal favourite, and the boys looked for her daily visits nearly, if not quite, as ardently as I did—crawled to the windows to see her.

What gladness was expressed in every movement! She would come prancing toward me, head and tail erect, and, pausing, rub her head against my shoulder, while I patted her glossy neck; then suddenly, with a sidewise spring, she would break away, and with her long tail elevated until her magnificent brush, fine and silken as the golden hair of a blonde, fell in a great spray on either flank, and, her head curved to its proudest arch, pace around me with that high action and springing step peculiar to the thoroughbred. Then like a flash, dropping her brush and laying back her ears and stretching her nose straight out, she would speed away with that quick, nervous, low-lying action which marks the rush of racers, when side by side and nose to nose lapping each other, with the roar of cheers on either hand and along the seats

295

above them, they come straining up the home stretch. Returning from one of these arrowy flights, she would come curvetting back, now pacing sidewise as on parade, now dashing her hind feet high into the air, and anon vaulting up and springing through the air, with legs well under her, as if in the act of taking a five-barred gate, and finally would approach and stand happy in her reward—my caress.

The war, at last, was over. Gulnare and I were in at the death with Sheridan at the Five Forks. Together we had shared the pageant at Richmond and Washington, and never had I see her in better spirits than on that day at the capital. It was a sight indeed to see her as she came down Pennsylvania Avenue. If the triumphant procession had been all in her honour and mine, she could not have moved with greater grace and pride. With dilating eye and tremulous ear, ceaselessly champing her bit, her heated blood bringing out the magnificent lacework of veins over her entire body, now and then pausing, and with a snort gathering herself back upon her haunches as for a mighty leap, while she shook the froth from her bits, she moved with a high, prancing step down the magnificent street, the admired of all beholders.

Cheer after cheer was given, huzza after huzza rang out over her head from roofs and balcony, bouquet after bouquet was launched by fair and enthusiastic admirers before her; and yet, amid the crash and swell of music, the cheering and tumult, so gentle and manageable was she, that, though I could feel her frame creep and tremble under me as she moved through that whirlwind of excitement, no check or curb was needed, and the bridle-lines—the same she wore when she came to me at Malvern Hill—lay unlifted on the pommel of the saddle. Never before had I seen her so grandly herself. Never before had the fire and energy, the grace and gentleness of her blood so revealed themselves.

This was the day and the event she needed. And all the royalty of her ancestral breed—a race of equine kings—flowing as without taint or cross from him that was the pride and wealth of the whole tribe of desert rangers, expressed itself in her. I need not say that I shared her mood. I sympathized in her every step. I entered into all her royal humours. I patted her neck and spoke loving and cheerful words to her. I called her my beauty, my pride, my pet. And did she not understand me? Every word! Else why that listening ear turned back to catch my softest whisper; why the responsive quiver through the frame, and the low, happy neigh? 'Well,' I exclaimed, as I leaped from her back at the close of the review—alas! that words spoken in lightest mood should portend so much!—'well, Gulnare, if you should die, your life has had its triumph. The nation itself, through its admiring capital, has paid tribute to your beauty, and death can never rob you of your fame.' And I patted her moist neck and foam-flecked shoulders, while the grooms were busy with head and loins.

That night our brigade made its bivouac just over Long Bridge, almost on the identical spot where, four years before, I had camped my company of three months' volunteers. With what experiences of march and battle were those four years filled! For three of these years Gulnare had been my constant companion. With me she had shared my tent, and not rarely my rations, for in appetite she was truly human, and my steward always counted her as one of our 'mess'.

Twice had she been wounded—once at Fredericksburg, through the thigh; and once at Cold Harbour, where a piece of shell tore away a part of her scalp. So completely did it stun her, that for some moments I thought her dead, but to my great joy she shortly recovered her senses. I had the wound carefully dressed by our brigade surgeon, from whose care she came in a month with the edges of the wound so nicely united that the eye could only with difficulty detect the scar.

This night, as usual, she lay at my side, her head almost touching mine. Never before, unless when on a raid and in face of the enemy, had I seen her so uneasy. Her movements during the night compelled wakefulness on my part. The sky was cloudless, and in the dim light I lay and watched her. Now she would stretch herself at full length, and rub her head on the ground. Then she would start up, and, sitting on her haunches, like a dog, lift one foreleg and paw her neck and ears. Anon she would rise to her feet and shake herself, walk off a few rods, return and lie down again by my side. I did not know what to make of it, unless the excitement of the day had been too much for her sensitive nerves. I spoke to her kindly and petted her. In response she would rub her nose against me, and lick my hand with her tongue—a peculiar habit of hers—like a dog.

As I was passing my hand over her head, I discovered that it was hot, and the thought of the old wound flashed into my mind, with a momentary fear that something might be wrong about her brain, but after thinking it over I dismissed it as incredible. Still I was alarmed. I knew that something was amiss, and I rejoiced at the thought that I should soon be at home where she could have quiet, and, if need be, the best of nursing.

At length the morning dawned, and the mare and I took our last meal together on Southern soil—the last we ever took together. The brigade was formed in line for the last time, and as I rode down the front to review the boys she moved with all her old battle grace and power. Only now and then, by a shake of the head, was I reminded of her actions during the night. I said a few words of farewell to the men whom I had led so often to battle, with whom I had shared perils not a few, and by whom, as I had reason to think, I was loved, and then gave, with a voice slightly unsteady, the last order they would ever receive from me: 'Brigade—Attention. Ready to break ranks—*Break ranks.*'

The order was obeyed. But before they scattered, moved by a common impulse, they gave first three cheers for me, and then, with the same heartiness and even more power, three cheers for Gulnare. And she, standing there, looking with her bright, cheerful countenance full at the men, pawing with her forefeet, alternately, the ground, seemed to understand the compliment; for no sooner had the cheering died away than she arched her neck to its proudest curve, lifted her thin, delicate head into the air, and gave a short, joyful neigh.

My arrangements for transporting her had been made by a friend the day before. A large, roomy car had been secured, its floor strewn with bright, clean straw, a bucket and a bag of oats provided, and everything done for her comfort. The car was to be attached to the through express, in consideration of fifty dollars extra, which I gladly paid, because of the greater rapidity with which it enabled me to make my journey. As the brigade broke up into groups, I glanced at my watch and saw that I had barely time to reach the cars before they started. I shook the reins upon her neck, and with a plunge, startled at the energy of my signal, away she flew.

What a stride she had! What an elastic spring! She touched and left the earth as if her limbs were of spiral wire. When I reached the car my friend was standing in front of it, the gang-plank was ready, I leaped from the saddle and, running up the plank into the car, whistled to her; and she, timid and hesitating, yet unwilling to be separated from me, crept slowly and cautiously up the steep incline and stood beside me. Inside I found a complete suit of flannel clothes, with a blanket and, better than all, a lunch-basket. My friend explained that he had bought the clothes as he came down to the depot, thinking, as he said, 'that they would be much better than your regimentals,' and suggested that I doff the one and don the other. To this I assented the more readily as I reflected that I would have to pass one night at least in the car, with no better bed than the straw under my feet. I had barely time to undress before the cars were coupled and started. I tossed the clothes to my friend with the injunction to pack them in my trunk and express them on to me, and waved him my adieu. I dressed myself in the nice, cool flannel and looked around.

The thoughtfulness of my friend had anticipated every want. An old cane-seated chair stood in one corner. The lunch-basket was large and well supplied. Among the oats I found a dozen oranges, some bananas, and a package of real Havana cigars. How I called down blessings on his thoughtful head as I took the chair and, lighting one of the fine-flavoured *figaros*, gazed out on the fields past which we were gliding, yet wet with morning dew. As I sat dreamily admiring the beauty before me, Gulnare came and, resting her head upon my shoulder, seemed to share my mood. As I stroked her fine-haired, satin-like nose, recollection quickened and memories of our companionship in perils thronged into my mind. I rode again that midnight ride to Knoxville, when Burnside lay intrenched, desperately holding his own, waiting for news from Chattanooga of which I was the bearer, chosen by Grant himself because of the reputation of my mare. What riding that was! We started, ten riders of us in all, each with the same message. I parted company the first hour out with all save one, an iron-grey stallion of Messenger blood. Jack Murdock rode him, who learned his horsemanship from buffalo and Indian hunting on the plains —not a bad school to graduate from. Ten miles out of Knoxville the grey, his flanks dripping with blood, plunged up abreast of the mare's shoulders and fell dead; and Gulnare and I passed through the lines alone. *I had ridden the terrible race without whip or spur.* With what scenes of blood and flight she would always be associated!

And then I thought of home, unvisited for four long years—that home I left a stripling, but to which I was returning a bronzed and brawny man. I thought of mother and Bob—how they would admire her!—of old Ben, the family groom, and of that one who shall be nameless, whose picture I had so often shown to Gulnare as the likeness of her future mistress; had they not all heard of her, my beautiful mare, she who came to me from the smoke and whirlwind, my battle-gift? How they would pat her soft, smooth sides, and tie her mane with ribbons, and feed her with all sweet things from open and caressing palm! And then I thought of one who might come after her to bear her name and repeat at least some portion of her beauty—a horse honoured and renowned the country through, because of the transmission of the mother's fame.

About three o'clock in the afternoon a change came over Gulnare. I had fallen asleep upon the straw, and she had come and awakened me with a touch of her nose. The moment I started up I saw that something was the matter. Her eyes were dull and heavy. Never before had I seen the light go out of them. The rocking of the car as it went jumping and vibrating along seemed to irritate her. She began to rub her head against the side of the car. Touching it, I found that the skin over the brain was hot as fire. Her breathing grew rapidly louder and louder. Each breath was drawn with a kind of gasping effort. The lids with their silken fringe drooped wearily over the lustreless eyes. The head sank lower and lower, until the nose almost touched the floor. The ears, naturally so lively and erect, hung limp and widely apart. The body was cold and senseless. A pinch elicited no motion. Even my voice was at last unheeded. To word and touch there came, for the first time in all our intercourse, no response. I knew as the symptoms spread what was the matter. The signs bore all one way. She was in the first stages of phrenitis, or inflammation of the brain. In other words, *my beautiful mare was going mad!*

I was well versed in the anatomy of the horse. Loving horses from my very childhood, there was little in veterinary practice with which I was not familiar. Instinctively, as soon as the symptoms had developed themselves, and I saw under what frightful disorder Gulnare was labouring, I put my hand into my pocket for my knife, in order to open a vein. *There was no knife there.*

Friends, I have met with many surprises. More than once in battle

*She was in the first stages of phrenitis, or inflammation of the brain.
In other words, my beautiful mare was going mad!'*

and scout have I been nigh death; but never did my blood desert my veins and settle so around the heart, never did such a sickening sensation possess me, as when, standing in that car with my beautiful mare before me marked with those horrible symptoms, I made that discovery. My knife, my sword, my pistols even, were with my suit in the care of my friend, two hundred miles away. Hastily, and with trembling fingers, I searched my clothes, the lunch-basket, my linen; not even a pin could I find. I shoved open the sliding door, and swung my hat and shouted, hoping to attract some brakesman's attention. The train was thundering along at full speed, and none saw or heard me.

I knew her stupor would not last long. A slight quivering of the lip, an occasional spasm running through the frame, told me too plainly that the stage of frenzy would soon begin. 'My God,' I exclaimed in despair, as I shut the door and turned toward her, 'must I see you die, Gulnare, when the opening of a vein would save you? Have you borne me, my pet, through all these years of peril, the icy chill of winter, the heat and torment of summer, and all the thronging dangers of a hundred bloody battles, only to die torn by fierce agonies, when so near a peaceful home?'

But little time was given me to mourn. My life was soon to be in peril, and I must summon up the utmost power of eye and limb to escape the violence of my frenzied mare. Did you ever see a mad horse when his madness is on him? Take your stand with me in that car, and you shall see what suffering a dumb creature can endure before it dies. In no malady does a horse suffer more than in phrenitis, or inflammation of the brain.

Had my pistols been with me, I should then and there, with whatever strength heaven granted, have taken my companion's life, that she might be spared the suffering which was so soon to rack and wring her sensitive frame. A horse labouring under an attack of phrenitis is as violent as a horse can be. He may kill his master, but he does it without design. There is in him no desire of mischief for its own sake, no cruel cunning, no stratagem and malice. He sees and recognizes no one. There is no method or purpose in his madness. He kills without knowing it.

I knew what was coming. I could not jump out, that would be certain death. I must stay in the car, and take my chance of life.

The car was fortunately high, long, and roomy. I took my position in front of my horse, watchful, and ready to spring. Suddenly her lids, which had been closed, came open with a snap, as if an electric shock had passed through her, and the eyes, wild in their brightness, stared directly at me.

The car suddenly reeled as it dashed around a curve, swaying her almost off her feet, and, as a contortion shook her, she recovered herself, and rearing upward as high as the car permitted, plunged directly at me. I was expecting the movement, and dodged. Then followed exhibitions of pain which I pray God I may never see again. Time and again did she dash herself upon the floor, and roll over and over, lashing out with her feet in all directions. Then like a flash she would leap to her feet, and whirl round and round until from very giddiness she would stagger and fall.

For some fifteen minutes without intermission the frenzy lasted. I was nearly exhausted. My efforts to avoid her mad rushes, the terrible tension of my nervous system, produced by the spectacle of such exquisite and prolonged suffering, were weakening me beyond what I should have thought it possible an hour before for anything to weaken me. In fact, I felt my strength leaving me. A terror such as I had never yet felt was taking possession of my mind. I sickened at the sight before me, and at the thought of agonies yet to come. 'My God,' I exclaimed, 'must I be killed by my own horse in this miserable car!' Even as I spoke the end came. The mare raised herself until her shoulders touched the roof, then dashed her body upon the floor with a violence which threatened the stout frame beneath her. I leaned, panting and exhausted, against the side of the car. Gulnare did not stir. She lay motionless, her breath coming and going in lessening respirations.

I tottered toward her, and, as I stood above her, my ear detected a low gurgling sound. I cannot describe the feeling that followed. Joy and grief contended within me. I knew the meaning of that sound. Gulnare, in her frenzied violence, had broken a blood–vessel, and was bleeding internally. Pain and life were passing away together. I knelt down by her side. I laid my head upon her shoulders and sobbed aloud. Her body moved a little beneath me. I crawled forward, and lifted her beautiful head into my lap. O, for one more sign of recognition before she died! I smoothed the tangled masses of her mane. I wiped, with a fragment of my coat, torn in the struggle, the blood which oozed from her nostril. I called her by name. My desire was granted. In a moment Gulnare opened her eyes. The redness of frenzy had passed out of them. She saw and recognized me. I spoke again. Her eye lighted a moment with the old and intelligent look of love. Her ear moved. Her nostril quivered slightly as she strove to neigh.

The effort was in vain. Her love was greater than her strength. She moved her head a little, as if she would be nearer me, looked once more with her clear eyes into my face, breathed a long breath, straightened her shapely limbs, and died. And there, holding the head of my dead mare in my lap, while the great warm tears fell one after another down my cheeks, I sat until the sun went down, the shadows darkened and night drew her mantle, coloured like my grief, over the world.

FAREWELL
TO THE ISLAND

Mary E. Patchett

The children sat down on the rocks by a small beach of the tiny island in the waters of Australia's Great Barrier Reef and waited for the outboard to bring their parents and Pauli, their dachshund.

'There they are!' called Danny, pointing towards the headland. Coming round it, the outboard chugged along. They waved to their parents, then ran to the other side of the island and mounted Cloud and Manta, the two wild young horses they had tamed. Old Bill, the third horse, seemed to have forgotten his hatred of mankind, but even so the children were a little worried about how he would receive their parents. When they rode over the rise towards the beach, Bill trotted behind. The Delaneys saw their son and daughter, saddle-less and bridleless, each astride a beautiful young horse, while the third horse they saw as a villainous-looking, four-legged Long John Silver.

Mr Delaney stopped the engine and the outboard drifted up on to the beach. He helped his wife out. This was the moment when Danny had feared Old Bill might forget his manners. She slipped off Cloud and put her arms reassuringly about Bill's neck. The man-eating gleam came into his eyes and his ears went back. Danny gave a spring

305

and landed on his back. Perhaps an audience meant something to Bill from his early days. The old horse pulled himself together and moved quietly and proudly as if he was in a showring.

'Aren't they lovely?' Danny asked. 'You can pat Cloud, but be careful of Bill—he doesn't like strangers.'

'What an understatement,' David thought, his anxious eye on the horse. But Mr Delaney had his own magic with horses. He had not been among them all his life for nothing. First he patted Manta, then Cloud, then he came over to Bill, and Danny's heart beat faster.

Bill stood proudly and only his eyes showed a flicker of concern, his stance obviously that of an old showring performer. Mr Delaney went to his head, stroked him and spoke quietly as a judge might speak to a nervous horse, running his firm hands over the scarred old hide.

'Come over here, Madge,' he called to his wife.

Mrs Delaney left Manta and came over to be introduced to Bill. He stood quietly and she exclaimed at his scars.

'What do you think made those scars, Daddy?' 'Danny asked.

'Some brutal rider made those on his ribs, but, if it is possible for him to have escaped them, I'd think those scars, the long ones, might come from sharks. I suppose you don't know how they got on the island, do you?'

'We thought they must've been shipwrecked.'

'That's possible. Many horse-carrying ships have foundered on the reefs. I'd say Bill got those long scars fighting sharks off himself and the youngsters, swimming to the island.'

Mrs Delaney broke in with, 'Wasn't the poor old fellow very wild when you found him, Danny?'

'Oh yes, he was, Mum. That's why it was so long before we could ask you and Dad to our island.'

'What are you going to do about them when we all leave?' Mr Delaney asked.

'Oh, Daddy, I'm sure Captain Morris'd ship them.'

'But you have your own horses at home. Anyway, your Old Bill wouldn't be much use to anyone——'

Danny gave a wail of protest. 'Oh you couldn't separate them,' she said. 'Bill'd die of loneliness. He adores the other two. Please, please don't leave him behind.'

'Well, we'll have to see. Now, let's take a look over the island.'

But the day was spoiled for Danny. It had never entered her head that the old horse might be left behind, deserted by everyone to die of loneliness. She followed the others tramping and scrambling to the top of the hill. Danny kept thinking of the quiet way her father had spoken. She knew he had really meant it.

Mr Delaney looked back and asked David, 'Where's Danny?'

'I expect she's with the horses.'

'I hope she's not sulking because I won't take Bill back with us. What could we do with an old crock like that?'

'Danny loves him because he *is* an old crock,' Mrs Delaney said quietly.

'Oh, Madge, be sensible. He'd be safe as houses here with the island all to himself.'

'He might be safe,' said David, 'but he wouldn't be happy without the others.'

Mr Delaney looked down at his son. 'Not you too, David. I thought you'd have some sense. You go on—I'm going to wait here to speak to Danny.'

'Dick, don't be hard on Danny—be gentle with her.'

'When have I ever been hard on Danny? But someone must show some common sense.'

David and his mother walked on, and Mr Delaney sat down on a tangle-topped log and waited. Danny, her feet dragging and her heart heavy, came up the hill. Old Bill walked behind her. Every now and again he bumped the back of her neck, nibbling at her so that she turned and stroked him, kissing his old scarred nose while the tears poured down her face. She didn't see her father until she was almost on top of him.

'Wait a minute, Danny, I want to talk to you,' he said.

She looked at him with sullen, red-rimmed eyes. At that moment he did not seem to her the father she knew. She felt very forlorn. She did not speak but sat stiffly on the log a little way from him. Pauli, panting furiously, climbed up the log, and walking along it she jumped into Danny's lap. Danny gathered the little dog into her arms and waited.

'Danny,' her father began in that quiet voice she dreaded and which made her look back at him defiantly because she felt helpless and alone. Why weren't David and her mother helping to save Bill after all the horrible things that men had done to him in the past?

Her father's voice went on, 'You know I'm not going to ship your old horse along with the other two. You're being very foolish. Perhaps you'd rather we left all three horses here?'

Suddenly Danny realized how much she loved the beautiful Cloud, and how David cared about Manta. But above everything else she thought of the bewildered loneliness of Old Bill, who had so much for which to forgive man. To it he would have to add something more: the breaking of his old heart.

'Yes, I would rather they all stayed here together,' she said in a tired little voice.

'Now, Danny, don't be silly. I'm willing to ship those two splendid young horses, but the old one must stay. There'll be plenty of feed for one horse and he'll be safe on the island. I'm sorry, but this is my final decision. I don't want to hear any more about it.'

Mr Delaney rose and walked after the others. Danny's tear-dimmed eyes watched his retreating back. Despair filled her heart. Pauli yawned and licked her chin, then yawned again and jumped off her lap and began sniffing about in the grass. Danny's eyes were blank. She was shut in in an unhappy world of her own. Then she heard Pauli's sharp yaps coming from the grass about ten yards in front of her.

Danny's eyes focused on Pauli's plump little back view, her tail wagging like a flag in her excitement, and making little forward bounces as she yapped. A copper-coloured head with cold eyes and flickering tongue rose in the air above Pauli. Danny knew the head belonged to that six feet of sinuous death that bushmen call a tiger-snake. Her sorrow-dulled mind became alert, as in a flash she remembered that the tiger-snake is one of the most venomous snakes in the world, and one of the very few that will follow and attack a retreating foe.

Danny did not even hear her own shout of 'Pauli! Pauli come here!' but something in her voice made that intrepid hunter turn and rush to her. She bent and swept Pauli up, her eyes on the snake; its strong muscles surged together and its wicked head dropped. The swirling body of the snake propelled it forward in a muscular movement of

Old Bill bore down on the muscular whiplash of copper . . .

grace and power. It was coming in to attack.

Like all snakes it was deaf and did not hear her shout, but another animal heard it. Danny sprang to her feet, clutching Pauli. Knowing it would be useless to run, she nevertheless turned and jumped on to the log. Then she heard a sound she had heard before: the screaming neigh of a charging horse.

For one awful instant she measured the onrushing, narrow copper head and estimated that it would strike midway up her shins. The next instant Barnacle Bill burst like a fury out of the bushes. He too had heard the fear in Danny's voice and he didn't hesitate. With pounding hooves and tossing mane he bore down on the muscular whiplash of copper that lifted a third of its long body and turned to meet him, its death-filled head swaying, poised for its lightning strike.

Danny's shout had been heard by more than the dog and the horse. It reached her parents' and David's ears. Without a word they all turned. Tearing their way through bushes and trailing vines, they rushed towards the sound. Reaching the edge of the clearing, they saw Old Bill, his own head fierce and flat as the head of some giant serpent, rushing in for the kill. He bared his yellow teeth, thrust his head forward and caught the copper body a few inches behind the head. Holding and shaking the snake, he reared and tore at the dangling body with his hooves, shaking and beating it until, with an upward fling of his head, he loosed his hold. The broken, pounded body of his enemy fell limply on to the ground a dozen feet away.

Now poor Danny was truly frantic. Bill had saved her life. Was it to cost him his own? Had the fang-filled head managed to inflict as much as a scratch during the snorting and shaking and pounding? If so, Barnacle Bill was doomed.

'Daddy—David—*do* something!' she wailed, flinging her arms about the shaggy neck. Her father and brother ran their hands carefully over the horse's neck and head, his chest and legs. Mr Delaney stood back.

'I don't know, Danny,' he said. 'It's impossible to find the fang-marks, but if he's bitten, there should be a damp patch of venom on his hide. Try not to be upset—we can only wait. In ten minutes we'll know.'

The family sat along the log, with Pauli in Mrs Delaney's lap, while Danny stood, her body trembling with fear, her arms about the horse's scarred neck. Cloud and Manta came to the edge of the clearing and began cropping the grass. Bill enjoyed the fuss Danny made of him; he sighed and snuffed and once he flung up his head as if he was listening, and Danny's heart missed a beat.

The minutes passed slowly. Mr Delaney stared at his watch. Ten minutes . . . Old Bill was still on his feet . . . Better give him another minute to be sure . . . Eleven minutes . . . Bill dropped his head and began to munch the grass.

'That's it! He's all right, Danny! Danny, listen to me, he's——'

Danny turned round, she saw her father's face and she knew. She ran to him and he put his arms round her and said, 'It's all right, Danny. Everything's all right.'

She lifted her tear-stained, freckled face. 'You won't leave him behind now?'

Her father pushed the damp streaks of hair away from her forehead and shook his head. 'I'll tell you what, darling: Bill's going to have the best accommodation the ship can offer. When we get home he's going to have the star loose box always and none of us is ever going to forget that he risked his life to save yours. But for him our summer on Wild Horse Island might have ended in tragedy. Now, whenever the *Captain Cook* arrives, we're taking home only the happiest memories.'

A PAIR

Phyllis Bottome

A little boy falls in love with the beautiful white horses of the Spanish riding school of Vienna. He longs to be able to work with them and, as soon as he is old enough, he sets about making his dream come true.

When Hans Kraus first heard of them he thought they must be angels. His father and mother had been to see them one Sunday morning for a treat. In the conversation that followed Hans gathered that these creatures had all the features of angels. They were pure white; they went like the wind; they were noble-hearted and obeyed the will of a god.

It was true that Hans had not grasped before that angels had long white tails. But why not tails? Are not feathery tails akin to wings, and perhaps even better adapted for dealing with flies?

When his father took Hans himself to see the Spanish riding school, the question was settled. Horses or angels stood for the same thing in Hans's mind for ever.

At four years old, Hans had made up his mind to become a rider in the Spanish riding school; and he never changed it, though it was a difficult problem. Such an occupation goes by favour, by heredity, by living within the charmed circle of people whose destinies are one with horses.

His father Kraus could help Hans only a little. He sold corn to the stables, and not always very good corn, and then there was trouble. However, Hans's father was more honest than most people, because he had the intelligence to realize that if he sold bad corn, he would soon be found out by the look of the horses, and lose his job. So he only sold rather less good corn than what he was paid for, and he, and any venal grooms there were, pocketed the difference.

When a little boy knows what he wants to be, and lives all day long with only that one end in view, miracles can be accomplished.

In a world of so many conflicting elements, where everybody is flying off at a tangent, steadiness is more of a miracle than magic, and Hans was miraculously steady. He hung all day long about the stables. He ran errands for the grooms; he brought them beer without secreting a drop for himself. At first they told him: 'No one is ever allowed to go into the riding school, except on show days, and only those who are employed with the horses may enter the stables at all. This is no circus, my boy—it is serious!'

Hans answered: 'But I will work for them, and for you, for nothing!'

His heart fixed itself upon the reluctant grooms through his bright blue eyes, and as he was such a little boy, and so accommodating about beer, in the end the grooms sacrificed their rigidity and let Hans into the stables.

Once there, they found him very useful. He helped to clean stalls, filled and emptied buckets, and was so industrious, quick and mild, that nobody had any interest in getting rid of him.

Hans played truant from school so that he could work all day long in the stables, until one day his teacher had the sense to tell him:

'To become a Spanish rider you must know something more than can be learned in a stable. You must be an educated man, capable of passing school tests!'

Hans saw at once that it would be worth while to stop playing truant until he had learned what was necessary for riders; and after all, he had the rest of his life in which to study horses.

Hans learned how to slip into their stalls without disturbing them; how to hold his hand out fingerless and flat so that they could eat apples or sugar off it without nibbling his fingers; how to check crib-biters, and how to persuade nervous horses that they were not really vicious.

313

Hans found that the great thing was always to trust any horse that could be trusted, and to depend on himself for getting swiftly out of the way of those who couldn't. There were border-line horses, of course, who could only be trusted every now and then; but by being very observant, Hans learned which was now and which was then.

Very soon all the well-meaning horses in the stables understood Hans and his small hands were so firm and gentle that they preferred his handling to that of any of the grooms.

It was a long while before Hans was allowed to groom a horse by himself. Fortunately he had watched the grooms for so many hours, and when they were in good-natured moods had asked them such intelligent questions, that he knew all the processes of a horse's toilette before his chance came to put them into practice.

One day he found his favourite groom drunk, at a convenient moment, and only too thankful for Hans's assistance; so the groom went to sleep in a corner of the horse-box, and Hans groomed his first horse. It was a *Lippizaner* and everybody knows what a *Lippizaner* can be made to look like, when he is well-groomed. It was a wonderful affair, and when Hans had finished grooming his horse no bright angel was ever more fit to ornament his corner of paradise; from henceforward, Hans was allowed to groom any horse in the stable.

Hans soon acquired the knack of making each horse in turn understand that what Hans was doing would always be favourable to him.

When a vicious stallion rolled the pupils of his eyes into their sockets, flattened his ears back and bared his teeth, Hans would say: '*Bitte schön! Moment?*' and the instant of malice would pass, the stallion decide *not* to obliterate this very small and polite fellow-creature, who was really only doing his best to make him smart and comfortable; and finally would even allow himself to be washed and hissed over; brushed and curry-combed until he realized that he had become a glory, though he would still have tried to kill any full-grown groom that came near him.

Hans knew very well that you must be careful with a vicious horse. Such a horse has no time to spare in which to learn good manners. He tries to savage anything that moves near him; afflicted by panic, he will take no risks himself, and give others very little chance to escape them. Hans treated such horses with infinite care and gentleness.

314

He would remain out of their reach until they had begun to trust him; and find ways of ministering to their comfort until, little by little, the most savage beast, fenced in by his raw and irritable nerves, began to let down his defences.

All horses, Hans learned, have their own little weaknesses, like all human beings. Nobility is a doubtful commodity and should never, either in men or horses, be too much relied upon.

One horse is afraid of being spoken to suddenly; another does not like to have his head touched; a third feels an irresistible desire to kick out at anything near his heels, but out of his sight.

After all, what are his heels for, Hans asked himself. One must look at it from the horse's point of view. If he wishes to defend himself, he has no teeth near his tail, but heels he has got, and he knows how to use them.

Quiet horses loved having Hans in their loose-boxes; they snuffed him all over with the velvet muzzles, and rested their heavy heads on his shoulders.

Hans could do anything he liked with them, if he went the right way about it; and even if he didn't know the right way at first, the horses would take pains to point it out to him, without any great risk to his existence. Of course Hans got stepped on sometimes by accident, and kicked occasionally on purpose, but you have to take the rough with the smooth in any profession.

It was his heart's desire to be with horses; and when once the heart's desire is gratified, one hardly notices which are kicks and which are ha'pence.

The school closed for the hottest of the summer months, and the horses, after their first three months on the Lounge, were taken back to Styria.

When Hans was thirteen years old, he was allowed to go with them. The grooms camped out in tents, and lived with the horses all day long, riding them gently, and gradually training them to definite tasks of obedience.

Hans rode each horse in turn, so that he might feel sure of himself as well as of any particular horse. 'If I ride only one,' he explained to the grooms, 'he will become too easy and I shall not know if I am a good rider, or only a bad rider riding a good horse.'

Hans rode softly, as if he were on velvet, until to ride became more natural to him than to walk; and until a horse was more like his mother than the summer earth.

It was a wonderful two months, and at the end of it the head of the school said to Hans: 'I thought you would make a good stableman, and even that is rare—but you will make something rarer than that—you have the seat, the hands and the heart of a rider. Now we shall have you trained for the school.'

Hans felt the earth grow unsubstantial under his feet, as if he were treading on light.

He was too young to begin his training, but three years passed in a flash; and every year he rode more, and studied with intensity the separate stages of trick-riding.

The horses began their training at four years old, and their education lasted three years; *Lippizaners* were slower to train, but lived longer than other horses.

The first year their training was general and they were ridden on the snaffle; but the second year their education became more severe, and the work between the pillars took place. This was the moment when the horses chose for themselves what their future speciality was to be. Only those horses that showed a natural disposition towards certain figures were trained in them.

There was no circus training, but a gradual, intensive development along the line of the horse's special talents. Whatever figure he showed a disposition for, became his by right; and although the obedience tests were common to all, no time was wasted in trying to force an unnatural talent upon an animal whose gifts lay in a different direction.

This had been the principle of the Spanish School since the sixteenth century, and the horses were still allowed to practise it, proving that any animal learns what he likes better than what he dislikes, and that force only becomes necessary when common sense breaks down.

The horses were still ridden on the snaffle during their second year, but with the beginning of the third year they had to accustom themselves to a double bridle.

When Hans was eighteen years old, he was given a special horse to train, a *Lippizaner*, a fine young stallion whose name was Emerald.

Emerald showed, from his first three months, an amazing confidence in his teacher. He was a big horse, with muscles like steel springs. He was white from stem to stern, with solid hindquarters and legs as thin as matches. The pink of his skin showed through the satin smoothness of his coat; and as he moved he glistened. Hans kept Emerald's long flowing tail as carefully trimmed as if it had been the coiffure of a court lady.

At the end of the second year horse and man seemed to read each other's mind, so securely did they work together, each prompting and sustaining the other.

With the beginning of the third year Hans had to do a lot of explaining to Emerald about the double bridle, for the great horse, accustomed to his freedom and proud of his docility, could not bear the sense of physical and spiritual restraint. Hans lay awake at night trying to think of ways to make the sense of forced servitude easier for Emerald.

'How can we do the *Levade*,' Hans would murmur into Emerald's ear, before he brought him out of his horse-box, 'if your neck isn't held tight? Think—how you must balance yourself on your hind-quarters, with your four legs held to the spot—and if your neck were loose—where wouldn't we be wobbling off to?—Just consider!' and in the end Hans believed that Emerald grasped that there was some support to be got out of the double bridle's fixed unpleasantness.

When it came to the *Capriole*, months and months were needed before Emerald mastered this incredible school jump.

In the *Capriole*, the leap on the spot has to be a metre high. Emerald must fold his forelegs under him, and kick out his hind legs so that the spectator could see his shoes, the line from hind leg to foreleg should be level; and what a business this was Hans's mother could have explained, because she heard him cry out about it in his sleep night after night. Perhaps Emerald's sleep was disturbed by it too; but *he* could not explain his dreams; Emerald could only learn how to please Hans by understanding the pressure of his knees, listening to his voice, and sweating to keep his restless nerves from slipping beyond his own control.

The last test of a perfectly trained horse is the *Quadrille*, which has to be ridden with faultless accuracy.

When Emerald took his place in it, and never missed a turn or a circle, then Hans knew that the first stage of their work together was over. They had taken the right direction and the rest of it was the same as any other artist's job: to advance along the road to perfection.

When Emerald's third year was completed there was very little that he could not do, with Hans's careful prompting, and he did it all with a passionate good will that almost burst Hans's heart with love and pride.

Sunday was the peak of their existence. Hans's father and mother never missed a performance.

They were allowed in, after all the paying people had taken their seats, and they would rather have missed their weekly *Schnitzel* and *Apfelstrüdel* than not have watched Hans and Emerald riding in their glory.

When Emerald first stepped delicately over the clean ribbed sand, he looked like any other fine horse that knows his manners.

He even moved a little nervously, though it was pride and not fear that inspired his restive carriage. He always kept well within the control of Hans's knees and hands, although sometimes, for the fun of the thing, he pretended to evade it.

When Emerald felt quite sure that nothing alarming or obstructive could interfere with their activities, he slid into the rhythm of the music, with unwavering steadiness.

The trumpets sounded, and one by one the riders approached the great box, which used to be the emperor's, and saluted.

The *Pas de Deux* followed—an intricate and tricky business, dependent on exact timing.

Neither turn nor circle must be interrupted by an impatient movement, and at the end Emerald was so at one with the music that he seemed to float down the length of the school and through the pillars, pacing now this way and now that, through or round the two central pillars, with the exquisite precision of a ballet dancer.

The other horses took their part, each in turn setting to his corner, and spreading out, or drawing together like a fan.

The *Quadrille* followed, in which the four best horses took part. For this figure, the excellence of one horse and rider was not enough; it was a perilous and difficult affair, as hard to correlate as the movements of migrating birds.

318

The music changed, and became more staccato and imperative. This was the moment for each horse to perform his chosen dance.

Emerald could take the *Levade*, but his speciality was the *Capriole*. He left to the other horses *Mezair*, *Courbette* and *Croupade*.

The *Ballotade* Emerald shared with one other horse; or rather they competed, for they had not learned to share, and were in fact highly jealous of each other; so that the breadth of the riding school was always put between them when it came to this performance.

When the *Quadrille* was over, Hans rode Emerald into an empty space. Emerald, his neck arched, his tail spreading, his nostrils crimson and dilating, his great eyes blazing with excitement, began to approach the *Capriole*.

Hans sat on the centre of his back straight as a sword from head to spine, and supple as the bend of a wave.

Once more they swept up towards the royal box; then Emerald, his hind legs arched, raised his forefeet to the height of a dog begging; and, motionless as a frozen leaf, he hung upon the air.

Hans sat light and firm, encouraging Emerald with the steady pressure of his knees, not letting his weight forward be a shade too much, and, above all, not letting Emerald slide too far back.

There was always great applause for the *Capriole*, for indeed it is a fine and moving sight when two fellow creatures master a difficult law by working together in harmony, neither taking precedence or advantage of the other.

Emerald always performed the *Capriole* at least once in each Sunday performance; but he could not always persuade himself to take it on the same spot. Sometimes he would be able to steady his nerves and muscles at the chosen moment before the royal box; but at others he would need the long swinging dance down the side of the school, before the nerve rose up in him, and in a burst of conscientious urgency he felt able to give Hans the final token of his confidence.

Hans never pressed or hurried Emerald. He let the great horse blossom into his act of grace at the time and place which best suited him.

When one of the other riders said to Hans: 'It seems to me you let your horse do what he likes!' Hans answered with pride: 'Yes—but, you see, I have first taught him how to like!'

When all the other horses had swung out in dignified triumph to the

Motionless as a frozen leaf, Emerald hung upon the air.

stables, Emerald was still fresh enough for the greatest feature of the school.

He went out, too, with the other horses; but only to return, on the snaffle, with Hans on his feet beside him, and the long rein lying close across his back, as his only guidance.

This was a nervous business for both of them. Emerald no longer had that sense of confident oneness with his rider; he was not half a horse and half a man any more: he was a horse alone.

Hans too, was forced into a double responsibility; he must neither move one step too fast, nor fall one inch behind; and he must hold back his over-eager friend, without breaking into his memory of their successive figures.

They must move faultlessly together, through altering measures of sound; slip exactly through the pillars, and be ready for the final salute—hooves in air, neck arched, with the spread tail a glory.

When the salute was over, Hans would whisper: '*Fertig!*' Emerald would turn, and side by side they would float down the school together, Hans darting one triumphant glance up towards his parents, who were nearly falling over the sides of the ring with pride and excitement.

Once in the stables, there was such a rubbing down, such splendid drinks and special mashes given to Emerald by Hans, with such praise and inarticulate love, as seldom falls to the lot of any but the best of horses from the best of masters.

But life cannot be lived for long on the peak.

The first break in Hans's unfettered joy was the death of his parents: his mother first, and his father a few months later.

No one would sit in the school again and thrill as violently, when Emerald and Hans rode in—nor would anyone sink back with such depths of gratified exultation when they rode out.

For a time Hans was low-spirited and Emerald felt that something disastrous had occurred, which no amount of carefully executed *Caprioles* could quite put right.

At last Hans's sadness lifted, and a fresh excitement, unlike the old, sober satisfaction of shared living, took its place.

A girl called Lisa Lotte came Sunday after Sunday to the riding school. She was a very pretty girl and felt that the best horse and the best rider were nothing but her due.

She took some trouble, through her eyes and the aimed emphasis of her person, to reach Hans's attention; and in this she succeeded perfectly. Hans thought that he had his audience back again. But this was where he made his mistake. Lisa Lotte was a performer, and not an audience.

She came to the Spanish School regularly for a year, until Hans married her, and then she very quickly stopped coming. She had got what she had gone for, a person who appreciated her charms and would earn her living for her. When you have bought a goose at the market you do not go back again—not, at any rate, for the same goose.

Hans was disappointed when Lisa Lotte ceased to come on Sundays, for he had wanted to share Emerald with his wife; it was easier to talk about a thing you shared.

But Lisa Lotte soon broke him of talking about Emerald. She told him that she never wished to hear about that tiresome horse again.

In spite of this painful shock, Hans loved Lisa Lotte very much. For a month or two after his marriage, he walked as if on light, as he had done when first he knew that he could be a Spanish rider.

All the world blossomed afresh for him, and if he could not share Emerald with Lisa Lotte, he found no difficulty in sharing Lisa Lotte with Emerald.

Emerald responded to Hans's happiness as if it were his own. It was almost a pity there was no one who loved them, to watch them in the school on Sundays; but the head of the school watched them, and all Vienna was proud of Hans and Emerald.

Still all this pride and satisfaction did not bring in any more money, and that was what Lisa Lotte most wanted.

There had to be sets of pink glass, like those her married sister possessed; and then her friend Elizabeth had silver dishes on the sideboard; and above all, Lisa Lotte herself must have more and finer clothes. A new hat can't cost much! Then silver sandals and a dress for dancing; and why not dancing? If Hans was too tired to dance in the evening, after all that stupid horse-riding, Lisa Lotte would find someone who was not tired.

It was very bewildering for Hans, because he had always supposed that marriage meant a very clean house, good food, and great kindness

—with, by and by, children to share it. But none of these things were included in his marriage. No kindness, no sign of a child, badly cooked food, and things swept up into corners.

Finally, at the end of two years there was even less, for Lisa Lotte ran away with an acrobat.

One might have thought this would be a relief to Hans, but unfortunately Hans was not acrobatic. Once fixed, his heart had a way of remaining fixed; and Hans had fixed it upon Lisa Lotte.

Any other horse but Emerald would not have put up with what followed for a moment; for Hans became listless, and even careless. He could not concentrate upon the intricate ardour of his profession. He left more than half of the work to Emerald, and gave him no gratitude for doing it.

Emerald knew well enough that Hans was suffering, and that he must stretch his nerves to take the place of his master's.

One day Hans let him down badly in the *Capriole*; the lovely turn was spoilt by his bad riding, and the audience hissed.

This was a shock to his pride, and it might have helped Hans if he had been in any need of discouragement, but he was already discouraged enough.

'This is the end,' Hans said to himself, as he rode out of the school with drooping head. 'No wonder Lisa Lotte left me! I must have failed her somehow, and now I have failed Emerald; it remains only to fail myself. This I shall do tonight!' and Hans decided to hang himself in the stables. He would have preferred to shoot himself, but that might startle the horses. To hang oneself is quite an easy thing to do in a stable, because there are plenty of strong leather straps about and good places to drop from.

That night Hans did not go home; he did not want to see again those ugly shiftless rooms which had held so short and beautiful a dream. He hid in the stables till all the grooms had gone home, and all the lights but one had been put out.

There was nothing left but the pungent smell of horses, and the quiet. The horses slipped or stirred a little; a hoof pawing in the straw clinked against the bricks beneath or a horse shook its ears and resettled itself; but these were all peaceful sounds that hardly broke the silence.

Hans thought, 'I will just look in at Emerald, before I do it!'

323

Emerald was in a large corner loose-box; he had no bad habits, so he was without restrictions and there was nothing that a horse could have which was not at his disposal.

When the gate of his box slipped back, he turned his head, and looked at his master.

He had forgotten the *Capriole*; perhaps he had never blamed Hans for their failure. When there is guilt, animals feel it, as some sensitive human beings feel thunder. It is a discomfort rather than a fault.

He was glad to see Hans in the middle of the night, and when Hans saw his gladness, the bitter stiffness of his anger unlocked itself within him. He cried with his head pressed against Emerald's glossy neck; and when he had stopped crying he no longer felt that life was a cheat.

It was true Lisa Lotte had cheated Hans; she had taken herself away, and with her all his dreams, but perhaps that was not altogether a disaster. For to live with a cheat is not only to lose one's dreams, but to cripple one's own sense of reality.

Reality was now uncrippled for Hans; all that he had had before Lisa Lotte stirred his heart, was his again.

The bond between him and Emerald was unbreakable. He had been faithful to Emerald for ten years, and faithless only for a moment; but if he had killed himself he would have been as faithless as Lisa Lotte herself, and perhaps more cowardly, for Lisa Lotte hadn't given up living; she had merely decided to live with someone else.

'This will never do,' Hans said out loud, half to himself and half to Emerald. 'What I was thinking of was a *Dummheit*. I can't keep house alone, but why should I? There is my widowed sister at Linz. I will send her a postcard—life can arrange itself differently!'

So he pulled a heap of straw into a corner of Emerald's loose-box, and slept there till morning, better than he had slept since Lisa Lotte left him.

His widowed sister consented very easily to give up a little shop in Linz, that had never paid very well, and to make her brother a home in Vienna instead.

Once more Hans had a clean room, well-cooked food, and kindness; and sometimes—but not very often, because his sister enjoyed cooking more than watching horses dance—his sister would come to the school on a Sunday morning.

Hans thought sometimes: 'It is funny, all my happiness and all my grief were quickly over! What I have now is neither happiness nor grief, but it is enough.'

The years slipped by like snowflakes, without noise or hurry or seeming to take up very much room in the air, until one day the new head of the school said to him: 'Hans, your hair is grey! You are sixteen years older than Emerald. *Lippizaners* retain their vigour and live longer than any other horses, but Emerald must have a younger rider. I do not say you ride less well than you did, in fact there is still no rider in the school to touch you; but the public likes to see a young man on a horse's back. Do not be afraid, you can have all the work you want in the stables, and be well paid for it, but you must stop riding.'

If he had said to Hans: 'Pray eat all you want for dinner, but stop breathing,' Hans would have felt much the same. He made no complaint. He said in fact nothing, but chewed a straw which he had just picked up and stuck in the corner of his mouth, to keep him in countenance.

He felt no different, neither younger nor older—fatter nor thinner—than he had always felt.

This particular blow as not like the loss of Lisa Lotte; nor did suicide again occur to him. Once you had lived through that sharp tearing of a breaking heart, you weren't going to make any more fuss when something else went through the same gap.

Hans went back and tried to eat his dinner, but he could not. He did not tell his sister what had happened. For a week or two he never went near the stables. He had never been sick before, so they allowed Hans a month's sick leave; and then Hans went back to work again, but he did not go to see Emerald. He knew the other grooms would look after him well, and they respected Hans's silence and his grief. None of them spoke to him of Emerald and his new rider.

Nothing in life seemed sensible to Hans any more, but he went on living, and he did his work well, because he thought: 'I was happy once, and for all those years I did what I had always wanted to do. Shall I not then do something that I don't want for the rest of the time, without being happy? Many men are not as lucky as I am even now, for I have work, and it has still to do with horses!'

It was almost a shock when only three months after Hans had given up riding, the head of the school once more approached him and said: 'Hans, it's an odd thing! That horse of yours won't work without you! I've tried him in turn with all the riders. It's not that he can't. He won't! He's waiting to get you back. Anyhow, I have the feeling that that is in his head. There isn't a horse we've got that can touch him. None of them do the *Levade* as he does, and he's the only horse who can do a *Capriole* at all, or the single, long-rein running. Take him into the school this morning, and we'll see what happens.'

Hans trembled all over as one trembles after an accident when one finds out that one is not dead.

He went into Emerald's loose-box and when Emerald felt the touch of his master's hand, he whinnied high and shrill; his ears pricked, and he too shivered and trembled.

Then they rode into the Lounge together. The school was empty except for the head and a curious groom or two; but it was as if every seat was filled, and in their ears the trumpets sounded.

Emerald stepped delicately up the ring. He danced, without the music, but with faultless precision, the *Pas de Deux*. He took the *Levade* next, then he floated through the pillars and set to corners for the *Quadrille*. In the centre of the Lounge he took the *Ballotade*. Then Emerald faced the royal box. They were both trembling still, but the trembling was ecstasy; it did not interfere with what they had to do.

Emerald took his leap for the *Capriole*, folding his forelegs neatly under him, kicking out his hind legs in an unbroken line. Hans sat motionless but supple with once more the unconquered wildness of youth in his heart.

'Well,' said the head of the school, as they came through the doors, 'I suppose the public will have to put up with that grey hair of yours, Hans, after all; for I see it was a mistake to try to break up a pair.'

HOW HEREWARD
WON MARE SWALLOW
Charles Kingsley

The adventures of Hereward, a Saxon living in the fens of eastern England who led a revolt against William the Conqueror, are told in a book called Hereward the Wake. *Charles Kingsley wrote a number of books of stirring adventure. Born at Holne, Devonshire, in 1819, he was at one time professor of modern history at Cambridge.*

On a bench at the door of his high-roofed wooden house sat Dirk Hammerhand, the richest man in Walcheren. From within the house sounded the pleasant noise of slave-women, grinding and chatting at the hand-mill; from without, the pleasant noise of geese and fowls without number. And as he sat and drank his ale, and watched the herd of horses in the fen, he thought himself a happy man, and thanked his Odin and Thor that, owing to his princely supplies of horses to Countess Gertrude, Robert the Frison and his Christian Franks had not yet harried him to the bare walls, as they would probably do ere all was over.

As he looked at the horses, some half a mile off, he saw a strange stir among them. They began whinnying and pawing round a four-footed thing in the midst, which might be a badger, or a wolf—though both were very uncommon in that pleasant isle of Walcheren; but which plainly had no business there. Whereon he took up a mighty staff and strode over the fen to see.

He found neither wolf nor badger: but to his exceeding surprise, a long lean man, clothed in ragged horseskins, whinnying and neighing exactly like a horse, and then stooping to eat grass like one. He advanced to do the first thing which came into his head, namely to break the man's back with his staff, and ask him afterwards who he might be. But ere he could strike, the man or horse kicked up with its hind legs in his face, and then springing on to the said hind legs ran away with extraordinary swiftness some fifty yards; after which it went down on all fours and began grazing again.

'Beest thou man or devil?' cried Dirk, somewhat frightened.

The thing looked up. The face at least was human.

'Art thou a Christian man?' asked it in bad Frisian, intermixed with snorts and neighs.

'What's that to thee?' growled Dirk; and began to wish a little that he was one, having heard that the sign of the cross was of great virtue in driving away fiends.

'Thou art not Christian. Thou believest in Thor and Odin? Then there is hope.'

'Hope of what?' Dirk was growing more and more frightened.

'Of her, my sister! Ah, my sister, can it be that I shall find thee at last, after ten thousand miles, and seven years of woeful wandering?'

'I have no man's sister here. At least, my wife's brother was killed——'

'I speak not of a sister in woman's shape. Mine, alas!—oh woeful prince, oh more woeful princess—eats the herb of the field somewhere in the shape of a mare, as ugly as she was once beautiful, but swifter than the swallow on the wing.'

'I've none such here,' quoth Dirk, thoroughly frightened, and glancing uneasily at mare Swallow.

'You have not? Alas, wretched me! It was prophesied to me by the witch that I should find her in the field of one who worshipped the old gods; for had she come across a holy priest, she had been a woman again, long ago. Whither must I wander afresh!' And the thing began weeping bitterly, and then ate more grass.

'I—that is—thou poor miserable creature,' said Dirk, half pitying, half wishing to turn the subject; 'leave off making a beast of thyself awhile, and tell me who thou art.'

'I have made no beast of myself, most noble earl of the Frisians, for so you doubtless are. I was made a beast of—a horse of, by an enchanter of a certain land, and my sister a mare.'

328

The thing began weeping bitterly, and ate more grass.

'Thou dost not say so!' quoth Dirk, who considered such an event quite possible.

'I was a prince of the county of Alboronia, which lies between Cathay and the Mountains of the Moon, as fair once as I am foul now, and only less fair than my lost sister; and by the enchantments of a cruel magician we became what we are.'

'But thou art not a horse, at all events?'

'Am I not? Thou knowest, then, more of me than I do of myself,' and it ate more grass. 'But hear the rest of my story. My hapless sister was sold away with me to a merchant: but I, breaking loose from him, fled until I bathed in a magic fountain. At once I recovered my man's shape, and was rejoicing therein, when out of the fountain rose a fairy more beautiful than an elf, and smiled upon me with love.

'She asked me my story, and I told it. And when it was told—"Wretch!" she cried, "and coward, who hast deserted thy sister in her need. I would have loved thee, and made thee immortal as myself: but now thou shalt wander ugly and eating grass, clothed in the horse-hide which has just dropped from thy limbs, till thou shalt find thy

329

sister, and bring her to bathe, like thee, in this magic well".'

'All good spirits help us! And you are really a prince?'

'As surely,' cried the thing with a voice of sudden rapture, 'as that mare is my sister;' and he rushed at mare Swallow. 'I see, I see, my mother's eyes, my father's nose——'

'He must have been a chuckle-headed king that, then,' grinned Dirk to himself. 'The mare's nose is as big as a buckbasket. But how can she be a princess, man—prince I mean? She has a foal running by her here.'

'A foal?' said the thing solemnly. 'Let me behold it. Alas, alas, my sister! Thy tyrant's threat has come true, that thou shouldst be his bride whether thou wouldst or not. I see, I see in the features of thy son his hated lineaments.'

'Why he must be as like a horse, then, as your father. But this will not do, Master Horseman; I know that foal's pedigree better than I do my own.'

'Man, man, simple though honest!—Hast thou never heard of the skill of the enchanters of the East? How they transform their victims at night back again into human shape, and by day into the shape of beasts again?'

'Yes—well—I know that——'

'And do you not see how you are deluded? Every night, doubt not, that mare and foal take their human shape again; and every night, perhaps, that foul enchanter visits in your fen, perhaps in your very stable, his wretched bride restored—alas, only for an hour!—into her human shape.'

'An enchanter in my stable? That is an ugly guest. But no. I've been into the stables fifty times, to see if that mare was safe. Mare was mare, and colt was colt, Mr Prince, if I have eyes to see.'

'And what are eyes against enchantments? The moment you opened the door, the spell was cast over them again. You ought to thank your stars that no worse has happened yet; that the enchanter, in fleeing, has not wrung your neck as he went out, or cast a spell on you, which will fire your barns, lame your geese, give your fowls the pip, your horses the glanders, your cattle the murrain, your children St Vitus's dance, your wife the creeping palsy, and yourself the chalf-stones in all your fingers.'

'All saints have mercy on me! If the half of this be true, I will turn Christian. I will send for a priest and be baptized tomorrow!'

'Oh, my sister, my sister! Dost thou not know me? Dost thou answer my caresses with kicks? Or is thy heart, as well as thy body, so enchained by that cruel sorcerer, that thou preferrest to be his, and scornest thine own salvation, leaving me to eat grass till I die?'

'I say, Prince—I say—What would you have a man to do? I bought the mare honestly, and I have kept her well. She can't say aught against me on that score. And whether she be princess or not, I'm loth to part with her.'

'Keep her then, and keep with her the curse of all the saints and angels. Look down, ye holy saints' (and the thing poured out a long string of saints' names), 'and avenge this catholic princess, kept in vile durance by an unbaptized heathen! May his——'

'Don't, don't!' roared Dirk. 'And don't look at me like that' (for he feared the evil eye), 'or I'll brain you with my staff!'

'Fool! If I have lost a horse's figure, I have not lost his swiftness. Ere thou couldst strike, I should have run a mile and back, to curse thee afresh.' And the thing ran round him, and fell on all-fours again, and ate grass.

'Mercy, mercy! And that is more than I ever asked yet of man. But it is hard,' growled he, 'that a man should lose his money, because a rogue sells him a princess in disguise.'

'Then sell her again; sell her, as thou valuest thy life, to the first Christian man thou meetest. And yet no. What matters? Ere a month be over, the seven years' enchantment will have passed; and she will return to her own shape, with her son, and vanish from thy farm, leaving thee to vain repentance; whereby thou wilt both lose thy money, and get her curse. Farewell, and my curse abide with thee!'

And the thing, without another word, ran right away, neighing as it went, leaving Dirk in a state of abject terror.

He went home. He cursed the mare, he cursed the man who sold her, he cursed the day he saw her, he cursed the day he was born. He told his story with exaggerations and confusions in plenty to all in the house; and terror fell on them likewise. No one, that evening, dare go down into the fen to drive the horses up; while Dirk got very drunk, went to bed, and trembled there all night (as did the rest of the household), expecting the enchanter to enter on a flaming fire-drake, at every howl of the wind.

The next morning, as Dirk was going about his business with a doleful face, casting stealthy glances at the fen to see if the mysterious mare was still there, and a chance of his money still left, a man rode up to the door.

He was poorly clothed, with a long rusty sword by his side. A broad felt hat, long boots, and a haversack behind his saddle, showed him to be a traveller, seemingly a horse dealer; for there followed him, tied head and tail, a brace of sorry nags.

'Heaven save all here,' quoth he, making the sign of the cross. 'Can any good Christian give me a drink of milk?'

'Ale, if thou wilt,' said Dirk. 'But what art thou, and whence?'

On any other day, he would have tried to coax his guest into trying a buffet with him for his horse and clothes: but this morning his heart was heavy with the thought of the enchanted mare, and he welcomed the chance of selling her to the stranger.

'We are not very fond of strangers about here, since these Flemings have been harrying our borders. If thou art a spy, it will be worse for thee.'

'I am neither spy nor Fleming: but a poor servant of the Lord Bishop of Utrecht's, buying a pony or two for his lordship's priests. As for these Flemings, may St John Baptist save from them both me and you. Do you know of any man who has horses to sell hereabouts?'

'There are horses in the fen yonder,' quoth Dirk, who knew that churchmen were likely to give a liberal price, and pay in good silver.

'I saw them as I rode up. And a fine lot they are: but of too good a stamp for my short purse, or for my holy master's riding—a fat priest likes a quiet nag, my master.'

'Humph. Well, if quietness is what you need, there is a mare down there that a child might ride with a thread of wool. But as for price—And she has a colt, too, running by her.'

'Ah?' quoth the horseman. 'Well, your Walcheren folk make good milk, that's certain. A colt by her? That's awkward. My lord does not like young horses; and it would be troublesome, too, to take the thing along with me.'

The less anxious the dealer seemed to buy, the more anxious grew

Dirk to sell; but he concealed his anxiety, and let the stranger turn away, thanking him for his drink.

'I say!' he called after him. 'You might look at her, as you ride past the herd.'

The stranger assented; and they went down into the fen, and looked over the precious mare, whose feats were afterwards sung by many an English fireside, or in the forest beneath the hollins green, by such as Robin Hood and his merry men. The ugliest, as well as the swiftest, of mares, she was, say the old chroniclers; and it was not till the stranger had looked twice at her that he forgot her great chuckle-head, greyhound-flanks, and drooping hind-quarters, and began to see the great length of those same quarters, the thighs let down into the hocks, the compact loin, the extraordinary girth through the saddle, the sloping shoulder, the long arms, the flat knees, the large well-set hooves, and all the other points which showed her strength and speed, and justified her fame.

'She might carry a big man like you through the mud,' said he carelessly; 'but as for pace, one cannot expect that with such a chuckle-head. And if one rode her through a town, the boys would call after one, "All head and no tail"—Why, I can't see her tail for her croup, it is so ill set on.'

'Ill set on, or none,' said Dirk, testily, 'don't go to speak against her pace, till you have seen it. Here, lass!'

Dirk was in his heart rather afraid of the princess: but he was comforted when she came up to him like a dog.

'She's as sensible as a woman,' said he; and then grumbled to himself, 'maybe she knows I mean to part with her.'

'Lend me your saddle,' said he to the stranger.

The stranger did so; and Dirk mounting galloped her in a ring. There was no doubt of her powers as soon as she began to move.

'I hope you won't remember this against me, madam,' said Dirk, as soon as he got out of the stranger's hearing. 'I can't do less than sell you to a Christian. And certainly I have been as good a master to you as if I'd known who you were; but if you wish to stay with me, you've only to kick me off, and say so; and I'm yours to command.'

'Well, she can gallop a bit,' said the stranger, as Dirk pulled her up and dismounted: 'but an ugly brute she is, nevertheless, and such an one as I should not care to ride, for I am a gay man among the ladies. However, what is your price?'

Dirk named twice as much as he would have taken.

'Half that, you mean.' And the usual haggle began.

'Tell thee what,' said Dirk at last. 'I am a man who has his fancies; and this shall be her price; half thy bid, and a box on the ear.'

The demon of covetousness had entered Dirk's heart. What if he got the money; brained, or at least disabled the stranger; and so had a chance of selling the mare a second time to some fresh comer?

'Thou art a strange fellow,' quoth the horse dealer. 'But so be it.'

Dirk chuckled. 'He does not know,' thought he, 'that he has to do with Dirk Hammerhand,' and he clenched his fist in anticipation of his rough joke.

'There,' quoth the stranger, counting out the money carefully, 'is thy coin. And there—is thy box on the ear.'

And with a blow which rattled over the fen, he felled Dirk Hammerhand to the ground.

He lay senseless for a moment, and then looked wildly round.

'Villain!' groaned he. 'It was I who was to give the buffet, not thou!'

'Art mad?' asked the stranger, as he coolly picked up the coins, which Dirk had scattered in his fall. 'It is the seller's business to take, and the buyer's to give.'

And while Dirk roared in vain for help, he leapt on Swallow, and rode off shouting.

'Aha! Dirk Hammerhand! So you thought to knock a hole in my skull, as you have done to many a better man than yourself? He must be a luckier man than you, who catches Hereward the Wake asleep. I shall give your love to the Enchanted Prince, my faithful serving man, whom they call Martin Lightfoot.'

Dirk cursed the day he was born. Instead of the mare and colt, he had got the two wretched ponies which the stranger had left, and a face which made him so tender of his own teeth, that he never again offered to try a buffet with a stranger.

A MAN AND HIS HORSE

Zane Grey

Toward evening of a lowering December day, some fifty miles west of Forlorn River, a horseman rode along an old dimly-defined trail. From time to time he halted to study the lay of the land ahead. It was bare, sombre, ridgy desert, covered with dun-coloured greasewood and stunted prickly pear. Distant mountains hemmed in the valley, raising black spurs above the round lomas and the square-walled mesas.

This lonely horseman bestrode a steed of magnificent build, perfectly white except for a dark bar of colour running down the noble head from ears to nose. Sweat-cake dust stained the long flanks. The horse had been running. His mane and tail were laced and knotted to keep their length out of reach of grasping cactus and brush. Clumsy home-made leather shields covered the front of his forelegs and ran up well to his wide breast. What otherwise would have been muscular symmetry of limb was marred by many a scar and many a lump. He was lean, gaunt, worn, a huge machine of muscle and bone, beautiful only in head and mane, a weight-carrier, a horse strong and fierce like the desert that had bred him.

The rider fitted the horse as he fitted the saddle. He was a young man of exceedingly powerful physique, wide-shouldered, long-armed, big-legged. His lean face, where it was not red, blistered and peeling, was the hue of bronze. He had a dark eye, a falcon gaze, roving and keen. His jaw was prominent and set, mastiff-like; his lips were stern. It was youth with its softness not yet quite burned and hardened away that kept the whole cast of his face from being ruthless.

This young man was Dick Gale, but not the listless traveller, nor the lounging wanderer who, two months before, had by chance dropped into Casita. Friendship, chivalry, love—the deep-seated, unplumbed emotions that had been stirred into being with all their incalculable power of spiritual change, had rendered different the meaning of life. In the moment almost of their realization the desert had claimed Gale, and had drawn him into its crucible.

The desert had multiplied weeks into years. Heat, thirst, hunger, loneliness, toil, fear, ferocity, pain—he knew them all. He had felt them all—the white sun, with its glazed, coalescing, lurid fire; the caked split lips and rasping, dry-puffed tongue; the sickening ache in the pit of the stomach; the insupportable silence, the empty space, the utter desolation, the contempt of life; the weary ride, the long climb, the plod in sand, the search, search, search for water; the sleepless night alone, the watch and wait, the dread of ambush, the swift flight; the fierce pursuit of men wild as Bedouins and as fleet, the willingness to deal sudden death, the pain of poison thorn, the stinging tear of lead through flesh; and that strange paradox of the burning desert, the cold at night, the piercing icy wind, the dew that penetrated to the marrow, the numbing desert cold of the dawn.

Beyond any dream of adventure he had ever had, beyond any wild story he had ever read, had been his experience with those hard-riding rangers, Ladd and Lash. Then he had travelled alone the hundred miles of desert between Forlorn River and the Sonoyta Oasis. Ladd's prophecy of trouble on the border had been mild compared to what had become the actuality. With rebel occupancy of the garrison at Casita, outlaws, bandits, raiders in rioting bands had spread westward. Like troops of Arabs, magnificently mounted, they were here, there, everywhere along the line; and if murder and worse were confined to the Mexican side, pillage and raiding were perpetrated across the border.

Many a dark-skinned raider bestrode one of Belding's fast horses; and, indeed, all except his selected white thoroughbreds had been stolen. So the job of the rangers had become more than a patrolling of the boundary line to keep Japanese and Chinese from being smuggled into the United States. Belding kept close at home to protect his family and to hold his property. But the three rangers, in fulfilling their duty, had incurred risks on their own side of the line, had been outraged, robbed, pursued, and injured on the other.

Some of the few waterholes that had to be reached lay far across the border in Mexican territory. Horses had to drink, men had to drink; and Ladd and Lash were not of the stripe that forsook a task because of danger. Slow to wrath at first, as became men who had long lived peaceful lives, they had at length revolted; and desert vultures could have told a gruesome story. Made a comrade and ally of these border-men, Dick Gale had leaped at the desert action and strife with an intensity of heart and a rare physical ability which accounted for the remarkable fact that he had not yet fallen by the way.

On this December afternoon the three rangers, as often, were separated. Lash was far to the westward of Sonoyta, somewhere along Camino del Diablo, that terrible Devil's Road, where many desert wayfarers had perished. Ladd had long been overdue in a prearranged meeting with Gale. The fact that Ladd had not shown up miles west of the Papago Well was significant.

The sun had hidden behind clouds all the latter part of that day—an unusual occurrence for that region even in winter. And now, as the light waned suddenly, telling of the hidden sunset. a cold, dry, penetrating wind sprang up and blew in Gale's face. Not at first but by imperceptible degrees it chilled him. He untied his coat from the back of the saddle and put it on. A few cold drops of rain touched his cheek.

He halted upon the edge of a low escarpment. Below him the narrowing valley showed bare, black ribs of rock, long, winding grey lines leading down to a central floor where mesquite and cactus dotted the barren landscape. Moving objects, diminutive in size, grey and white in colour, arrested Gale's roving sight. They bobbed away for a while, then stopped. They were antelope, and they had seen his horse. When he rode on they started once more, keeping to the lowest level. These wary animals were often desert watchdogs for the ranger;

337

they would betray the proximity of horse or man. With them trotting forward, he made better time for some miles across the valley. When he lost them, caution once more slowed his advance.

The valley sloped up and narrowed, to head into an arroyo where grass began to show grey between the clumps of mesquite. Shadows formed ahead in the hollows, along the walls of the arroyo, under the trees, and they seemed to creep, to rise, to float into a veil cast by the background of bold mountains, at last to claim the skyline. Night was not close at hand; but it was there in the east, lifting upward, drooping downward, encroaching upon the west.

Gale dismounted to lead his horse, to go forward more slowly. He had ridden sixty miles since morning, and he was tired, and a not entirely healed wound in his hip made one leg drag a little. A mile up the arroyo, near its head, lay the Papago Well. The need of water for his horse entailed a risk that otherwise he could have avoided. The well was on Mexican soil. Gale distinguished a faint light flickering through the thin, sharp foliage. Campers were at the well, and, whoever they were, no doubt they had prevented Ladd from meeting Gale. Ladd had gone back to the next waterhole, or maybe he was hiding in an arroyo to the eastward, awaiting developments.

Gale turned his horse, not without urge of iron arm and persuasive speech, for the desert steed scented water, and plodded back to the edge of the arroyo, where in a secluded circle of mesquite he halted. The horse snorted his relief at the removal of the heavy, burdened saddle and accoutrements, and sagging, bent his knees, lowered himself with slow heave, and plunged down to roll in the sand. Gale poured the contents of his larger canteen into his hat and held it to the horse's nose.

'Drink, Sol,' he said.

It was but a drop for a thirsty horse. However, Blanco Sol rubbed a wet muzzle against Gale's hand in appreciation. Gale loved the horse, and was loved in return. They had saved each other's lives, and had spent long days and nights of desert solitude together. Sol had known other masters, though none so kind as this new one; but it was certain that Gale had never before known a horse.

The spot of secluded ground was covered with bunches of galleta grass upon which Sol began to graze. Gale made a long halter of his lariat to keep the horse from wandering in search of water. Next Gale kicked off the cumbersome chapparejos, with their flapping, tripping folds of leather over his feet, and drawing a long rifle from its saddle sheath, he slipped away into the shadows.

The coyotes were howling, not here and there, but in concerted volume at the head of the arroyo. To Dick this was no more reassuring than had been the flickering light of the campfire. The wild desert dogs, with their characteristic insolent curiosity, were baying men round a campfire. Gale proceeded slowly, halting every few steps, careful not to brush against the stiff greasewood. In the soft sand his steps made no sound. The twinkling light vanished occasionally, like a Jack-o'-lantern, and when it did show it seemed still a long way off. Gale was not seeking trouble or inviting danger. Water was the thing that drove him. He must see who these campers were, and then decide how to give Blanco Sol a drink.

A rabbit rustled out of brush at Gale's feet and thumped away over the sand. The wind pattered among dry, broken stalks of dead *ocatilla*. Every little sound brought Gale to a listening pause. The gloom was thickening fast into darkness. It would be a night without starlight. He moved forward up the pale, zigzag aisles between the mesquite. He lost the light for a while, but the coyotes' chorus told him he was approaching the campfire. Presently the light danced through the black branches and soon grew into a flame. Stooping low, with bushy mesquites between him and the fire, Gale advanced. The coyotes were in full cry. Gale heard the tramping, stamping thumps of many hooves. The sound worried him. Foot by foot he advanced, and finally began to crawl. The wind favoured his position, so that neither coyotes nor horses could scent him. The nearer he approached the head of the arroyo, where the well was located, the thicker grew the desert vegetation. At length a dead *palo verde*, with huge black clumps of its parasite mistletoe thick in the branches, marked a distance from the well that Gale considered close enough. Noiselessly he crawled here and there until he secured a favourable position, and then rose to peep from behind his covert.

He saw a bright fire, not a cooking fire, for that would have been low and red, but a crackling blaze of mesquite. Three men were in sight, all close to the burning sticks. They were Mexicans and of the

339

coarse type of raiders, rebels, bandits that Gale had expected to see. One stood up, his back to the fire; another sat with shoulders enveloped in a blanket; and the third lounged in the sand, his feet almost in the blaze. They had cast off belts and weapons. A glint of steel caught Gale's eye. Three short, shiny carbines leaned against a rock. A little to the left, within the circle of light, stood a square house made of adobe bricks. Several untrimmed poles upheld a roof of brush, which was partly fallen in. This house was a Papago Indian habitation, and a month before had been occupied by a family that had been murdered or driven off by a roving band of outlaws. A rude corral showed dimly in the edge of firelight, and from a black mass within came the snort and stamp and whinney of horses.

Gale took in the scene in one quick glance, then sank down at the foot of the mesquite. He had naturally expected to see more men. But the situation was by no means new. This was one, or part of one, of the raider bands harrying the border. They were stealing horses, or driving a herd already stolen. These bands were more numerous than the waterholes of northern Sonora; they never camped long at one place; like Arabs, they roamed over the desert all the way from Nogales to Casita. If Gale had gone peaceably up to this campfire there were a hundred chances that the raiders would kill and rob him to one chance that they might not. If they recognized him as a ranger comrade of Ladd and Lash, if they got a glimpse of Blanco Sol, then Gale would have no chance.

These Mexicans had evidently been at the well some time. Their horses being in the corral meant that grazing had been done by day. Gale revolved questions in mind. Had this trio of outlaws run across Ladd? It was not likely, for in that event they might not have been so comfortable and carefree in camp. Were they waiting for more members of their gang? That was very probable. With Gale, however, the most important consideration was how to get his horse to water. Sol must have a drink if it cost a fight. There was stern reason for Gale to hurry eastward along the trail. He thought it best to go back to where he had left his horse and not make any decisive move until daylight.

With the same noiseless care he had exercised in the advance, Gale retreated until it was safe for him to rise and walk on down the arroyo.

He found Blanco Sol contentedly grazing. A heavy dew was falling, and, as the grass was abundant, the horse did not show the usual restlessness and distress after a dry and exhausting day. Gale carried his saddle, blankets, and bags into the lee of a little greasewood-covered mound, from around which the wind had cut the soil, and here, in a wash, he risked building a small fire. By this time the wind was piercingly cold. Gale's hands were numb, and he moved them to and fro in the little blaze. Then he made coffee in a cup, cooked some slices of bacon on the end of a stick, and took a couple of hard biscuits from a saddlebag. Of these his meal consisted. After that he removed the halter from Blanco Sol, intending to leave him free to graze for a while.

Then Gale returned to his little fire, replenished it with short sticks of dead greasewood and mesquite, and, wrapping his blanket round his shoulders, he sat down to warm himself and to wait till it was time to bring in the horse and tie him up.

The fire was inadequate, and Gale was cold and wet with dew. Hunger and thirst were with him. His bones ached, and there was a dull, deep-seated pain throbbing in his unhealed wound. For days unshaven, his beard seemed like a million pricking needles in his blistered skin. He was so tired that, once having settled himself, he did not move hand or foot. The night was dark, dismal, cloudy, windy, growing colder. A moan of wind in the mesquites was occasionally pierced by the high-keyed yelp of a coyote. There were lulls in which the silence seemed to be a thing of stifling, encroaching substance—a thing that enveloped, buried the desert.

Judged by the great average of ideals and conventional standards of life, Dick Gale was a starved, lonely, suffering, miserable wretch. But in his case the judgement would have hit only externals, would have missed the vital inner truth. For Gale was happy with a kind of strange, wild glory in the privations, the pains, the perils, and the silence and solitude to be endured on this desert land. In the past he had not been of any use to himself or others; and he had never known what it meant to be hungry, cold, tired, lonely. He had never worked for anything. The needs of the day had been provided, and tomorrow and the future looked the same. Danger, peril, toil—these had been words read in books and papers.

In the present he used his hands, his senses, and his wits. He had a duty to a man who relied on his services. He was a comrade, a friend, a valuable ally to riding, fighting rangers. He had spent endless days, weeks that seemed years, alone with a horse, trailing over, climbing over, hunting over a desert that was harsh and hostile by nature, and perilous by the invasion of savage men. That horse had become human to Gale. And with him Gale had learned to know the simple needs of existence. Like dead scales the superficialities, the falsities, the habits that had once meant all of life dropped off, usless things in this stern waste of rock and sand.

Gale's happiness, as far as it concerned the toil and strife, was perhaps a grim and stoical one. But love abided with him, and it had engendered and fostered other undeveloped traits—romance and a feeling for beauty, and a keen observation of nature. He felt pain, but he was never miserable. He felt the solitude, but he was never lonely.

As he rode across the desert, even though keen eyes searched for the moving black dots, the rising puffs of white dust that were warnings, he saw Nell's face in every cloud. The clean-cut mesas took on the shape of her straight profile, with its strong chin and lips, its fine nose and forehead. There was always a glint of gold or touch of red or graceful line or gleam of blue to remind him of her. Then at night her face shone warm and glowing, flushing and paling, in the campfire.

Tonight, as usual, with a keen ear to the wind, Gale listened as one on guard; yet he watched the changing phantom of a sweet face in the embers, and as he watched he thought. The desert developed and multiplied thought. A thousand sweet faces glowed in the pink and white ashes of his campfire, the faces of other sweethearts or wives that had gleamed for other men. Gale was happy in his thought of Nell, for something, when he was alone this way in the wilderness, told him she was near him, she thought of him, she loved him. But there were many men alone on that vast southwestern plateau, and when they saw dream faces, surely for some it was a fleeting flash, a gleam soon gone, like the hope and the name and the happiness that had been and was now no more.

Often Gale thought of those hundreds of desert travellers, prospectors, wanderers who had ventured down the Camino del Diablo, never to be heard of again. Belding had told him of that most terrible of all desert trails—a trial of shifting sands. Lash had traversed it, and brought back stories of buried waterholes, of bones bleaching white in the sun, of gold mines as lost as were the prospectors who had sought them, of the merciless Yaqui and his hatred for the Mexican. Gale thought of this trail and the men who had camped along it. For many there had been one night, one campfire that had been the last. This idea seemed to creep in out of the darkness, the loneliness, the silence, and to find a place in Gale's mind, so that it had strange fascination for him. He knew now as he had never dreamed before how men drifted into the desert, leaving behind graves, wrecked homes, ruined lives, lost wives and sweethearts. And for every wanderer every campfire had a phantom face. Gale measured the agony of these men at their last campfire by the joy and promise he traced in the ruddy heart of his own.

By and by Gale remembered what he was waiting for; and, getting up, he took the halter and went out to find Blanco Sol. It was pitch-dark now, and Gale could not see a rod ahead. He felt his way, and presently as he rounded a mesquite he saw Sol's white shape outlined against the blackness. The horse jumped and wheeled, ready to run. It was doubtful if any one unknown to Sol could ever have caught him. Gale's low call reassured him, and he went on grazing. Gale haltered him in the likeliest patch of grass and returned to his camp. There he lifted his saddle into a protected spot under a low wall of the mound, and, laying one blanket on the sand, he covered himself with the other, and stretched himself for the night.

Here he was out of reach of the wind; but he heard its melancholy moan in the mesquite. There was no other sound. The coyotes had ceased their hungry cries. Gale dropped to sleep, and slept soundly during the first half of the night; and after that he seemed always to be partially awake, aware of increasing cold and damp. The dark mantle turned grey, and then daylight came quickly. The morning was clear and nipping cold. He threw off the wet blanket, and got up cramped and half frozen. A little brisk action was all that was necessary to warm his blood and loosen his muscles, and then he was fresh, tingling, eager. The sun rose in a golden blaze, and the descending valley took on wondrous changing hues. Then he fetched up Blanco Sol, saddled him, and tied him to the thickest clump of mesquite.

'Sol, we'll have a drink pretty soon,' he said, patting the splendid neck.

Gale meant it. He would not eat till he had watered his horse. Sol had gone nearly forty-eight hours without a sufficient drink, and that was long enough, even for a desert-bred beast. No three raiders could keep Gale away from that well. Taking his rifle in hand, he faced up the arroyo. Rabbits were frisking in the short willows, and some were so tame he could have kicked them. Gale walked swiftly for a goodly part of the distance, and then, when he saw blue smoke curling up above the trees, he proceeded slowly, with alert eye and ear. From the lay of the land and position of trees seen by daylight, he found an easier and safer course than the one he had taken in the dark. And by careful work he was enabled to get closer to the well, and somewhat above it.

The Mexicans were leisurely cooking their morning meal. They had two fires, one for warmth, the other to cook over. Gale had an idea these raiders were familiar to him. It seemed all these border hawks resembled one another—being mostly small of build, wiry, angular, swarthy-faced, and black-haired, and they wore the oddly styled Mexican clothes and sombreros. A slow wrath stirred in Gale as he watched the trio. They showed not the slightest indication of breaking camp. One fellow, evidently the leader, packed a gun at his hip, the only weapon in sight. Gale noted this with speculative eyes. The raiders had slept inside the little adobe house, and had not yet brought out the carbines. Next Gale swept his gaze to the corral, in which he saw more than a dozen horses, some of them fine animals. They were stamping and whistling, fighting one another, and pawing the dirt. This was entirely natural behaviour for desert horses penned in when they wanted to get at water and grass.

But suddenly one of the blacks, a big, shaggy fellow, shot up his ears and pointed his nose over the top of the fence. He whistled. Other horses looked in the same direction, and their ears went up, and they, too, whistled. Gale knew that other horses or men, very likely both, were approaching. But the Mexicans did not hear the alarm, or show any interest if they did. These mescal-drinking raiders were not scouts. It was notorious how easily they could be surprised or ambushed. Mostly they were ignorant, thick-skulled peons. They were wonderful horsemen, and could go long without food or water; but they had no other accomplishments or attributes calculated to help them in desert warfare. They had poor sight, poor hearing, poor judgment, and when excited they resembled crazed ants running wild.

Gale saw two Indians on burros come riding up the other side of the knoll upon which the adobe house stood; and apparently they were not aware of the presence of the Mexicans, for they came on up the path. One Indian was a Papago. The other, striking in appearance for other reasons than that he seemed to be about to fall from the burro Gale took to be a Yaqui. These travellers had absolutely nothing for an outfit except a blanket and a half-empty bag. They came over the knoll and down the path toward the well, turned a corner of the house, and completely surprised the raiders.

Gale heard a short, shrill cry, strangely high and wild, and this came from one of the Indians. It was answered by hoarse shouts. Then the leader of the trio, the Mexican who packed a gun, pulled it and fired point-blank. He missed once—and again. At the third shot the Papago shrieked and tumbled off his burro to fall in a heap. The other Indian swayed, as if the taking away of the support lent by his comrade had brought collapse, and with the fourth shot he, too, slipped to the ground.

The reports had frightened the horses in the corral; and the vicious black, crowding the rickety bars, broke them down. He came plunging out. Two of the Mexicans ran for him, catching him by nose and mane, and the third ran to block the gateway.

Then, with a splendid vaulting mount, the Mexican with the gun leaped to the back of the horse. He yelled and waved his gun, and urged the black forward. The manner of all three was savagely jocose. They were having sport. The two on the ground began to dance and jabber. The mounted leader shot again, and then stuck like a leech upon the bare back of the rearing black. It was a vain show of horsemanship. Then this Mexican, by some strange grip, brought the horse down, plunging almost upon the body of the Indian that had fallen last.

Gale stood aghast with his rifle clutched tight. He could not divine the intention of the raider, but suspected something strikingly brutal. The horse answered to that cruel, guiding hand, yet he swerved and bucked. He reared aloft, pawing the air, wildly snorting, then he plunged down upon the prostrate Indian. Even in the act the intelligent animal tried to keep from striking the body with his hooves. But that was not possible. A hideous yell signalled this feat of horsemanship.

345

The Mexican made no move to trample the body of the Papago. He turned the black to ride again over the other Indian. That brought into Gale's mind what he had heard of a Mexican's hate for a Yaqui. It recalled the barbarism of these savage peons, and the war of extermination being waged upon the Yaquis.

Suddenly Gale was horrified to see the Yaqui writhe and raise a feeble hand. The action brought renewed and more savage cries from the Mexicans. The horse snorted in terror.

Gale could bear no more. He took a quick shot at the rider. He missed the moving figure, but hit the horse. There was a bound, a horrid scream, a mighty plunge, then the horse went down, giving the Mexican a stunning fall. Both beast and man lay still.

Gale rushed from his cover to intercept the other raiders before they could reach the house and their weapons. One fellow yelled and ran wildly in the opposite direction; the other stood stricken in h's tracks. Gale ran in close and picked up the gun that had dropped from the raider leader's hand. This fellow had begun to stir, to come out of his stunned condition. Then the frightened horses burst the corral bars, and in a thundering, dust-mantled stream fled up the arroyo.

The fallen raider sat up, mumbling to his saints in one breath, cursing in his next. The other Mexican kept his stand, intimidated by the threatening rifle.

'Go, Greasers! Run!' yelled Gale. Then he yelled it in Spanish. At the point of his rifle he drove the two raiders out of the camp. His next move was to run into the house and fetch out the carbines. With a heavy stone he dismantled each weapon. That done, he set out on a run for his horse. He took the shortest cut down the arroyo, with no concern as to whether or not he would encounter the raiders. Probably such a meeting would be all the worse for them, and they knew it. Blanco Sol heard him coming and whistled a welcome, and when Gale ran up the horse was snorting war. Mounting, Gale rode rapidly back to the scene of the action, and his first thought, when he arrived at the well, was to give Sol a drink and to fill his canteens.

Then Gale led his horse up out of the waterhole, and decided before remounting to have a look at the Indians. The Papago had been shot through the heart, but the Yaqui was still alive. Moreover, he was conscious and staring up at Gale with great, strange, sombre eyes,

346

*Gale could bear no more. He took a quick shot at the Mexican. There was a
bound, a horrid scream, a mighty plunge, then the horse went down . . .*

black as volcanic slag.

'Gringo good—no kill,' he said, in husky whisper.

His speech was not affirmative so much as questioning.

'Yaqui, you're done for,' said Gale, and his words were positive. He was simply speaking aloud his mind.

'Yaqui—no hurt—much,' replied the Indian, and then he spoke a strange word—repeated it again and again.

An instinct of Gale's, or perhaps some suggestion in the husky, thick whisper or dark face, told Gale to reach for his canteen. He lifted the Indian and gave him a drink, and if ever in all his life he saw gratitude in human eyes he saw it then. Then he examined the injured Yaqui, not forgetting for an instant to send wary, fugitive glances on all sides. Gale was not to be surprised. The Indian had three wounds—a bullet hole in his shoulder, a crushed arm, and a badly lacerated leg. What had been the matter with him before being set upon by the raider Gale could not be certain.

The ranger thought rapidly. This Yaqui would live unless left there to die or be murdered by the Mexicans when they, found courage to sneak back to the well. It never occurred to Gale to abandon the poor fellow. That was where his old training, the higher order of human feeling, made impossible the following of any elemental instinct of self-preservation. All the same, Gale knew he multiplied his perils a hundredfold by burdening himself with a crippled Indian. Swiftly he set to work, and with rifle ever under his hand, and shifting glance spared from his task, he bound up the Yaqui's wounds. At the same time he kept keen watch.

The Indians' burros and the horses of the raiders were all out of sight. Time was too valuable for Gale to use any in what might be vain search. Therefore he lifted the Yaqui upon Sol's broad shoulders and climbed into the saddle. At a word Sol dropped his head and started eastward up the trail, walking swiftly, without resentment for his double burden.

Far ahead, between two huge mesas where the trail mounted over a pass, a long line of dust clouds marked the position of the horses that had escaped from the corral. Those that had been stolen would travel straight and true for home, and perhaps would lead the others with them. The raiders were left on the desert without guns or mounts.

Blanco Sol walked or jog-trotted six miles to the hour. At that gait fifty miles would not have wet or turned a hair of his dazzling white coat. Gale, bearing in mind the ever-present possibility of encountering more raiders and of being pursued, saved the strength of the horse. Once out of sight of Papago Well, Gale dismounted and walked beside the horse, steadying with one firm hand the helpless, dangling Yaqui.

The sun cleared the eastern ramparts, and the coolness of morning fled as if before a magic foe. The whole desert changed. The greys wore bright; the mesquites glistened; the cactus took the silver hue of frost, and the rocks gleamed gold and red. Then, as the heat increased, a wind rushed up out of the valley behind Gale, and the hotter the sun blazed down the swifter rushed the wind. The wonderful transparent haze of distance lost its bluish hue for one with tinge of yellow. Flying sand made the peaks dimly outlined.

Gale kept pace with his horse. He bore the twinge of pain that darted through his injured hip at every stride. His eye roved over the wide, smoky prospect, seeking the landmarks he knew. When the wild and bold spurs of No Name Mountains loomed through a rent in flying clouds of sand he felt nearer home. Another hour brought him abreast of a dark, straight shaft rising clear from a beetling escarpment. This was a monument marking the international boundary line. When he had passed it he had his own country under foot. In the heat of midday he halted in the shade of a rock, and, lifting the Yaqui down, gave him a drink. Then, after a long, sweeping survey of the surrounding desert, he removed Sol's saddle and let him roll, and took for himself a welcome rest and a bite to eat.

The Yaqui was tenacious of life. He was still holding his own. For the first time Gale really looked at the Indian to study him. He had a large head nobly cast, and a face that resembled a shrunken mask. It seemed chiselled in the dark-red, volcanic lava of his Sonora wilderness. The Indian's eyes were always black and mystic, but this Yaqui's encompassed all the tragic desolation of the desert. They were fixed on Gale, moved only when he moved. The Indian was short and broad, and his body showed unusual muscular development, although he seemed greatly emaciated from starvation or illness.

Gale resumed his homeward journey. When he got through the pass he faced a great depression, as rough as if millions of gigantic spikes had been driven by the hammer of Thor into a seamed and cracked floor. This was Altar Valley. It was a chaos of arroyos, canyons, rocks, and ridges all mantled with cactus, and at its eastern end it claimed the dry bed of Forlorn River and water, when there was any.

With a wounded, helpless man across the saddle, this stretch of thorny and contorted desert was practically impassable. Yet Gale headed into it unflinchingly. He would carry the Yaqui as far as possible, or until death made the burden no longer a duty. Blanco Sol plodded on over the dragging sand, up and down the steep, loose banks or washes, out on the rocks, and through the rows of white-toothed *choyas*.

The sun sloped westward, bending fiercer heat in vengeful, parting reluctance. The wind slackened. The dust settled. And the bold, forbidding front of No Name Mountains changed to red and gold. Gale held grimly by the side of the tireless, implacable horse, holding the Yaqui on the saddle, taking the brunt of the merciless thorns. In the end it became heart-rending toil. His heavy chaps dragged him down; but he dared not go on without them, for, thick and stiff as they were, the terrible, steel-bayoneted spikes of the *choyas* pierced through to sting his legs.

To the last mile Gale held to Blanco Sol's gait and kept ever-watchful gaze ahead on the trail. Then, with the low, flat houses of Forlorn River shining red in the sunset, Gale flagged and rapidly weakened. The Yaqui slipped out of the saddle and dropped limp in the sand. Gale could not mount his horse. He clutched Sol's long tail and twisted his hand in it and staggered on.

Blanco Sol whistled a piercing blast. He scented cool water and sweet alfalfa hay. Twinkling lights ahead meant rest. The melancholy desert twilight rapidly succeeded the sunset. It accentuated the forlorn loneliness of the grey, winding river of sand and its greyer shores. Night shadows trooped down from the black and looming mountains.

AN APPLE –
A MEASURE OF OATS

Cecilia Dabrowska

The spring comes to this far country of New Zealand from out of the soft, phantom rains of September and the prodigal flames of the sun in Libra.

Burgeoning up out of winter's bitter and frost-seared depths, the lush young crops heel over in the wind and the hand of man can reap the things it has sown. But it is not in the reaping that death lurks in the furrow, but in the planting time of autumn. Then a man in peril might have to snatch his own life out of the harsh, dusty pit of the season, foiling death by word of command.

Coming down through the dew-wet grass towards the ploughed field, Tom Davis whistled gently and continuously to himself and to the three-horse team walking at his shoulder. The knobbed points of the hames bobbed above their silhouettes like the horns of huge snails, while the jingling harness-music clashed all round them, rhythmic with the tread of their giant, feathered hooves.

Immense and curiously protective, the near- and off-side chestnut horses flanked the beautiful bay middle mare. Tom Davis felt the willing strength of them vibrant in the air, and his pride in them was at once a thing fierce and gentle. An old man's wisdom and belief and faith he had put into the training of these ones, when others had forsaken their like for mechanization, leaving behind the jingle of bit-ring and harness, and great hearts that drive a full and valiant pulse.

At the closed gate to the paddock he spoke to the horses, saying, 'Whoa there,' automatically and unnecessarily, because repetition bound, they had stopped a fraction of time before he spoke. He opened the gate and they followed at his call, halting while he closed it— waiting as he hung the three nosebags on the fence and the kit with his own meal in alongside them. They went forward again across the field.

The old man took hold of a coupling-rein and brought them round, arranging them in front of the discs. Not until he spoke and said, 'Whoa back,' did they back, and then each stopped after the requisite number of paces. They waited while he picked up the chains that lay where they had dropped the evening before, and fastened each to the hames; they stood quietly while the long plough-lines were unhooked from the points of the hames.

Tom Davis's hands, bronzed and blunt-fingered, gathered the plough-lines up, genetly shaking and lifting them through the air until one on each side of the three horses was correctly angled from the bit-ring, coming over the great quarters into his fingers in a triangle shape. 'Gidup,' he said, clicking his tongue, and the three threw their weight into the collar as one. Each leaned forward and lifted a great hoof with almost telepathic synchronization, and the discs eased forward, not jerking, but taking hold deep in the dark earth, cutting straight and true behind them.

Somewhere in the middle of the morning they heard the train whistle, shrill as an angry stallion. Turning, Tom Davis saw it coming towards them—the groaning of its wheels was like a living thing in travail. Fleetingly he wished that he had been on the far side of the paddock when it made its sporadic run to the hydro station. The slow, crawling terror dragged its great length up the gradient, coming upon the team from behind, huge wheels grinding in a shuddering frenzy, while the sulphur-tainted smoke eddied across the paddock, wreathing itself about the horses. It smote at their senses with a treble menace, sight, sound and scent. Like things beleaguered they stood uncertain.

The old man tied the reins back tight to the discs and went and stood by them, where they could sense his nearness though they did not look at him. There was a faint tremor among the three that grew to a visible quiver of still-leashed apprehension. The near-side chestnut lifted a tentative hoof and reefed at the bit. The mare swung her head high in a half-circle towards the railwayline—pulling the near-side chestnut's bit askew until he complied and stared likewise. The off-side chestnut leaned into the collar a little and stared apprehensively at all that the blinkered bridle would allow him to see.

'Easy now, easy now,' intoned the familiar voice alongside them, and the near-side chestnut dropped his great fore-hoof again. Some of the loose earth crumbled in, falling against it like a wavelet against a rock. The mare continued to stare ahead when she could no longer see anything, ears pricked against the sound.

When the engine with the curious men in the cab was gone, and the last truck went past with a clanking blur of indifferent wheels, the old man loosed the reins and urged the horses forward again, smiling a little to himself, pleased that there had been others to see the proof of his lore with the team.

He was something rare now, an anachronism on the landscape, but the might of the three had the power to turn eyes for another backward look. The deep solidity of the plough-gashed earth was a fitting thing to take their leviathan stride. They moved with powerful dignity in their vast amplitude of strength—stepping freely with a strong, slinging action.

Tom Davis would watch them as they worked, knowing the satisfaction of an artisan seeing his craft fulfilled. He had been careful in the breaking of the three, careful that they should never learn defiance—believing that no horse knows its own strength until it has resisted and conquered a man, and so they never learned the truth of that.

When they were younger and in training, after the day's work was over, he had sponged their shoulders with a lukewarm solution of salt and water, washing away the sweat-stained collar-marks to prevent galling. Knowing that he had no cause for wariness he could walk behind each of them to adjust an S-hook and keep his mind only on that, or stand level with their great quarters and run a hand down their lower legs, and say, 'Lift up,' and the big hoof would come up easily

353

into his hand and lie across his knee without more than its own weight while he tended the hoof. He would talk to them quietly and his voice reached down into them, infiltrating the pits of their brains— they understood its tone, just as they could read the wind, or be suddenly panicked by the contagion of terror in their kind.

As one who studies these things he knew the indisputable truths about the great horses, and he built his code of rules round those truths. He knew that a horse does not pull by instinct, but through training; that he learns firstly of fear from another's flinching; that if anyone plays a practical joke on him he only feels the torment and does not understand the humour; and when urged he will pull till his great heart breaks and he goes down on his knees, unable to rise again, still willing, still believing that the possessor of the whip-hand comprehends the limits of his endurance. 'No,' the old man thought, saddened, 'there are times when the beasts of God are better creatures than those who have dominion over them.'

When finally it was time for the longer midday break, the sun was at its zenith, its molten fervour filtered by a humid cloud layer. Tom Davis halted the team and went to fetch the three nosebags and the kit from off the fence. He loosened the bridle-straps, slipping the bits from the horses' mouths, and placed the nosebags, filled with chaff and oats, over their heads. He collected his own meal and sat down near them to eat it.

The sea-birds that had followed after him all morning swooped closer in mewling, dark-pinioned flight. He threw the crusts to them, watching them squabble. He looked away at the lowering sky. The clouds lay in a vast grey pall. Leaning over the horizon in mock largesse they taunted the bleak and parching earth. Far away on the mountain range their shadows played in empty buffoonery. The old man said, 'They all reckon it's going to rain, but it won't. About an hour from now that wind will go round to the north-west and it won't rain for weeks. Always does when the clouds lie like that at this time of the year.'

The three flicked an attentive ear towards his voice and continued feeding—the muscles bulging in the sides of their heads. Irregularly they were forced to lower their heads as one or the other sought the gleanings in the bottom of the nosebag by pressing it against the ground and lipping lightly at it. When they had finished they stood, all three of them, staring mutely towards the willow-bordered water-hole in the far corner of the paddock. Spring fed, it was deep and secret and cold, and the fallen feathers from the wild geese lay on its banks in slender gashes of colour like a random guerdon left for some dark genie. There was water there they knew, and out of the heat and burning toil the knowledge of it came to them, cool on the wind, so that they yearned after its thirst-slaking promise.

Tom Davis got up and took off the nosebags, rubbing each head affectionately, and said apologetically, 'No drink for you yet, and not for a while after I get you home. Any man who has seen a horse in trouble with colic isn't going to let it happen to one of his own.' He adjusted the last bit again, and his hands, old, sun-darkened and large-veined, lingered there; his fingers curved, cupping memory, ghost-filled with labours long done. 'No, I never want that trouble on my conscience,' he reflected.

And then as old men do, he became troubled and distracted over the things he had seen, and he said aloud to the three, 'There are people who say animals don't feel pain—they try and fool themselves that life for you is just a sort of blur and it doesn't matter what happens— that you don't understand. None of us really understands pain, but anything that is flesh and blood must feel it, and if animals don't, then the whole of creation is out of order.'

Filled with a kind man's wrath at irreparable damage, the indignation worked in him for a while, and he finished by saying angrily, 'And it's not for any of us to be trying to criticize the works of God.' To him such talk was criticism, a fool's babbling to stifle conscience; a deliberate denial of the might and beauty and perfect sensitivity of an Almighty handiwork. For they were perfect, he knew that. In a strange way all animals were entirely complete in themselves, and into the careless hands of the imperfect their time span is delivered.

The old man walked over to the fence and hung up the nosebags and kit. Then he urged the team on again. The great legs, wide-angled from solid breadth of body, lifted largely and thrust against the earth, straining and powerful. About their hooves the long fetlock hairs creamed in a flurry of endeavour. Trace-chains grinding, swingle-trees lifted, quivering taut, and the discs took their hold of the earth.

He worked the team up the side of the hill, walking alongside the discs, following the crumbling earth that churned darkly beneath the blades in rapid wake. The three breasted the slope with vigorous endeavour, coming into the wind earnestly, benign of expression, ears slightly lopped. Each strong forehand lifted for the next step, great wide knee bent, arched to its zenith, then plunged down in leviathan accord with the other two.

When they had disc'd the whole of the small sloping hillside, Tom Davis spelled the team, and they went down onto the flat that was smooth and level as the back of a hand, and which he knew like his own. A while after that, because he was tired, and because he had never really believed or witnessed such a thing as anyone being thrown off the discs, the old man did as he usually did and climbed into the seat perched above the blades.

In front of him the three pulled steadily, and behind him the seagulls wheeled and settled to earth spasmodically. Sitting there he felt the gentle bumping of the discs, slicing the furrow. Above him the cloud wrack had dispersed in the changing wind. He was pleasurably aware of the relief that riding had given to his aching legs. He looked about him, studying the slow dehydration of the grasses beneath the drought. He calculated that it would last another three weeks. After an hour he spelled the team and then rode on again behind them.

Lulled by the rhythmic stride of the three and the quiet of the land about him, Tom Davis was utterly unprepared for the incredible thing when it happened. Almost he accepted it passively, as one accepts the terrible inconsequence of an evil dream. There was a sudden, wrenching, concerted movement beneath thim and he was flung bodily from the seat, catapulted in a sickeningly rapid parabola—thrown down like any other portion of earth before the still-turning blades winking their steel mockery of the sun.

As he felt himself leave the seat, and the reins slackened in his grasp, the old man called to the three, automatically, and once only, 'Whoa there!' His voice was loud and forceful with surprise and anguish that death should approach him thus. Then he hit the ground, sprawled on the furrow, the breath gone from his lungs and fear in his heart. He lay immobile, gasping, the reins still clenched in his fist.

But the three did hear him. Over the thin cries of the following sea-birds they heard and heeded, and the leviathan thrust of their effort-

356

One of the steel discs touched his forehead with the bare promise of death.

grooved quarters stopped on the instant; each great hoof, caught in midstride, finished that one step, sank into the loose earth with finality and stayed there motionless.

After a long moment Tom Davis looked up. Above him the steel discs made a gleaming row of multiple moons to eternity, and one of them touched his forehead with the bare promise of death. Sprawled on the dusty earth he raised his head, and the blade bit a thin red line on his forehead for his unwariness. He writhed himself away from it and sat up. One booted foot lay between the giant, hairy fetlocks of the middle mare. She eased her weight off one of them and rested it on the point of the hoof. Not a fraction more of the ground in front of the hoof was imprinted by the movement. Like a rock she stood. Incurious, impassive, the three still held his life in their care, and training fettered, they waited motionless for the word of command. For God did not give to these placid ones of cold-blooded lineage a soul wherewith to comprehend the terror sudden death holds for a man with all eternity waiting.

Trembling, the old man trod blindly over the slackened trace-

357

chains, and found his way to their heads. The three stared at him, square blinkered, and now mildly curious. On each in turn he laid a shaking hand, and no words could he find now to say to them. He who had always talked to his horses stood before them numbly. The heat from their great bodies, sweated out in their furnace of toil, glowed against him, easing the cold fright from his bones. He stood there, his head bowed a little, overcome by the strange imponderability that the beasts of God in their mortality can be rewarded only by man for what they do. And the three did not know, would never know, that because they halted to the word of command he had not died beneath the glittering disc knives.

An apple—a measure of oats, the brief pleasure of a small reward, was all he had to offer in return for his life. He was hurtfully conscious of the inability to communicate his reason for gratitude, acutely aware of the impeachable trust that is given to those with dominion over the beasts of the earth.

Tom Davis walked round the team, gratitude welling within him, and gathered up the plough-lines. His hands firmed upon them, steady now, and the three came to attention dutifully. 'Gidup,' he said, and clicked his tongue. The three pressed into their collars, humble and willing, and the discs slashed into the dusty imprint where his body had lain.

AN OLD WAR HORSE

Anna Sewell

Black Beauty was to know many masters in his long life and some were very cruel. But in Jeremiah he found a gentle, understanding friend—and in Captain a fascinating colleague.

My new master's name was Jeremiah Barker, but as every one called him Jerry, I shall do the same. Polly, his wife, was just as good a match as a man could have. She was a plump, trim, tidy little woman, with smooth dark hair, dark eyes, and a merry little mouth. The boy was nearly twelve years old; a tall, frank, good-tempered lad; and little Dorothy (Dolly they called her) was her mother over again, at eight years old.

They were all wonderfully fond of each other; I never knew such a happy, merry family before or since. Jerry had a cab of his own, and two horses, which he drove and attended to himself. His other horse was a tall, white, rather large-boned animal called Captain. He was old now, but when he was young he must have been splendid; he had still a proud way of holding his head and arching his neck; in fact, he was a high-bred, fine-mannered, noble old horse, every inch of him. He told me that in his early youth he went to the Crimean War; he belonged to an officer in the cavalry, and used to lead the regiment; I will tell more of that hereafter.

The next morning, when I was well groomed, Polly and Dolly

359

came into the yard to see me and make friends. Harry had been helping his father since the early morning, and had stated his opinion that I should turn out 'a regular brick'. Polly brought me a slice of apple, and Dolly a piece of bread, and made as much of me as if I had been the 'Black Beauty' of olden time. It was a great treat to be petted again, and talked to in a gentle voice, and I let them see as well as I could that I wished to be friendly. Polly thought I was very handsome, and a great deal too good for a cab, if it was not for the broken knees.

'Of course, there's no one to tell us whose fault that was,' said Jerry, 'and as long as I don't know I shall give him the benefit of the doubt; for a firmer neater stepper I never rode; we'll call him 'Jack', after the old one; shall we, Polly?'

'Do,' she said, 'for I like to keep a good name going.'

Captain went out in the cab all the morning. Harry came in after school to feed me and give me water. In the afternoon I was put into the cab. Jerry took as much pains to see if the collar and bridle fitted comfortably as if he had been John Manly over again. When the crupper was let out a hole or two, it all fitted well. There was no bearing rein—no curb—nothing but a plain ring snaffle. What a blessing that was!

After driving through the side street we came to the large cabstand where Jerry had said 'Good-night'. On one side of this wide street were high houses with wonderful shop fronts, and on the other was an old church and churchyard surrounded by iron palisades. Alongside these iron rails a number of cabs were drawn up, waiting for passengers; bits of hay were lying about on the ground; some of the men were standing together, some were sitting on their boxes reading the newspaper, and one or two were feeding their horses with bits of hay and a drink of water. We pulled up in the rank at the back of the last cab. Two or three men came round and began to look at me and pass their remarks.

'Very good for a funeral,' said one.

'Too smart-looking,' said another, shaking his head in a very wise way; 'you'll find out something wrong one of these fine mornings, or my name isn't Jones.'

'Well,' said Jerry pleasantly, 'I suppose I need not find it out till it finds me out; eh? and if so, I'll keep up my spirits a little longer.'

Then came up a broad-faced man, dressed in a great grey coat with great grey capes, and great white buttons, a grey hat, and a blue comforter loosely tied round his neck; his hair was grey too, but he was a jolly-looking fellow, and the other men made way for him. He looked me all over as if he had been going to buy me; and then straightening himself up with a grunt, he said, 'He's the right sort for you, Jerry; I don't care what you gave for him, he'll be worth it.' Thus my character was established on the stand.

This man's name was Grant, but he was called 'Grey Grant', or 'Governor Grant'. He had been the longest on that stand of any of the men, and he took it upon himself to settle matters, and stop disputes. He was generally a good-humoured, sensible man; but if his temper was a little out, as it was sometimes when he had drunk too much, nobody liked to come too near his fist, for he could deal a very heavy blow.

The first week of my life as a cab horse was very trying; I had never been used to London, and the noise, the hurry, the crowds of horses, carts, and carriages that I had to make my way through, made me feel anxious and harassed; but I soon found that I could perfectly trust my driver, and then I made myself easy, and got used to it.

Jerry was as good a driver as I had ever known; and, what was better, he took as much thought for his horses as he did for himself. He soon found out that I was willing to work, and do my best; and he never laid the whip on me unless it was gently drawing the end of it over my back when I was to go on; but generally I knew this quite well by the way in which he took up the reins; and I believe his whip was more frequently stuck up by his side than in his hand.

In a short time I and my master understood each other as well as horse and man can do. In the stable, too, he did all that he could for our comfort. The stalls were the old-fashioned style, too much on the slope; but he had two movable bars fixed across the back of our stalls, so that at night, and when we were resting, he just took off our halters and put up the bars, and thus we could turn about and stand whichever way we pleased, which is a great comfort.

Jerry kept us very clean, and gave us as much change of food as he could, and always plenty of it; and not only that, but he always gave us plenty of clean fresh water, which he allowed to stand by us both night and day, except, of course, when we came in warm. Some people say that a horse ought not to drink all he likes; but I know if we are allowed to drink when we want it, we drink only a little at a time, and it does us a great deal more good than swallowing down half a bucketful at a time, because we have been left without till we are thirsty and miserable. Some grooms will go home to their beer and leave us for hours with our dry hay and oats and nothing to moisten them; then, of course, we gulp down too much at once, which helps to spoil our breathing and sometimes chills our stomachs.

But the best thing that we had here was our Sundays for rest; we worked so hard in the week that I do not think we could have kept up to it but for that day; besides, we had then time to enjoy each other's company. It was on these days that I learned my companion's history.

Captain had been broken in and trained for an army horse; his first owner was an officer of cavalry going out to the Crimean War. He said he quite enjoyed the training with all the other horses, trotting together, turning together, to the right hand or to the left, halting at the word of command, or dashing forward at full speed at the sound of the trumpet, or signal of the officer. He was, when young, a dark, dappled iron-grey, and considered very handsome. His master, a young, high-spirited gentleman, was very fond of him, and treated him from the first with the greatest care and kindness. He told me he thought the life of an army horse was very pleasant; but when he came to being sent abroad, over the sea in a great ship, he almost changed his mind.

'That part of it,' said he, 'was dreadful! Of course we could not walk off the land into the ship, so they were obliged to put strong straps under our bodies, and then we were lifted off our legs in spite of our struggles, and were swung through the air over the water to the deck of the great vessel. There we were placed in small close stalls, and never for a long time saw the sky, or were able to stretch our legs. The ship sometimes rolled about in high winds, and we were knocked about, and felt bad enough. However, at last it came to an end, and we were hauled up and swung over again to the land; we were very glad, and snorted, and neighed for joy when we once more felt firm ground under our feet.

362

'We soon found that the country we had come to was very different to our own, and that we had many hardships to endure besides the fighting; but many of the men were so fond of their horses that they did everything they could to make them comfortable, in spite of snow, wet, and all things out of order.'

'But what about the fighting?' said I. 'Was not that worse than anything else?'

'Well,' said he, 'I hardly know; we always liked to hear the trumpet sound, and to be called out, and were impatient to start off, though sometimes we had to stand for hours waiting for the word of command; and when the word was given, we used to spring forward as gaily and eagerly as if there were no cannon balls, bayonets or bullets. I believe so long as we felt our rider firm in the saddle, and his hand steady on the bridle, not one of us gave way to fear, not even when the terrible bombshells whirled through the air and burst into a thousand pieces.

'I, with my noble master, went into many actions together without a wound; and though I saw horses shot down with bullets, pierced through with lances, and gashed with fearful sabre-cuts; though we left them dead on the field, or dying in the agony of their wounds, I don't think I feared for myself. My master's cheery voice, as he encouraged his men, made me feel as if he and I could not be killed. I had such perfect trust in him that whilst he was guiding me I was ready to charge up to the very cannon's mouth. I saw many brave men cut down, many fall mortally wounded from their saddles. I had heard the cries and groans of the dying, I had cantered over ground slippery with blood, and frequently had to turn aside to avoid trampling on wounded man or horse; but, until one dreadful day, I had never felt terror; that day I shall never forget.'

Here old Captain paused for a while and drew a long breath. I waited, and he went on:

'It was one autumn morning, and, as usual, an hour before daybreak our cavalry had turned out, ready caparisoned for the day's work, whether it might be fighting or waiting. The men stood by their horses waiting, ready for orders. As the light increased there seemed to be some excitement among the officers; and before the day was well begun we heard the firing of the enemy's guns.

'Then one of the officers rode up and gave the word for the men to mount, and in a second every man was in his saddle, and every horse stood expecting the touch of the rein or the pressure of his rider's heels, all animated, all eager; but still we had been trained so well, that, except by the champing of our bits, and the restive tossing of our heads from time to time, it could not be said that we stirred.

'My dear master and I were at the head of the line, and as all sat motionless and watchful, he took a little stray lock of my mane which had turned over on the wrong side, laid it over on the right, and smoothed it down with his hand; then patting my neck, he said, 'We shall have a day of it today, Bayard, my beauty; but we'll do our duty as we have done.' He stroked my neck that morning, more, I think, than he had ever done before; quietly on and on, as if he were thinking of something else. I loved to feel his hand on my neck, and arched my crest proudly and happily; but I stood very still, for I knew all his moods, and when he liked me to be quiet and when gay.

'I cannot tell all that happened on that day, but I will tell of the last charge that we made together: it was across a valley right in front of the enemy's cannon. By this time we were well used to the roar of heavy guns, the rattle of musket fire, and the flying of shot near us; but never had I been under such a fire as we rode through on that day. From the right, from the left, and from the front, shot and shell poured in upon us. Many a brave man went down, many a horse fell, flinging his rider to the earth; many horse without a rider ran wildly out of the ranks: then terrified at being alone with no hand to guide him, came pressing in amongst his old campanions, to gallop with them to the charge.

'Fearful as it was, no one stopped, no one turned back. Every moment the ranks were thinned, but as our comrades fell we closed in to keep them together; and instead of being shaken or staggered in our pace, our gallop became faster and faster as we neared the cannon, all clouded in white smoke, while the red fire flashed through it.

'My master, my dear master, was cheering on his comrades, his right arm raised on high, when one of the balls, whizzing close to my head, struck him. I felt him stagger with the shock, though he uttered no cry. I tried to check my speed, but the sword dropped from his right hand, the rein fell loose from the left, and sinking backward from the

'One of the balls struck my master. I felt him stagger with the shock . . .'

saddle he fell to the earth; the other riders swept past us, and by the force of their charge I was driven from the spot where he fell.

'I wanted to keep my place by his side and not leave him under the rush of horses' feet, but it was in vain; and now, without a master or a friend, I was alone on that great slaughter ground; then fear took hold on me and I trembled as I had never trembled before; and I too, as I had seen other horses do, tried to join in the ranks and gallop with them; but I was beaten off by the swords of the soldiers. Just then a soldier, whose horse had been killed under him, caught at my bridle and mounted me; and with this new master I was again going forward. But our gallant company was cruelly overpowered, and those who remained alive after the fierce fight for the guns came galloping back over the same ground. Some of the horses had been so badly wounded that they could scarcely move from the loss of blood; other noble creatures were trying on three legs to drag themselves along, and others were struggling to rise on their forefeet, when their hind legs had been shattered by shot. Their groans were piteous to hear, and the beseeching look in their eyes as those who escaped passed by, and left them to their fate, I shall never forget. After the battle the wounded men were brought in, and the dead buried.'

'And what about the wounded horses?' I said. 'Were they left to die?'

'No, the army farriers went over the field with their pistols and shot all that were ruined; some that had only slight wounds were brought back and attended to, but the greater part of the noble willing creatures that went out that morning never came back! In our stables there was only about one in four that returned.

'I never saw my dear master again. I believe he fell dead from the saddle. I never loved any other master so well. I went into many other engagements, but was only once wounded, and then not seriously; and when the war was over I came back again to England, as sound and strong as when I went out.'

I said, 'I have heard people talk about war as if it was a very fine thing.'

'Ah!' said he, 'I should think they never saw it. No doubt it is very fine when there is no enemy, when it is just exercise and parade, and sham-fight. Yes, it is very fine then; but when thousands of good brave men and horses are killed, or crippled for life, it has a very different look.'

'Do you know what they fought about?' said I.

'No,' he said, 'that is more than a horse can understand, but the enemy must have been awfully wicked people if it was right to go all that way over the sea on purpose to kill them.'

THIEF IN THE NIGHT

Helen Griffiths

The bay mare, Candyfloss, raised her head with pricked ears. The darkness of the stable enveloped her but her eyes gleamed as a strange desire rose within her. Outside, calling softly to her, was a stallion and she was eager to answer his call.

Candyfloss belónged to an Englishman called Ridgeway, who owned a small ranch several miles north of the Coronado *estancia*. She was an English cob, a sturdy, friendly creature with four fine foals to her credit. She loved her master and was obedient to him but her first natural instincts caused her to obey the stallion's demands and so she listened to him and made her reply.

She struggled to free herself from the head-rope but to no avail. She backed away and tugged hard; she reared up, but the rope remained firm. The eager snuffles of the stallion outside urged her to make more effort and frantically she dragged the rope this way and that. The block at the end bumped against the wooden manger with crashes that resounded through the stillness of the night and the stallion grew afraid at the noise.

He hesitated before calling again to her and then trotted away. She

It was midnight when the stallion returned to the hut and the roan was expecting him. They greeted one another in a careless manner and it did not take the stallion long to tear through the rough rope which tied her. Unwillingly she trotted away from her master and unwillingly she accepted his command . . .

In the morning the young gaucho examined the chewed-up rope with rising anger. He examined the many hoofprints which surrounded his home and cursed with violence. Then he went back into the hut and searched round until he found the rifle he was looking for. It was old and dirty, but it was with grim pleasure that he set about cleaning it. The job done, he set out to follow the trail of hoofprints leading across the vast pampa in search of a thief who had stolen his friend . . . There was black revenge in the heart of one Pascuel Jerez.

In this manner, Pampa, the chestnut stallion, gradually collected together a small band of mares. They grazed contentedly on the flat, endless grassland, filling their bellies with the tall green grass, sunning themselves beneath azure skies, growing sleek and strong, carefree and wild.

Pampa, his restless cravings satisfied, watched over them anxiously. Engraved upon his mind were many memories: memories that brought fear to his heart when in the distance he espied a horse and rider; memories that made him cunning and watchful; memories which, added to his instinctive knowledge, made him a fine protector for his dependent mares.

But the stallion was not eager to linger long in the district he knew so well. He was too near to mankind to rest contented and much to his mares' displeasure he insisted on wandering farther afield.

They travelled in a northerly direction, towards warmer skies and more undulating land, with scrubby bushes and trees to break the monotony of the skyline. For several months they grazed without sighting a single person and gradually the stallion's fears subsided as contentment overtook him . . .

The chestnut stallion was perturbed. He and his mares had dwelt in the district for several months, becoming increasingly aware of another stallion who inhabited the same area. This knowledge both angered and excited him for he knew that there was room for only one leader. But Pampa never saw his adversary and he grew restless thinking about him.

The winter passed slowly. It was warmer in the north and the horses had no problems. Only the two percherons were discontented; they did not get on well with the mustangs. They stood together on the outside of the herd, defying Pampa to molest them, and moodily passed their days, staring longingly at the horizon as if some better life called them from afar.

Pampa hazed the two mares day after day but they ignored him. Eventually he left them alone but he was anxious. The other stallion was an enemy and Pampa hated him.

As the spring days advanced Pampa became conscious of new feelings rising within him. He became aggressive and ugly-tempered and the knowledge that somewhere he had a possible rival forever rancoured in his mind. The wind blew to him all news of the other's whereabouts, but he kept himself well hidden, and Pampa never met him.

He first saw his adversary one afternoon in late spring. His mares were dozing but for him there was no rest. Only the occasional squawk of an overhead bird broke the silence and the bright sun, burning in an azure sky, shone down on their sleek, fat hides.

Pampa stirred suddenly, detecting a warning note in the bird's cry. He stared across the plain as he heard a low nicker. There was his rival at last—a big, black, well-muscled creature intently watching the now wakened mares, seemingly ignorant of the chestnut's presence. He trotted forward and was soon in among them, nuzzling and grunting.

The mares were confused and half afraid. The newcomer was enticing them away, dividing their affections, stealing them under the very eyes of their protector.

Suddenly Pampa shot forward, nostrils distended, eyes showing white with rage. He skidded to a halt a few yards from the intruder, stamping his hoof, snorting heavily.

The black stallion transferred his gaze from the mares to the young chestnut. He was of a strong, regal appearance with several deep scars on his flanks and shoulders. His muzzle and eyebrows were turning grey and he was a good many years older than his challenger. He was

Ricardo Coronado's black thoroughbred, Tarquin.

Pampa challenged the black and Tarquin surveyed him with mild contempt. The chestnut was arrogant, with the confidence of a youngster and too sure of success. Tarquin felt only the confidence of one who has been victorious in a hundred similar battles. He had no fear or excitement, only rising anger and eager desire.

The chestnut squealed and tossed his shaggy head, hesitant now that the issue had come. He stamped his hoof again then flung himself at the aggravating black, his teeth bared, his ears flat against his skull. Tarquin sprang aside, his eyes alight with anger, then wheeled sharply to follow his opponent. He ripped a chunk of flesh from Pampa's withers and reared over him, a fearful whirlwind of flesh and fury.

Pampa retreated from the flailing hooves, renewing his attack with a scream of rage. He grabbed a mouthful of black mane and then a torn black ear. Tarquin whirled sharply from his grasp, tearing at the chestnut's thickly muscled neck. He reared up again and Pampa shrank from his threatening hooves. He could not dodge the striking blows.

Beaten and disconcerted he fled, pursued closely by the other. He slowed to make a final stand but thought better of it and redoubled his pace.

Tarquin grew weary of the chase and turned back to the mares he had won, wielding his authority over the interested but unconcerned mares.

For several days Pampa followed the herd. The black stallion ignored him until he drew too close then chased him off again. But the chestnut soon tired of this new manner of living and eventually he accepted the facts and left the mares alone . . .

Meanwhile, Pascuel Jerez, the young gaucho, bought himself a pony and for several months covered the vast trackless countryside looking for his roan mare. Sometimes he made good progress, on other days he would lose all sign of his quarry, but he did not despair. He had his gun, his knife and his poncho and even if he had to cross the whole of the pampa he was determined to regain his mare.

By early spring he had travelled far. The northern country was new to him but he had high hopes of success. The pony he rode was a filly and he knew that if any stallion existed in this district he would be

Pampa flung himself at the black, his teeth bared . . .

tempted to come close and reveal himself.

At night he hobbled her and let her roam a wide range, watching eagerly for his 'bait' to attract the prey.

Soon Pascuel became aware of a young chestnut stallion who, though interested, kept his distance. He followed them during the day, stopping when they stopped, curious but wary.

Pascuel was disappointed. This stallion could have no mares of his own and therefore was not the beast he was searching. He seemed well acquainted with humans, however, and the gaucho was curious. His filly was nervous and excited at the nearness of the stallion but Pascuel was not satisfied.

His rifle was loaded, ready to shoot. All he had to do was release the catch and pull the trigger. But he was not sure; he could not shoot until he was sure.

On the third morning after his meeting with the stallion Pascuel reached a decision. He would catch the chestnut and see what happened from there.

Pampa grew suspicious when those he was trailing turned in his direction. For several minutes he watched the filly approach, torn between two desires: a desire to flee and a desire to touch her and rub noses.

He stood his ground. Pascuel called to him and noticed how quickly the stallion pricked and flattened his ears.

'You're no more a bronc than I am,' he thought, as, halting his filly, he looked the chestnut over. 'My, you've been in a battle! There *must* be another stallion around here. You couldn't have got those cuts falling over your shadow.'

The stallion grew restless at the closeness of the stranger and the sound of his voice. But the young filly called him and he did not back away.

Suddenly Pascuel acted. Pampa was not quick enough to dodge the noose as the gaucho, standing in his stirrups, circled it over him. For a moment he struggled then stood defiantly surveying his captor as he was drawn close.

'You're acquainted with ropes then? That's just as well because you'll know this one pretty well before I've finished with you,' Pascuel muttered, and he slipped from the filly's back, tied her reins to a tussock of grass, and mounted the stallion. Pampa trembled as he felt the pressure of the man's knees against him. He gave a wild buck and sprang forward. Pascuel did not want to check him, even if he could have done so. He clung to the stallion's back as he raced over the ground, puzzled and amazed. This was more than he had expected, hoped for, and he was thrilled.

Suddenly Pampa skidded to a halt. He flung his head up high, distended his wide, pink nostrils, and nickered deep in his throat. There was a rise in the ground ahead of him and Pascuel experienced some of his mount's eagerness as, firmly and deliberately, the chestnut mounted the slope.

Pascuel gave a gasp of triumphant surprise as he saw the mares lift their heads at the sudden appearance of the solitary horse and rider on the ridge. Immediately, Black Tarquin began rounding them up.

He recognized his roan mare at once. She no longer wore a bridle round her head, Pampa had torn that off long since, but she recognized his piercing whistle and faltered in her stride as she heard it. She turned, looked back at her master who called her name, and with ears forward, staring right at him, she trotted up her side of the rise.

Pampa lunged forward to meet her. Pascuel sprang from his back and bounded down the hill. The chestnut halted and watched uncertainly as they met. It was not for him that she had left the herd. Now was his chance to escape. The man had forgotten about him.

He wheeled away and cantered back the way he had come. He heard a shout. Pascuel was chasing after him. The roan mare was fast and the stallion's escape but a half-hearted affair. He was conscious of the trailing rope; he was afraid of it.

He swerved away as the mare drew level with him but Pascuel, leaning forward, grabbed the lasso. Pampa did not stop. The gaucho had to loose the rope or be dragged from the roan. He was not perturbed. Round his waist was wound his *boleadoras*, a kind of sling made of three balls attached to leather thongs tied in a star shape. He unwrapped it, swung it in a wide arc, and sent it spinning after the galloping horse. It entangled his hind legs and he turned a somersault as he crashed to the ground.

By the time Pampa had scrambled up the gaucho had reached him. He fashioned the rope into a halter and, relying on his roan mare to

375

follow him, mounted the stallion. The chestnut was stunned or he might have protested. Instead he allowed the gaucho to guide him back to where he had left the filly tied to the tuft of grass.

Pascuel decided to continue riding the filly on the return journey as he could rope the stallion to his saddle and trust the roan to keep up with them. He did not start back that day but made camp and settled himself for the night. He looked at his rifle, then at his mare. He smiled. He had known all along that he would not use it, now he could afford to admit it. He hobbled the chestnut and the filly but left the roan loose. She would not run away and he doubted if the black stallion would try to regain her.

He examined the stallion with some disappointment. His white knees were ugly and scarred, spoiling his otherwise handsome appearance. He had no idea what to do with him. That he belonged to someone was obvious, but Pascuel was not particularly worried about finding the owner. He did not want the horse so he decided to sell him at the earliest opportunity.

'I don't suppose I'll get much for you,' he told the stallion. 'Still, you didn't cost me anything.'

With this he made himself comfortable beside the flickering campfire, rolled himself into his poncho and, using his saddle as a pillow, fell asleep . . .

DRUMMERBOY AND THE GYPSY

Fiona Citroen

Drummerboy hated horse-boxes. And he particularly disliked this one because he was receiving such rough treatment from one of his travelling companions, an Irish mare. She had grown very restless and was furiously kicking and biting the horses around her.

Drummerboy was one of a number of horses and ponies that Madge and Tom had bought at an auction in a nearby town. It had been a long day and it was dark as they drove back to Applegate Stables with their purchases in the horse-box behind.

The Irish mare's bad manners so affected the other horses that they too became excited and caused the whole box to lurch dangerously and Tom was forced to pull over to the side of the road. While he and Madge were trying to sort out the trouble, Drummerboy made his escape. Drummerboy had been the mount of one of the leading international riders but his jumping career had ended when he strained his front tendons and never regained his old form. Since then he had worked in a riding school and Madge had thought he would be an asset to Applegate. But now, frightened and excited, he threw up his head and jerked the halter rope from Tom's hand and then thundered away into the dusk.

Madge wanted to go after him but Tom dissuaded her. 'We will never catch him now, it's too dark,' he said. 'Anyway, we can't just leave the others standing here. We'll bring the horse-box out first thing in the morning and organize a proper search.' Madge realized that this was the best course of action and dejectedly they loaded the problem mare back into the horse-box, separating her from the other horses with a barricade, and drove off, leaving the little roan pony alone in the darkness.

At first Drummerboy thought only of putting as much distance as possible between himself and the hateful horse-box, and its equally hateful inmates. He galloped noisily along the tarmac road, sparks of fire erupting from his steel shoes, and his mane blowing free in the night wind. Once he saw a car and swerved to avoid the yellow head-lights that blazed like a tiger's eyes out of the black and silver shadows. Once he ducked, terrified, as a huge owl blundered out of the dark hedgerow.

Then, slowly, the hot fear left him and he slowed to a walk. The warmth of the day had long since gone with the setting sun, and cold little breezes whipped about his damp coat, making him shiver. The pony halted, and dropped his head. He felt lost and frightened, and missed his warm stable at Covercote, with its deep golden straw and oat–filled manger.

For a time, he just stood dejectedly in the blustery, wide roadway, but then instinct slowly took over, and he stumbled towards a large hawthorn bush that loomed against the dark sky. Once enveloped in its thick, prickly branches, the pony felt both safer and less windblown and, pressing himself yet deeper into the leafy greens, he settled down to sleep.

He was still there when Billy Hackett came whistling down the lane on his way to school. Billy Hackett was a gypsy boy with black curly hair, and equally black eyes, which were as bright and as quick as those of a thrush. He hated school, but the council man was always coming to the camp and making trouble if the children there didn't attend, so his father insisted on his going. Not that he ever learned anything, he thought with a grin. Still, he was almost old enough to leave now, and soon he'd be saying goodbye to the rotten dump for ever. He was thinking happily about this when he saw the roan pony.

As Billy approached the animal his whole face lit up with joy. If there was one thing he loved best in all the world it was horses. His father did not keep them any more, nor did any of the other gypsies. The piebald ponies that had once been their pride and joy had been exchanged for cars, and now even the caravans were motorized. Instead of horse dealing, they now dealt in scrap and spare engine parts. But Billy was a throwback to the old type of Romany. He had horse fever in his blood.

'Whoa, my lad! Whoa there, my feller!' he whispered, laying a sunburnt hand on Drummerboy's neck. 'We're going to be friends, you and me.' The pony snorted and arched his neck. Here was a human at last, and humans meant warm blankets and sweet hay; he was sick of a night of fending for himself. Billy, seeing how willing he was, quickly slipped his belt around the roan's neck. Once again he patted him, and noticed how the animal's coat stared with cold, and he saw the torn skin where the Irish mare had sunk her teeth. 'Poor old feller,' he said. 'We'd better get you home and patched up. You shouldn't be wandering around in that condition.'

Billy turned and began to walk back to camp with the pony following him like a large and bumbling puppy. The gypsy camp was situated in a field just off the main road. There were no painted caravans, camp-fires and Spanish-looking girls in swirling scarlet dresses. This modern gypsy camp looked more like a breaker's yard, with shabby metal caravans dotted among the rusting bodies and innards of old cars and lorries. A few grubby babies played among the rubbish, and in a corner women were doing their washing in an old oil drum.

Billy carefully avoided the women, one of whom was his mother and, skirting round huge piles of tawny copper wire, he led the pony towards a strikingly painted caravan which stood out like a bright flower from among the peeling cream-coloured trailers that surrounded it. He knocked on the door, and waited.

It was answered by his great-grandmother, a gypsy of the old school, who still wore the long flannel petticoats and delicately crocheted shawl that were so much associated with her people. 'What have you got there?' she asked, peering intently at the pony. 'Stolen him, have you? Good boy!'

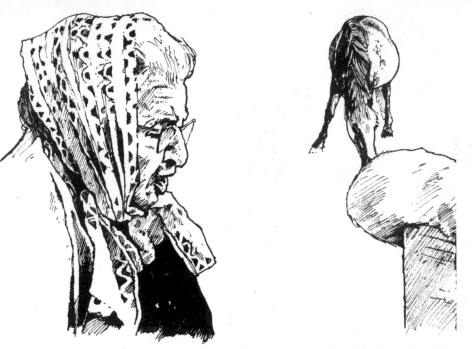

'What have you got there?' asked the old gypsy,

Billy looked embarrassed. His great-grandmother had funny ideas on honesty. 'I didn't steal him, I found him,' he said.

The old lady chuckled. 'Found, stole, it's all the same.' She suddenly glanced up sharply, her face hawk-like with its hooked nose and glittering eyes. 'You didn't take him from another Romany, did you? If you steal from a Brother, you're cursed.'

'I keep trying to tell you,' her great-grandson sighed, 'I found him up by the Luckton Road. He's been pretty badly knocked around somewhere, and I thought you might be able to doctor him.'

'Oh, aye, aye. I can do that still. I may be old, but my hands haven't lost their cunning. Now, bring the animal round to the back, out of sight. We don't want your father to see.'

When Billy arrived with the pony, the old lady was waiting for him with a bottle of evil-smelling liquid. 'What's that?' asked the boy.

'Never you mind. It's my own special recipe for putting life into horses, or into anyone else for that matter.' She took a swig at the bottle and Billy watched fascinated as the green, treacly brew bubbled down her throat. 'Now that you're satisfied that it's not poison,'

peering intently at the pony. 'Stolen him, have you?'

went on his great-grandmother sarcastically, wiping her lips, 'perhaps you'll open the animal's mouth so I can give him some.'

Drummerboy was too far gone to object, and soon he was dosed and lying down gratefully on a pile of old flock mattresses and sacks. 'Just leave him there for a while,' said the old gypsy. 'I've put some ointment on his cuts, and within the hour he'll be as good as new again.'

The boy settled down beside the pony, determined to keep an eye on him until he had completely recovered. He was still sitting there, dreamily stroking Drummerboy's forelock, when his father appeared.

Norman Hackett was a giant of a man, dark faced and blue jowled. 'What's that horse doing here?' he roared in a voice that made his son tremble. Billy started to explain how he'd found the pony, but the tall gypsy cut him short. 'You get that animal away from here now, this minute. I don't want no trouble with the police. Parish council's always looking for an excuse to move us on, and horse stealing would just suit their book nicely.'

'But I didn't steal him,' Billy yelled back in desperation. 'Anyhow, I can't turn him loose to wander round the roads.'

Norman Hackett, who was not really the hard man he liked to make out, wavered. 'Well, in that case you'd better take him down the local nick. They'll look after him until his owner turns up.'

His son cheered up considerably at this suggestion. 'Perhaps, if nobody claims him, they'll let me keep him,' he said, urging the pony to get to its feet. 'They do that if you find money, or dogs.'

'You can put that idea right out of your mind,' scowled his father. 'We ain't got no room here for horses.' And with that depressing information he stamped off, leaving his son staring mutionously after him.

'Billy!' It was his great-grandmother calling. She poked her head out of the caravan door and, after assuring herself the coast was clear, beckoned him with a crooked talon of a fingernail. 'Come in here, boy! I've something to show you.' Billy knew better than to disobey the fierce old lady and, tying Drummerboy to a car bumper, he climbed the steps and entered the caravan.

His great-grandmother was hunched over an old carved chest, from which she drew a bundle, wrapped in dirty newspaper. With almost religious respect she slowly unwrapped the crumpled yellow folds until she held in her weather-beaten hands the most beautiful bridle that Billy had ever seen.

'It was your great-grandfather's,' she said, stroking the soft leather straps and the gleaming silver bit. 'He was a real king of the Romanies, who never owned less than thirty or forty horses at a time. This was made for his favourite stallion just before he rode him in the Ballydoyle races.' Her eyes misted over as she remembered the wild days of her youth.

'He had a bet with my father that day, and if the stallion won the race I would be allowed to marry him. Of course, the stallion did win and Jem came galloping back to my father's caravan, swept me up on the back of that big bay horse, and off we rode.'

Billy shuffled his feet uncomfortably. He wasn't very keen on romance. In fact, he would much rather have heard the story of how his hard-riding ancestor had actually won the race. Great-grandmother had told him the tale once before—of galloping rivals into the rails, foul play on the starting line, and the gouging of one jockey's eyes with another's whip handle.

The old lady sensed that his attention was wandering, and she thrust the bridle into the boy's arms with a snort of annoyance. 'Now you look after it, do you hear! One scratch on that leather and the ghost of Jem Hackett will come back to haunt you, and he was a terrible violent man. On the other hand, treat it well and it will bring you luck.'

Billy could hardly stammer enough thanks. 'Can I try it on the roan pony?' he asked.

'Of course,' answered the old lady. 'That's what it's for. You weren't thinking of wearing it around your own neck, were you?'

They went out into the sunlight and, after some adjustment, managed to fit the well oiled straps to Drummerboy's small head. 'There, it fits perfectly!' Billy said. Then he sighed. 'But I don't know why I'm getting pleased about it—I won't even have a pony tomorrow!'

His great-grandmother gave a wicked chuckle. 'That's up to you, my boy, but I know what Jem would have done. Once he'd put his mark on a horse, that horse was his, even if he had to cross the Irish Sea to keep it. That's the trouble with you youngsters . . . you've no proper respect for the law of nature. Remember, finders is keepers!' And with that, she scuttled back into her caravan like a rheumatic black beetle.

Billy would have given the old lady's last remark some consideration, but just then his father appeared, bellowing like a wounded animal. 'Ain't you on your way yet? Do you want me to give you the end of my belt as a going away present?'

The boy didn't wait to hear any more, as with one easy movement he gathered the reins, leapt on to the pony's back, and was off at a canter out of the camp.

Young Billy Hackett had learned to ride in the days before the car had ousted horses from the gypsy camp. He had a strong natural seat and good balance, so that when the roan pony put in a couple of cat-like bucks, he merely dug his knees in harder. This annoyed Drummerboy and he started to gallop along the roadside verge. But Billy let him . . . he was enjoying himself! A little way down the road from the gypsy caravans was a bridle-path which cut across country, roughly in the direction of Luckton. Luckton was where Billy was supposed to be heading, containing as it did the county police station. Therefore, he turned on to the grassy track without any stir of conscience.

help but, every time he tried to move, the pony began to struggle again. So he contented himself by yelling as loudly as he could for help, until his voice finally gave out.

Evening came, and with it the gnats. They fluttered in a haze over the pool, and the gypsy boy had just resigned himself to drowning or being bitten to death by invading insects, when suddenly from overhead he heard the bark of a dog. At first, he thought his ears were playing tricks but then, twisting his face painfully to look upwards, he saw a large black Labrador hovering on the edge of the quarry.

In a voice shaking with emotion, Billy called to the dog. To his utter delight, it scrambled down towards him, panting and grinning like an excited child. The dog obviously regarded the whole thing as a huge joke. When it reached the boy, it fell upon him in delight, wriggling so much that Billy was hard put to get hold of its fat black body. At last, he managed to grab the dog's collar, but how was he to get a message back to its master? Then he remembered the exercise book.

It was in his back pocket, and was supposed to have been handed in that day for a history essay to be marked. Billy pulled the book out and tore off the last page. He held the squirming dog between his knees and, with the stub of a pencil, he quickly wrote his message for help, and tied it firmly to the dog's collar.

'Off you go, then! And for heaven's sake find your owner,' he said, giving the Labrador a hefty whack on the rump to speed it on its way. The dog needed no second bidding. In a trice it was off, climbing up the quarry side, and kicking about a ton of chalk dust back into Billy's face. But he hardly noticed. He was too busy swatting insects, which was another use he had found for his invaluable school book.

The Labrador's owner, when at last he arrived, turned out to be a slim, military-looking man with a bristling ginger moustache. He took charge right away. 'Soon have you out of there,' he said briskly and, thanks to the fact that besides being very competent he was also a retired air vice-marshal, his words were soon proved correct.

In less than half an hour, an RAF rescue helicopter was lowering its winch, first to take up the astonished gypsy boy, and then to raise the equally astonished roan pony. After that, everything happened in a kind of hazy whirl of cocoa, blankets, Land-Rovers, trailers and a lot of military orders laced with rough kindness.

Billy and Drummerboy were whisked off to the vice-marshal's palatial home on the edge of the moors, and there they were housed in luxury that neither thought really existed. It was in these pleasant surroundings that Billy at last had to face the police. The ordeal didn't turn out too badly, for they accepted the story that he had been on his way to the police station when the pony had fallen. When they left, however, Billy didn't feel any happier, for they had gone to fetch his father, and he knew for certain that Ned Hackett would never accept such a feeble tale; he'd soon realize that the chalk quarry was nowhere near the bridle-path to Luckton.

He was saved, surprisingly enough, by the arrival of Madge Summers when she came to collect Drummerboy. She received such a glowing report of the young gypsy's courage from the air vice-marshal that she was determined to thank him herself. Billy was a little embarrassed by this, seeing that the whole thing was his fault anyway, and he spoke modestly. But this only served to impress the girl even more, so that by the end of the interview, Billy found himself being offered a job at Applegate stables.

Billy jumped at it. For not only would it mean that he could be near his beloved pony, but it would also provide an escape from his father's wrath.

And so the young gypsy boy joined the staff of Applegate, and a good worker he proved to be.

THE LAST OF THE TROUBADOURS

O. Henry

The real name of this famous American writer was William Sydney Porter. Some of his funniest and wittiest stories were collected and published in 1904, six years before his death in 1910. Porter's stories were renowned both for their wit and surprise endings, and this selection is no exception.

Inexorably Sam Galloway saddled his pony. He was going away from the Rancho Altito at the end of a three-month visit. It is not to be expected that a guest should put up with wheat coffee and biscuits yellow-streaked with saleratus for longer than that. Nick Napoleon, the big Negro cook, had never been able to make good biscuits. Once before, when Nick was cooking at the Willow Ranch, Sam had been forced to fly from his cuisine, after only a six-week sojourn.

On Sam's face was an expression of sorrow, deepened with regret and slightly tempered by the patient forgiveness of a connoisseur who cannot be understood. But very firmly and deliberately he buckled his saddle-cinches, looped his stake-rope and hung it to his saddle-horn, tied his slicker and coat on the cantle, and looped his quirt on his right wrist. The Merrydews (householders of the Rancho Altito), men, women, children, and servants, vassals, visitors, employees, dogs, and casual callers were grouped in the 'gallery' of the ranch-house, all with faces set to the tune of melancholy and grief. For, as the coming of Sam Galloway to any ranch, camp, or cabin between the rivers Frio and Bravo del Norte aroused joy, so his departure caused mourning.

388

And then, during absolute silence, except for the bumping of a hind elbow of a hound dog as he pursued a wicked flea, Sam tenderly and carefully tied his guitar across his saddle on top of his slicker and coat. The guitar was in a green duck bag; and if you catch the significance of it, it explains Sam.

Sam Galloway was the last of the troubadours. Of course you know about the troubadours. The encyclopedia says they flourished between the eleventh and the thirteenth centuries. What they flourished doesn't seem clear—you may be pretty sure it wasn't a sword; maybe it was a fiddlebow, or a forkful of spaghetti, or a lady's scarf. Anyhow, Sam Galloway was one of 'em.

Sam put on a martyred expression as he mounted his pony. But the expression on his face was hilarious compared with the one on his pony's. You see, a pony gets to know his rider mighty well, and it is not unlikely that cow ponies in pastures and at hitching racks had often guyed Sam's pony for being ridden by a guitar player instead of a rollicking, cussing, all-wool cowboy. No man is a hero to his saddle-horse. And even an escalator in a department store might be excused for tripping up a troubadour.

Oh, I know I'm one; and so are you. You remember the stories you memorize and the card tricks you study and that little piece on the piano—how does it go?—ti-tum-te-tum-ti-tum—those little Arabian Ten-Minute Entertainments that you furnish when you go up to call on your rich Aunt Jane. You should know that *omnes personae in tres partes divisae sunt*, namely: barons, troubadours, and workers. Barons have no inclination to read such folderol as this; and workers have no time: so I know you must be a troubadour, and that you will understand Sam Galloway. Whether we sing, act, dance, write, lecture, or paint, we are only troubadours; so let us make the worst of it.

The pony with the Dante Alighieri face, guided by the pressure of Sam's knees, bore that wandering minstrel sixteen miles south-eastward. Nature was in her most benignant mood. League after league of delicate, sweet flowerets made fragrant the gently undulating prairie. The east wind tempered the spring warmth; wool-white clouds flying in from the Mexican Gulf hindered the direct rays of the April sun. Sam sang songs as he rode. Under his pony's bridle he had tucked some sprigs of chaparral to keep away the deer flies. Thus crowned, the long-

389

faced quadruped looked more Dantesque than before, and, judging by his countenance, seemed to think of Beatrice.

Straight as topography permitted, Sam rode to the sheep ranch of old man Ellison. A visit to a sheep ranch seemed to him desirable just then. There had been too many people, too much noise, argument, competition, confusion, at Rancho Altito. He had never conferred upon old man Ellison the favour of sojourning at his ranch; but he knew he would be welcome. The troubadour is his own passport everywhere. The workers in the castle let down the drawbridge to him, and the baron sets him at his left hand at table in the banquet hall. There ladies smile upon him and applaud his songs and stories, while the workers bring boars' heads and flagons. If the baron nods once or twice in his carved oaken chair, he does not do it maliciously.

Old man Ellison welcomed the troubadour flatteringly. He had often heard praises of Sam Galloway from other ranchmen who had been complimented by his visits, but had never aspired to such an honour for his own humble barony. I say barony because old man Ellison was the last of the barons. Of course, Bulwer-Lytton lived too early to know him, or he wouldn't have conferred that soubriquet upon Warwick. In life it is the duty and the function of the baron to provide work for the workers and lodging and shelter for the various troubadours.

Old man Ellison was a shrunken old man, with a short, yellow-white beard and a face lined and seamed by past-and-gone smiles. His ranch was a little two-room box house in a grove of hackberry trees in the lonesomest part of the sheep country. His household consisted of a Kiowa Indian man cook, four hounds, a pet sheep, and a half-tamed coyote chained to a fence-post. He owned 3,000 sheep, which he ran on two sections of leased land and many thousands of acres neither leased nor owned. Three or four times a year someone who spoke his language would ride up to his gate and exchange a few bald ideas with him. Those were red-letter days to old man Ellison. Then in what illuminated, embossed, and gorgeously decorated capitals must have been written the day on which a troubadour—a troubadour who, according to the encyclopedia, should have flourished between the eleventh and the thirteenth centuries—drew rein at the gates of his baronial castle!

Old man Ellison's smiles came back and filled his wrinkles when he saw Sam. He hurried out of the house in his shuffling, limping way to greet him.

'Hello, Mr Ellison,' called Sam cheerfully. 'Thought I'd drop over and see you awhile. Notice you've had fine rains on your range. They ought to make good grazing for your spring lambs.'

'Well, well, well,' said old man Ellison. 'I'm mighty glad to see you, Sam. I never thought you'd take the trouble to ride over to as out-of-the-way an old ranch as this. But you're mighty welcome. 'Light. I've got a sack of new oats in the kitchen—shall I bring out a feed for your hoss?'

'Oats for him?' said Sam derisively. 'No, sir-ee. He's as fat as a pig now on grass. He don't get rode enough to keep him in condition. I'll just turn him in the horse pasture with a drag rope on if you don't mind.'

I am positive that never during the eleventh and thirteenth centuries did baron, troubadour, and worker amalgamate as harmoniously as their parallels did that evening at old man Ellison's sheep ranch. The Kiowa's biscuits were light and tasty and his coffee strong. Ineradicable hospitality and appreciation glowed on old man Ellison's weather-tanned face. As for the troubadour, he said to himself that he had stumbled upon pleasant places indeed. A well-cooked, abundant meal, a host whom his lighest attempt to entertain seemed to delight far beyond the merits of the exertion, and the reposeful atmosphere that his sensitive soul at that time craved united to confer upon him a satisfaction and luxurious ease that he had seldom found on his tours of the ranches.

After the delectable supper, Sam untied the green duck bag and took out his guitar. Not by way of payment, mind you—neither Sam Galloway nor any other of the true troubadours are lineal descendants of the late Tommy Tucker. You have read of Tommy Tucker in the works of the esteemed but often obscure Mother Goose. Tommy Tucker sang for his supper. No true troubadour would do that. He would have his supper, and then sing for art's sake.

Sam Galloway's repertoire comprised about fifty funny stories and between thirty and forty songs. He by no means stopped there. He could talk through twenty cigarettes on any topic that you brought up.

391

And he never sat up when he could lie down; and never stood when he could sit. I am strongly disposed to linger with him, for I am drawing a portrait as well as a blunt pencil and a tattered thesaurus will allow.

I wish you could have seen him: he was small and tough and inactive beyond the power of imagination to conceive. He wore an ultramarine-blue woollen shirt laced down the front with a pearl-grey, exaggerated sort of shoe-string, indestructible brown duck clothes, inevitable high-heeled boots with Mexican spurs, and a Mexican straw sombrero.

That evening Sam and old man Ellison dragged their chairs out under the hackberry trees. They lighted cigarettes; and the troubadour gaily touched his guitar. Many of the songs he sang were the weird, melancholy, minor-keyed *canciones* that he had learned from the Mexican sheep herders and *vaqueros*. One, in particular, charmed and soothed the soul of the lonely baron. It was a favourite song of the sheep herders, beginning '*Huile, huile, palomita*', which being translated means, 'Fly, fly, little dove'. Sam sang it for old man Ellison many times that evening.

The troubadour stayed on at the old man's ranch. There was peace and quiet and appreciation there, such as he had not found in the noisy camps of the cattle kings. No audience in the world could have crowned the work of poet, musician, or artist with more worshipful and un-flagging approval than that bestowed upon his efforts by old man Ellison. No visit by a royal personage to a humble woodchopper or peasant could have been received with more flattering thankfulness and joy.

On a cool, canvas-covered cot in the shade of the hackberry trees Sam Galloway passed the greater part of his time. There he rolled his brown paper cigarettes, read such tedious literature as the ranch afforded, and added to his repertoire of improvisations that he played so expertly on his guitar. To him, as a slave ministering to a great lord, the Kiowa brought cool water from the red jar hanging under the brush shelter, and food when he called for it. The prairie zephyrs fanned him mildly; mocking-birds at morn and eve competed with but scarce equalled the sweet melodies of his lyre; a perfumed stillness seemed to fill all his world.

While old man Ellison was pottering among his flocks of sheep on his mile-an-hour pony, and while the Kiowa took his siesta in the burning sunshine at the end of the kitchen, Sam would lie on his cot thinking what a happy world he lived in, and how kind it is to the ones whose mission in life it is to give entertainment and pleasure. Here he had food and lodging as good as he had ever longed for; absolute immunity from care of exertion or strife; an endless welcome, and a host whose delight in the sixteenth repetition of a song or a story was as keen as at its initial giving. Was there ever a troubadour of old who struck upon as royal a castle in his wanderings? While he lay thus, mediating upon his blessings, little brown cottontails would shyly frolic through the yard; a covey of white-topknotted blue quail would run past, in single file, twenty yards away; a *paisano* bird, out hunting for tarantulas, would hop upon the fence and salute him with sweeping flourishes of its long tail. In the eighty-acre horse pasture the pony with the Dantesque face grew fat and almost smiling. The troubadour was at the end of his wanderings.

Old man Ellison was his own *vaciero*. That means that he supplied his sheep camps with wood, water, and rations by his own labours instead of hiring a *vaciero*. On small ranches it is often done. One morning he started for the camp of Incarnación Felipe de la Cruz y Monte Piedras (one of his sheep herders) with the week's usual rations of brown beans, coffee, meal, and sugar. Two miles away on the trail from old Fort Ewing, he met, face to face, a terrible being called King James, mounted on a fiery, prancing, Kentucky-bred horse.

King James's real name was James King; but people reversed it because it seemed to fit him better, and also because it seemed to please his majesty. King James was the biggest cattleman between the Alamo plaza in San Antone and Bill Hopper's saloon in Brownsville. Also he was the loudest and most offensive bully and braggart and bad man in south-west Texas. And he always made good whenever he bragged; and the more noise he made the more dangerous he was. In the story papers it is always the quiet, mild-mannered man with light-blue eyes and a low voice who turns out to be really dangerous; but in real life and in this story such is not the case. Give me my choice between assaulting a large, loud-mouthed rough-houser and an inoffensive stranger with blue eyes sitting quietly in a corner, and you will see something doing in the corner every time.

King James, as I intended to say earlier, was a fierce, two-hundred-

393

'*I'm putting up a wire fence, forty by sixty miles,*' said King James, '*and if there's a sheep inside of it when it's done it'll be a dead one.*'

394

pound, sunburned, blond man, as pink as an October strawberry, and with two horizontal slits under shaggy red eyebrows for eyes. On that day he wore a flannel shirt that was tan-coloured, with the exception of certain large areas which were darkened by transudations due to the summer sun. There seemed to be other clothing and garnishings about him, such as brown duck trousers stuffed into immense boots, and red handkerchiefs and revolvers; and a shotgun laid across his saddle and a leather belt with millions of cartridges shining in it—but your mind skidded off such accessories; what held your gaze was just the two little horizontal slits that he used for eyes.

This was the man that old man Ellison met on the trail; and when you count up in the baron's favour that he was sixty-five and weighed ninety-eight pounds and had heard of King James's record, and that he (the baron) had a hankering for the *vita simplex* and had no gun with him and wouldn't have used it if he had, you can't censure him if I tell you that the smiles with which the troubadour had filled his wrinkles went out of them and left them plain wrinkles again. But he was not the kind of baron that flies from danger. He reined in the mile-an-hour pony (no difficult feat) and saluted the formidable monarch.

King James expressed himself with royal directness.

'You're that old snoozer that's running sheep on this range, ain't you?' said he. 'What right have you got to do it? Do you own any land, or lease any?'

'I have two sections leased from the state,' said old man Ellison mildly.

'Not by no means you haven't,' said King James. 'Your lease expired yesterday; and I had a man at the land office on the minute to take it up. You don't control a foot of grass in Texas. You sheep men have got to git. Your time's up. It's a cattle country, and there ain't any room in it for snoozers. This range you've got your sheep on is mine. I'm putting up a wire fence, forty by sixty miles; and if there's a sheep inside of it when it's done it'll be a dead one. I'll give you a week to move yours away. If they ain't gone by then, I'll send six men over here with Winchesters to make mutton out of the whole lot. And if I find you here at the same time this is what you'll get.'

King James patted the breech of his shotgun warningly.

Old man Ellison rode on to the camp of Incarnación. He sighed many times, and the wrinkles in his face grew deeper. Rumours that the old order was about to change had reached him before. The end of free grass was in sight. Other troubles, too, had been accumulating upon his shoulders. His flocks were decreasing instead of growing; the price of wool was declining at every clip; even Bradshaw, the storekeeper at Frio City, at whose store he bought his ranch supplies, was dunning him for his last six months' bill and threatening to cut him off. And so this last greatest calamity suddenly dealt out to him by the terrible King James was a crusher.

When the old man got back to the ranch at sunset he found Sam Galloway lying on his cot, propped against a roll of blankets and wool sacks, fingering his guitar.

'Hello, Uncle Ben,' the troubadour called cheerfully. 'You rolled in early this evening. I been trying a new twist on the Spanish fandango today. I just about got it. Here's how she goes—listen.'

'That's fine, that's mighty fine,' said old man Ellison, sitting on the kitchen step and rubbing his white, Scotch-terrier whiskers. 'I reckon you've got all the musicians beat east and west, Sam, as far as the roads are cut out.'

'Oh, I don't know,' said Sam reflectively. 'But I certainly do get there on variations. I guess I can handle anything in five flats about as well as any of 'em. But you look kind of fagged out, Uncle Ben— ain't you feeling right well this evening?'

'Little tired; that's all, Sam. If you ain't played yourself out, let's have that Mexican piece that starts off with "*Huile, huile, palomita.*" It seems that that song always kind of soothes and comforts me after I've been riding far or anything bothers me.'

'Why, *seguramente, senor*,' said Sam. 'I'll hit her up for you as often as you like. And before I forget about it, Uncle Ben, you want to jerk Bradshaw up about them last hams he sent us. They're just a little bit strong.'

A man sixty-five years old, living on a sheep ranch and beset by a complication of disasters, cannot successfully and continuously dissemble. Moreover, a troubadour has eyes quick to see unhappiness in others around him—because it disturbs his own ease. So, on the next day, Sam again questioned the old man about his air of sadness and abstraction. Then old man Ellison told him the story of King James's threats and orders and that pale melancholy and red ruin appeared to have marked him for their own. The troubadour took the news thoughtfully. He had heard much about King James.

On the third day of the seven days of grace allowed him by the autocrat of the range, old man Ellison drove his buckboard to Frio City to fetch some necessary supplies for the ranch. Bradshaw was hard but not implacable. He divided the old man's order by two, and let him have a little more time. One article secured was a new fine ham for the pleasure of the troubadour.

Five miles out of Frio City on his way home the old man met King James riding into town. His majesty could never look anything but fierce and menacing, but today his slits of eyes appeared to be a little wider than they usually were.

'Good day,' said the king gruffly. 'I've been wanting to see you. I hear it said by a cowman from Sandy yesterday that you was from Jackson County, Mississippi, originally. I want to know if that's a fact.'

'Born there,' said old man Ellison, 'and raised there till I was twenty-one.'

'This man says.' went on King James, 'that he thinks you was related to the Jackson County Reeveses. Was he right?'

'Aunt Caroline Reeves,' said the old man, 'was my half-sister.'

'She was my aunt,' said King James. 'I run away from home when I was sixteen. Now let's re-talk over some things that we discussed a few days ago. They call me a bad man; and they're only half right. There's plenty of room in my pasture for your bunch of sheep and their increase for a long time to come. Aunt Caroline used to cut out sheep in cake dough and bake 'em for me. You keep your sheep where they are, and use all the range you want. How's your finances?' The old man related his woes in detail, dignifiedly, with restraint and candour.

'She used to smuggle extra grub into my school basket—I'm speaking of Aunt Caroline,' said King James. 'I'm going over to Frio City today, and I'll ride back by your ranch tomorrow. I'll draw two thousand dollars out of the bank there and bring it over to you; and I'll tell Bradshaw to let you have everything you want on credit. You are bound to have heard the old saying at home, that the Jackson County Reeveses and Kings would stick closer by each other than chestnut burrs. Well, I'm a King yet whenever I run across a Reeves. So you look out for me along about sundown tomorrow, and don't worry about nothing. Shouldn't wonder if the dry spell don't kill out the young grass.'

Old man Ellison drove happily ranchward. Once more the smiles filled out his wrinkles. Very suddenly, by the magic of kinship and the good that lies somewhere in all hearts, his troubles had been removed.

On reaching the ranch he found that Sam Galloway was not there. His guitar hung by its buckskin string to a hackberry limb, moaning as the gulf breeze blew across its masterless strings.

The Kiowa endeavoured to explain. 'Sam, he catch pony,' said he, 'and say he ride to Frio City. What for no can damn sabe. Say he come back tonight. Maybe so. That all.'

As the first stars came out the troubadour rode back to his haven. He pastured his pony and went into the house, his spurs jingling martially.

Old man Ellison sat at the kitchen table, having a tin cup of before-supper coffee. He looked contented and pleased.

'Hello, Sam,' said he, 'I'm darned glad to see ye back. I don't know how I managed to get along on this ranch, anyhow, before ye dropped in to cheer things up. I'll bet ye've been skylarking around with some of them Frio City gals, now, that's kept ye so late.'

And then old man Ellison took another look at Sam's face and saw that the minstrel had changed to the man of action.

And while Sam is unbuckling from his waist old man Ellison's six-shooter, that the latter had left behind him when he drove to town, we may well pause to remark that anywhere and whenever a troubadour lays down the guitar and takes up the sword trouble is sure to follow. It is not the expert thrust of Athos nor the cold skill of Aramis nor the iron wrist of Porthos that we have to fear—it is the Gascon's fury—the wild attack of the troubadour—the sword of D'Artagnan.

'I done it,' said Sam. 'I went over to Frio City to do it. I couldn't let him put the skibunk on you, Uncle Ben. I met him in Summer's saloon. I knowed what to do. I said a few things to him that nobody else heard. He reached for his gun first—half a dozen fellows saw him do it—but I got mine unlimbered first. Three doses I gave him—right around the lungs, and a saucer could have covered up all of 'em. He won't bother you no more.'

398

'This—is—King—James—you speak—of?' asked old man Ellison, while he sipped his coffee.

'You bet it was. And they took me before the county judge; and the witnesses what saw him draw his gun first was all there. Well, of course, they put me under $300 bond to appear before the court, but there was four or five boys on the spot ready to sign the bail. He won't bother you no more, Uncle Ben. You ought to have seen how close them bullet holes was together. I reckon playing a guitar as much as I do must kind of limber a fellow's trigger finger up a little, don't you think, Uncle Ben?'

Then there was a little silence in the castle except for the spluttering of a venison steak that the Kiowa was cooking.

'Sam,' said old man Ellison, stroking his white whiskers with a tremulous hand, 'would you mind getting the guitar and playing that "*Huile, huile, palomita*," piece once or twice? It always seems to be kind of soothing and comforting when a man's tired and fagged out.'

There is no more to be said, except that the title of the story is wrong. It should have been called 'The Last of the Barons'. There never will be an end to the troubadours; and now and then it does seem that the jingle of their guitars will drown the sound of the muffled blows of the pickaxes and trip-hammers of all the workers in the world.

Acknowledgements

The editors would like to thank the following authors, publishers and literary agents for their kind permission to include the following copyright material in this book:

Mollie Hunter and A. M. Heath & Co. Ltd., for THE SILVER BRIDLE from *Patrick Kentigern Keenan*, published by Blackie & Son Ltd.

Jack Schaefer and A. D. Peters & Co. Ltd. for THAT MARK HORSE.

Michael Williams and *Pony Club Annual* for A HORSE CALLED GEORGE; and Bess Leese and *Pony Magazine* for SONG AND DANCE (published by D. J. Murphy Ltd.)

Rosemary Sutcliff and Oxford University Press for ROYAL HUNT from *The Mark of the Horse Lord*, © Rosemary Sutcliff 1965; reprinted by permission of Oxford University Press.

James Herriot, Michael Joseph Ltd. and St Martin's Press Inc. for the extract, presently entitled THE PENSIONERS, from *It Shouldn't Happen to a Vet*. (*All Creatures Great and Small* © 1972 American edition).

Ruby Ferguson and Brockhampton—now Hodder & Stoughton Children's Books—for AND AS FOR PEDRO from *A Stable for Jill*.

John Murray (Publishers) Ltd. for THE TALKING HORSE from *The Talking Horse and other Tales* by F. Anstey.

O. M. Salter for RESCUE PARTY and Berwyn Jones for THE RACING GAME (abridged) previously entitled *A Day in the Life of a Trainer*; both stories reprinted from *Riding Cavalcade* by courtesy of J. A. Allen & Co. Ltd.

Caroline Baxter and Jonathan Cape Ltd. for THE UNICORN-STONE from *The Times Anthology of Children's Stories*.

The Hutchinson Publishing Group Ltd. for IN PURSUIT OF A WILD STALLION from *Dark Fury* by Joseph E. Chipperfield.

William Heinemann Ltd. and The Viking Press Inc. for JODY AND THE RED PONY from *The Red Pony* by John Steinbeck © 1933, 1937, 1938 © renewed 1961, 1965 by John Steinbeck.

Monica Edwards and William Collins Sons & Co. Ltd. for LANTERN LIGHT TO MOONLIGHT from *Cargo of Horses*; © Monica Edwards 1951.

Dorian Williams and John Farquharson Ltd. for PANCHO from *Pancho, the story of a horse* published by J. M. Dent & Sons Ltd.

Longmans Group Ltd. for DON QUIXOTE AND ROZINANTE from *The Red Romance Book* (1905) ed. Andrew Lang.

The National Trust and the Macmillan Co. of London & Basingstoke for THE MALTESE CAT from *The Day's Work* by Rudyard Kipling.

Mary E. Patchett and Bolt & Watson Ltd. for FAREWELL TO THE ISLAND from *Summer on Wild Horse Island* published by Brockhampton, now Hodder & Stoughton Children's Books.

Phyllis Bottome, The Condé Nast Publications Ltd. and David Higham Associates Ltd. for A PAIR.

Zane Grey Inc. for A MAN AND HIS HORSE (Chapter 6, *The Yaqui*) from *Desert Gold* by Zane Grey.

William Blackwood & Sons Ltd. for AN APPLE—A MEASURE OF OATS by Cecilia Dabrowska, reprinted from *Tales of the Horse*.

Helen Griffiths and the Hutchinson Publishing Group Ltd. for THIEF IN THE NIGHT from *Horse in the Clouds*.

Fiona Citroen and Thomas Nelson & Sons Ltd. for DRUMMERBOY AND THE GYPSY from *Applegate*.

Every effort has been made to clear all copyrights and the publishers trust that their apologies will be accepted for any errors or omissions.